COLD-BLOODED

AN 'OHANA NOVEL

Book Two

BY
KENDALL GREY

Published by
Howling Mad Press, LLC
P.O. Box 660
Bethlehem, GA 30620
United States of America
howlingmadpress.com

Edited by Jenn Sommersby Young

Cover Design by Emma Rider at Moonstruck Cover Design & Photography

Additional graphics by Renee Coffey

ISBN 10: 1-947830-17-1
ISBN 13: 978-1-947830-17-2

Published in the United States of America
First Paperback Edition: February 2019

TO MY READERS ...

I'm not a Native Hawaiian, but I conducted extensive research for the 'Ohana series in order to portray the characters and places in these books as accurately as possible. That said, I may have gotten some things wrong. I apologize in advance if I did.

The island of Kaho'olawe is mentioned several times within these pages. It has a fascinating history, and I encourage you to visit www.kahoolawe.hawaii.gov to learn more about it. I borrowed the chants that visitors must recite to approach and leave the island from www.protectkahoolaweohana.org.

COLD-BLOODED is best read after HOT-BLOODED, book 1 in the 'Ohana series. If you've read my *Just Breathe* urban fantasy series, you might notice a few similarities between that world and this one. Keep your eyes peeled. Clues to the mystery bridging the two series hide in every shadow. ☺

Mahalo for reading. I hope you enjoy Manō's story.

—Kendall

Everyone carries a shadow, and the less it is embodied in the individual's conscious life, the blacker and denser it is.

—Carl Jung

CHAPTER ONE

Thursday, October 2—Maui

Manō Alana toed the crumpled body at his feet. Blood from the crater in Blake Murphy's head oozed slowly across the dry grass, staining it glossy red.

It was a pity Keahilani had to kill him, but Blake was not his victim to mourn. Manō had someone else to mourn, and this was not the time for it. This was a time for damage control.

Though his name meant "shark," Manō had little interest in dead things. He preferred things pulsing with life. They carried power in their blood.

"I'll take care of this," he said to his sister Keahilani, who still held the gun that relieved Blake of the lower portion of his face. Though her fingers were clamped tight around the stock, her hand didn't tremble. Keahilani rarely trembled at anything anymore. She found too much comfort in the dark and what it had forced her to do over the last several years.

And the shadows found comfort in her.

As she stared through blank green eyes at her dead lover, those shadows clung to her shoulders and calves like children playing hide-and-go-seek. They moved just slow enough to make a man question what his eyes registered, but not enough to drag him against his will into the realm of disbelief.

Manō wished they would leave her alone.

Too late for that.

A fleeting memory from childhood swished across his vision. He'd been four or five, at a street party shortly after their father died. A human-shaped shadow chased him into a copse of palm trees after dark. It shouldn't have been there. By definition, shadows had a source—a person, a tree with wind tickling its leaves—something that blocked the light to make darkness. This one didn't.

Teeth clenched, he tripped over his own clumsy feet and tumbled to the ground, shaking. Snot bubbled from his nose. Terror weighed heavily against his arms and legs, holding him down. The taunting, man-shaped monster darted this way and that among the trees, too fast to track. Whispers fell around him like black feathers. The soft, otherworldly voices seemed to chant, *Blood, blood, blood.*

Mustering what little courage he could find, he ran inside, so scared he couldn't even scream. His legs burned with the burst of adrenaline powering them. Panic rippled through his chest.

Keahilani came into the apartment to check on him, her long black hair tied in braids on either side of her head. Behind her, the shadow flirted with the plaits as she bent down to talk to Manō. She didn't notice it.

The thing had said it wanted blood. Manō thought it might try to hurt his sister. He assured her he was only thirsty and came in for a drink of water. Once she seemed satisfied he was okay, she went back outside.

He found a knife in the kitchen. He cut a line down the center of his palm and watched with pained fascination as blood rose within the skin trench. The man-sized shadow grew bigger, hungrier. Manō held out his shaking hand to it, hoping to distract it from his sister. The creature lapped at his blood slowly, its razor-sharp black tongue draining life from him. He actually felt it. Manō pissed himself in the middle of the kitchen, unable to move or even cry out. But Keahilani was safe while the monster focused on his offering. That was all that mattered.

'Ohana is everything, their mother Mahina used to say. After Mahina's death, Keahilani, the new matriarch of the family, transformed the expression into an Alana mantra. Manō lived and breathed it to this day.

He shook his head and jerked back to the present. When he looked up, Keahilani's normally green eyes assumed an unnatural shroud not so different from Manō's. The inky blackness taking her over worried him far more than any trouble the corpse lying on the grass between them might bring.

There were no new shadows.

The Alanas had become the shadows.

Their brother Kai, Keahilani's twin, jogged up to join them, his long dreadlocks flopping with the exaggerated movement. With sea-green eyes that matched their sister's, he assessed Blake's unfortunate state. A note of pity turned down the corners of his lips, but it flitted away almost as fast as it landed.

"What can I do?" Kai's words floated out on a sigh. Dirty work fell under Manō's domain, and Kai complained whenever he got lured into helping with it. But not today.

"Let's wrap him up and put him in the canoe. I'll handle the rest." Manō quickly scoped their surroundings. The family's safe house lay far off the beaten path of nearby Kula, but that didn't mean no one heard the gunshot.

Kai and Keahilani knew better than to ask about Manō's plans for the corpse. The less they knew, the less likely they were to be thrown in jail if the truth ever came out. Manō was as good at evading the truth as he was at evading the light, but he wouldn't put his 'ohana—his family—at risk.

He slid the gun from Keahilani's blood-spattered hand. She didn't seem to notice. Shoulders slumped, she turned and trudged slowly to the drab two-bedroom house set against the rust-colored backdrop of the sleeping Haleakalā volcano a few miles away. Her expression was blank, distant. Manō couldn't blame her. She'd lost both her little brother and her lover in the last twenty-four hours, and one of those deaths had been by her hand. But she'd be okay. She had to be.

Manō emptied the magazine of its remaining bullets, stuffed the gun in his back pocket, and headed over to the ramshackle shed infected with rotting boards and scarred by a broken window. He pulled out a length of tarp, spread it over the grass, and with Kai's help, gently dragged Blake's body onto it. Then he thoroughly wiped the gun down, careful to ensure no prints remained, and fixed it in Blake's cooling hand. In the highly unlikely event the body was ever discovered, it would look like he committed suicide.

Kai mutely helped roll up Blake's corpse, and the brothers lugged it to the trailer cradling a small canoe that had been passed down through at least four generations of Alanas.

His mother Mahina inherited the koa wood outrigger from her father, a powerful and well-respected *kahuna*—or spiritual leader—with ties to Hawaiian royalty. His father got it from his father before him, and he from his father. Family legend held that the canoe was originally a gift from King Kamehameha V himself to one of his most trusted *kahunas*, Great-Great Grandpa Alana. Why Mahina's father left it to her and not her brother, Manō wasn't sure, but he thought it was because Mahina had stronger *mana*, or spiritual power.

Manō doubted either his mother or the great king would approve of the way the canoe had been used in recent years. Manō had buried a lot of bodies across the 'Alalākeiki Channel on the uninhabited island of Kaho'olawe, and traveling by boat or helicopter was the only way to get there. Sometimes you had to utilize whatever means were at your disposal for the sake of your *'ohana*, even if it meant defiling a precious family heirloom for the greater good.

Once Kai and Manō settled the body into the carved-out wood, Kai laid a hand on the tarp and bowed his head. Of the surviving Alanas, he was the most sensitive. He did what he had to for the family, but he didn't always like it.

He lifted his sad green eyes to Manō and said, "Why do I get the feeling this is just the beginning?"

By "this" he meant the blazing turf war Keahilani had just thrown gasoline on by killing Blake. But it was so much bigger.

Manō saw things his siblings did not. They hadn't just lost their brother Bane today. Manō feared Bane's death had opened the floodgates for something far worse.

"Trying times lie ahead," Manō said.

Kai nodded and returned to the house without another word.

Manō sighed heavily. It had been a brutal day that took its toll on all three of the remaining Alanas, and it wasn't over yet.

Keahilani and Kai would make funeral arrangements for their youngest brother while Manō handled sanitation and body-disposal duties. Violence like this didn't bother him. On the contrary, his only regret was that he hadn't had the pleasure of pulling the trigger on Blake himself. He might sleep tonight if he had.

As it was, his demons would have to be content to feed off death's scraps on his trip to Kaho'olawe after dark. And he'd feed himself the only way he could that didn't involve violence: by staying awake.

Manō cast his eyes upward to check the sun's position. Night would fall in a couple hours. Though his body craved a nap at the prospect of paddling seven miles across the channel each way, he couldn't afford that luxury. The best he could do was eat a filling meal and rest in quiet meditation in hopes of staving off sleep and the nightmares that accompanied it.

A distant rumble and a shift in the prevailing trade winds warned of a far-off storm. Manō sniffed the air, but all he got was a sense of confusion among the thick, humid breezes, like they couldn't agree on which way to go. The smaller winds merged into one and initiated a fist fight with the bigger.

Lightning zapped above the restless horizon. Thunder bellowed its ominous laughter. And below Manō's feet, the earth grumbled, injecting a searing itch through his veins. He scratched the insides of his arms, but the untouchable poison within had to run its course.

Manō gritted his teeth as he trudged toward his pickup truck. He cranked the engine and backed the vehicle up to the canoe-laden trailer. Once everything was hooked up, he went inside the safe house where he found Keahilani sitting at the kitchen table, hands cleaned of blood, their mother's journals stacked before her. Her elbows planted on the old wood, Keahilani grasped a hank of black hair and held it on top of her head while staring out the window to the truck.

She didn't look at him. Her voice was low and threatening as she said, "We need to find Scott. He owes our 'ohana a debt. I will take payment in full."

The biggest drug dealer in Hawai'i, Scott Harris—or someone Scott Harris hired—had shot their youngest brother. Bane survived the shooting and made it to the hospital, but the son of a bitch had smothered him to death in the ICU. Scott sought vengeance for his wife's death at Bane's hands, an incident the Alanas were still trying to unravel. Bane had killed Lori Harris, but their little brother must have had good reason. Manō just hadn't dug it up yet.

Keahilani didn't jerk with tears. Her shoulders didn't hunch under the unbearable weight of grief. Instead of falling apart, her resolve deepened. Under great pressure, rocks became even stronger. So was the case with his sister.

The darkness had seeped into her just as it had done to him the first time he saw the shadow and gave it a taste of his blood. Once you fed them, they always came back, usually with death in tow.

Death, death, and more death. It clung to the Alanas like a putrid perfume. First their father, then Mahina, now Bane. When would it retract its talons and leave them the hell alone?

When the secrets under Haleakalā shake loose and crawl to the surface for all to see, his mother echoed through his thoughts.

Until then, it seemed death was fully entwined with life.

Manō followed Keahilani's gaze to the truck outside.

"We'll find Bane's killer," he said. "And he'll pay."

Keahilani laid her cheek on folded arms in front of her and closed her eyes. Manō reached over to pat her head but stopped before touching her. The only way past the cascade of tragedies she'd experienced was through it, and it was a one-way, solo trip to the other side where Manō had been standing for years. Keahilani had to work through the grief and find the light. Or the darkness, as the case may be.

"I love you, Keahilani," he said.

She lifted her head, pressed her lips together tightly, and closed her face off from whatever emotions lurked beneath the skin with a determined nod. "Love you too, little brother," she said coldly.

Two hours later, Manō exited his truck at a hidden ramp off Makena Beach and dragged the canoe to the water's edge. He squatted on the sand, uttered a silent prayer, and ran his hands through the brine to cleanse the blood no one but him saw.

In the times before colonization, the Hawaiian people used salt to purify dead bodies and to keep evil spirits from haunting them. As he stared at his two great brown fists, Manō questioned the wisdom of bothering with such ceremonial niceties. It wasn't like the spirits that had dogged him all these years were going away now. He had too much to give them. Yet, here he sat, asking the ocean for … what? Happiness? Forgiveness? Pity?

Peace.

Manō just wanted peace. From the darkness constantly threatening to swallow him. From the shadows urging him to do bad things. From all the death life had dealt him.

The wind whipped up in a frenzied lash across his face. He stood, dusted off, and accepted his fate. No matter how much he wanted it, peace wouldn't make an appearance in his life any time soon.

He laid a hand on Blake's wrapped remains and felt a pang of jealousy tinged with a hint of sadness. "No rest for the wicked."

CHAPTER TWO

Seven miles separated the island of Maui from Kaho'olawe. Seven miles and a swelling tropical storm on this October night. Under calm maritime conditions, it took Manō a little more than two hours to reach the deserted island that once served as a weapons range for US Navy aircraft, post-World War II. With the wind determined to blow him back two yards for every three he gained, it would take far longer tonight.

At least he didn't need any light to see where he was going. The shadows were useful for a few things, like imbuing their hosts with sharp night vision.

Manō removed a small packet of tinfoil from his pocket and unfolded it. He tore off a corner of the tiny paper within and dropped the microdose of LSD onto his tongue to keep him focused and awake. And, if he were honest with himself, to keep his mind off the thought of paddling across the basin of an ocean that had killed his father and stoked nightmares in his subconscious every night for the last twenty years.

He closed his eyes as the chemical bonded with his saliva, and then he swallowed. Dipping his oars into the water, he cast off into the incoming squall. He was used to the intense paddling workout, but the storm tested his bulging muscles. With practiced, smooth motions, he focused his full attention on safely navigating the sixteen-foot canoe across the torrents of angry ocean.

About a mile into the journey, a trio of large, inky shapes appeared in the water, two on his right and one on the left. Triangles of black dorsal fins sliced through the surface above them. Manō grinned at his namesakes.

These were his *'aumākua*—family spirits who had gone to their deaths but remained with the *'ohana* to protect them, give them advice, and to warn them of their own unfavorable actions that needed correcting. They offered assistance, and they expected a libation in return. They appeared in the form of an animal or something in nature—sharks for Manō.

Perhaps these shadowy sharks were his Hawaiian grandparents. Or Bane's recently departed spirit come back to taunt him. Or Mahina herself. He had no way of knowing, but whoever the *'aumākua* were, Manō always welcomed them when they joined him on his trips across the channel. They only wished to protect him, and he accepted any help they offered.

"Aloha." He bowed his head respectfully and greeted the sharks by tossing them several fish he'd brought along to thank them. They gobbled their meals, acknowledged him with satisfied splashes, and continued their escort service to the imposing island in the distance.

More lightning woke the night, followed by insurgent thunder. The clouds were heavy with rain, but no drops had fallen yet. It seemed like the thunderheads were gathering more ammunition to use against him.

Manō shivered. Kaho'olawe's fortress of sand and secrets seemed to smile with frightening tiki teeth as more winds gathered in an effort to knock Manō off course.

The foreboding island made him uneasy. The sharks didn't like it either. On every trip he made, they tried to steer him away from Kaho'olawe. But coming here wasn't Manō's choice. Too many people had seen Blake with Keahilani. If Blake's body turned up on Maui, Kai's girl Ret at the police department might not be able to stifle any investigations into Keahilani or her connection to the deceased. The Alana *'ohana* and their legal business, Mahina's Surf and Dive Shop, could both be implicated.

Manō got the eerie sense that anger lay fuming under Kaho'olawe's rocks, under pressure with nowhere to go but nuclear. Much like the anger fuming under dormant Haleakalā and Mahina's miracle garden, which had become a blessing and a curse for the family after she died.

Out of necessity, Keahilani, Kai, and Manō had turned to a life of crime and used Mahina Surf and Dive as a legitimate front for their illegal business. With little insurance money to collect after their mother's car accident, the Alanas capitalized on the one thing of value she left behind: a small field of extremely potent marijuana they dubbed Pāhoehoe.

Manō yearned to investigate whatever lurked under the mountain, but not until Bane had been buried and the 'ohana had enough time to properly grieve his loss. There were only so many priorities one could juggle simultaneously, and Keahilani as the new matriarch had shifted their brother's death to the top of the list, where it should be.

The sharks continued their watchful procession alongside Manō. Their presence gave him comfort amid an underlying fog of agitation. With so many things in his life going wrong lately, it was nice to share a few hours of silence with other beings that didn't talk back or have an opinion about everything.

As the wind and sea kicked up stronger with each thump of his heart, the LSD slowly blossoming toward full potency inside his cranium shot his senses into overdrive. The shadowy world before him transformed into something vivacious, dynamic, hungry.

Colors bled into the night, casting rich blue and green layers into the sunless, restless realm. Manō *felt* the ocean breathing, seething, stretching around him like a cool cape. He lifted his koa wood paddles in sync with the sea's grand inhales and exhales, mimicking its steady rhythm, imagining himself a shark like the great fish swimming on either side of him. With each swing, he inflated and deflated his lungs, savoring the rush of salty, crisp air even as it worked against him.

The ancestors made the trip bearable.

A couple hours later, he stopped paddling. About a quarter mile offshore, the outrigger bobbed heavily on the rising and falling sea. Out of respect, Manō struggled to his feet. Leaning on his oars like canes pressed to the bottom of the canoe, he found his balance, which would've been difficult even without the strong winds and the microdose in full swing. He lifted his arms toward Kaho'olawe and respectfully sang the *Oli Kāhea*, the chant required to approach the island:

> *He haki nu'anu'a nei kai*
> (Indeed, a rough and crashing sea)
> *'O 'awa ana i uka*
> (Echoing into the uplands)
> *Pehea e hiki aku ai*
> (How is it that one lands?)
> *'O ka leo*
> (It is the voice)
> *Mai pa'a i ka leo*
> (Please don't hold back the voice)

If this were a normal situation, the lord of the island would respond with another chant to welcome him, but no one had lived on Kaho'olawe since the 1960s, and the few people who came here today were only allowed to visit the island at certain times as prescribed by Hawaiian law and cultural protocols. Manō was always a little surprised when the island seemed to answer him in whispers surfing the whipping currents:

> *'Ane hiki mai*
> (You are almost here)
> *'Ane hiki mai 'oukou*
> (Almost here)
> *Lehua lanalana o Kanaloa*

(You brave ones so buoyant on the sea of Kanaloa)
E pae, e pae
(Land, land)
Eia lā ka leo, 'ae
(Here is the voice, yes)

Then again, it might've been the drugs talking.

Either way, Manō resumed his paddles, sensitive to the hour and the impending tropical storm. He had a lot of work to do and not much time.

The sharks tightened their formation. When he closed in on the beach, they hung back, waiting. Fretting.

Don't go to Kaho'olawe, Manō, they begged through the frothy currents. They went through this ritual every time he came here, but it was no less jarring after several visits. *We can't protect you there. Come back where it's safe.*

Manō wasn't keen about going ashore with yet another dead body and bad weather to top it off, but he didn't have a choice.

"I'm sorry, *'aumākua,*" he said. "I respect your wish to protect me. I appreciate your offer."

The sharks seemed more distraught about his approach than usual, lashing the water with their tails and lunging aggressively in front of the canoe. He wasn't sure why until something red atop the eroded watershed snagged his attention. Manō did a double take and swallowed hard when he determined the red wasn't one spot. It was two.

Eyes?

It was hard to see this far away, but there were definitely two tiny glowing red dots right where a pair of eyes would be on a person.

Manō wasn't easily frightened. He'd stared death in the face countless times and probably intimidated the Grim Reaper more than the other way around. But something about the two pinpricks of crimson heat carried a palpable power that scared and awed him all at once. Scared him because he didn't know what the fuck it was. Awed him because it was familiar.

Like the thrum he felt every time he set foot in Mahina's garden at the base of Haleakalā.

Everything always came back to that damn mountain.

A certain *awareness* had overcome him the day he and his siblings brought Mahina's ashes to her garden, and he sensed it every time he returned since then. It was a subversive kind of warmth—tricky and untrustworthy, like sweat on a cold day. A massive, ancient presence folded and melded into the rock like crystals of olivine sprinkled through andesite. Despite not knowing how to define it, he felt a disturbing connection to whatever lay underfoot. It called to him on a subatomic level.

What the hell are you?

The sore muscles strapped across his ribs tightened. He balled his hands into fists, ready to fight anything that might come at him, natural or supernatural.

Darkness shifted with the rising wind. The sharks behind him thrashed, insisting he return to them. Much as he wanted to, he couldn't.

The two dots disappeared, taking their heat with them. Manō ground his teeth. Not knowing where the creature went made him even more jittery, but he'd come this far. It was too late to chicken out.

Everything clutched in the night's grip shimmered with energy—the agitated ripples on the ocean, the fish carrying on beneath it, the red wrinkles of Kaho'olawe's furrowed plains. Microdosing gave Manō the feeling of being in tune with nature, but this was different. He wasn't just in tune. He was *part* of nature.

Manō resumed paddling and made it to shore a few minutes later. He lugged the canoe onto the beach, away from the reaching fingers of sea. His body wired and primed for a confrontation, he scanned the area for the red lights but found nothing.

Offshore, the sharks flailed as if in a feeding frenzy, their dark bodies illuminated by sparks of darting lightning when they broke the surface.

Come back. It's not safe.

"I'll be okay," Manō shouted to them over the rising wind as he dragged the tarp-covered corpse from the outrigger onto the sand. He grabbed his shovel and strung a pair of binoculars around his neck.

He carefully lifted Blake. His thick, tired arms straining under the dead weight, Manō hoisted him up and over one shoulder and slung the shovel over the other.

His shadow stretched to an unnatural length as Manō plodded with his heavy load up the beach. There were a few areas on this part of the island that volunteers and other ordnance-removal personnel hadn't yet cleared. Those were the places where he'd laid half a dozen souls to rest. Tonight, Blake would join them.

On high alert, Manō studied the horizon as he trudged. The shadows were awake and playful. They crawled up his arms, draping across his shoulders, darting in and out of his peripheral vision.

Manō relied on the drugs to help him dismiss it, focusing instead on finding a proper spot to bury Blake. The wind slapped his cheeks hard; the fat nimbus clouds above, ripe with unshed rain, hung low and threatening.

After walking several minutes, he lifted his binoculars to check on the outrigger. The waves crashing on the beach inched higher and higher, much faster than he'd expected. They threatened to drag his canoe into their giant maws. Manō tensed. If that canoe went adrift, he'd have no way home. No one knew he was here, he had no cell service, and there wouldn't be another cohort of volunteers arriving for a couple weeks. He'd be as dead as Blake, which might not be so bad.

He glanced at the heavy load digging into his shoulder. A bead of sweat rolled down his temple.

Hawaiian tradition passed down from his mother said that unattended or improperly buried bodies attracted evil spirits. Manō wasn't big on superstition, but Mahina knew things others didn't. He trusted her judgment even when it conflicted with his personal beliefs.

Regardless of any spiritual implications, Manō's sister had murdered Blake in cold blood. No one could find out about her crime. That meant Manō had to ensure the body would never be discovered.

Judging by the tide's increasingly fast approach, he had about fifteen minutes—twenty tops—to get back to the outrigger before the sea whisked it away.

With improved night vision from the LSD and the shadows guiding his way like mischievous little gremlins, he picked up the pace toward a small expanse of red dirt at the foot of the island's craggy, rootlike rock protrusions. There was enough soft ground there to dig a shallow grave. It wouldn't be deep enough to conceal the body from the elements indefinitely, but it should keep Blake covered well enough in case someone else decided to visit Kaho'olawe before Manō could return.

He didn't like leaving a job unfinished, but it was that or be stuck on an island with no known fresh water sources and limited food options.

The choice was clear.

He excavated a hole big enough to lay Blake's body within and hastily covered it with stray rocks, building an inconspicuous shrine he'd easily be able to locate later.

As he worked, Manō wondered who, if anyone, Blake had left behind. Did he have a family? Friends who would miss him?

Mahina had taught Manō that all people projected varying shades of light and darkness. There was some of both in everyone, no matter how pious or how criminal. His twenty-year-old brother Bane had been a good kid, one Mahina would've been proud of, but he got caught doing business with the wrong person, most likely a third party who stood to gain where Scott Harris lost. Scott had plenty of enemies, many of them his own distributors, who might've orchestrated the hit on Lori. A calculating and cruel drug lord,

Scott wasn't hated by just the Alanas. He was universally despised.

Manō wrapped up his crude, impromptu burial with a quick whispered prayer spoken in Hawaiian for Blake's spirit to find peace.

Churning gusts and raging sea ratcheted up like a supercharged game of hide-and-seek between air and water. Loose soil and bits of shrub flung into the air. Waves crashed the beach like a barrage of grenades. Manō had to return to his canoe, and fast.

Using the shovel as a staff to help navigate the dips and divots underfoot, Manō hurried down the beach to where he'd left the outrigger. Along the way, he couldn't shake the feeling that someone was watching him. A fresh shiver crawled up his spine on centipede legs as he searched Kaho'olawe's rocky gradient for red eyes, but nothing turned up.

With a seductive voice, the thrashing sea that had murdered his father whispered promises of bashing him on the rocks until he was nothing but a bag of blood and broken bones. Manō had no doubt it would carry out those threats if he stuck around much longer.

He sang the chant requesting permission to leave Kaho'olawe:

'O 'awe kuhi, 'o kai uli
(Pointing tentacle of the deep sea)
Kuhikau, kuhikau
(Direct, direct)
E hō mai i 'a'ama, i 'a'ama aha
(Grant also an 'a'ama, 'a'ama for what purpose?)
I 'a'ama 'ia au
(For releasing me from my obligations as your guest.)

The island seemed all too happy to oblige. The land gave its permission for him to go with its own chant. The words weren't spoken, of course, but Manō felt them in his blood:

Ku 'oe a hele,
(Rise up and take leave,)
Noho au
(I will remain)
Ua hele 'oe, ua hele 'oe
(Go, go see)
A, ua hele lā
(You have left already.)

He guessed he was cleared for takeoff.

As Manō worked the paddles, muscles fighting against nature's relentless resistance, the shadows elongating around him unfurled their wings and danced in celebration. Of what, he didn't know, but all signs pointed to the Alanas' latest victim's death.

Manō frowned at the darting, inky blobs and paddled harder.

Feed us, the shadows whispered as they oozed past his ears and taunted the startled sharks who rejoined the canoe as tentative escorts. Tightening their formation, the sharks seemed leery of the black forms.

The protective sharks nudged him east with sudden but calculated lunges, insistent splashes, and bared teeth breaking the raucous surface. *This way. Hurry, Manō.*

What was their problem? Their high energy blended with his, creating a frenzy of urgency he couldn't dismiss.

Another earth-shaking bellow of thunder silenced his racing thoughts. He didn't have the time or patience to puzzle out the addled musings of his fried gray matter when the world was falling apart around him.

He had one goal: to make it home.

Blood surged cold in his veins as the shadows he despised but couldn't shake cloaked him in the kind of darkness even an ominous, dead volcanic island couldn't penetrate. He rowed like his life depended on it. Because it did.

About a mile out, he took a quick break to swig some

water from the bottle he'd brought and chanced a final glance through the binoculars to the shore fading behind him.

He could've sworn he saw a figure—an actual *person* with the dull aura of life—easing down to the rocks he'd used as a marker for Blake's body.

He blinked. The figure disappeared just as the rain began to fall.

Manō shook his head and resumed paddling. If exhaustion and sleep deprivation didn't get to him, the hallucinations would.

CHAPTER THREE

Friday, October 3

By the time Manō unlocked the door to his tiny house in Pā'ia on the north shore, dawn had broken, though you wouldn't know it from the darkness outside. Storm clouds draped most of Maui's lush windward side in capes of gray. The pounding, heavy rain sounded like a waterfall. It was unusual for storms to come in from the west like this, but it didn't surprise Manō. What better way for Kaho'olawe to make its displeasure known than to try to drown him so he'd stop littering its slopes with dead bodies?

Near the point of collapse from paddling countless hours, Manō closed the door and leaned against it.

And then it hit him from out of the blue.

His brother was dead.

In the midst of nonstop chaos, he had somehow forgotten that his little brother had been murdered. He felt like shit for focusing his energy everywhere but on Bane.

Though they hadn't been as close as Manō and Keahilani were, he loved Bane deeply. The thought of never seeing him surf again or schooling the rest of them about finance or watching him turn a scant few dollars of Mahina's insurance money into enough for a down payment on the shop—it crushed him like a tidal wave. The storm surge welled up the column of his throat, sparking prickles at the corners of his eyes.

We'll find Bane's killer. And he'll pay, Manō had promised Keahilani.

He clenched his fists. He fucking meant it.

Anger eclipsed the pain of loss. If he let it grow too big, bad things would happen.

Blinking, he banged the base of his skull on the wood several times to clear his head. He looked down at himself. His clothes were soaked from the storm and sea, yet he didn't feel any colder than usual. The high from the LSD was waning, but he still picked up tracers here and there in the subtle shifts of the shadows.

He sighed. Shadows weren't supposed to move on their own. According to science, they didn't have free will. They could only do what the light told them to. But his shadows didn't obey the rules of physics. They were slaves to some other, darker master within him. He lifted his paddle-blistered hands and stared at them.

At the far edge of his range of vision, a shadow that didn't belong there moved. Manō's gun was out of his waistband and in his grip before he finished inhaling. His eyes were all-seeing, thanks to the lingering bump from the LSD. Streaks of weak color darted across his vision and swirled to life in the form of a body. A female one he knew intimately. His shoulders relaxed, but he kept her in his sights.

The spiky-haired blond stood slowly from the old, threadbare couch where she'd apparently been sleeping. She looked at the gun, but she either didn't care that it was trained on her or didn't think he'd actually use it. His black satin robe clung to her shoulders, its sleeves too wide and hem too long. The sides split open just below the crux of her thighs as she sauntered toward him.

She leaned her hip against a bar stool, crossed her arms over her ample breasts, and tipped her head to the side as she took in his drenched clothes and hair. "You okay?"

Manō didn't ask how she got in. He assumed she either picked the lock or left a window cracked the last time she was here and climbed through. He cursed himself for not paying closer attention to security around his house. Though, he'd been more than a bit distracted lately.

"Fine," he mumbled, flipping his keys onto the hook by the door. He walked into the open dining/living/kitchen area and set the gun on the bar.

She slunk away from the stool, reaching for him.

He was tired. Of crime. Of death. Of life. But he let her take his hand because he didn't know what else to do.

Inside, he was empty. Inside, he had only shadows and cobwebs to keep him company. He liked it better on the outside. With people he cared about.

"I'm so sorry. Bane was a great kid. Whoever killed your brother will get his due," she said, her topaz eyes sparkling. They were beautiful. How had he never noticed before?

He tentatively stroked her face from cheekbone to chin. She nuzzled into his palm. He wished things were different between them.

"I don't want to talk about my brother. Either of them," he added softly, redirecting the flow of energy in the room from her to him. With each inhale, he sucked more light into his lungs until the darkness shifted in his favor and he was in control of everything. He blocked her forward motion with his big body and herded her into the wall.

This was the power the shadows gave him. As he took, so did they.

Light eater.
Darkness dweller.
Dead-eyed killer.

His calloused fingers twitched as they traced a line down her arm over a smattering of fresh goose bumps and lifted her wrist above her head. He matched and pinned the other arm, forcing both wrists to the wall as he thrust his hips against the flimsy fabric of the robe. Her tough body melted into lava under his touch.

"I'll respect your wishes for now because you're grieving," she whispered, gazing hungrily through hooded lids at his lips, "but we do have to talk about at least one of your brothers sooner rather than later."

He kissed her harsh Boston accent quiet, sampling her drying vanilla lip gloss and snapping open the robe with a rough jerk. Her barely contained breasts spilled into his waiting hand. He stroked her exposed skin, trailing fingers across flesh and reveling in the feel of another human's heat sparking against his.

He needed this.

"If you want Kai, then have him," Manō said, gruffly exhaling the words up the column of her neck. He let her arms drop.

She twisted away with a shiver and a smile and planted both palms on his chest, warm against his cold. "If only it were that easy. Besides," she added, tugging open his belt, "I'm not sure I'm ready to give up this new thing I got on the side."

He caught her lips with his, rougher this time, greedy for whatever she offered. Her mouth ebbed and flowed, following a half step behind his lead. Easing closer, he covered her with his black-inked flesh and the shadows he couldn't escape, activating pressure points and lighting up nerve centers from every angle. Desperate to connect with a human being, to be free of the heavy burdens of dealing with the dead and running from the light, he fumbled his fly open and buried himself inside her.

She was very willing and very wet.

She clutched his shoulders, hiking a leg around his pumping thigh and gasping heavily beside his ear. "Yes," she murmured, her hot breath amplifying his desire.

He was so ready for release, he couldn't even be bothered to push his soggy pants off his hips. Manō emptied his mind of all thoughts and worries and focused solely on *feeling*, something he'd never been much good at. Right now, he needed to feel something other than loss and duty to his 'ohana. He needed to *be*.

The acid still singing quietly in his veins lent him the

freedom and colors his mind craved. Guiding him on a frenetic journey along a roller coaster of pleasure, the drug provided just the distraction he craved, if only for a short time.

Manō climbed higher and higher, scaling a volcano on the verge of eruption. With each thrust, more pressure escaped containment, spinning his head in dizzying ecstasy. When he reached the peak, a rainbow explosion ensued.

On an island that boasted rainbows practically every day, such beautiful displays were common fixtures in Manō's world. Yet drug-induced moments like these were the only times he noticed colors. When the shadows receded under the threat of too much light. When happiness snuck up on him unexpectedly.

The release rippled cascading waves of red, orange, yellow, blue, green, and purple across his vision and through his body. He clung to the crest as long as it would support him and mourned the moment when the brightness faded into varying shades of gray.

The vivid hues shone only as long as the afterglow, yet long enough to remind him that he could indeed still feel, despite the fact it was getting harder and harder.

She let go of him, dropping her hands to her sides. He disengaged and stuffed himself back into his jeans. She didn't look at him as she lowered her head and smudged his kiss off her lips with her knuckles.

They'd only done this twice, and now, like before, he wanted her gone right after. But the truth was, they needed each other. She reminded him that the world was not all black and white, and he gave her something his brother couldn't: satisfying release with no emotional strings attached.

Manō didn't care that he was nothing more than a stand-in for her idealized version of Kai, nor did it bother him that she fantasized about his brother while she fucked him. She might've even mumbled Kai's name once in the heat of the moment. She provided a service as much as he did.

Whatever their respective reasons for continuing the

unusual "relationship," neither would tell a soul about the other. They were both dirty little secrets nobody else needed to know about.

She tugged the robe around her chest and retied it. Stepping back, she blew a short, stray wisp of blond hair out of her eyes with a quick puff and settled her hands on her hips.

"I know this isn't the time," she began slowly, "but a couple items of interest came across my desk today."

Manō cocked a brow.

She worried her bottom lip between her thumb and index finger. "The dealer who bit it last week. Butch?" she said. "Keahilani told me what happened with him when I had lunch with her and Kai on Saturday."

Keahilani had blown off Butch's balls with a stolen SIG Sauer after he'd tried to rape her. Manō was still kicking himself for not accompanying her to the meeting that night. He and Kai *always* backed up Keahilani at drug deals, but she hadn't told them about this one.

"And?" Manō said.

"The sheriff's division got a whiff of what went down, and their noses are twitching. Homicides have that effect on them."

Manō nodded. The cops must've accessed the security feeds at the resort where it happened. It wouldn't be long before they linked Keahilani to Butch's murder.

"I'll do my best sleight of hand to make shit go away," she continued, "but I'm low on the chain of command."

"I understand," Manō said. "You mentioned a *couple* items of interest?"

She straightened. "I tried your weed. It's top of the line, without a doubt, but your Pāhoehoe might have some competition."

Manō quirked a brow. As far as he knew, nothing on the market came close to producing the intense sexual high the Alanas' Pāhoehoe gave its users.

"The good news is, this other shit is hard to find, and it's ridiculously overpriced. No one can afford it. The bad news is, there are at least three local chemists trying to reverse engineer it. This drug produces effects identical to Pāhoehoe, but it's super concentrated. All it takes is 150 micrograms administered sublingually to send you on a round-trip ticket to the dark side of the moon. The high is instantaneous and lasts a solid six hours. Erections can go even longer."

"What is this miracle drug?" he asked.

"The kids are calling it Ambrosia," she said.

"Can you get me a sample?"

Kai had friends in high places who not only worked on the weekends but who might also be able to crack the drug's code faster than whoever was already on it.

A slow smile crept across her lips. She swaggered over to the purse she'd left on the floor, dug around inside it, and produced a tiny vial about half the size of her pinkie. Inside was a milliliter of diluted red liquid. She sidled up to him and waved the bottle between them.

"Be careful with this. It's five doses."

He snapped the vial from her fingers and studied it. The Ambrosia shimmered under the faint light. Presentation was everything these days. Manō supposed even illicit drugs needed proper branding, hence the flashy, glitter-like swirls.

He tipped the glass to the side. It held only a few drops of fluid, but the Ambrosia rolled in a strange, almost intelligent way, defying gravity as he twisted the bottle. The viscous red curled around itself, its glitter forging patterns like a kaleidoscope with one color but an infinite number of shades.

The substance hummed and churned with subtle vibrations that shuttled from the glass into his fingers. It was mesmerizing. And warm.

Manō glanced at his hand. His pulse thrummed in an accented rhythm that matched the red chemical's swirling beats.

The drug *called* to him. To his blood.

"Ambrosia," he mused softly, hunger awakening in his gut. The ever-present shadows that clung to his feet loosened their grips, stretching beyond their usual size. Heat flooded Manō's eyes.

"If you plan to try it, I advise doing it when you don't have anywhere to be for a while," she said.

That ruled out this weekend. According to the voice mail Keahilani left, Bane's funeral would be tomorrow, and Manō needed to clear his schedule for something as important as Ambrosia.

If Kai's subcontractors could reverse engineer the drug, the Alanas might be able to shift their Pāhoehoe operation to something less obvious. Though the Alanas tried desperately to keep it hidden, the marijuana farm in Kula wouldn't remain a secret forever, especially if Scott Harris had his way. He'd made it clear through Blake he intended to assume control of it. With money like his, it was only a matter of time until he found it.

And when he does, you'll be there to claim vengeance for what he did to Bane, a tinny voice in his head whispered. *A kill for a kill.*

Manō pushed the thought away. For now.

He'd send half of the drug to Kai's friends and keep the rest for a day when he could devote his full attention to it.

She curled her arms around his neck and nipped at the gape-mouthed shark below his ear as she whispered, "And if you need a body to test-drive it on …"

"We need to keep this"—Manō gestured between them—"under the radar. Indefinitely."

"I ain't telling him shit," she said. "It would break his heart."

Jealousy fluttered in a teasing arc in front of his face. Manō mentally batted it away.

"But what he doesn't know can't hurt him," she mumbled before tagging his lips and dragging him toward the couch.

At least Manō didn't have to worry about falling asleep. Officer Beretta "Ret" Rogers of the Maui County Police Department was a woman of many talents, not the least of which was keeping men awake.

CHAPTER FOUR

Saturday, October 4

Bane's funeral was a somber affair, but the many friends who came to pay their respects and share stories about his life made it bearable. Manō enjoyed seeing a different side of his little brother through other people's memories, but it also made him ache like a healed wound sliced open anew. Bane, with his college education and a promising future in applied business and information technology, was supposed to be the Alana who would break out of poverty and make something of himself. He was the good one. When he died, hope for the rest of them died with him.

Manō was not a man who let emotions get the better of him, but today, he felt deeply. Mourning his lost brother was a private thing he didn't wish to share with his *'ohana*, let alone anyone else. He'd deal with his grief later. Preferably standing over Scott Harris's corpse, smoking gun in hand.

He drifted among the attendees after the service concluded, quietly thanking them for coming, accepting condolences, and listening for chatter that might provide clues about Bane's killer. As per a prior agreement, Tua, an associate of Manō's, was hanging in the periphery listening too.

"Keahilani?" someone said at the back of the church.

He turned around. A tall, lean, familiar-looking man

stood before Keahilani. He had short, neatly cropped blondish hair, a gaunt but angular face, and wore a designer suit that probably cost more than the funeral. Manō scanned his memory banks for his identity. When he got a hit, it felt like a punch in the gut.

Scott Harris.

After the initial shock of recognizing the kingpin who ordered their brother's death, Manō's brain lurched into action.

His first instinct was to strangle the son of a bitch with his bare hands, but as much as he wanted to take this motherfucker out, he couldn't do it in such a public setting.

Sure you can, the shadows nipping at his ankles goaded. *Slip a blade between two ribs and watch the blood spill.*

"Shut up," he whispered, slinking toward his sister.

Scott was rich. He probably brought backup. Manō scanned the attendees for signs of trouble. Most of the mourners had left, but a dozen or so lingered. He didn't see anyone who didn't belong.

"Do I know you?" Keahilani asked, her brow creased as Harris offered his hand to shake.

"Scott Harris," he said.

Keahilani visibly tensed, and so did the tiny butterfly shadows flitting around her feet, defying the light sneaking through the stained glass. Her voice chilled to subarctic. "What the *hell* do you think you're doing here?"

"Paying my respects to my half brother," Harris replied.

Manō paused his steps. All the air left the room. Everything that remained became kindling for Keahilani's hot-blooded rage as the mourners' mouths dropped in unison.

"Excuse me?" she demanded, bowing up like a tiger defending its territory. The temperature in the church seemed to jump a couple degrees.

"My condolences on your loss. I didn't know him, but I just learned he was family," Scott said, casually scoping the people around him with intense blue eyes.

Half brother? Family? What the fucking hell?

Manō cleared the distance to Keahilani's side, practically leaping over one of Bane's friends from college.

"How *dare* you. How fucking *dare* you show up at my brother's funeral after you murdered him in cold blood, you pig!" Keahilani shrieked, her words pinging off the high church ceiling and echoing around the sacred space.

Manō didn't think. He reacted, grabbing her fist before she could strike Harris. He clamped an arm around her middle as her tears flew. She pinwheeled, trying to get at Scott, her carmine nails primed and ready for slashing.

Kai and Ret darted over to intervene.

"This is the piece of shit you need to be checking out," Keahilani fumed to Ret. "He's the one who smothered Bane at the hospital." She turned back and spat in Scott's face.

Throwing down in the middle of a church would likely get them kicked out, if not tossed in jail. He subtly nodded to Tua, who slunk around the pews toward the exit.

"I think you should leave," Ret said to Scott, her voice low and cool. It matched her soft hair, tamed from its usual spikes. She subtly flashed her police badge from her hip pocket. "You're upsetting the bereaved. I'd be happy to escort you to your hotel."

Scott wiped the blob of Keahilani's spit away with a handkerchief. The smarmy asshole grinned. "No need for that. I'm heading to the airport momentarily. But before I go, there's one more thing I'll say."

Harris met Keahilani's gaze with the unmistakable blue eyes of their father. Manō suppressed a shiver. Having been only three when Justin Jacobs died, he didn't remember much about his father in real life, but he'd memorized every line of Dad's face from the handful of pictures Mahina kept. The resemblance was uncanny.

Jesus, it was true. Scott Harris was their half brother.

Scott's jaw clenched for a long moment before he spoke. "Bane got what he deserved. I only wish I'd been the one who'd done it. See, I'd have drawn it out and made it hurt.

Just like he did to my Lori and our unborn child. He didn't tell you that part, did he? It's the inconvenient truth no one wants to face. Your brother murdered an innocent woman and her baby. Live with that, *sister*. I hope the weight of it drowns you as it does me every day of my life."

Shit. Killing someone's wife was bad enough, but a baby took Lori Harris's murder to a new level. Now Manō understood why Scott was so dead set on revenge. It gave him pause.

"No," Keahilani cried, her face streaked with matching salt water rivers. "He didn't do it. He was a good man."

"He was his mother's son," Scott shot back with disgust.

Though Manō agreed, Scott meant it as a slur. The darkness clinging to Manō surged and swelled, staining his vision black. Blind fury claimed his blood.

Kill him, the prickly voices taunted.

An intense and sudden desire to commit murder overwhelmed him. The reins on his control loosened.

Driven by rage at this asshole's insults to their beloved mother's and brother's memories, he shoved Keahilani out of the way, flung his arm back, and plowed his fist into Scott's face.

Blood gushed from the corner of Scott's mouth. Manō scented it. Saliva flooded his tongue. A wave of satisfaction washed over him.

The sky rumbled from the west. His muscles flexed.

Kill him, the voices begged, more urgently this time.

Weakened by grief and lack of sleep, he wanted to oblige, but left unchecked, Manō's wrath would create a lose-lose situation for everyone.

Thankfully, Ret hooked a strong arm through Scott's, urging him toward the door. "Time to go."

"Get your hands off me," he said and jerked away. "This is only the beginning, my brothers and sister. Justin Jacobs's legacy will live on."

Manō's resolve shook like an earthquake and shattered.

This couldn't be happening. If Justin Jacobs was his

father, why hadn't Mahina told them about Scott? Had she even known?

Too many directions for his racing thoughts to run.

Scott made a quick escape through the stained-glass doors to a waiting limo at the church's curb, leaving the stunned Alanas on the steps watching after him. A moment later, Tua pulled out of the parking lot in a nondescript black sedan and followed him. Good. Tua would send updates, and with a little luck, Manō would personally close the deal on Scott Harris later. That ought to make the shadows happy.

Keahilani's lip curled as the cars drove away. "Let's get out of here."

Manō nodded, laid a hand on his sister's back, and guided her through the exit, past Ret and Kai, who were talking anxiously. Manō was careful to avoid Ret's gaze.

Grateful for the fresh air, he inhaled a deep breath and let it out slowly. Beside him, fury sizzled like lightning across Keahilani's skin.

"Walk with me," he said, heading toward the cemetery behind the church.

Keahilani followed, anxious and visibly upset.

Scott's DNA held something in common with Manō's. It wasn't exclusive to his surfer-body build or eyes that were clones of their father's. No, Manō sensed in Scott the same, familiar darkness that lurked in himself. And Keahilani. And Kai.

But not Bane.

Though she rarely talked about their father when the kids were growing up, Mahina had revealed secrets about Justin Jacobs in her journals Manō wished he'd never learned. If Manō was cold-blooded, then Justin had been just plain evil-blooded. And it appeared Scott inherited plenty of Dad's darkness too.

Manō stopped at a memorial with a flat granite stone embedded in the grass. It read, "Justin Jacobs, January 3, 1958 – December 19, 1993." He'd spent many nights here, sitting beside his father's marker, wishing for answers to questions he'd never receive. He'd been a toddler when Justin died and knew very little of the man aside from what old pictures and his frequent nightmares told him.

What he did know was that Justin got what he deserved: a gruesome drowning at the whims of the ocean, by way of Mahina's natural powers. That was enough.

Keahilani shunned the marker and narrowed her sea-green eyes on Manō. "Tell me about Lori Harris's murder."

He sighed. They'd been through this before, but he indulged her. "Bane intercepted one of my hit jobs a year ago. While on O'ahu for a surf competition, he pulled the trigger on Lori and confessed everything to me when he got home. Bane never said another word about it."

"So, you just buried our baby brother's dirty little secret?" Keahilani demanded. "It never dawned on you to tell me?"

"I didn't tell you because I knew you'd react like this."

"Bullshit," she snapped.

When he didn't answer, Keahilani continued. "Mahina wrote something in her diary that's been bugging me." She'd been devouring their mother's old journals since Manō found them a couple weeks ago. "A fortune-teller told her, 'When the third son is conceived, your shackles will fall away.' What did she mean?"

Bane was Mahina's third son, and their father died before he was born.

"Was his death the 'shackles' the woman spoke of?" Keahilani asked.

"Yes," Manō said. "And no."

"Enough with the riddles, brother. Spill it. I know something is going on with us. It has to do with Dad. I feel it inside me."

She raked her arms with her nails, leaving behind long red scratches. When she tipped her head back to meet his gaze, black throbbing lines circled her irises.

The change was overcoming her like it had overcome him after the incident in the kitchen when he was a boy. He never fully understood what he was, only that he had some deep connection to these ever-present shadows that made him want to do bad things.

Manō should have been terrified for his sister. Selfishly, he was relieved he was no longer alone.

"Kai's falling prey to the darkness too. Like us," Keahilani said.

Manō had to agree. He'd seen little signs here and there— shadows hanging too heavily on Kai's lanky frame, bursts of aggression at odd times, black circles around his irises after dark.

"But Bane escaped it," Keahilani continued. "Why is that?"

Manō pressed his lips together. He couldn't keep the truth from her anymore. "Because he wasn't born with it."

Keahilani stared at him, slack-jawed. The turning wheels picked up speed as she processed the secret that had been dangling over her head for years, just out of reach.

"Because he wasn't Justin's son," she whispered.

Now she understood.

"But if he wasn't Justin's," she said, sifting through the puzzle pieces, "then whose was he? And why would he kill an innocent woman who happened to be our half brother's wife?"

These were the same questions Manō had been asking himself.

Keahilani's eyes darted back and forth as she tossed out hypotheses. "Mahina hooked up with someone else and got pregnant with Bane. She raised him as our full-blooded brother. After her death, someone hired Bane to execute a hit on Lori Harris for reasons we still don't understand. If Scott is our half brother, then why isn't his last name Jacobs?"

"Mahina refused to give us Justin's surname because they weren't married. Maybe Scott's mother felt the same," Manō said, toeing the edge of their father's marker.

If Bane had lived, would he be joining the rest of them as a new inductee into the Alana Shadow Society? Despite him killing Lori, Manō didn't think so. He would have sensed the shadows cavorting inside his little brother. Truth was, Manō had sensed only light in Bane. That light had come from Mahina, and it seeped into every aspect of Bane's life. It made him better than the rest of them.

It was now clear Justin Jacobs was not Bane's father. The Alanas' shadows were tied to Justin, not Mahina.

"So, Justin fathered the three of us, but not Bane," Keahilani repeated, seemingly unsatisfied by the knowledge.

Manō nodded.

She still hadn't so much as glanced at the granite on the ground bearing Justin's name. She must've been angry at him for treating Mahina like shit, and hurt, perhaps, that Manō had kept secrets from her and Kai.

But he couldn't have told her. For one, she wouldn't have believed him about Bane back then any more than she did now. Secondly, the shadows would make their full presence known at a time of their choosing. It wasn't his decision. They'd show her and Kai what they were when they were damn well ready, just as they'd done with Manō in the kitchen that day when he cut his hand to keep the shadow away from Keahilani.

Snaps of twigs and dried leaves alerted Manō to Kai's presence. Keahilani turned to Kai and her gaze fell to the wooden box urn cradled in his hands. Their little brother, the brilliant, vibrant surfer with everything going for him, reduced to a few pounds of ash and stray bone fragments.

"So senseless," she muttered. Water filled her eyes again. She wiped away the falling tears, smudging her mascara, making the black circles around her irises even more striking. She turned her back on Justin's marker and started toward the parking lot. "Tonight, we take Bane home. To Haleakalā. To Mahina. Tonight, we end the curse on the Alana *'ohana.*"

Manō would like nothing better. Only problem was, their curse was just waking up.

CHAPTER FIVE

Haleakalā's foothills rippled with heat. The day's ultraviolet rays contributed most of it, but now that dusk had come and gone, another source joined forces with the electromagnetic spectrum to keep the mountain's feet warm: body heat.

The sounds of car wheels rolling out of the freezing clouds and down the drought-bleached slopes were typical for this post-twilight stretch. The sun—the mountain's center-stage attraction—had just faded like an out-of-breath lullaby falling into sleep. The tourists would soon join their mighty star in slumber, but first, they had ten thousand feet to scale down and traffic to navigate along the winding pavement. By ten or eleven, the House of the Sun would be quiet save for the heartbeats of those few souls who lived on her lower extremities in the warmer climes closer to sea level.

Life on the mountain swelled in a backward-flowing cascade from her toes up to the puffy skirt made of white clouds ringing her hips. Little flourished up high, but a horn of plenty drenched the land in green down low. There was always *something* moving, breathing, or thinking on her side of the thriving volcanic island. A puff of breeze through leaves in need of watering. A scuttle of pollen-tipped insect feet over a flower's stamen. The settling of a corpse in its repose as microbes and worms had their way with it.

Haleakalā knew such delicate sounds because she listened.

But tonight, not even the bugs feasting on the decomposing body of a meth head named Pekelo in the trunk of the car Blake Murphy had left at Haleakalā's foothills dared to move. Something bigger than the mountain, bigger than death had spooked them into stillness.

Haleakalā had been dormant since the 1700s, but she hadn't been quiet. Not with all the activity disturbing the underside of her slopes.

An unexpected chill shivered upward from deep under the mountain's sleeping crags, neutralizing the heat the day had collected. The earth that held its roots in place cracked open. Inky, amorphous shapes oozed out of the rift, slinking around the darkest bits of night, seeking shelter in them. The remnants of green in the grass turned a malevolent gray under the encroaching shadows.

Something stunk there. Pekelo 'Ōpūnui's corpse. Or perhaps, what had gotten inside it.

A lone car's lights approached the spot and slowed to a bumpy stop. Three presences with tenuous connections to corporeal form exited the car.

Haleakalā recognized them.

They were Alanas.

But also something else.

They were linked to the darkness through the "something else" portion of their heritage. The mountain did not know through whom or why. She only knew Pekelo's body had to go, and its escorts to permanent accommodations in the land of the dead had arrived.

The deceased was tainted by violence, and on this mountain, violence was met with silence of the eternal variety.

From the rift, part of the other world leached into this one in a long stream of mist. The fog expelled tiki-faced spirits tapping drums and wielding torches that ate light rather than projecting it. The delegation float-marched toward the car and circled it with increasing speed as the Alanas watched with wide, black-rimmed eyes.

Haleakalā shifted under the putrid-smelling vehicle,

barely kissing its underside. The spirits of the Night Marchers continued, singing a chant that could be felt deep in the bones, but not heard by human ears.

Haleakalā opened her mouth and sucked the car into a sinkhole.

Then she swallowed.

All traces of the car, Pekelo ʻŌpūnui, and Blake Murphy's guilt over killing him disappeared.

Mahina was dead. Bane killed. Blake was gone now too. He didn't matter any more than the tweaker he'd murdered for his secrets.

The surviving Alanas probably wouldn't matter either.

In the grand scheme of things, the lives that touched the mountain were as dust: small, fleeting, and wholly insignificant.

Haleakalā prevailed no matter what direction fate decided to lean toward.

Life came and went. The mountain was forever.

And so was what lived under it.

* * * *

Manō, Keahilani, and Kai stood slack-jawed, staring at the Night Marchers—ghosts of slain Hawaiian warriors from ancient times. Mahina had taught Manō that these spirits roamed the land between sunset and sunrise, bashing war drums and blowing conches to warn humans of their approach. It was said that anyone who looked upon the face of a Night Marcher would die unless a relative marched within their ranks.

The tiki-masked apparitions could shoot deadly bolts of heat and light from their empty eyes. They could travel through any substance, and their hunger for death was insatiable.

Few things scared Manō. The Night Marchers were second on his list after threats to his ʻohana.

The scene was something out of a horror movie. Mere

minutes before, the Alanas had ridden the shadows from their parked car. Manō had performed the feat—stepping onto the back of the corporeal darkness that always seemed to surround him and letting it guide him toward his destination—countless times before. His siblings had not.

Kai's and Keahilani's newfound ability to shadow surf had been the night's first surprise. The second came when they arrived at the foot of Haleakalā. The ground opened like a maw and devoured an abandoned car with what must've been a dead body in it, judging by the smell. Manō had never seen anything like it.

The tiki-headed spirits followed the siblings to Mahina's garden, squared off around it, and waited motionless, their war drums now silent.

Holding Bane's ashes, Keahilani stared them down, her chin lifted proudly, irises ringed in black. Only Manō's fearless sister had balls big enough to look a Night Marcher in its dead eyes and not run away screaming.

Respect.

Once it became obvious Keahilani wasn't going to die, some of the tension surrounding Manō lifted. He relaxed a little but slipped closer to his brother and sister in case the Night Marchers decided they wanted a closer look at the woman who had defied them.

A butterfly landed on Keahilani's finger, and Manō's heart leapt. The insect was a manifestation of their mother's spirit. Keahilani seemed to commune quietly with it for a moment.

A pang of jealousy hit Manō between the ribs, but he blew it off. Keahilani and Mahina had a special connection in life that even death couldn't touch. Mahina always showed up at the right moments to comfort her children, and man, did they need her now.

When the butterfly flew away, Keahilani shook Bane's ashes out of the urn near the spot where they'd done the same for their mother after her death years before. She said, "You're free, Bane. Find Mahina and ride the surf together."

Kai sniffled, kissed the tips of his fingers, and lowered his head. Manō said a quick prayer for his brother, found his siblings' eyes in turn, and nodded. The Night Marchers gathered their torches and glided away from the garden, feet never touching the ground.

The Alanas stared through the mist after the tiki spirits until the drumbeats could no longer be heard. Then they turned to one another and exchanged incredulous expressions. They'd just witnessed some hardcore supernatural shit, and Manō for one had no words.

"Let's go home," Keahilani said. She gathered the night around her like a cloak and melted into the darkness.

Manō was impressed, yes. Surprised, no.

Kai snapped his head up. "Where'd she go?"

"To the car, I assume," Manō answered.

"How?"

"Same way we got here."

"By surfing the darkness?" Kai scoffed.

"Yes," Manō said, clapping his brother on the back and guiding him toward a stand of trees heavy with darkness.

Kai dug his heels in and faced him. "You can't ride a shadow." He didn't seem convinced by his own statement.

"You did."

Kai shook his head. "You slipped me a drug or something. You must've. We were driving down from the top of the mountain. I was tired—exhausted after losing our little brother. I noticed we were being followed, so Keahilani pulled off the road. You told us to meet you at the garden."

"Which you did."

"Obviously," Kai said, "but I still don't understand how I got here."

Manō flashed a rare smile and resumed his trek toward the trees, waving Kai along. "Something life-changing is happening to you, brother. Come on."

Kai caught up. "What is it? I feel … different since Bane's death. I can see better in the dark. The night molds around me like a second skin." He smoothed a palm down his arm. When he looked up, black ringed his eyes. "I'm stronger in darkness."

Manō shrugged. "That's exactly how I felt when it happened to me."

"How long … have you been like this?" Kai's brows tightened.

"Since I was three."

"Fucking *three?* What the—" Kai sputtered. "You gotta tell me everything. Am I going crazy? Is something wrong with me? Am I gonna disappear forever?"

Manō shook his head. "No, no, and no." He paused when they reached the trees and turned to Kai. Holding his shoulders, Manō looked him in the eyes. "I don't know what the shadows are, where they come from, or why they're attracted to us. But now that they're following all three of us, maybe we can figure it out together."

Kai paused, looked away nervously, then returned his gaze to Manō. "I'm scared, brother."

"I was too." Manō understood his fear intimately. It had dominated his entire childhood. "But they won't hurt you." *Not directly.* "They aren't leaving, so you might as well learn how to use them to your advantage. You can start by letting them take you back to the car."

If Manō had learned anything from decades of being cloaked in writhing, sentient darkness, it was acceptance. He could resist a lot of things in this world, but his shadows were *very* persuasive.

Kai sighed. "I'm just supposed to close my eyes, click my heels, and I'll be home?"

"Just like slipping into the barrel, man."

Manō smacked the back of Kai's arm and took the Nestea plunge into the darkness behind him. Once incorporeal, he lingered hidden among the shadows for a moment to see if Kai would follow.

His brother's shoulders rose and fell with several breaths. Kai glanced toward the spot where they'd scattered Bane's ashes, pressed his lips together, and stepped into the black.

So it began.

CHAPTER SIX

Manō was disappointed not to be greeted by a sexy cop wearing his robe when he arrived home well past his bedtime. It wasn't just because she was a good lay. After a week like this one, he was afraid to go to sleep.

But damn, he was exhausted. His life was a bubbling cauldron of what-the-fuckery on the verge of boiling over.

His phone buzzed with a call from Tua. Finally, an update on Harris.

The shadows sidled up to Manō with interest as he lifted the phone to his ear. "Where is he?"

"Followed him across the island and back for hours. Never lost sight of him," Tua said. "He stopped at a gas station in Pā'ia about thirty minutes ago. The driver filled up, then he returned to the limo company. He got in his car and drove home. Never saw your boy get out."

"You check the limo?"

"Yeah. It was empty."

Manō started to protest. People didn't just disappear into thin air.

Except for people like him.

He rubbed his forehead.

"My gut told me to try the airport," Tua went on. "I didn't see him, but I had a guy I know who works for Hawaiian Airlines check the passenger manifests for all flights to O'ahu. He was on the six o'clock. I swear, Manō, he didn't stop anywhere near the airport, and I never lost sight of the limo. He *might* have snuck out of the car in Lāhainā traffic when I had my head turned, but I doubt it."

"Don't worry about it," Manō said gruffly. "*Mahalo.*" He ended the call and tossed his phone on the coffee table with irritation.

He'd been close enough to kill Scott Harris and missed his opportunity.

Fuck.

Despite all the excitement, or perhaps because of it, Manō wouldn't make it ten minutes longer in the realm of the conscious. Dreamland was calling, and no amount of caffeine or LSD or cocaine would stop him from landing there soon, regardless of how much he needed to stay awake.

It had been five days without sleep.

If the internet was to be trusted, he'd start hallucinating soon. Assuming he hadn't been already.

He sunk into Mahina's old Barcalounger in front of the blank television, bent over his knees, and laughed.

The tattered arm covers irritated his skin. He laughed harder. The lights were too bright, though none were on. He laughed some more. He thought about Blake's dead body, rotting and exposed to the elements on the hostile island across the channel. No relatives or friends could mourn him *because they didn't know he was dead.*

Laugh, laugh, laugh.

Tonight, Manō had laid his baby brother's ashes to rest and watched phantoms send an entire car containing yet another dead body into the pit of hell, and all he could do was laugh.

If he hadn't lost his mind already, he was on the verge of going bat-shit crazy.

Wrenching gasps of uncontrollable laughter made his stomach hurt. He could hardly breathe, but he couldn't stop laughing. Just as he'd slow down, another volley of ammunition hit him.

He was fucking his brother's ex-girlfriend. Why? To spite

Kai? To make himself feel better? Because he was a real piece of shit, that's why.

Ha, ha, ha!

He missed his mother. His brother. And, even to a small degree, his father.

Worst of all? He could do nothing to stanch the free-bleeding wounds eating away at his soul.

Manō Alana, drug-thug extraordinaire, was powerless in the face of the shitshow that was his life.

Ha, ha-ha, ha-ha!

Ha, ha-ha, ha-ha!

Bone-weary, he rubbed his eyes. So many people he could have cried real tears for, yet here he sat, cry-laughing at himself, floating away on some deranged, hysterical fugue.

With effort, he pushed up to stand. His legs barely supported his weight as he shuffled to his bedroom, dreading what would come, but desperate to lighten the load of madness taking its toll on his soul.

Out of the frying pan and into the bubbling lava pit.

You could kill yourself, he thought, not for the first time. *It would bring you peace.*

People said suicide was a cop-out, but Manō kind of respected those who took their lives into their own hands. What freedom it must be to control your destiny, to give Death the middle finger as you stripped his prize right out of his hands.

It would only take a single bullet. Or a jump off the cliffs of Hāna onto the rocks below. Then he'd be food for the sharks he was named after. His final act on earth would be one of kindness, a perfect bookend to his humble beginnings as a good boy who loved his *'ohana* more than anything and wanted only happiness for them.

Manō winced. How far he'd fallen.

He shoved the thoughts aside, tumbled into bed without taking his shoes off, and was asleep the instant his eyes closed.

Mahina and Bane were waiting for him on the other side.

You look like hell, Mahina chided. *As you should.*

She was as beautiful as he remembered with long black waves of hair like Keahilani's and warm brown eyes that sparkled.

He tried to embrace his mother, but his hands slipped through her wispy form. He nodded to Bane, who only smiled. He was the same twenty-year-old kid with surfer-tight muscles, dark hair, and nearly black eyes, but he had a distant affect that saddened Manō.

You found her, Manō said to his little brother.

Bane nodded.

And the Night Marchers found you, Mahina said to Manō.

Behind her, Haleakalā shimmered in lusty red hues draped in shadows. Neither his mother nor his brother had shadows. They seemed to be made of light.

A pang of bone-deep pain struck Manō's chest, caving it in. Everywhere he turned, darkness closed. Everywhere except straight ahead where his lost family hovered much like the Night Marchers had earlier on Haleakalā.

You must resist the shadows, Mahina said.

In life, Mahina had been called many names, including *kahuna kilokilo,* the title of a respected Hawaiian diviner. She could predict the future and did so with perfect precision. Was this advice a warning of what would come? Were he, Keahilani, and Kai stuck to destiny's path like insects to fly paper?

Resist the shadows, or what? Manō challenged as the darkness settled around him like a black-feathered cape, its oily barbs deceptively seductive. It would be so easy to let the shadows have all of him.

Mahina stepped forward and tried to grab his hand, but her fingers passed through him. She scowled. *Resist them or become them. Your choice.*

So, I have a choice? He shook his head bitterly.

Fate had kept him chained up in its backyard like a mangy, starving dog since the day his father died. When you were inextricably tied to darkness, immune to tears, you did bad things because your genetic code told you to.

The time for choice had long since passed.

Darkness is a part of you, Mahina reminded, *but don't allow it to eclipse the light. 'Ohana comes from both sides. Separate, but equal.*

Mahina had uttered these words to her children almost every day when they were growing up. Manō knew the lines backward and forward to the point where they lost their original meaning. But hearing the statement again after his mother's long absence brought a fresh ring of truth.

Separate, but equal, he repeated.

His father was the reason he was cold-blooded. His mother was the reason he needed to return to Kaho'olawe and put Blake Murphy to rest properly.

He'd trusted that as long as he held on to the part of him—however small—that came from Mahina, the shadows couldn't break him. He'd believed Mahina's blood would do what it could to protect him from the darkness if he allowed himself permission to draw on it when shit got tough.

Now he wasn't sure.

Darkness and light swirled in his chest, each taunting the other, the shadows filling more of the space. Manō rubbed his sternum as his inky comrades slipped up behind him, whispering directives.

Scott must die for what he did to Bane.

Blow his brains out.

Your brother must be avenged.

What has Kai done for you lately? He treats Ret badly. Make him pay.

Madness descended as the whispers cranked up to shouts and eventually screams. Manō covered his ears and shut his eyes.

This was the nightmare that filled him with bloodthirsty rage goading him to hurt someone, *anyone* for any reason or none at all when he woke up. The urge to commit violence was too powerful to overcome. He had to find a way around it, but the only path he saw ended with his demise or someone else's.

He couldn't keep hurting people to satisfy the darkness.

He couldn't keep hurting himself, refusing to sleep, or

dosing drugs, either.

Something had to go, and he knew damn well what something it was: him.

He had to die to put an end to the violence.

Manō. Mahina's firm voice demanded his attention.

He opened his eyes and lowered his hands. The shadows were still there, but they were quiet. For now.

You can't go on like this, baby, his mother said, reaching for him. Her head tipped sadly to the side when her fingers passed through his hand a third time.

In that fleeting moment, Manō believed that if he could have touched her—truly felt the warmth of her sun-drenched skin, a little sticky from the splash of coconut water she used to indulge in on special occasions and fragrant with her favorite plumeria lotion—she would've saved him.

He stared at the lack of physical connection between their overlapping palms. He could no longer remember what his mother's warmth had felt like when she had been real.

A better man might've shed a tear over such a loss. But Manō was not a good man.

I'll be fine, Mahina.

Manō, please. Don't go, she begged, her eyes soft and round with worry.

He shook his head. *It's not my choice.*

The shadows dragged him into a cave of fidgeting blackness—a new dream where fresh monsters would have their way with him. As the sinister darkness loomed, anguish exploded across Mahina's face.

Her grief broke him.

Manō! she screamed, grabbing for him, her ghostly hands passing through his flesh, the desperate frenzy of a mother trying to protect her son.

His name echoing off her lips followed him all the way down into the oubliette of nightmares where blobby black hellions filled him with malevolent intentions to be executed immediately upon his return to the Waking.

CHAPTER SEVEN

Sunday, October 5

Manō woke to taunting hisses from under the closet door, under the bed, between his ears. *Kill. Kill. Kill,* the shadows whispered.

He rolled over and immediately tossed an arm over his searing eyes, willing the sun to fuck off. God, the burn was intense. A breath later, a different kind of fire joined the sun, sparking a dark, lusty urge to hurt something. The desire flared deep in his gut, a hunger that wouldn't be denied.

Kill. Kill. Kill.

He clenched his right fist and squinted at its roughness. How many people had he killed with this hand? Twenty? Thirty? He stopped keeping track after ten. How many deserved it? He liked to think they all did, but there was no way to know.

Scott Harris would definitely deserve it. If only Manō could find him.

Another flare of insatiable hunger tore through him. He sat up and scooted off the mattress only to be accosted by a sudden, debilitating headache. Unsteady, he grabbed his forehead with one hand and the wall with the other.

Kill. Kill. Kill.

Dark blobs ventured out from hiding places along the floor. Their tinny voices demanded his attention.

It's time to kill, Manō.
Feed us the flesh we crave.
Get dressed and murder someone, you sorry piece of shit.

"No," he said, his voice weakened by the dueling pains in his head and stomach. A fault line nestled behind his eyes shifted, tilting half of his brain into a panic with fresh throbbing that expanded outward, growing with each axon of cerebral real estate it swallowed. He slapped a palm to the spot and tried to find his breath.

He had to get to the surf shop. Maybe if he was with Keahilani or Kai, he'd be able to control his urges better.

You will kill.
If you don't, we'll feed you pain like nothing you've ever known.
Kill for us, Manō. Kill.

Nausea under pressure climbed the vent of his throat, seeking release. He swallowed several times, but that only made it worse.

"Stop it," he gasped, doubled over in agony.

One of the shadows hopped onto his foot and grinned up at him with a mercury smile. *We'll stop when you give us blood.*

Scott Harris would've made perfect shadow fodder, but he was two islands away. That meant someone else had to die.

Manō stumbled into the bathroom to splash water on his face. He stared at his reflection, disgusted by the blackness clinging to his skin. No matter how much he washed, it never disappeared.

He quickly brushed his teeth, got dressed, and grabbed a burner from the drawer full of untraceable cheap phones in the kitchen. Stuffing his hoodie pockets with an assortment of other supplies he used to cover his tracks, he devised a plan. He'd head to the warehouse district and find a scumbag there to plug. With no paying jobs currently on deck, it was his only option. He just hoped Mahina wasn't watching.

Thirty minutes later, clothed in shadow and driven to the edge of madness by an insatiable need for violence, Manō slipped into an alley where a known crack dealer usually hung out. He didn't know the guy's name, but he'd seen him roughing up customers more than once. Word was the dealer accepted various forms of payment, most notably in unprotected sex, sometimes not entirely consensual.

Stomach screaming and blood on the verge of boiling, Manō had to feed his demons before they destroyed him. Pulling up his hood and lowering his sunglasses, he stomped down the gray alley and caught sight of the dealer in question fucking a limp woman like he intended to nail her to the wall. Her head hit the bricks repeatedly as the man thrust violently into her. His victim appeared too dazed to react. She might've even been unconscious.

Manō's throat tightened. He felt even sicker than before.

The shadows writhed, became more animated. Metallic drool leaked from the corners of their mouths. Their dagger-teeth shone dull gray as their lips pulled back in cruel, sick grins.

Kill him. Kill her. Feed us. Their throaty whispers bordered on sexual, which made the scene even more disturbing.

"Just him," Manō whispered, licking his dry lips. He buried his hands into a new pair of black suede work gloves— his preferred type for killing because they didn't hold fingerprints.

Sweat slid down the side of his face as he checked the security of the weapon tucked into his waistband. Though he planned to employ a very personal touch for this particular shitbag, the gun served as insurance in case things went south.

He approached the dealer slowly, using the shadows for cover. The guy was so zonked out on whatever filth polluted his veins, he didn't even notice until Manō was on him.

He looked up at Manō through cloudy eyes, rimmed with red. His pumping hips didn't miss a beat. "Want a piece?" the prick asked. "Sell you some Ambrosia to go with it." *Thrust, thrust, thrust.*

Manō's lip curled. The hunger gnawing his belly reached its crescendo. He summoned the power of darkness to keep him hidden from potential passersby—not that anyone around here would care about a drug dealer raping a crack whore—and channeled the shadows' strength into cold-cocking the fucker in the face.

Now the druggie's hips did stop. He stumbled away, leaving his victim to crumble to the ground. She was so far gone, she didn't even moan when her head hit the pavement.

Blood spilled. The shadows pounced. Enraged, Manō stepped over the woman and zeroed in on his kill.

"Where'd you get the Ambrosia?" he asked, stalking toward the dealer, whose dick pointed straight at him, maybe from the drugs, maybe from fear. Whatever the case, the shadows purred their approval.

Sick fucks.

The guy turned and ran, but Manō was faster and had a hell of a lot of motivation. He and his army of darkness easily grabbed the man and yanked him back into the shadows. The inky demons surrounded him, shimmying up and down his body with malevolent, sexual delight. The man's erection was erotically distracting.

Bile rose up Manō's gullet. What the fuck was wrong with him? He tried to focus on the rapist's scabbed face, unkempt hair, and dirty skin. He grabbed the dealer by the shirt and shoved him into the wall with a crack, pinning him there by the throat.

"Who's your source?" he demanded through gritted teeth.

The tweaker struggled against him, but he was much smaller than Manō. "Get the fuck off me, man!"

"Tell me who's supplying you, and I'll consider making this quick."

The guy's eyes went wide and wild, darting left and right. "I—I got the shit off Prince Seamus. See. It's right here." He reached for his pocket, but Manō batted his hand aside and dug in himself.

His fingers came away with a vial similar to the one Ret had given him. Thick, glittery red fluid swirled within. It was sealed with a white sticker stamped with a red crown and the initials P.S.

How very interesting. "Prince" Seamus was one of the Hawaiian underworld's top cocaine dealers and an occasional hitman. According to Manō's contacts, he had ties to Scott Harris, but not many people knew about it. Scott was careful to keep his two businesses completely separate from one another.

"Seamus only deals in coke," Manō said, testing the tweaker. "Try again."

The man violently shook his head. Somehow his eyes got even bigger. "Not anymore. He's Ambrosia exclusive now. Got a line to some subverse where the trains come and go, their cars loaded up with riches." Spittle flew from the corner of his mouth as he spoke. His maniacal laugh sounded almost as shrill and grating as the shadows' titters.

"Stop talking shit and tell me where I can find him." Manō tightened his grip on the guy's throat.

"You can't find him," the tweaker said. "He's a ghost. Casper. Boo! But I'll tell you something else, and you'll want to hear this. Trust me. If you want Ambrosia, talk to Malware. He got the mainline to the source, baby. He'll get your limp dick hoppin'." He thrust his hips aggressively at Manō, his bobbing erection slapping his lower belly.

The shadows writhed with ecstatic delight, slithering across Manō's skin like snakes made of night.

That was it.

Manō grabbed the tweaker's chin and mushed the guy's mouth. He shoved his head into the bricks again. And again. And again.

This was more like it. Manō flashed a cruel smile.

Light faded from the dealer's eyes, and he mumbled more incoherent gibberish about Ambrosia and secrets and the underground. As his life slipped away, it bled into Manō and gave the shadows something to crow about. The energy invigorated him like nothing else. He was ashamed to get such a rush from killing, but shame didn't stop him.

"Fucking piece of garbage." Manō turned his head, spat on the ground, and jabbed his fist into the tweaker's jaw with an uppercut that split bone. The guy's mouth hung open, blood pouring out like a macabre waterfall.

And the shadows feasted.

Mahalo, *Manō*.

More ...

So hungry ...

Manō turned away from the scene, shaking out his bloodied fist. The burn of freshly torn and bruised knuckles inside the glove brought him back to reality. He ran over to the woman crumpled beside the wall and shooed the shadows away. Red pooled around her. She was still breathing, but she didn't look good.

Pity panged around the echo chamber of his heart, conjuring an ache he couldn't ignore. Keahilani had recently been sexually assaulted by Butch Kelly. This woman could've been his sister. Or Ret. He wanted to help her, but if she saw him, she might identify him to the cops, and the Alanas already had two too many recent murders under their belts for comfort.

Using the burner, he dialed 911, reported two bodies in the alley, and hung up before the operator could ask any further questions. Then he faced the dying woman. Brows creased, he whispered, "I'm sorry," and turned away.

He quickly wiped the phone clean of any lingering oils his face might've left behind and tossed it into the first trash can he came upon. The gloves went into a plastic baggie from his pocket. He'd destroy them when he got home.

He'd be long gone by the time help arrived. He only hoped it would come quick enough for the woman.

As he staggered numbly toward his bike, he glanced over his shoulder to the dead man. A shadow lifted its black, bulbous head from the body and grinned at him, blood cascading down its face.

Manō had gotten a lead on Ambrosia. The pain hammering in his head and stomach had dissipated. Why did he suddenly feel worse than before?

CHAPTER EIGHT

"You look like hell," Kai said as Manō dragged ass into Mahina Surf and Dive later that morning.

"So I've been told," Manō grunted, rubbing his eyes. It felt like he was staring into a solar eclipse. He squinted at the ceiling, wondering if they could install lower wattage bulbs. Then he realized the lights weren't on and disgustedly resumed rubbing.

Kai crossed to the customer side of the counter. The shop would open soon, but for now, it was just the two of them.

"Hey, man, I spoke to my botanist buddy about the Ambrosia sample you gave me the other day," Kai began, his dreadlocks scratching against the blue polyester rash guard clinging to his wiry shoulders. "Your anonymous tipper was right about that shit being similar to Pāhoehoe. More than right. His drug and our drug are chemically identical."

Manō blinked. "That's impossible."

Kai nodded knowingly. "I thought so too. The only difference is the sample has a super concentrated amount of whatever the substance is. And the really interesting news? He can't identify the chemical. He's never seen anything like it."

Kai pulled a clear plastic baggie from his shorts pocket, peeled its wings open, and withdrew a fat, fragrant bud of Pāhoehoe. He held it out to Manō and said, "Notice anything about the color of our weed?"

Manō drew it closer and peered at the intricacies and mini highways weaving among the small leaves. "No."

Kai took the bud back and broke off a bit. "That's because you're only looking at the outside parts. You haven't seen what's inside."

He rolled the leaves between his fingers, gently crushing them into a loose powder in his palm. He lifted it for Manō's inspection. "What do you see now?"

Manō blinked a few times to clear the blurriness from his vision and focused on the tiny pile. At first, he didn't see anything, but when he turned his head slightly, the sun eavesdropping through the window behind him lit up a bit of reflective particulate and activated a cascade of flashing red glitter.

And it moved.

Like the liquid Ret had given him and the shit he took off the tweaker, this stuff seemed to have a mind of its own. It crept in directions gravity didn't normally allow.

What the fuck?

"Is it alive?" Surely not.

Kai shook his head. "Not by any definition modern science uses. But this chemical is so new, it's hard to define it with existing terms. My friend wants to dig a little deeper into its code. You cool with that?"

Manō nodded, his thoughts flickering to the mutterings of the madman he'd just killed. He didn't know what to make of all the new information being thrown at him. Two identical chemicals—one from their farm, the other from an unknown source. Coincidence? Unlikely.

"You know a dealer named Prince Seamus?" Manō asked.

"No," Kai replied. "Should I?"

"Maybe," Manō said. He tossed Kai the vial he'd taken off the crackhead. "He's running Ambrosia exclusively. Recently made the switch from coke."

Kai whistled appreciatively. "He must have deep-ass

pockets."

"Or he knows someone with deep-ass pockets," Manō agreed. "Like Scott Harris."

"I'll ask around about him. Speaking of Scott, have you talked to Keahilani today?" Kai asked, glancing to the door.

"No."

"I happened to be looking over her shoulder when she booked a ticket to O'ahu in the car last night."

Shit. Harris's resort was on O'ahu. "When?"

"Probably on her way to the airport now for a noon flight. I think she gets home tomorrow." Kai slid him a sheepish look. "You think we should go after her?"

"Keahilani is her own woman. If she wanted help, she'd have asked."

"Last time we weren't with her, she went off on a deal she didn't tell us about and killed a guy," Kai said.

As if Manō needed a reminder. "She won't make that mistake again. Leave it alone. She's fine."

"You know she's going straight to Scott," Kai blustered.

"Let's hope so."

Kai's green eyes widened, and his hair shook with his jaw drop. "You *want* her to go? There's no telling what she'll do."

A satisfied grin crawled over Manō's lips. "Maybe she'll kill him too and save me the trouble."

Kai opened his mouth to speak and promptly shut it.

In daylight, he lost some of the intensity Manō had witnessed last night. The darkness had a way of wearing a person down slowly. Kai would probably backslide into the light. Maybe it would even stick. If at least one of the Alanas could be saved, Manō would welcome it. Keahilani, however, appeared to have passed the point of no return.

Two murders under her belt with a possible third on the horizon were pretty clear indicators the shadows had gotten under her skin for good. Yet another loss to mourn. Manō would hold out hope for Kai, but he didn't expect a happy ending there. The Alanas were what they were. They couldn't fight their own blood.

"I talked to Ret at the funeral yesterday." Kai straightened to his full height and pretended to busy himself with a stack of flyers on the counter.

Manō couldn't tell if he brought up Ret to fill in the silence or because he legit wanted to talk about her. Kai had never been a fan of silence, much to Manō's irritation.

Manō grabbed the pricing gun from the counter and ripped open a box of surfboard leashes. He dragged both to the wall display that hadn't changed in the five years they'd owned the place.

Kai continued. "I think she's seeing someone."

Why Kai felt the need to bellyache about his woman—a problem they shared in more ways than one—escaped Manō's grasp. Unless Kai suspected he was the other man. Manō pressed his lips together, squatted down to tag the merchandise, and let his brother unload.

"We haven't been together-together since high school, so I don't know why it bothers me. We're not an item, but I …" Kai trailed off.

Manō mentally finished the sentence for him: *I want to be.*

Kai inhaled deeply and let out his breath in a gust. "I made a mistake."

Manō had never cared enough to inquire further, but Keahilani said Kai cheated on Ret in high school, and things between them hadn't been the same since. That was ages ago, but apparently, neither party had let go of the pain the breakup had caused. They both still pined and whined to everybody but each other.

"So, tell her," Manō said, irritated at being dragged into the drama.

"I've tried," he admitted. "She doesn't want to hear it."

Manō shrugged. "Then quit bitching about it and move on."

Kai knelt beside him at the display and tacked the leashes onto their pegs as Manō finished tagging them.

"I'm not like you," Kai said. "I can't let her go. It's been years, but I still think about her all the time."

"Even when you're banging someone else?"

Kai's cheeks colored, and he looked down at the shiny package of cord in his hands.

"If you want her, you know what you have to do," Manō said. He let the "*Or stop doing*" hang unspoken in the air between them.

Manō didn't care if Kai and Ret got together. They'd be perfect for each other if she'd stop being so goddamn passive-aggressive, and he'd put his dick on notice.

The bell above the door jangled. Manō looked up. Drowning his surprise under his usual mask of cold calm, he murmured, "Speak of the devil."

Kai hopped to his feet like a jackrabbit and grinned. "Ret. What are you doing here?"

Manō stood slowly. He nodded at Ret dressed in her navy-black Maui police uniform with a gold emblem embroidered on the left sleeve. The shiny silver badge over her breast pocket caught the sunlight and winked at him. She avoided Manō's gaze and faced Kai with a smile.

"I'm here on business," she said, removing her hat and laying it on the counter. She snapped her gum with a loud pop. "Just got a missing persons report on a guy named Pekelo 'Ōpūnui. Didn't he work for you? At your *other* business?" She lifted a brow, emphasizing the word "other."

"Uh, maybe," Kai said. "Hard to remember. They come and go so fast …"

Kai's memory was just fine. He remembered Pekelo as well as Manō did. The guy was a hardcore tweaker, but the meth made him work fast. Pekelo was one of the Alanas' best harvesters.

Ret removed a piece of paper from her pocket and unfolded it. "Says here someone matching his description and driving a rusted-out green 1985 Fiesta was last seen at a bar in Lāhainā on Friday. You guys know anything about that?"

Manō and Kai exchanged glances. The Night Marchers had escorted a vaguely green POS Fiesta into the mouth of madness last night at the foot of Haleakalā.

Both brothers shook their heads. If the implications weren't so serious, their synchronized movement would've been comical.

Shit. Shit. Shit.

What the hell was one of their Pāhoehoe employees doing at the farm without them? They always blindfolded their workers and personally transported them to the site to keep its location hidden. And why was he—Manō now assumed the awful stink last night was Pekelo—dead in his own car, which happened to be swallowed by the land itself?

They should've opened it to see who was inside. But they wouldn't have had enough time. The vehicle was devoured moments after they got there.

Damn it.

Manō would ask Kai to put in a call to Jezzy as soon as Ret left. Jezzy was the Alanas' on-retainer hacker and general fixer. Maybe she knew something about how Pekelo got dead. If not, she could find out.

A ripple of unease climbed Manō's spine. Jezzy said she was working for someone whom she dubbed a "conflict of interest" with the Alana 'ohana. Manō was reasonably sure Scott was the conflict.

Jezzy worked both sides, but as long as the Alanas' requests for information didn't overlap with Scott's, she'd play ball fair and square. But that also meant whatever info the Alanas asked her for could get back to Scott.

Ret studied Kai with detached interest. She didn't believe him.

"If you hear anything, let me know," she said. Then she leaned closer to Kai. "And it might behoove you to remember that information *does* flow both ways." She whacked his arm twice with the back of her hand, grabbed her hat, and fixed it on her head.

She swaggered to the door. She must've been aware of both sets of eyes on her retreating form because she took her sweet time getting there. Manō started to chub up. He quickly averted his gaze from her ass.

When her fingers settled on the bar, she paused and turned to Kai. "Oh, and I can't make it tomorrow night after all. Something else just came up."

Manō willed her not to look at him. She didn't. But he knew exactly what had come up: him.

He'd have to do some serious laundry when he got home. Nobody needed to see the fresh blood stains on the clothes he'd left on the floor after the morning's outing, least of all a cop who suspected his family of covering up a possible murder.

CHAPTER NINE

Monday, October 6

Sure enough, Ret showed up at Manō's house in Pā'ia shortly after ten next night with a bottle of wine in one hand and clutching a paper takeout bag from the local hole-in-the-wall Italian place in the other.

"Special delivery," she said when he opened the door. She wore jeans, slippas that showed off her freshly painted pink toenails, and a tight Maui High T-shirt that probably fit when she and the Alanas attended the school several years ago. Now, it looked two sizes too small, and that was just fine with Manō.

He quickly scanned the street for anyone who might've followed her. No car in his driveway. She either parked elsewhere or arrived by taxi. Seeing nothing unusual, he stepped out of the threshold and waited for her to come in before shutting the door.

His house was about 400 square feet. Rented, not owned. White walls. Beige carpet. Open floor plan with combined living room and kitchen on one side of the front entrance, bedroom on the other. Basic, utilitarian furniture. Only the necessities. He didn't spend enough time here to warrant extravagances, nor did he care for them. The king-sized bed that dominated the bedroom was his only real luxury. Manō moved a lot in his sleep. When he slept.

Ret's topaz eyes roved over the scattering of candles providing just enough light to navigate the living room. He'd lit them as a courtesy in anticipation of her arrival. If he'd thought he'd be sleeping alone tonight, he wouldn't have bothered. He was much more comfortable without them.

She flashed a seductive smile. "Were you expecting someone?"

Manō skimmed his gaze meaningfully down her front hard enough for her to feel it and made no effort to hide the growing bulge in his pants. She noticed. Her grin widened.

Without a word, he took the food and wine from her and set them on the small kitchen table. Then he laid a deep kiss on her, drilling deep with his tongue, biting into her like a ripe papaya. She leaned into his chest, heavy breasts warm against him.

Ret was sexy and feminine despite the hard muscles and brash talk. Her lips joined his in a forbidden dance, tasting. Testing. He allowed himself to enjoy it.

He knew carrying on with her was wrong. Deep down, she loved Kai. She was using him to make Kai jealous. But Manō was using her too. She served as both a sounding board for the dark side of his soul and a mirror to his retreating light. It didn't take a genius to know the former part wanted a permanent piece of her. The latter secretly hoped she'd save him.

Ret broke the kiss and tipped her head back to study him. Her eyes shone like liquid amber with sharp edges in the low light. Her fingers skimmed through his short black hair, and she curled her arms around his neck, fingering the inked shark's teeth there.

"Are you hungry?" she purred demurely.

He arched a brow. The microdose of LSD he'd taken an hour before said hell yes. "Insatiable."

She smiled. "Lucky for you, I came prepared."

Ret opened the bag. The delicious smell of pasta prompted a growl from his stomach. She set out two to-go boxes on the table while Manō snagged a corkscrew from a drawer and went to work on the wine bottle.

The shadows drifted from the corners of the room toward him and pooled around his feet. They'd been temporarily sated by the drug dealer that morning, but now they wanted someone else's blood.

Not her, he silently warned and shooed them away.

The puddle of darkness below him seemed to glower as it separated like oozing beads of black mercury. Its blob-like pieces reluctantly retreated under furnishings, through door cracks, and behind a couple of boxes containing some of Mahina's old mementos he'd found at the safe house.

As he popped the cork on the wine, Ret's gaze snagged on the bandage awkwardly taped across his knuckles. He quickly lowered his hand to cover it up, but it was too late. Ret caught his arm.

"What happened?" Concern rounded her eyes.

He shook his head. "Surfing accident this morning. I'm fine."

Her fingers slid gently over the tape. A patch of broken, raw skin peeked out the side. Manō snatched his arm away.

"Who was on the other end of this?" she said, eyes narrowing with suspicion. All the flirtatiousness left her voice.

"Like I said. Surfing accident."

She hitched her hands to her hips. "Shark?" The word came out like an accusation rather than a question.

He shrugged noncommittally.

"Where were you surfing?" Ret had left the premises. Officer Beretta Rogers was in charge, practicing her detective moves in preparation for the upcoming exams, no doubt.

He poured two glasses of wine and offered one to her. "Kīhei," he fibbed.

"You're full of shit," she said, accepting the glass. The Boston accent strengthened when she smelled a lie. It added to the overall hard-ass attitude, which he found vaguely arousing.

He blew off her accusation. Manō didn't want to talk about it, though he appreciated her persistence. It was an endearing quality he admired in her.

A staredown ensued.

When she realized he wasn't budging on the subject, she seemed to let it go. She brought the wine to her lips and watched him through the glass as she swallowed.

Ret wasn't a problem at the moment, but she could easily become one if he wasn't careful. That persistence he admired could turn into a royal pain in his ass if she caught wind of some of the more questionable pies he had his fingers in.

On the other hand, she was no angel either. She'd admitted to smoking the illegal weed she'd gotten from Keahilani and Kai, and she'd likely hit some of the Ambrosia she'd given to him. Drug possession was bad enough for a cop, but it wouldn't be nearly as much of a big deal to her bosses as her failure to report what she knew about Butch the drug dealer's death at Keahilani's hands a week ago.

Candidates for detective had to pass psych tests and polygraphs. If they caught her lying, she could forget about a promotion. She'd be kicked to the curb and likely indicted, assuming the assholes she worked with were on the level.

Then again, Ret was almost as good at lying as Manō.

Yeah, he knew a few things about her he was sure she didn't want out in the wild.

He was safe with her. For now.

That didn't mean he trusted her.

Their takeout boxes open, they sat across from each other and ate. The food was more amazing than usual, thanks to the acid. The company didn't hurt either.

Ret didn't say much, which was fine with him. After she finished her last bite and laid her fork on the table, she picked up her wine glass and casually swirled its contents.

"You gonna tell me what happened to Pekelo?" she asked and downed the last gulp.

"You wouldn't believe me."

"So, you do know."

He gave her a dark look.

"Come on, Manō. I'm trying to impress the chief. Throw

me a bone."

"You'll have your bone soon enough," he replied, glancing to his lap.

Smiling, she stood, circled the table, and stopped behind him. Easing her arms around his neck, she whispered in his ear, "I was hoping you'd say that." She licked a line from the stubble on his chin up to his earlobe. A jolt of need shot through him.

Tracers spawned by the LSD kicked in, and everything in the world slid into a hyperreal state of flux. His senses jacked in to the pulse of the universe. Ret's closeness lit up his skin. The lingering smells of pasta and wine flooded his nose and merged with her scent—a clean, no-nonsense lemony fragrance. So Ret.

He turned his head into hers. Nuzzled her cheek. He wanted to taste her. Her insides. Her blood. Her soul.

Some small part in his own blood boomed, *No*.

That authoritarian voice brought him back to his senses. *Mahina?*

His scattered thoughts drifted to Blake's corpse, left alone on an angry island, vulnerable to the elements. He shouldn't have cared what happened to the body, but the truth was, Manō didn't dislike Blake. Blake had a thing for Keahilani, and Manō's gut told him he wouldn't have had the stones to do the deed even if someone else hadn't murdered Bane first.

He had to go back to Kaho'olawe and bury the body properly, if for no other reason than to minimize the chance a future visitor might find it. He'd do it tomorrow. No. Tonight. After he finished with Ret. He would go tonight. He owed it to Keahilani. She'd entrusted him with a task, and he'd done a half-assed job—

"Manō," Ret said softly, redirecting his attention to the hand rubbing his crotch.

When had that happened?

He closed his eyes, focused on the pleasure, and the bad things drifted away. "Hmm?"

"Let's go to bed." She wove her fingers between his and pulled him up.

He stood as if in a dream. The shadows ventured out from their various hidey-holes, slinking toward him tentatively, and gathered around his feet like a school of black piranhas with razor-sharp fangs and a hellish thirst for blood.

Could Ret see them?

He floated like a balloon tethered to Ret's wrist into the bedroom. Everything felt distant, like he was high above the earth, looking down at the beautiful woman disrobing him. Her creamy white shoulders shrugging out of a gem-studded bra. Her toned legs kicking back the covers on the bed. The blond spikes of her hair tamed by his eager fingers. The soft smacks of lips colliding and retreating, tasting, testing. The box springs protesting with gentle squeaks.

The shadows slunk up the bed's legs. They scaled the mattress and hung back at the edges, watching with quicksilver eyes. Hungry.

Don't eat her, he thought. *That's my job.*

He burst out laughing.

Straddling him, Ret jerked away from kissing his neck to look at him. Her shoulders rose and fell with rushed breaths. Her big breasts and their rosy nipples taunted him. "You okay?"

She was beautiful. Kai was a fucking idiot.

"Yes, *eleu,*" he said.

Spirited. She said she liked it when he called her that.

He lowered his hands to her naked waist and yanked her closer, spearing her to the hilt. She gasped as if in pain, but then her surprised expression transformed into one of loose enjoyment. Need sprouted in the lines of her face. She quickened her pace and rode him hard.

All around them, the shadows watched and writhed. And with their increased movements, Manō's desire demanded a sacrifice.

Or maybe that was the shadows projecting on him.

Either way, he sat up lightning fast, shoved Ret to her

back, and pounded her. Her lip curled in a furious snarl.

"Yeah, fuck me like that," she growled between her teeth. "Harder."

He pumped into her with renewed vigor. The headboard smacked and dented the wall. The legs of the bed lifted off the floor.

"Harder!" she commanded.

More shadows appeared, darkening the room, snuffing out the light, licking their trembling matte-black lips as if trying to quell a fever. They swelled into bloated monsters, preying, devouring, destroying. Manō felt them burrowing into his skin.

He channeled all the violence and rage and fire he could muster and cut it loose on her. Her legs split wider. Her eyes begged for more. The shadows encouraged it.

Hurt her, they whispered. *Give us her pain.*

Closing a hand around her throat, he stared down at Ret, her skin flushed red, damp with sweat. Tears collected at the corners of her bulging, bloodshot eyes.

He squeezed harder.

She didn't resist.

A black storm gathered within him, creating a high far grander and more pervasive than any drug could give. It coursed through him from the tips of his fingers, up his arm, down his chest, and exploded at the root of his cock.

Was this the kind of power trip Bane's killer had felt when he strangled him at the hospital?

Yesssss, the shadows moaned.

Manō tightened his grip. His upper lip curled with the effort. He felt the air within the column of her throat stop moving.

She clamped a hand on his forearm, meeting his pelvic blows, but her resolve seemed to weaken.

This moment was a line in the sand between darkness and light.

Manō could maintain his grip and suffocate her as he filled her with his seed, or he could release her and let the day get away with one less murder in the greater good's tally box.

Ret uttered a *kuh-kuh-kkkkk* sound. Water escaped from her dimming eyes. The strain in her muscles loosened.

Take her, the shadows goaded.

His need for release outweighed his need to please the little monsters who'd taken up residence in his head.

Upping the ante on his thrusts, he yanked his hand away. Ret sucked in a fast breath that seemed barely adequate. She wheezed again and again and again, slowly refilling the empty tanks of her lungs. Her thighs crushed around his in a painful squeeze, and he felt her inner walls collapse under the weight of his darkness.

He unleashed hell on her. Over her. In her.

Gritting his teeth as he released, Manō bludgeoned her with crushing lunges. She snatched the sheets either side of her and balled them till her knuckles whitened. She blew out her freshly caught breath in a hiccupping stream as she bucked under him, inciting him to hold her down and drown her with his body while leaving a string of alternating bites and vicious kisses across her flushed neck, shoulders, and breasts.

His strength waned as the shadows sipped their fill of his corruption and slowly dissolved back into the cracks and crevices from which they'd come, satisfaction plain on their glossy black faces.

Ret's heaving chest slowed as she regained control of her lost breath. Manō toppled to the mattress beside her, drained.

Regret at having nearly choked Ret to death set in just as a hail of bullets shattered the window on the other side of the room, spraying fragments of glass across the bed.

CHAPTER TEN

Ret Rogers sprung from her lover's bed and dropped to the floor in a crouch, keeping her head low. A car's engine revved. Tires squealed on the street.

"Son of a bitch!" she shouted, adrenaline and endorphins battling for control in her veins. Law enforcement training prepared her for situations like this, but on Maui, she rarely had to rely on it.

She scrambled over to her purse and grabbed her Beretta as Manō rifled through the bedside table. He found his gun, and together they army-crawled to the window. A thick layer of glass shards on the carpet glinted under the streetlights flooding the room. They split up to cover either side of the giant hole where the window had been. The bullets had stopped flying.

Shadows bathed Manō in an ethereal darkness. His black eyes shone under lush lashes. His tan skin glistened with sweat. Back pressed to the wall, he held up three fingers. She nodded. He mouthed the count.

One. Two. Three.

They swung their gun arms through the hole in sync. Humid air clung to her naked flesh. Lights from the surrounding houses flicked on. Manō ducked his head and squinted through the dark. A dog barked.

Another screech accompanied a set of fading brake lights as a midsize car careened around the corner at the end of the street and disappeared into the night. The stench of burning rubber infiltrated Ret's nose. She swiped at her nostrils.

At least she caught the last two digits of the license plate. Not much to go on, but something.

"What the fuck?" Her shoulders hitched up and down as adrenaline had its way with her nervous system. Expression blank and hands steady, Manō seemed unfazed by the drive-by.

Ret lowered her weapon and loosened her firing stance. She looked around for her clothes, shrugged on the shirt and punched her legs into the pants. No time for bra or underwear.

She grabbed her phone and started to dial 911, but then she remembered she wasn't supposed to be here.

"Shit." She turned to Manō. "You gotta call this in. Tell them you saw a dark-colored midsize SUV, probably a Nissan Pathfinder. The last two digits on the license plate were 46."

He nodded. He was still naked. If they hadn't just been targeted for death, she probably would've pushed him to the bed and demanded another go with that glorious body of his. As it was, she averted her gaze and swallowed hard.

Manō made the call. His voice remained calm as he explained what happened to the 911 operator. Ret stuffed the rest of her clothes in her bag and quickly disposed of the takeout boxes in the kitchen while Manō waited on the line. No need to give her comrades any reason to believe he'd had guests tonight.

And since they'd be here momentarily, she had to bolt.

Slipping her shoes on, she gestured to the door with a head jerk. Manō covered the phone speaker with a palm and nodded. "Go," he whispered.

A distant siren wailed, growing louder. Torn between wanting to stay with him and needing to cover her ass, Ret mouthed, "I'm sorry."

He shooed her toward the door.

She hesitated for a second, then ran over and planted a quick kiss on his lips. He stared after her as she backed up.

Heart pinging against her ribs in a frenetic rhythm, she ached to protect him, but if there was one person in the world who *didn't* need protection, it was Manō Alana. He could handle the cops.

Ret cracked open the back door, looked around. Seeing no one, she snuck into the night and trotted through the yard toward her car parked a block up and over.

Her gut tightened as she ran. Exposed and vulnerable were two adjectives she wasn't keen on having attached to her. Ret stuck to the shadows as best she could. By the time she reached her Mazda CX-5, the spinning blue and white lights of three Maui police cars had lit up Manō's street like a football stadium on Super Bowl night.

Theorizing that the gunner had continued north on Manō's street, she headed that way, scoping for anything that seemed unusual. Every driver became a suspect, every shadow a potential hiding place. She saw nothing out of the ordinary, so she went back for another look.

Nope.

Fingers itching to call Manō to make sure he was all right, she convinced herself to drive home instead. Of course, he was all right. He was Manō.

By the time she got inside her apartment in Wailuku about twenty minutes later, she'd received a text from Kai: *Drive by at Manō's. He's fine. We need to talk.*

Well, wasn't that the damn truth?

She plugged the phone into its charger and got ready for bed. Kai could wait until morning.

She pulled up the covers, but sleep eluded her. Her mind wouldn't stop running through the details of her night. Manō's turn toward violence in bed took her by surprise, but she kind of liked it. The pressure of his big hand on her throat, clamping down to the point of pain, robbing her of life-giving oxygen, combined with the eroticism of his brutal thrusts had been orgasmic even before the orgasm.

She'd put her life in his hands for those few precious moments. The intense pleasure that came from flirting with disaster had been epic. At first, she'd imagined looking up into Kai's face, but the picture didn't last. Manō owned her body, and his control over her made her want to break the lease on the heart that belonged to his brother.

And damn if the butterflies in her stomach didn't go bonkers every time he called her *eleu*. The morning after their first tryst, Manō had told her the word meant "spirited" in Hawaiian. She caught herself scribbling it on scraps of paper when she got bored at work. Her cheeks warmed.

In many respects, Kai was fading into the background, but in others, he wouldn't leave her alone. They had history. The kind that stuck between your ears and rattled your rib cage long after all was said and done.

After chatting at Bane's funeral, Ret had reluctantly agreed to a date with Kai, but she got cold feet when old, familiar insecurities crept up. Kai had been unfaithful to her not once, but twice before. And those were the two times she knew about. It had probably been far more than that.

And then, there was the pain that flooded her every time she saw a mom or dad playing with their kid at the park, teaching them how to surf on the beach, or kissing a boo-boo after a stumble. Those kicks to the gut always shook Kai to the surface of her thoughts, and sometimes they were too much to bear, even after all these years.

She couldn't afford the handling fees for the extra baggage she dragged around courtesy of Kai Alana.

Fool me once, shame on you. Fool me twice, shame on me.

So, back to Manō she went. He was a simple, what-you-see-is-what-you-get kind of man. And boy, did she get it.

She mentally cracked open the lantern door surrounding her tender heart and let a sliver of light shine from it. She considered leaving it unlocked, barely ajar, in case Manō decided to come a little closer, but then she hit the pause button on that idea. If he wanted to open up to her, he would. Until then, he was a booty call, nothing more. Whatever they had would *not* be a replay of her and Kai's fucked-up relationship.

As for the shooting tonight, any number of people could've been responsible, but Ret's Spidey sense leaned toward someone from Scott Harris's menagerie. After his dramatic reveal at Bane's funeral, it was obvious Scott's and the Alanas' interests were in direct conflict. Drug dealers-turned-unexpected-family had become hated enemies thanks to the tit-for-tat hits each had executed on the other.

This Mafia-style warfare put Ret in the center of some really bad shit. While she wanted to help the Alanas, she also had to look out for herself. Now that she was gunning for detective, the chief was watching her like a hawk. She either had to wash her hands of the Alanas completely or find a way to cover up the dirty deeds she'd been doing for them lately.

Hell of a choice with no good answer. Sure, there was a *right* answer, but right had a strong possibility of going very wrong.

Her phone dinged with another text, this one from Keahilani: *Scott issued hits on Manō and Kai.*

Ret sat up straighter and threw the covers off. A fresh burst of energy flooded her chest. Kai had messaged her only minutes ago. He either didn't want to worry her, or Scott's thugs had just reached his house. Shit, she should've texted him right after the drive-by at Manō's. Or told Manō to warn Kai himself. Scott had already taken out one Alana. Of *course* he'd go after the others.

"Stupid, stupid, stupid," she scolded herself.

She frantically typed, *Is Kai OK?* Then she deleted it in favor of, *Are they OK?*

For now, came Keahilani's reply.

Where are you? Ret sent back.

Just got home. Police here after the attempts on Kai and Manō.

If Ret went to Keahilani's on her own, her coworkers might suspect she'd rekindled friendships with the Alanas. That could be dangerous. But anyone who'd been to Bane's funeral knew of Ret's connection to them. They'd just lost their brother, for fuck's sake. In that context, her showing up at Keahilani's wouldn't seem that strange. In fact, it might seem off if she *didn't* go check on a friend who'd recently lost her brother.

I'm coming over, Ret typed and quickly got dressed.

On her way out, she grabbed her phone. A new message popped up from Keahilani: *This is war.*

Ret pressed her lips together. Keahilani was wrong. This wasn't war. It was fucking Armageddon.

CHAPTER ELEVEN

Ret arrived at Keahilani's apartment in Kīhei in record time. A squad car sat in the parking lot with its lights off. The complex was quiet.

Ret hopped out, slammed the door shut, and shouldered her bag. The weight of the gun within swung heavily at her side. She headed up to Keahilani's door, subtly swiveling her head in search of movement, glinting metal in shadows, anything out of the ordinary.

Keahilani welcomed her in. She wore sweatpants and a nondescript gray T-shirt, but she was fully made up—heavy black eyeliner, fake lashes, the works—as if she'd just gotten home from a grand gala but hadn't taken off her face yet. Even with all the makeup, though, she had slight bags under her muted green eyes.

"Ret Rogers, this is Sergeant Haoa."

"Pleased to meet you." Ret shook Haoa's hand, which was almost as big as a bear's paw. He was a massive Hawaiian dude, not an ounce of fat on him. A slightly beefed-up version of Manō, but not as sexy.

He nodded. "Likewise. Miss Alana tells me you're with the Wailuku district."

"That's right," Ret said.

"Tell Chief Hale he might want to wear earplugs at this year's baseball tournament. He's gonna need it when District VI brings the thunder."

With a wide grin, she snapped her gum and casually swiped her nose. "That so? You must be new."

"Why's that?" Haoa asked.

Ret leaned back on her heels and crossed her arms over her chest, flexing. "Because Officer Ret Rogers *is* the thunder."

Beside her, Keahilani snickered.

Haoa boomed a hearty laugh. "I'll remember that." He gestured to Keahilani. "Seems your friends have attracted the notice of some unsavory types."

"I heard. Any leads?" Ret asked.

"Her brother"—he paused to consult his little notebook—"Manō got a partial on a license plate, but other than that, nothing. We haven't received any other calls about shots fired, so we're working on the theory that this was a targeted attempt on the family."

Ret turned to Keahilani. "So, who'd you piss off this time?" she joked.

Keahilani smiled tersely. The lines on her face put her tiredness and worry on bold display.

"Kai's place was hit too, but he wasn't home when it happened," Keahilani clarified.

Jealousy wielded its ugly knife and sliced Ret across the chest. So, Kai had been out late too. She refused to speculate as to where, with whom, or what he'd gotten up to.

"We're coordinating with the Wailuku department since the hit on Manō took place in Pā'ia," Haoa said.

"I want to help. I'll ask the chief to put me on the case tomorrow," Ret told Keahilani. "We'll get to the bottom of this."

"Is there anything else, Sergeant?" Keahilani asked, rubbing her forehead.

He looked over his notes. "I don't think so. I'll stick around, patrol the lot and street. We've got a couple other cops on duty who are aware of what's going on. You should be fine tonight."

"I'll stay if it would make you feel better," Ret offered.

Keahilani nodded eagerly. "Yes. It would." Ret couldn't tell if the tremble in her voice was genuine or engineered for the benefit of the sergeant.

"We'll check into this Scott Harris you mentioned tomorrow," Haoa said.

"See that you do," Ret said. "I already escorted that asshole out of their brother's funeral after he waltzed in and made a scene, upsetting everyone. My gut tells me if he had something to do with Bane's death, he was damn sure behind the attempts on Kai and Manō tonight too. He's dangerous, Sarge."

Haoa nodded curtly and retreated to the door. He replaced his hat. "We'll be in touch."

"*Mahalo*," Keahilani said and saw him out. Ret tugged down the corner of the blinds overlooking the parking lot and scanned for activity. Haoa got in his car, but he didn't leave. Good. Ret was completely capable of keeping Keahilani safe, but it was nice to know she had backup in case trouble arose. The squad car itself should make a strong deterrent for anyone who dared to get sassy with the Alanas.

Keahilani dropped onto the couch. "I appreciate you staying."

"Where'd you go today?" Ret asked, taking a seat across from her in a beige wingback chair.

Keahilani's eyes flashed. "Who says I went anywhere?"

Ret pointed to her face. "Your makeup."

Keahilani sighed and yanked off the fake lashes. "The truth would probably get us both in trouble."

"Lay it on me."

Her friend paused as if trying to decide whether to spill. Then she said, "I went to O'ahu. To see Scott."

"Shit," Ret spat.

Of all the *stupid* things Keahilani could do—

Ret sprung to her feet and paced. "Why the hell would you go and do something like that?"

Pools of shadow fell over Keahilani's green eyes, filling them with threat. "Because he fucking killed Bane."

Ret pressed her lips together and stood over her with hands on her hips. "Do you have evidence? Because in Hawai'i, the police don't arrest people without that shit."

"He did it," Keahilani said in a resolute, cold voice.

Ret sat beside her on the couch. "I happen to believe you, but you can't take matters into your own hands. You have more pressing issues to worry about than taking revenge on your brother's killer. Let me handle that. It's what they pay me for."

"You're handling enough of our problems already," Keahilani said. "There are some things you don't need to be involved in. This is Alana 'ohana business."

The flippant comment stung like a slap to the face. "I'm sorry you feel like I'm butting into your personal space. If you want me to back off, say so. I just assumed you liked having my protection. Maybe I was wrong."

The tight screws on Keahilani's harsh expression loosened a tad. "I do. Sorry, Ret. It's been a shitty week."

Ret laid a hand on her arm. "Yes. It has. And you're allowed to feel bad. Maybe you should give yourself a little time to heal before you charge back in to work. You've been through a major traumatic event."

Keahilani's brows pinched together in a knot. Her shoulders tensed as if she was holding her breath. For a moment, Ret thought she might cry, but her friend quickly corralled her emotions and exhaled heavily.

A moment of silence fell between them, and then Keahilani changed the subject. "Scott's going to send more people after us. Not only do we have this ongoing feud about Bane and Scott's wife, but he also wants our product. From what I've seen, he'll stop at nothing to get it.

"I'm in a pinch, Ret. Distributors are moving our stuff, but the money's not coming in as we'd hoped. I have to pay our investors next Thursday, and now the police are involved in this drive-by, which puts us directly under their microscope. If I don't unload all of this product fast, we're in a world of hurt."

She paused for a few seconds and then looked Ret directly in the eye. "I know you care about Kai. If those feelings mean anything, help us shake off the cops and anyone else who comes sniffing around our business."

Ret knew Keahilani wasn't talking about the surf shop. And Ret's growing feelings for Manō complicated things even more than her feelings for Kai. Alana brothers aside, Ret didn't like the pressure Keahilani put on her.

"I adore you guys," she began, choosing her words carefully. "We've known each other since high school when Mom and I moved here. You befriended me when other kids picked on me for being from Boston and made fun of my accent. That shit meant the world to me. I'd give my left tit to help you out. But I'm in a delicate position with this opportunity to make detective—"

"I know," Keahilani cut in. She paused as if gathering her thoughts. "Maybe you could make evidence disappear on the sly if it comes to you. You know, misplace it. Or point them in a different direction. It doesn't have to be anything overt. Every little bit helps."

Ret sighed. She didn't want to get more deeply involved in the Alanas' shit. If anything, she needed to step back. But they'd been through the ringer, and she loved them like family. And sometimes you had to make sacrifices for those you loved, even when they didn't have much to give in return. Call it naivete, but Ret genuinely cared about her friends and wanted to keep them out of trouble. If they were using her, so be it. She was doing the right thing.

"If you want my help, you're gonna have to come clean. About everything. The better I understand your situation, the better I'll be able to assist."

"Everything?" Keahilani lifted a brow.

"Everything," Ret replied.

"It's heavy."

"I got strong arms. I can handle it."

Keahilani inhaled a full breath, pressed her lips into a thin line, and let the air out slowly. "Butch the drug dealer isn't the only guy I … took care of."

Ret had to work at maintaining a neutral expression. "Okay."

Keahilani wet her lips. "I was sort of seeing a guy who turned out to be one of Scott's men. His name was Blake Murphy. He came to Maui posing as a tourist surfer, but he was really looking for our farm. I gave him surfing lessons. Things heated up between us.

"I found out Scott sent him to kill Bane. Blake went to do the deed, but someone else had already plugged him and left him for dead. I shot Blake in the leg and took him to the safe house in Kula. Manō roughed him up some more, but Blake wouldn't talk."

She paused again, her face flushed. A little crack threatened to split her wavering demeanor, putting her emotions on display for a fraction of a second.

Another deep breath. "When the ambulance came, I warned Blake that if Bane died, he would too. But if he'd just tell us where Scott was, we'd …" She shook her head. When she looked at Ret again, defeat marred her beautiful face. "Anyway, when someone else smothered Bane to death at the hospital, I had to follow through."

The hairs on Ret's arms stiffened at her friend's admission. A spike of ice settled into the base of her spine. She swallowed hard. "How'd you do it?" she asked softly.

Keahilani made a gun out of her hand and pointed two fingers under her chin.

Damn. Ret thought *she* was tough, but she had nothing on Keahilani.

"Where's the body?"

"I don't know. Manō said he'd handle it. I don't get involved with his business. But this trip to O'ahu today—"

"Jesus Christ," Ret exclaimed and quickly made the sign of the cross, "please tell me you didn't brag about Blake's death to Scott."

"I may have … alluded to something of the sort." Keahilani shifted her gaze to the hands in her lap. She didn't fidget like a guilty person would, which made Ret wonder just how dark and twisted her friend really was. And how deeply the darkness had scarred her.

Ret considered herself a pretty good judge of character. She'd known all of the Alanas, including their mother, for years. Though work and Kai's shenanigans forced them to grow apart after graduation, they'd stayed in contact. Ret had never gotten any bad vibes off them. If anything, they seemed to be unlucky people driven by outside forces to do bad things.

"Keahilani, this is serious. If Blake had hurt you or your brothers, if he'd murdered or assaulted someone, a court of law might judge your actions as justifiable. But you're walking in some ill-lit alleys with this shit. It's gonna be hard for others to view your actions as anything other than cold-blooded murder."

Keahilani slowly turned her head to Ret. A strange expression fell over her face. Ret couldn't tell if it was revenge or satisfaction. Either way, it scared her a little.

"Then, I guess we'll have to make sure no one finds out."

Keahilani's hooded eyes glittered from the shadows falling over her head. Only problem was, with all the light in the room, there shouldn't have been any shadows there.

A tremor raced from Ret's feet to her scalp. Heavy black circles edged the outer ring of Keahilani's irises. Ret was certain they hadn't been there when she arrived. Her entire body bloomed with goose bumps.

Something really bad was going down with her friends, and it wasn't related to just the drugs and murders. The growing darkness surrounding them threatened to stretch beyond the kind she witnessed every day in the killers, rapists, and child molesters she encountered on the job. Left unchecked, this kind of darkness would penetrate soul-deep. It was the stuff of horror movies made real.

She should get the hell out of there. Run far away and never look back.

Officer Beretta Rogers was many things, but a coward

wasn't one of them. She'd become a cop to help people. And to redeem herself for the bad things she'd done herself.

She'd always walked a fine line between right and wrong, but she tried to lean right as much as she could. The Alanas were good people who were forced to commit bad deeds to get by. Her gut told her Scott Harris was a bigger criminal than her friends were. That was all she needed to know.

Sometimes you had to abandon your morals in deference to the bigger picture. And in that moment, Ret got the distinct feeling that helping her friends overcome their own darkness was far more important than her job or even her future.

"Okay," she said with a sigh. "I'm in. If Scott wants a fight, let's give it to him, Alana style."

CHAPTER TWELVE

Tuesday, October 7

Scott Harris did not want to go to work.

He couldn't. Not today.

He rolled over miserably in bed and stared at the ceiling. His palms were sweaty. His heart raced. He hadn't slept a wink last night. A perfect shitstorm converged above his head and unleashed its fury.

Not only was today the one-year anniversary of his wife's and unborn baby's deaths, but his half sister Keahilani had waltzed into his office yesterday, throwing her weight around, alluding to his best friend and right-hand man Blake in the past tense.

Dread sunk into his gut, decomposing him one cell at a time. He closed his lids and pictured Lori, her long brown hair kissed by the sun, sweet eyes of a fawn, a hand lying low on her belly, standing at the door to the afterlife. Blake stepped into the space beside her. The only two people in the entire world he trusted were gone.

Their faces morphed into those of rotting corpses, teeming with maggots and worms, skin sloughing off in bloody sheets, exposing raw muscle and sinew until nothing but bones remained. Tears burned hot trails down his temples into his ears.

"No," he moaned, palming the liquid away. "I can't. I

can't …"

He tried to inhale a breath, but his entire frame shook with the effort. He couldn't escape the macabre images that held him hostage. He couldn't see past the agony that seemed intent on consuming him.

"Why do you torture me?" he demanded of God or whatever cruel deity ruled the cosmos.

The morning of the shooting, Lori had learned she was pregnant. For the first time in his life, Scott had a sense of true accomplishment. It was a feeling that couldn't be bought or duplicated. One he'd earned through unconditional love and devotion and a vehement commitment to giving his beautiful wife the best things he could. Lori's pregnancy brought him hope—a belief, however false, that goodness really did exist inside him and that it would be passed along to his son or daughter.

He remembered in vivid detail standing up from this same bed, dressed in the same pajama pants, at the same time a year ago, looking down at Lori and marveling at his good fortune. He'd been born into his wealth, given everything a man could ever need to be successful in business. He owned a multimillion-dollar resort on O'ahu. Until he met Lori, his business had defined him.

But she showed him he was more than his three-letter title or a bank account balance with too many zeroes in it to count. *I can't be bought*, she'd told him on their first date, meeting his gaze head-on. She hadn't been coy or submissive like the other women he'd dated. They were only interested in his money. But Lori was resolute. Proud. *If you want me, you have to fight for me.*

And he did.

Lori taught him that success in relationships had to be carefully cultivated and continuously nuanced. She wasn't some deal to be brokered or an employee to be hired for his personal amusement. She was the love of his life. The thing that kept him going from day to day. When he'd humbly asked for the honor of her hand in marriage, her affirmative answer was a gift no amount of money could top.

They'd been trying to conceive a child for over a year. When she showed him the positive pregnancy test, he'd been so moved by the swell of love he felt for her and their unborn baby, he had actually cried. The idea of becoming someone's parent and of sharing that duty with the woman who made his heart race every time she walked into a room transformed him into something bigger than he could ever be without her.

Lori made him better. She might've even made him human.

Through the tears blurring his vision, he remembered Lori's vibrant smile. Her reaching for him. Holding him tight as they cried happily together over the baby news. She grazed her nose across his neck to smell the cologne she loved. Kissed him. When she smiled up into his face, he was so taken by the beauty and purity of the moment, he broke down again.

Hours later, his joy turned to panic when a knock on the door from the police destroyed him.

The officer removed his hat and tucked it under his arm. *Are you Scott Harris?* When he answered yes, the officer lowered his head. *I regret to inform you that your wife has been killed.*

At first, the words didn't make sense. The universe must've suffered from a bout of dyslexia. There was no way his Lori could be dead. They'd made a mistake.

But it wasn't a mistake. He went to the hospital morgue to identify her, but he still couldn't believe it. Blake stood outside, faithful as ever, while Scott carried on and yowled and threw things.

I have a wife. And a child. And this is a twisted joke.

Blake hugged him in a vise grip like he was afraid he'd lose Scott to madness or suicide or worse if he let go.

Lori and the baby were everything.

A year ago today, Scott's soul died with theirs.

And now he had Blake's loss to add to Lori's.

He could not bear the weight of either.

You don't have a choice. Get your ass up and deal with it. The people you love must be avenged.

His throat tightened with choking sadness. His head hurt. But he conjured the strength to sit up.

The universe has made you its bitch three times over.

He wiped his eyes with shaking fingers.

When Bane killed his family, he killed Scott too. Scott had been little more than a shell ever since, going through the motions at work, delegating tasks to his staff, staying hidden in the shadows where it was safe.

Blake's loss was icing on the cake, but it was all the motivation he needed to shuck this feeble armor of self-loathing and sorrow in favor of a sharper variety fashioned in razor-blade-scale mail and fully funded retribution.

He deserved better than this. He was Scott Harris. Bad things didn't happen to him. He made bad things happen to others.

Around him, the bedroom darkened as if storm clouds had suddenly gathered outside his window. Or the moon had eclipsed the sun.

Keahilani and her brothers weren't worthy of the privilege of sharing blood with him.

Scott looked at his hands. Turned them over. Faint veins of black throbbed under the skin. This was *his* blood, not theirs.

Take it back, a chorus of hissing voices whispered between his ears.

An oiliness crept over him, clogging his pores and stifling his skin's access to air. Light dove for cover as the room darkened further until nothing but shadows skittered over his flesh, digging into his soul for a bite.

Scott dropped his hands to his sides and let the darkness feast. There was nothing left of his heart to protect anyway. The swarm penetrated him and rose to the surface in an explosion of hatred. Pins of anger shot outward, prickling nerves, dousing him in blackness.

He fell into the cold, waiting arms behind him, soft as feathers. The shadows grinned and caressed him, mussing his short hair, licking his face like loyal dogs.

But he wasn't their pet. Not anymore.

He shook off their black wings and sharp talons and stood.

He had no one left to give a single fuck about. And a man with nothing to live for was dangerous indeed.

The gloves were coming off. No more taking shit from unworthy siblings. No more sucker punches to the balls.

His phone chirped from its charger beside the bed. Scott snatched it up.

"Jezzy," he said, his tone so cold he didn't recognize it. It was about time his personal assistant for his illegal business called.

"Scott, darling." The low purr of her familiar voice sounded a half-step higher than usual. That was bad news.

"You'd better have something good for me," he said. "I'm not in the mood for anything less than success."

A pause followed. "The hits you ordered last night were unsuccessful."

"So, my men still can't find an Alana to save their lives. Why am I not surprised?" That was fine. Their souls were now forfeit for all the ineptitude they'd shown.

"If you want a job done, you have to do it yourself," Jezzy remarked offhandedly.

He grinned. "You're absolutely right."

Another pause. "You're not gonna do something stupid, are you?"

"No, for once I'm doing something smart," he said. "Set up a fake ID and book me on a commercial flight to Maui tonight. No electronic footprints or paper trails leading back to me. And find me a hotel. Where did you say Keahilani lives?"

"Kīhei," came Jezzy's slow, suspicious answer. It sounded as if she were turning the word over in her mouth, testing it for soft spots she could exploit.

"A hotel in Kīhei," he continued. "The scummier, the better."

"You're not going into the office today?" she asked.

"I'm not going into the office ever."

"As your personal hacker and sometime sounding board, I strongly advise you to rethink your last statement." She cut the shit with the breathy voice theatrics and dropped all pretense of maintaining her usual sexy mystique.

"And as your employer, I advise you to get your nose out of my goddamn business and do your fucking job. Unless, of course, you don't need the million I'm about to transfer."

Her pauses were becoming a habit.

"Scott. Please. Be reasonable." A hint of desperation underscored her voice.

"I'm seeing things much more clearly this morning, and my newly corrected 20-20 vision is showing me a side of you I don't care for," he warned.

"I just," she began, then stopped herself and sighed. "I heard about what happened to Blake." Her voice wobbled over his name. Even though she and Blake had never met, they'd always shared a playful, flirtatious camaraderie in their communications. She must've been upset about his death too.

"Then you know what I have to do."

"No," she said firmly. "You don't *have* to do anything. This tit-for-tat between you and the Alanas has gotten out of control."

Fury rose from his chest and spewed like acid out his mouth. "As far as I'm concerned, no amount of vengeance I could heap upon Bane Alana's siblings is enough to pay back what he took from me."

"I get it. I do," she said.

"No. You don't. Stick to sneaking around in dark corners, Jezzy. It's what you do best. You'll have your money momentarily." He hung up.

No more failures.

He scrolled through his contact list, found Prince Seamus's number, and dialed.

"Good morning, Mr. Harris. What can I do for you?" his Ambrosia dealer said.

"How are sales going?" Scott asked.

"Very well. Despite the steep price, the addictive nature of our product makes for quite a few returning customers." Seamus hesitated. "You need a bump?"

"Not the kind you mean," Scott said dryly. "How much do you have in stock?"

"It's not easy to come by," Seamus hedged. "My source is still scrambling to refine the raw product, which is rare enough. The distillation process hasn't been perfected—"

"How much?" Scott interrupted, irritated.

"Half a liter."

"Speak in terms I understand."

"About 2500 doses at a hundred bucks a pop … Two hundred and fifty grand."

"I want you to flood the market on Maui," Scott said. "Halve your prices if you have to. I'll cover your losses."

The Alanas were struggling to pay their Pāhoehoe investors, a couple of whom Scott knew personally. The lenders were cutthroats who had no qualms about ordering hits on anyone who displeased them, and their assassins had far better track records than Scott's pay-to-slay mercenaries, Blake notwithstanding.

By dramatically dropping Ambrosia prices, he'd create fierce competition and start a price war with Pāhoehoe. With their looming deadline only days away, the Alanas couldn't afford to drop their prices to match his. In business, Scott had always been a big fan of watching his foes sweat before he swept in and devoured his weakened prey. Let Keahilani and her brothers live in terror for their lives for a while. That would make the moment when he crushed them in his talons even sweeter. It would also give him time to arrange his remaining chess pieces on the board before the final match.

"You sure?" Seamus asked uncertainly.

"Absolutely. Invoice me at your leisure." Scott smiled as he laid track for the next stage of his plan to destroy his siblings. "By the way, how are things between you and our big Hawaiian friend on Maui?"

"Lui bends to my will—in more ways than one," Seamus said with a chuckle.

"I always suspected he was a bottom under all that raging, desperate need for control," Scott replied.

"And what a beautiful bottom he is."

"I may need to book your *other* services through him soon."

"Book away. Lui suspects nothing," Seamus said.

"Keep it that way." With that, Scott hung up.

He picked up the picture of him and Lori smiling from his bedside table and rubbed a thumb across his wife's image. It was past time to take matters into his own hands. Keahilani and her brothers—*his* brothers—were going to suffer and die for what they stole from him, even if it killed him too.

CHAPTER THIRTEEN

Meeting at the usual spot, usual time, Keahilani's text read.

The sun streaming through the slight gap in the hotel curtains amplified Manō's headache. He got up from the bed and made coffee in the mini pot. Its glass bore hints of reddish water stains, the kind you couldn't scrub out, no matter how hard you tried.

Like his soul stains.

He walked over to the other bed where Kai slept and stared down at his older brother. A flash of memory trailing a mischievous thought in its rearview crossed his mind. When they were kids, they used to pile-drive each other at every opportunity. If Kai was busy reading a book, Manō would sneak up and attack him from behind. Kai would get payback when Keahilani sat with Manō, telling him ghost stories or singing Hawaiian songs to him.

They wrestled all the time. Mahina would shake her finger and shout for them to stop, but she liked that they were so playful. She and Keahilani often exchanged secret smiles when they thought he wasn't looking.

Manō was tempted to jump Kai's sleeping form now, but that was childish. They were adults with adult problems. Manō nudged him in the shoulder instead. "Wake up."

Kai rolled onto his back and threw his forearm in front of his squinting eyes. "Jesus, what time is it?"

"Seven."

Kai snorted. "Fuck you. Way too early." He curled onto his side.

"Keahilani called a meeting." Manō yanked off the sheets. "You got fifteen."

Kai protested weakly by pulling the linens back into place around his hips, but he was awake and getting more so by the second. Sunlight had an annoying way of squashing all hope of peace for people like them. He sighed, grabbed his phone off the table between the beds, and read the same message Manō had received.

With an annoyed huff, Kai tumbled out of bed, his bare feet avoiding the sun's sprawl across the floor on his way to the toilet.

Manō sat on the made-up bed near the window. He hadn't bothered pulling the covers down. He knew he wouldn't sleep last night. He couldn't afford to with everything that was going on.

Thanks to the drive-by and a couple hours spent talking to police between his house and Kai's, Manō hadn't made it to Kaho'olawe. He seriously doubted anyone would go there, let alone find Blake's body in the near future, but the red-eyed man—Creature? Monster? Hallucination?—he'd seen on the island's slopes haunted his subconscious with increasing regularity.

No one should've been there, yet, someone clearly was.

That bothered Manō. A lot.

The water shut off in the bathroom, and Kai came out wiping his face with a towel, dreadlocks spilling over his broad, bare shoulders. His green eyes still shone with light that didn't carry over anywhere else.

He wasn't completely gone. Yet.

Manō exhaled a quiet sigh of relief.

Kai checked his phone again and frowned. "I called Jezzy like you asked to get information about Pekelo and also enquired about Scott's whereabouts last night. She hasn't responded."

"She's a busy woman."

"Yeah," Kai agreed, pulling on a pair of shorts, "but she usually acknowledges messages even if she can't get to the job right away. Something seems off."

Manō had to agree. It wasn't like Jezzy not to reply within a few hours. Based on his limited interactions with her, he'd come to believe Jezzy slept about as much as he did.

None of the Alanas had ever met the mysterious tech guru. She'd been recommended by one of Keahilani's contacts in the drug world a couple years before, and all of their transactions had been conducted electronically, usually over the phone.

As far as Manō could tell, Jezzy had always been forthright with the 'ohana. When she couldn't do a job, she said so. Manō never got the feeling she meant to harm them, but he'd been annoyed on the few occasions when her intel would've been a hell of a lot handier had she only shared it an hour or two sooner.

He understood that in illegal business, precautions and fail-safes were essential. He just wondered how long it would take for her to cross a point of no return. She worked for Scott and the Alanas. Conflicts of interest figured prominently in her central operating system. They certainly made for strange bedfellows.

"If we don't hear from her by tonight, we'll cut her loose," Manō said.

"Be a shame to lose her." Kai shrugged on a Mahina Surf and Dive T-shirt and stubbed his feet into a pair of slippas.

"Just business," Manō said with a shrug.

"Speaking of business, it looks like Ret's trying her damnedest to be assigned to our case." Kai avoided Manō's gaze as he gathered his keys and wallet.

Manō nodded. He'd tired of Kai's attempts to engage him on the subject of their mutual affection. Or attraction. Or whatever Ret was. "You ready?"

"Yeah," Kai said.

"You're driving."

A grin wiped the concern off Kai's face, and the pair left

the hotel for his black Mustang. It was an older model with a few dings and scrapes, but the beast drove well. Kai was proud of the car, and that pride swelled anytime his siblings wanted a ride in it.

The low growl of the engine cranked up, and they headed toward their secret meeting place off Honoapi'ilani Highway's beaten track.

"I've been thinking about what you said about us. About the shadows," Kai said after several minutes of silence. "And I've started paying more attention, noticing things I didn't see before. It started off as a stray movement from the corner of my eye, like a black cat darting behind me that I could never quite track. I figured my mind was playing tricks. But now that I'm keyed in, I see so much more."

A bubble of worry rose in Manō's throat. He saw Kai's shadows, but he couldn't make them go away. Manō's only goal in life was to protect his 'ohana. Now he couldn't even protect himself.

"They're most active at twilight," Kai continued. "They haunt my dreams. When I wake up, my arms and legs ache with a driving need to do *something*, but I'm not sure what. I want to fight and feed and fuck." He turned to Manō, black rings vibrant in his eyes. "I want to do bad things."

Manō's pulse picked up. This was the moment he was afraid of. After Mahina's death, Keahilani fell into depression and developed a dark streak. But nothing bothered Kai. Like Bane, he'd been the happy-go-lucky guy who got along with everyone. Sure, he smoked too much pot and banged too many women, but his heart was good.

When the siblings conducted their drug deals in elaborate Hawaiian costumes as Pele and her Enforcers, Kai was visibly uncomfortable. He disliked donning his giant tiki-head mask. He said it brought to mind violence, which he wanted nothing to do with.

It hurt Manō to see his brother transforming into something he feared. It hurt worse that he couldn't do anything to stop it.

"Don't give in," Manō said quietly, knowing his advice was useless. The shadows would have their way with Kai and Keahilani as they'd done with Manō. Just a matter of time.

Gazing out the window, he couldn't look his brother in the eye. The truth was like an axe to the heart. If he could've taken on all the *'ohana's* shadows so his brother or sister wouldn't have to deal with them, he'd have done it without question. But each of the Alanas had their own cross to bear.

"Whatever they are, the shadows are here to stay," Manō said. "Keep to the light. As long as you can."

"What if I can't?" Kai asked, his voice cracking.

"If the light becomes too much, then embrace the shadows while you cling to your morals," Manō said.

Kai slowed to a stop on the dirt by the beach and swiveled his head toward Manō. "That's some heavy shit, bruh."

"Yeah." Manō hesitated. His fingers twitched. He wanted to hug Kai like Keahilani used to hug him. Instead, he popped the door handle and stepped out.

Keahilani stood on the sand, arms crossed over her chest, her hair tangling with the gentle winds playing along the shore. Invasive kiawe trees with their long thorns framed her slender figure. She didn't offer any sign of recognition when the brothers joined her. Her eyes seemed distant as she stared across miles of ocean to Kaho'olawe's whale-shaped form.

The trio remained silent for a short eternity. Under the shade of the trees, Manō's hyper senses snaked out and sampled the familiar tang in his siblings' blood. It was like the call of a siren. He heard it, felt it, smelled it, and tasted it. He realized then that he'd been aware of the dark link among them ever since they were children. Whether he was tackling Kai in the apartment complex yard or sitting with Keahilani as she read him bedtime stories, he'd always sensed their connection.

It had been different with Bane. When he was around, the darkness retreated. Maybe that was why they hadn't been close. Whatever clicked among the older siblings had missed the mark when it came to the youngest Alana.

"Ever wonder if Bane was Justin's son," Manō asked, keeping his expression neutral and eyes fixed on the horizon, "or someone else's?"

Kai whipped around to face Manō, but Keahilani's reaction was slower, more calculated. They had to be careful with Kai. Despite him and Keahilani being the oldest, he was the most impressionable and sensitive of the bunch. He didn't respond well to change. Questioning Bane's lineage was a touchy subject.

"No," Kai spat defensively. "He was Justin's son. Mom wouldn't have cheated on Dad."

"He cheated on her regularly," Keahilani countered. "Bane's name means 'long-awaited child.' In her journal, Mahina called him her salvation. Right after she killed Justin."

A sad smile fell on Manō's lips. "Salvation," he echoed, barely shaking his head. Some savior. Bane killed their half brother's wife and got the same in return.

"Mahina kept too many secrets," Keahilani murmured, turning away from the beach. "And what does it matter whose son Bane was? He's dead. Mahina's dead. It's just us."

She had been holding in too much after the losses of her brother and her lover. Manō worried she was on the verge of a breakdown. She was angry and heartbroken over Bane, but she'd barely mentioned Blake in the days since she'd pulled the trigger on him. It wasn't normal or healthy.

Maybe she'd plunged deeper into the darkness than he thought.

"The time for mourning is over," she said. "Two more attempts on our lives last night. No more complacency. We need a plan for how to deal with our problems. I propose we conduct some heavy research, starting with the hits. Once we find out where Scott is and what he's up to, we'll have an idea about where to go from there."

Kai nodded. "I think we also need to look into a couple of other leads that might be related." He marked off each idea with a finger tick. "The coffee company, Waialua Kope, has some connection to Scott. Might be able to dig up some answers there. Also, this new Ambrosia drug is directly related to Pāhoehoe, but we don't know how. It's niggling my brain. And it's in high demand. Several customers messaged me yesterday, asking if we had some."

"You mentioned Mahina's journals," Manō said to Keahilani. "Have you finished reading them?"

She shook her head. "Haven't had time."

"Make it a priority," he said. "Maybe you'll find something there that'll unravel some mysteries."

"I'll tackle that as soon as I can," she agreed. "There's also the matter of the business. Both of them. I think it would be wise to take production of Pāhoehoe underground. We'll tell our employees we no longer need their services."

"Who's gonna work the field, harvest, dry, and package?" Kai asked.

She met his eyes. "We are."

"So, three of us are going to do the work of ten people," Kai challenged. "By ourselves."

"We're strong and have plenty of motivation. We can handle it," she said confidently.

"And the shop?"

"We hire a manager and split rotating shifts to support him or her as needed. During busy times, one of us watches the shop and the other two work the field."

"In broad daylight?" Kai protested. "Between Scott and the cops, we got eyes all over us."

Keahilani smiled briefly. "Which is why we only go to the garden at night from now on. To prevent being followed, we need the shadows to cover us. Use them to our advantage."

"So, we just tap in to our 'powers,'" Kai made air quotes and then dropped his hands to his sides, shooting side-eye at Manō, "and teleport over there?"

She stared at him as if she wanted to say something but decided against it. Instead, she slipped under the shade of the nearest tree. The canopy hung thick in the spot above her. Very little light filtered down to touch her. She laid a hand on the bark and closed her eyes. Nothing happened for several seconds, but then an odd gray shimmer fell across her shoulders. She tilted her head into the tree, and it seemed as if she were melting into it.

She wasn't, of course. But by some trick of the light, her skin faded slightly. When she lifted her eyes to Kai, they were rimmed with black. She blinked, and everything returned to normal as if nothing had happened.

"Yes. We'll use our 'powers.'" She mimicked Kai's air quotes.

Kai grunted. "I've been trying to shadow surf, but it hasn't worked since Bane's funeral."

"Me too," Keahilani said. "I can't force it, but if I leave myself open to the darkness, it finds a way in. Or out."

"The mountain," Manō said tersely, tipping his head in the direction of Haleakalā watching from a distance.

Keahilani met his gaze and nodded once. "It's a lot easier when we're there."

Because whatever lives under Haleakalā controls it. Controls us.

"Scott is sure to ramp up his search for us," Keahilani said. "He has the means to take us out, as he proved last night. We have to stay one step ahead of him and out of his sights."

"Jezzy isn't responding to requests for assistance," Kai said.

Keahilani pulled out her phone, dialed a number, and held the device to her ear. Several seconds passed. She hit the end button and tucked the phone in her pocket. A wrinkle marred the space between her brows. "Her number's been disconnected."

A slow shiver like the sensation of someone walking over his grave climbed the rungs of Manō's spine. He briefly wondered if something had happened to Jezzy. She could've easily gotten caught in the crossfire between Scott and the Alanas.

"Shit," Kai said.

"That marks her off our list of people to trust," Keahilani sighed.

Assuming she's still alive, Manō thought with a twinge of

regret.

"Not that I trusted her much anyway," Keahilani said.

As far as Manō was concerned, the "trust list" had officially dwindled to the three of them. Ret was the only one close to being added, but he still wasn't sure of her motivations either.

"So, where do we go from here?" Kai asked.

"Nobody leaves Maui until the police close the shooting case and things blow over. We're under too much scrutiny. I say we move into the safe house in Kula and run operations from there," Keahilani said. "We can keep an eye on each other, and it's not far from Mahina's garden."

Manō enjoyed his privacy, but Keahilani was right. He'd best protect his siblings if they were close. "Agreed."

Kai seemed less than enthused, but he didn't protest.

"I'll set up new security cameras at the shop in case we get any unwanted visitors there. Manō, ask around about the drive-by," Keahilani continued. "Maybe one of your contacts heard something. Kai, get us an update on Ambrosia. I'll give Lui a call and find out what he knows. I need to see how his distributor is doing with Pāhoehoe sales anyway."

"What about Ret?" Kai asked.

Manō's question too. He was fine to share space with his siblings, but it would put his liaisons with Ret in a stranglehold.

"She's on a need-to-know basis," Keahilani said.

That was that. Damn it.

"I'll handle hiring someone to manage the shop," she said. "Take only necessities to the safe house for now and meet at the garden tonight after dark. We have a lot of work to do."

With a grim expression, she faced her brothers in turn. "For Mahina."

"For 'ohana," Kai said.

"For Alana," Manō said.

Keahilani's throat bobbed with a swallow. "For Bane," she added, expanding their end-of-meeting ritual to include their lost brother.

Manō looked across the water to Kaho'olawe. A hint of a dare hung heavy in the mists shrouding it. So much for taking care of Blake today.

Why did he get the feeling the island was pleased with his unease?

CHAPTER FOURTEEN

Ret spent the morning dealing with the cranked-up addict she'd hauled in who tried to sexually assault a homeless woman in Wells Park, but she kept an ear open as she processed him. The police station was abuzz with activity over the attempts on the Alanas' lives last night. Maui was generally a quiet place as far as crime went. Lots of crackheads like the douchebag sitting across from her now, some drunk drivers, a smattering of aggravated assaults and thefts. Very few murders or gun-related violence, though. Two separate drive-bys were something to talk about.

So far, she'd learned exactly nothing about the shootings. Her boss, Chief Hale, was in contact with Sergeant Haoa's people in the Kīhei office. Ret had made it clear the case was personal, and the chief liked her. She hoped that was enough to get her on board the investigation.

As Ret wrapped up her report, Hale stopped at her desk. He was a slight Hawaiian man in his midfifties with sharp eyes and a soft voice. "Come see me before you go to lunch."

"You got it," she replied, crossing her fingers that this was the call to action she'd been waiting for.

She straightened her files, poured some water from her thermos into the peat cushioning the orchid sitting beside her computer, and stood.

"Come on, asshole," she said to the would-be rapist, dragging him to his feet.

His face was bright red, he stunk to high hell, and he was sweating profusely. He kept mumbling overtly sexual comments under his breath that skeeved Ret out. She hadn't found any drugs on him, but if the rigid bulge in his pants and his attempted crime were indicators, she guessed he'd ingested either Ambrosia or Pāhoehoe. Either way, it wasn't good. Keeping her nose pointed away from him to avoid the smell, she lugged him off to holding and promptly detoured to the bathroom on her way out to wash her hands.

When she got to the chief's office, he motioned for her to shut the door. "Have a seat," he said.

She did.

He opened the thin folder on his desk and settled his glasses into place. Scrutinizing the papers before him, he said, "Your friends, the Alanas. They've had a run of bad luck lately. They recently lost a brother."

"Bane was murdered at the hospital." Ret looked away and swallowed back her sadness. She still wasn't used to talking about Bane in the past tense. "Choked to death after someone shot him in his home."

Hale nodded, flipping pages. "I've read the reports. What did you see at the funeral?"

Ret shifted in her seat. "A half brother they didn't know about on their dad's side showed up and made a fuss. Name is Scott Harris. He owns Rainbows Resort on O'ahu. Keahilani thinks he had something to do with Bane's murder, but I haven't seen any evidence to that effect."

"Eyewitnesses say there was an altercation between Harris and the Alana woman."

"A minor one. Things heated up. Empty threats were made—"

Hale removed his glasses and leveled his heavy gaze on her. "What makes you think they were empty?"

She shrugged and crossed a foot over her knee, attempting to appear casual. "People say things they don't mean in the heat of the moment."

"Such as?"

"Harris said Bane got what he deserved and that he'd have killed Bane himself if he could have."

Hale consulted his notes. "And what about the suggestion that Bane killed Harris's wife?"

Ret shook her head slowly. "I don't know anything about that. Bane was a good kid. Seems pretty out of character to me. But even if he did do it, the point's moot. He's dead. Speaking of, have we made any progress on his case or the other victim at the hospital?" This was the perfect opportunity to flip the tables and reposition the spotlight to shine on Bane's killer.

"The sister said she saw a white guy running from Bane's house, and she shot him. None of the local hospitals admitted any patients with gunshot wounds aside from Bane, but we retrieved some blood samples from the kid's front yard. We're running the DNA. If we're lucky he'll be in the system.

"Forensics found little evidence at the hospital. The surveillance feed in ICU was cut just before the incident," Chief continued. "The nurse who saw the phlebotomist who entered both victims' rooms didn't recognize him. She only noticed that he was white with short hair and had a Waialua Kope keychain dangling from his pocket. She said it was too dark to make out facial details, which I find puzzling."

Waialua Kope was an interesting lead Ret hadn't heard about. She'd do a little snooping around the coffee company's digital trail later.

"We're checking into the background on the other patient who died," Chief went on. "There may be a separate motive we missed, but it would be a hell of a coincidence to have two unrelated but suspicious deaths on the same floor within minutes. My gut tells me the other guy was a distraction, and Bane was the main target. We'll know more when we get the autopsy reports."

Hale paused for a moment and fixed his gaze on the blank spot above the door as if in deep thought. "Something doesn't feel right." He jammed the arm of his glasses in his mouth and bit the end.

Ret glanced at the stack of papers, hoping for a tidbit of information, a warning, anything she could share with the Alanas. No love. "What do we know about Harris?"

The chief laid the glasses on his desk and leaned back in his seat, propping folded hands on top of his head. "According to the Honolulu police, he has an alibi. He was on O'ahu until the morning of the funeral. Plenty of witnesses at his resort office."

"He's a rich man," Ret said. "Who's to say he didn't hire someone to take out Bane?"

"We're looking into that possibility," the chief said guardedly. "But Harris also requested that the Maui police investigate Keahilani Alana. He claims she might be responsible for that drug dealer murder a week ago. Brian 'Butch' Kelly."

Ret nodded. She'd already laid the groundwork for an alibi for Keahilani, and now was the perfect opportunity to exploit it. "That case rings a bell. What was the date?"

Hale closed the top folder and opened the one underneath it. His finger eased up the page and stopped at a line of text at the top of a police report. "September 26."

Ret pretended to think. "I'm pretty sure that was the night we went to the movies." She pulled out her phone, opened the calendar, and flashed it at the chief. The 7:15 slot read, *Casablanca w/ Keahilani.*

Chief didn't miss a beat. "Where did you see it?"

"The dollar theater in Kahului."

Truth was, she'd gone to see the movie that night by herself. If Chief dug deeper, he'd find that the movie had indeed played at 7:15. Kahului was nearly thirty miles and a forty-five-minute drive from Kā'anapali where Butch's murder happened. No way Keahilani could've been in both places with only a fifteen-minute window.

He nodded, apparently satisfied with her answer. He removed a page from the folder and scrutinized it. "She also flew to O'ahu on Sunday. Returned yesterday. Any idea what that was about?"

Ret's palms sweated in her lap. She shook her head. "You'd have to ask her."

"This is turning into a very complicated case with lots of 'he said, she said' and few clear answers. There are allegations of murder on both sides, and the possibility of a drug war whose generals are unclear. I need to know where your loyalties lie, Rogers," Hale said, targeting her in his sharp gaze.

Ret cocked her head, mildly hurt by the insinuation that her allegiance would be anywhere but here. Especially after the incident a couple years ago when Ret was a rookie cop. She'd been patrolling on third shift when she pulled over a driver swerving all over the road. When the guy unrolled his window, she'd been shocked to see Chief behind the wheel. With a woman who wasn't his wife in the passenger seat.

"My loyalty is to this police department. To the law. Where else would it be?"

"You have history with this family," he said, measuring his words. "Maybe you feel a need to protect them."

Ret cut him off and laid on a thick layer of personal affront. "With all due respect, sir, you're wrong. They're my friends, yes, but I'm committed to justice. Have my actions in the last four years here ever given you reason to believe anything different?"

He studied her for a long moment, his face inscrutable. "I need to get to the truth. Your friends have some shady acquaintances, and a cursory look at their financials raise more questions. They own a surf shop that, based on the emptiness of the parking lot, doesn't appear to bring in a lot of business. Yet they rent separate living spaces in Kīhei and Pā'ia where average one-bedrooms go for over a thousand a month. Something isn't adding up."

Ret sighed. "They got some insurance money from their mother's accidental death a few years ago. They're good people, Chief. What do you want me to do?"

He leaned forward, eyes narrowed, and rested his elbows on the desk. "I need facts. What's real and what's fiction? Is there more to this relationship with Scott Harris? His wife's murder was never solved. Now we have him showing up to the dead Alana brother's funeral claiming *he* killed the wife, and we got a dead drug dealer who he says the sister murdered. Lots of accusations but not much evidence.

"The Alanas trust you. I need you to leverage that trust. Find out what they know. Report back." He paused. "I'm counting on you to help me get to the bottom of this, Rogers."

Ret straightened. Her heart felt as if it were about to beat out of her chest. She hated being torn apart by her conscience. She was caught between her job on the right side of the law and her friends—her *'ohana*—on the wrong.

"I won't let you down," she said, unsure whether the words were a lie or the truth. She couldn't decide which way to lean.

But one thing was sure: Hale was setting her up to see what she'd do. He was testing her in more ways than one, and if she passed this part of the challenge, it would lead to bigger, more profitable opportunities down the road.

Which meant Ret would have to play both sides to get what she wanted.

She could do that. For the Alanas.

Ret stood up and headed to the door.

"And Rogers?" Hale said.

She faced him. "Sir?"

"If anyone on this case comes knocking on your door, give them whatever they want." He jutted his chin, directing her attention through the glass walls to Detective Blasingame, a smartly dressed woman with an even smarter brain. She could be trouble.

A spring of ice-cold water burst up the column of Ret's spine. A host of necessities to pick up after work formed a to-do list in the back of her mind: burner phone, burner email account, changes of clothes to stash in her car. If she was gonna do this, she had to see the Alanas ASAP so they could strategize and develop contingencies.

"Yes, sir," Ret said. She pulled the door open and returned to her desk, smiling briefly at the watchful detective as she passed.

CHAPTER FIFTEEN

The bell above the door to Mahina Surf and Dive jingled loudly, startling Keahilani. Every time the damn thing rang, she thought of the day Blake Murphy strode in, pretending to want surfing lessons. Seemed like ages ago. In reality, it had been only a week and a half.

She nearly fumbled the screwdriver she was using to install a new security camera, but she caught it before it fell. From her perch atop the ladder in the corner, she tossed over her shoulder without looking, "We're closed. Running a little late. Open in ten minutes."

"I'm here about the job?" a high-pitched voice said directly behind her.

Keahilani twisted around, and her gaze landed on a young white woman of slight build, more willowy than wispy. She had heavily kohled light eyes of indeterminate color and wore her long, ultra-black-dyed hair like a mop with the front strands tied at the top of her head. The rest cascaded around her shoulders in a flowing fountain of shiny keratin.

Leather slippas, black tank top, khaki shorts, and two arms with full tattoo sleeves and black rubber bracelets topped off the look. Her tan was at odds with the goth style, but with the exception of the fish-belly-white tourists on vacation from colder climes, everyone on Maui was at least some shade of tan.

Keahilani tightened the last screw and descended the

ladder. She dusted off her hands and offered the right one to the woman. "Keahilani Alana," she said. "I'm the owner."

"Sophia," answered the woman as she shook. "Black. Sophia Black."

Keahilani waved her toward the cash register. There, she pulled out an application form she'd downloaded from the internet that morning. She handed it to the girl and said, "We're looking to hire a full-time manager. Retail experience is preferred. College degree optional. You do need at least a high school diploma, though."

Sophia planted an elbow on the glass counter and studied the form. "I got a master's in business."

"Ever worked in retail?"

"No."

Not surprising. The girl looked like she'd barely graduated high school, let alone earned a master's degree.

"You surf?" Keahilani settled her hands on her hips.

Sophia shook her head. "No, but I paddleboard and snorkel on occasion."

Well, that was better than nothing. Keahilani passed her a pen. This kid didn't have the skills they needed, but it might not matter. It wasn't like customers were banging down the door to get in here.

"There's only four—*three* of us." Keahilani winced at the correction. A fresh rush of anger rose at the thought of never seeing Bane sitting on the stool up front again, flipping through surfing magazines or hitting the books for an upcoming test. Never again scolding him for being too lazy or lost in his own little world to deal with customers. Never again ruffling his hair—a gesture she'd substituted in later years for planting a kiss on his forehead, which he always wiped off and scrunched up his face over.

Gross, she could hear him complain.

What she wouldn't give to hear him utter that word again. Just once.

She shook out of her reverie. "There are three of us who work here. If I were to hire you, it would be full-time managing the day-to-day operations. We're open every day, ten to six with an hour for lunch whenever you feel like it as long as there aren't any customers, which," she glanced around the empty store, "shouldn't be a problem. Pay is minimum wage for now."

Sophia hit the brakes on the pen and looked up. "For now, meaning if I show promise, you'll give me a raise? I got student loans out the ass."

She was probably thinking it shouldn't be too hard to improve things around the shop. For one, it was in desperate need of customers. If Sophia—or whoever the Alanas hired—could bring some of those in, hell yeah, they'd give her a raise. But part of the reason business sucked was because none of them had invested much effort into improving the store. It had always been a side thing, the legal arm of their mostly illegal operations. A front for the *real* business of keeping people high and happy.

If she were here, Mahina would've scolded them for their apathy and lack of pride. And she'd have been angry they slapped her name on a place they didn't believe in.

For a moment, Keahilani envisioned the shop transformed into a welcoming space with fresh, boldly displayed products and a Hawaiian flare. She glanced at young, inexperienced Sophia and decided it was a pipe dream.

Sorry, Mahina.

"Sure," Keahilani said doubtfully. "You turn this place around and find us some customers, and you'll get a big raise."

A lopsided smile cracked the smooth lines of Sophia's face. "Does that mean I'm hired?"

Keahilani inhaled a full breath and let it out slowly. She'd have to check this girl's references and ensure she wasn't on some criminal watchlist. And consult with Manō and Kai, of course.

"If you pass the brother test, you're in," Keahilani said.

Sophia arched a pencil-thin brow. "Brother test?"

Keahilani grabbed her phone and texted the boys, asking

them to drop by if they were in the neighborhood. "This is a family business. Everything goes through the *'ohana*."

Because 'ohana was still everything, even when two-fifths of its members were gone.

Sophia returned to filling out her application. "I'm confident we'll get along just fine. When can I start?"

Amused by Sophia's brazenness, Keahilani shrugged. She pointed to the new security cameras. "I have one more of those to install outside. Make yourself at home. Have a look around and familiarize yourself with the merchandise. When I get finished, I'll show you how to work the register. We'll move on from there."

Sophia smiled. "Sounds good, boss."

Boss. Sophia was no Bane, but her smart-ass attitude would fit right in at Mahina Surf and Dive.

Keahilani grabbed the camera box, screwdriver, and ladder, and dragged the lot outside. Her phone buzzed in her back pocket. The text from Kai said he'd be here momentarily. A few minutes later, Manō parked his motorcycle on a patch of cracked, overgrown blacktop and ambled over.

Keahilani started a mental list of tasks for the new girl, the first of which involved a lot of weed killer.

Manō stood at the base of the ladder, holding it steady. She passed the screwdriver to him as she wrangled the box into place and lined up holes for the screws. "New girl is Sophia. She's inside."

Manō gave the tool back when she held out her hand. "I'll run a background check."

Keahilani knew what he meant. He wouldn't go through police or FBI records. He'd run her name by his associates and check it against known douchebags who'd done the Alanas wrong in the past. If she came up squeaky clean, they'd keep her.

Trying to forget about the huge dent the new equipment had put in the shop's pitiful bank account, Keahilani gestured to the camera and then pointed to the opposite side of the roof. "I think I've covered all the angles outside. Replaced the old one inside and added another two above the register and on the door."

Manō nodded. "I took the bag you packed to the safe house and boarded up the windows at Kai's place and mine."

She was grateful for his help, especially with little details like boarding windows. Manō knew how to handle shit. No one ever had to ask him. He just did what needed to be done.

"Any news about the drive-by?" she asked.

He shook his head. "None of my contacts have heard anything."

If his people hadn't heard about it, the attack on the 'ohana hadn't come from this island. O'ahu was the likely culprit, as Keahilani had already surmised.

"You know anyone on O'ahu?"

"I'll see what I can find out." Manō narrowed his black eyes, and something in them made Keahilani shudder. It wasn't the darkness that had been haunting her day and night. It was the emptiness.

She started to ask how he was doing since Bane's death, but the black Mustang's throaty growl announced Kai's arrival. She'd talk to Manō later.

Kai hopped out and joined them as Keahilani climbed down the ladder.

"Come on," she said, gathering her tools. Manō took the ladder from her. "I'll introduce you to the new girl, pending your approval, of course."

The three of them entered to the jangle of the bell, but this time Keahilani was prepared for the memories it elicited. Sophia stood in front of the bathing suit display, scribbling in a notebook. She spun around as the trio approached.

"Sophia, these are my brothers, Kai and Manō," Keahilani said, nodding to each.

"I see the family resemblance," Sophia said, gesturing between her and Kai. Then she turned to Manō. "Him, not as much."

Kai grinned and flung an arm around Keahilani's

shoulder. "Twins."

She playfully shoved it off. "Gross." Then she swallowed, remembering Bane again. She turned her head and blinked away the sudden wetness flooding her eyes.

"Ah," Sophia said. "That explains a lot." She faced the display and drew an invisible box around the women's wear with her pen. "I think you'd do better if you clearly separated the women's clothing and accessories from the men's. Put them on opposite sides of the store." She indicated the north-facing wall for female and south for male. "It's a tribe thing."

"Tribe thing?" Keahilani cocked her head, unsure what Sophia meant.

"People love to have something to rally for or against. When it comes to others that aren't like them, they grab their pitchforks and gather the troops," Sophia explained. "I call it tribalism. Us-versus-them mentality." She tapped her temple with the pen. "Men versus women, *haole* versus Hawaiian, the Rainbow Warriors versus the Wyoming Cowboys. Humans are masters at finding *something* to divide them."

"So, you're suggesting we prey on this human need for conflict by creating a male wall and a female wall," Kai said, admiring her appreciatively.

"Exactly," Sophia agreed.

Kai flung his hands in the air and skimmed his gaze down Sophia's assets. "Well, I'm sold."

Sophia laughed.

Keahilani side-eyed Kai and flashed him a *You'd better not be flirting with the help* look. He ducked his head and reined in his grin.

Manō looked bored by the conversation. He rounded the corner with the ladder in tow and made for the office. Kai took his cue and followed. "Nice to meet you, Sophia," he said over his shoulder.

Keahilani jabbed a thumb in their direction. "Sorry about Kai. He's mostly harmless."

Sophia resumed the sketch she was working on for the swimwear treatment. "No worries. I'm a lesbian." She winked.

The corners of Keahilani's mouth pulled into a wide grin, and for the first time in days, she didn't feel like the world was falling around her. "Perfect. You're officially hired."

Sophia smiled and carried on with her drawing as if she'd known she'd get the job all along.

CHAPTER SIXTEEN

As soon as Keahilani joined Manō and Kai in the office, she rounded on her twin and spoke in rapid-fire Hawaiian. "What part of 'keep your dick in your pants' do you not understand?" She thumped Kai on the side of his head.

"Oww," he protested, pushing her hand away and rubbing the offending spot.

Manō coughed over a laugh.

"What happened to Ret?" Keahilani demanded. "I thought you liked her. We need her help, asshole. You running around like a tomcat isn't doing the rest of us any favors." She glanced down at his zipper. "For fuck's sake, stop thinking with your meat stick."

"What? Sophia's cute." Kai gestured innocently to the door.

Keahilani leaned close and said in a low, cold voice, "She's a lesbian. Leave her alone."

"Hmph," Kai grunted, crossing his arms over his chest.

Manō found himself strangely lightened by Kai's interest in someone other than Ret.

The conversation continued in Hawaiian.

"I told Sophia she was hired," Keahilani said. "Anyone got a problem with that?"

Manō and Kai shook their heads.

"Good. Item one, done." Keahilani ticked off an invisible list. "How's the safe house looking?"

"I call the guest bedroom," Kai blurted, raising his hand like a kid in class. "Already dropped my shit in there, so don't even think about it." He shot a pointed glare at Manō. All traces of the darkness clinging to Kai a couple days ago were gone.

"As long as we're clear that I have the master bedroom, I don't give a shit where you two sleep," Keahilani said.

With the ever-present threat of shadows lurking in the darkest corners of his dreams, Manō didn't plan on sleeping anytime soon. If he had to pretend, he could do it on the couch.

Outside the office, the bell jangled. Keahilani visibly tensed and turned her head to the sound. "I gotta help Sophia with customers. You two figure out what needs to be done on the mountain tonight." Then she left the brothers staring at each other.

"There aren't many plants left at the garden. We can harvest the last few stragglers when we get there," Kai said softly in Hawaiian. "We can get a new crop going while we wind down sales on the existing stuff sitting in the warehouse. If we keep things in motion, we can produce four or five crops a year. Once people get a hold of our shit, they'll never want anything else."

"Yeah, until Ambrosia gets cheaper," Manō murmured, thoughts flickering to the stoned rapist-dealer he'd murdered earlier.

Kai held up a finger. "About that."

He pulled his phone from his back pocket. Leaning closer to Manō, he flashed a screen full of formulas and gobbledygook. Manō waited for him to explain.

"My botanist friend sent a more detailed analysis with side-by-side comparisons of Ambrosia and Pāhoehoe's chemical structures." Kai indicated the two drugs in left and right columns and scrolled down. "Everything matches up. Here's the really interesting thing." He pointed to a detailed network of chemical symbols and numbers.

Chemistry had never been Manō's strong suit. "I don't get it."

"Nobody does," Kai laughed. "Because it hasn't existed until now. The fact that our weed and Ambrosia have identical biochemistry and neither has ever been seen before now makes me wonder if the mountain is the missing link."

Before Ambrosia made its appearance, Manō had never heard of any other drug that came close to matching the intense sexual high Pāhoehoe provided. What if the source that "fed" Pāhoehoe also fed Ambrosia? And if the source *was* the same, where was the Ambrosia growing? They'd never seen anyone near Mahina's garden before. It was secluded, nowhere near anything, and not easy to get to.

"You may be right," Manō agreed.

A chorus of female laughter rang out from the shop floor. Ret's voice had joined Keahilani's and Sophia's.

Kai perked up and pointed a thumb their way. "I gotta talk to Ret. I'll do some scoping on the mountain for Ambrosia after we finish harvesting tonight."

Manō nodded as Kai headed out of the office toward the shop floor. He leaned against the wall beside the jamb and listened to the conversation. Ret's New England accent thickened when she was at work. He pictured her in her navy-black uniform, wild blond hair minimally contained by styling product.

The more he tried to shake her out of his mind, the deeper she planted her flag in his gray matter. And the more jealous he became of his brother's hold over her.

They made small talk about the weather and how awful the traffic was on Honoapi'ilani Highway today, thanks to an accident. After a few minutes, the bell rang, and the chatter quieted. Keahilani's and Sophia's were the only voices left.

Manō's stomach knotted at the sudden thought of Ret getting back together with Kai. He cracked the back door. Shadows gathered around him like a cloak as he spied Kai and Ret talking outside.

Look at him, trying to steal your woman from you. A real man would put him in his place, the darkness whispered. *Let him have a piece of your mind. Or your fist.*

Ret stood with her butt against the Mustang's door and her chest poked out. Kai leaned toward her, telling a joke or paying a compliment, Manō couldn't tell, but Ret laughed.

Anger simmered quietly in his blood, contained for now. *He's trying to seduce her. He wants to fuck her. That's your job.*

A cold, black, gelatinous protrusion circled his feet, clinging to him with a vacuum-tight seal, oozing slowly upward.

Manō closed his eyes, willing the darkness away. But it wasn't going anywhere, not with a front row seat to the main event.

The furnace inside him climbed to a low boil. His veins itched; marrow stewed in its calcium casings. He curled his hands into fists and opened his eyes.

Kai stood inches away from Ret, his lips hovering over hers. Manō couldn't tell by her body language whether she welcomed Kai's intrusion or not. If she did, he'd respect her wishes, but if she didn't …

Her cheeks colored as Kai moved in for the kill. She planted her palms on his chest just as he made contact with her lips.

Kai's dreads fell around them like a curtain, enclosing them in a wall that kept the rest of the world out.

The triggered shadows shimmied down Manō's legs and through the cracked door. A muffled choke escaped him as the shadows slunk along the tarry pavement, turning it blacker everywhere they touched.

Come back, he mentally commanded, but they refused. The twisted fuckers *smiled* as they slithered toward his brother and his lover.

Panic ripped the cord on his control. Manō inhaled, clasped the doorknob, and started to push it open.

Just then, Ret broke the kiss, shaking her head. Manō

paused, drawing the door back enough to watch through the crack. The shadows paused too, marking time for a couple seconds.

Manō concentrated on Ret's voice and picked up a few words.

"—can't do this. I'm sorry," she said. Her fists balled against Kai. She gently pushed him out of her personal space but not completely away.

Kai remained still, looking puzzled.

He said something Manō couldn't make out. Then, "—force me to find out who he is on my own, then?"

"You don't own me," Ret shot back, thrusting a finger in his face. She turned her head, targeting her sights on the police car parked out front.

The shadows retreated into the office, scurrying for cover like roaches caught in a spotlight.

The corners of Manō's lips curled into a satisfied smile.

"Come on, Ret." Exasperation weighted Kai's words.

She lowered her voice a half step. "For a guy who's so smart about so many things, you never learn, do you, Kai? Contrary to popular belief, the world doesn't revolve around you. Now's not the time for flirtation. Do you even care that your brother was just murdered?"

Darkness fell over Kai's eyes. It was black enough to see from this distance. And was that a shadow where one shouldn't be? Manō peered painfully through the glaring daylight. Considering the angle of the sun approaching noon, the shadow should've fallen on the ground in a slightly westerly direction. Instead, the shade pooled around Kai's feet and seemed to stand up in slow motion, stealing his light. Devouring it.

If Ret noticed the growing darkness, she didn't show it.

Kai leaned in to Ret, close and almost threatening. "I care more than you'll ever know. And I'm handling it."

Ret shrunk back and stared at him, eyes wide, lips parted in surprise. "Your judgment is a little cloudy. Always has been."

Kai's lip curled, but Ret turned away before she could see it. Good thing too. Manō didn't think she'd have taken kindly to the gesture.

As Ret made for her car, the shadow surrounding Kai reached its full height. It formed the shape of a huge, hulking thing that would give a nightmare nightmares.

Manō cocked a brow. Now, that was some shit.

The amorphous creature shifted and stretched, testing the confines of reality. It seemed unsure of this time and place, as if it knew it didn't belong here but was curious enough to stick around to learn more. The slam of Ret's car door elicited a shiver from the beast.

A pair of black, blob-like arms slid down Kai's shoulders from behind him like a lover's caress. He tipped his head back as if leaning into the thing. Man and shadow watched with detached interest as Ret's tires squealed, leaving a cloud of dust hovering over the parking lot.

Manō thought his shadows were a problem. He didn't know the half of it.

CHAPTER SEVENTEEN

That night, while waiting for her brothers to arrive at the safe house, Keahilani tossed a bag of popcorn in the rickety microwave. The bulky old appliance was on its last leg, clunking and sputtering with odd noises. It was probably spraying radiation on her like a fake tan. The sickly smell of burnt imitation butter permeated the air.

For as good as she was at running drugs and shooting people, Keahilani sucked at a lot of things. Top of the list was cooking. She couldn't even do microwave popcorn right. If she ever decided to look for a man worthy of settling down with, the first prerequisite would be his ability to cook.

Had Blake been a good cook? she wondered. She hadn't known him long enough to find out.

Because you killed him, she reminded herself.

She shook the bag and opened it, turning her head away from the rancid puff of smoke that billowed out. She reached in, grabbed a handful speckled with half-popped kernels, and shoved the wad into her mouth.

She'd killed Blake because she had to. She warned him not to cross her, but he did. In a big way. She had to prove she meant business, otherwise no one would ever take her seriously. The Alanas weren't drug dealers for the fun of it. They owed bad people a lot of money. Owing meant you sometimes had to collect on shit yourself to save your own ass.

Which reminded her …

She grabbed her phone and dialed Lui's number.

"*C'est moi,* Lui," answered an effeminate voice. "To what do I owe the pleasure so soon after you last came calling?"

"I'm fine," Keahilani said sarcastically. "And you? Oh, good. Glad you're doing well."

"What do you want?" Lui replied coolly.

"Full moon's tomorrow," Keahilani said. "Wanna go stargazing with me?"

"Ooh, I just *love* staring at the stars. Let me see if I can find my muumuu. Or shall we go skyclad?" Playfulness sunk into Lui's tone, and Keahilani relaxed a touch.

"The last thing I want to see is you naked," she grumbled.

"You're not helping with my body image issues, Pele."

And in the blink of an eye, she was on the defensive. "Don't call me that."

"Why?" he asked, tapping the receiver. "Is someone listening? Hello? NSA? FBI? CIA? DEA? ATF? DIX? COX? Or any other three-lettered acronym that passes for intelligence. Is that you?" His crooning voice sounded very close to the speaker. Distortion muddied the words. "I'm not worried about anyone tracking me down. But if you are, perhaps you should invest in a burner. Or a Jezzy."

"I have a Jezzy," she snapped, irritated by the lie. It cut a little too close for comfort. Who the hell *didn't* that bitch work for, anyway?

"You mentioned some skyclad stargazing," Lui prompted. "How many stars are you expecting to count?"

"If I remember correctly, you promised several hundred thousand. The sky's a big place, my friend."

"Weather report predicts lots of clouds tomorrow."

Keahilani put a chokehold on the growl poised to pounce from her throat. "Then you'd better bring your high-powered binoculars."

"No can do, buttercup."

"We had a deal," Keahilani snarled.

From the corner of her eye, a rip curl of black sneaked

into her periphery and caressed her back like a lover.

"I'm tired of the games, Lui. What's the hold up?"

Lui grunted a couple times like he was trying to get comfortable in a seat, but he was probably searching for the right angle from which to launch whatever lies he'd loaded onto the platform for takeoff.

"Everything was going fine until you made your little trip to O'ahu," Lui huffed. "Your new brother must've been put off by the visit. He decided to look a little deeper into your dealings on Maui. I guess he didn't like what he found."

"Meaning?" A lump of cold, hard desolation formed in the center of her chest. She shut her eyes.

The shadows consoled her with murmured platitudes and soft suggestions of violence. *Pretty Pele. You should kill Lui like you did Blake. He doesn't care about you. He just wants your money. They're all out to get you. Gather your Enforcers and make him pay.*

Lui dropped all pretense and said with exasperation, "Meaning the nice housewife who was helping us out suffered an accident in her Honolulu kitchen this morning."

Shit. She rubbed her forehead.

"How bad was she injured?" This distributor was the Alanas' last shot at moving the Pāhoehoe before the deadline to pay their investors.

"Real bad. Dead-bad."

"Fuck," she said, shoving a handful of long, dark hair out of her eyes. "Just fuck."

More of her shadow pets crawled up her legs and enfolded her in their black wings.

"Where's the product?" she asked, afraid of the answer.

"That's the good news in this incredibly regrettable story. See, you should always look at the bright side—"

"Where is it?" she demanded through clenched teeth.

"I had my boy run over and fish it out of her underwear drawer," he said. "Well, most of it, at least."

Triple fuck. If Scott got hold of even a little bit of Pāhoehoe, he'd have it tested. And if he was hooked in to the newly developing Ambrosia network, he'd uncover the connection between the two drugs in no time. Keahilani had no doubt Scott would ramp up his attacks on her and her brothers until he got what he wanted.

The end game wasn't the weed. It was the mountain. It had always been the mountain.

The Alanas could *not* let him find Mahina's garden.

"Wire me whatever you've collected," she said.

"Minus my fee," Lui reminded.

"I need it tonight." She ended the call. If she spent another second on the line with him, she would completely lose her shit. The shadows would like that too much.

The door opened, and Kai strutted in, carrying bags of groceries. "What up?"

Keahilani stood to help him put the food away, fuming the whole time.

"Who pissed in your surf wax?" Kai asked. He scrunched up his nose. "And why does it smell like ass in here? Have you been cooking again?"

Keahilani pulled one of his dreadlocks a little harder than necessary. "Lui. And popcorn."

Kai paused his unloading. "What did he say?"

"We're fucked."

"That sums it up succinctly."

The roar of Manō's motorcycle interrupted their conversation. A few seconds later, he wandered in and tossed his keys on the counter. He looked tired. Keahilani couldn't remember ever seeing him with bags under his eyes. Maybe the stress of losing Bane had finally caught him in its net. She too had experienced frequent moments of sudden, debilitating despair since his and Blake's deaths.

"Keahilani was just telling me about how Lui fucked us," Kai said.

"Without lube," she added dryly.

The three of them unpacked the remaining groceries in silence. When everything was put away, Keahilani held out the partially eaten bag of popcorn. Her brothers dipped in and joined her in eating the disgusting stuff. No one complained, despite the unpopped kernels and burnt bits. No one spoke, which was fine with her. Keahilani needed this moment of quiet communion with her brothers—the two most important people left in the entire world.

She leaned tentatively on Manō's shoulder. He didn't pull away like she expected. His hand came up and settled on her back. Gentle. Understanding. Kai eased closer, and she and Manō dragged him all the way into the circle.

The painfully *incomplete* circle.

The shadows slunk away, leaving the trio alone with their grief.

Keahilani's breath caught on a sudden choke of tears. One second she was fine; the next, she was in full-blown snot-bubble meltdown. Her sorrow swirled into a perfect storm that flooded her from the inside out.

Trapped in the safety of her brothers' arms, she let everything out. All the pain and anger and hurt and sadness. All the regrets.

She'd wondered why she couldn't seem to cry over her brother's death, but she realized now she simply hadn't had time to process it.

And then, there was Blake. The man she'd thought she might have just enough space in her heart to share a small part of herself with.

She had killed Blake.

Murdered him.

In cold blood.

From crown to toes, her body wracked with sobs. She cried into Kai's hair, "I'm a bad person. I brought this on our family."

Kai hugged her tighter, smashing her face to his chest, his fist a ball on her shoulder. He was hot and trembling.

Was he crying too? She couldn't look. Couldn't bear to see his tears.

So, she lifted her eyes to the *'ohana's* rock. Manō stared back at her, his craggy face unreadable, yet she sensed empathy from him. From his surprising lack of ever-present shadow.

The three of them huddled together, weathering a storm of flowing tears, their bodies bathed in a sea of light.

Maybe the shadows didn't like families or the unconditional love that encircled them.

'Ohana is everything.

Keahilani sniffled, wiped away the lines of water streaming down her hot cheeks, and made a half-hearted attempt at laughing.

"Some Pele, huh?" she said.

In the stories Mahina had told the kids when they were growing up, the volcano goddess Pele didn't put up with shit. She didn't whine about mistakes she made. She got up when she fell down and fixed them. And she looked like a badass when she did.

Keahilani straightened her spine, inhaled a full breath, and reluctantly let go of her brothers. Kai blinked a few times, shouldered his eyes dry, and looked away. Manō stepped back, the possessive shadows reclaiming him in silent victory.

"Even Pele is allowed to have a moment," Kai teased, "as long as it's quick."

She smiled gently at her twin and nodded. Head bowed, she said, "Lui's dealer in Honolulu is dead. He recovered some of her product, but not all of it. Scott likely has what's missing, and he's coming for us. We have to protect the mountain and figure out its connection with Ambrosia."

"Only one way to get there," Manō said quietly, shadows bobbing around him like negatives of twinkling Christmas lights, siphoning color from the air.

Keahilani swallowed hard. "It's high tide, brothers."

The shadow riders would surf tonight.

CHAPTER EIGHTEEN

Manō slipped off the wave of darkness like stepping off a surfboard into the shallows. He landed in the middle of Mahina's garden, illuminated by bright moonlight. Mahina's name meant "moon." Seemed appropriate that her namesake would be smiling through the clouds at this particular moment. He and his siblings could use all the light and love they could get.

He was worried about Keahilani. She wasn't one to melt down. It took a lot to break her, and he feared she might be on the verge. Yet he didn't know how to help her. He couldn't even help himself.

The star-shaped tops of the marijuana plants shone a matte silver. He wandered among the rows as he waited for his siblings, the fronds tickling the tips of his outstretched fingers. Beneath his feet, the ground shifted. The movement was subtle, but his drug-induced, alert senses caught it like a scent on a breeze.

A million years ago, Haleakalā had been an active volcano that shaped three quarters of Maui's current landscape. Its last eruption was in the seventeenth century, but the volcano was far from extinct, as the unobtrusive heat rising from the ground through Manō's shoes proved. If he hadn't been looking for it, he wouldn't have noticed it.

Maybe it was looking for him.

He'd learned via his mother's journals that Mahina and

Justin had once spent the day having a picnic in her garden. When a lone hiker stumbled upon them, Justin went after him and mowed him down with his car to keep the man from exploiting the illegal treasure trove growing there.

That was the beginning of the end for his parents' seventeen-year affair. Shortly after, Mahina used her powers to drown Justin. The newspapers labeled his death a tragic surfing accident. Mahina's journal told a different story.

Manō had learned more about his mother by reading her diaries than he ever had by breathing the same air. And he had yet to peruse several of her newly discovered journals. Imagine what other secrets lay within those pages.

He wasn't sure he wanted to know.

He scanned the darkness for signs of his siblings, but they hadn't arrived yet. It was just him and the volcano and the shadows.

Maybe he could ride the shadows to Kaho'olawe and finish putting Blake to rest. That would be a hell of a lot easier than paddling there and back for hours, and it wouldn't leave a trace anyone could follow.

He faced the direction of the distant island. He pictured the beach, the red dirt transformed by darkness into the color of dead blood, and the furrows on the slope where he'd left Blake. He remembered laying the body in a shallow hole, piling rocks on top of it, and concentrated on those shadows.

He reached out and touched them through the lens of his memory. They startled, backed away, then paused as if curious. Like they sensed familiarity in his touch. They inched closer. He petted them.

The familiar sensation of melting into night's cradling arms overcame him. A blanket of jet folded him into himself and pushed him from one shadow to the next like he was running a relay race.

No longer corporeal, he skated along the currents surrounding Haleakalā, but he couldn't reach escape velocity, no matter how hard he willed himself away from the volcano.

The red eyes he'd seen on Kaho'olawe surged out of the

blackness, jostling him. They widened on seeing him.

He lost hold of the shadows and crashed to the ground with a thud.

Lying there, he stared up at the sky and its millions of stars. The volcano's shadows blanketed him again, a shiver of black sharks weighing him down, and whispered in a persuasive chorus, *Stay*.

They didn't want him to leave. They wouldn't *let* him leave.

What the—

"Manō," Keahilani called in a stage whisper.

He sat up and spotted her coming from the west. He quickly stood and walked over to meet her.

"What happened?" she asked. "You look like you saw the Night Marchers."

Though the moon was full, she shouldn't have been able to see his expression. But darkness was more their friend these days than light. The Alanas saw better here, clearer, because this mountain was their point of connection to darkness. To their father.

Mahina's garden served as the entrance to their heavenly hell on Earth.

"Nothing," Manō said. He diverted his gaze to Kai, who ambled up behind Keahilani.

"You guys start harvesting," Kai directed. "I'm gonna collect some dirt from the vicinity. It'll help us understand Pāhoehoe's composition better and maybe provide some leads about where to look for Ambrosia."

Kai pulled out his phone, a couple sample containers, and a Sharpie from the pack slung over his shoulder. He wrote something on one of the cups. After consulting the GPS and noting coordinates, he scooped some earth into a plastic container.

Keahilani touched Manō's elbow and guided him toward the crops while Kai worked.

"I'm worried about him." She nodded toward her twin and spoke in quiet tones. "Whatever happened to you and me is happening to him too."

"And?"

"And I don't like it."

"Kai can handle it," Manō said, irrationally irritated. Kai's confrontation with Ret earlier had soured Manō's mood all day. "He can make his own choices."

"Yes, but what's changing us isn't a choice, is it?" Keahilani's green eyes sparked with Pele's fire. "This"—she looked down at herself and held out arms bathed in unnatural darkness—"whatever *this* is, came from within, not without. It's embedded in our DNA. We got it from Justin."

Manō folded his arms over his chest.

"You feel it." Her voice turned quiet. Haunting. She looked around at the inky blobs cavorting over the gray-green landscape. "The shadows like us here. They want us to stay. They keep pulling us back to this place. When we come here, they welcome us. They open some kind of … of *portal* that allows us to slide through them to get here. It's like we're balanced on the edge of a giant funnel, and they're the wind, pushing us down the side into the maw waiting below."

She might've still been sliding, but Manō had found that maw long ago and already made himself at home in its depths.

"What is it?" she whispered, as if trying to grasp the logic behind a complicated calculus problem. She stared at the ground, past the ground, under the ground. "What's down there?"

"I don't know." He honestly didn't. He wasn't inclined to believe in mumbo jumbo, but enough weird shit had happened in his life to leave him cautiously open to the possibility of supernatural forces *if* it could be backed up with evidence. Even shaky evidence was better than none at all.

The more he aligned the stories in Mahina's journals with his perception of reality, the more strongly he believed their mother really did have powers over certain aspects of nature. And the more he believed their father had a connection to opposing dark forces that he'd passed on to his children.

Keahilani loosened her tough stance and ran her fingers

through her hair. "I'm going crazy here. It's like puberty all over again, except instead of raging hormones, I'm dealing with a ravenous desire to hurt things under the cover of darkness."

Manō's heart sunk.

"Something's taken over my body, mind, and soul." She angled her face up to his. Worry carved creases into her forehead.

His sister was one of the strongest people he knew. She believed wearing her heart on her sleeve was weak. Putting her fears on display couldn't have been easy, but it showed how much she trusted Manō. If only he had answers that would soothe her uneasiness.

"You're not alone, Keahilani." Manō gave her shoulder a quick squeeze. It was the only comfort he could offer. "We'll get through this together."

She closed her eyes for a moment, leaned into him, and nodded.

While Kai wandered the grounds, collecting dirt, Manō and Keahilani snapped on latex gloves and combed the garden's plants for ripe buds. Years ago, Kai had taught them how to harvest the buds and manicure the leaves. They snipped quickly, dropping their pruned treasures into a sack they'd brought along. They worked mostly in silence, exchanging a few words here and there.

About an hour later when all the usable parts were collected and Kai had finished gathering samples, he assessed the plants in the back section of the garden. "We need trim these guys to force bigger cola tops," Kai said. He bent down to one of the plants and waved Manō and Keahilani over. "See, these little buds at the bottom aren't getting sunlight, and they're sucking up nutrients the bigger ones need." Using his pruning shears, he snipped off the smaller leaves near the ground, leaving behind clean stems.

Keahilani squatted and followed Kai's directions, trimming a plant at her feet. "This good?"

Kai nodded bent down for a closer look. "Perfect. Let's

knock these out," he drew a square in the air around a swath of about twenty plants, "and we'll be done."

When the three of them finished the remaining plants, Kai stood and slung the bud bag over his shoulder. "I'll take these over to the warehouse for drying."

"I'll meet you there," Keahilani said.

"I'm gonna have a look around," Manō said. "See if there are any signs of activity in the vicinity. I'll catch up later."

Keahilani rested her hands on her hips and looked up at him. "You think someone's growing Ambrosia out here?"

He nodded. "The similarities between Ambrosia and Pāhoehoe are too close to be a coincidence."

A muscle ticked in her cheek. "Be careful."

"I will."

Keahilani hooked an arm around Kai's shoulder, and they wandered into the shadows.

Manō slipped into a shadow of his own and commanded it to take him on a tour of the adjacent environs. Melted into the darkness, he surfed from one patch of blackness to the next, slowly spiraling outward from Mahina's garden, looking for other marijuana crops and signs of human presence.

He found nothing.

Not so much as a footprint or an out-of-place twig.

He widened his search radius, his senses on high alert to anything that seemed out of order.

Still nothing.

When the first fingers of sunlight tickled the eastern horizon, he returned to Mahina's garden and sat on the grass next to the decapitated stalks of freshly culled crops. He was puzzled. He'd been certain he'd find Ambrosia *somewhere* around here. His sweeps of the area had been thorough. Had he missed something?

A lone shadow frolicking through a copse of nearby trees grinned at him. It faced east and shrunk back from the lightening sky. Then it sunk into the dirt, leaving no traces it had ever been there.

That gave Manō an idea.

He laid back under the shade of the plants and fingered the earth beside him. Instead of concentrating on what was above the ground, he closed his eyes and turned his focus downward to what lurked below the ground.

Using his inner shadow as a guide, he connected with a swath of darkness that mirrored his own, except this one was tinged red. He pressed deeper, mapping the boundaries of this underground … presence. As he felt his way around its perimeter, he realized the expanse of red-haloed blackness stretched to almost the exact dimensions of Mahina's garden.

Red.

Like the glitter in Ambrosia. And the miniscule flecks of red in crushed Pāhoehoe.

But there was no evidence of other crops, no Ambrosia nearby. He supposed Ambrosia *could've* come from Pāhoehoe bought off the Alanas' dealers, but someone would've had to figure out how to condense it to get such a high concentration. And with very few dealers selling it, there wasn't that much Pāhoehoe on the streets to begin with.

Nothing made sense.

Manō sat up and dusted off his hands.

He was suffering from a combination of exhaustion and drug-induced hallucinations. His addled mind couldn't be trusted in this state. Yet, the reddish black mass he'd "seen" under the ground seemed to resonate with the shiver of shadow sharks swimming lazily around him. Their noses bobbed up and down as if nodding their approval.

The scrap of a forgotten story Mahina had once told him when he was a boy stoked a tiny fire of recognition. Something about the goddess Pele making a deal with shadows to save her daughter from the water goddess Nāmakaokaha'i … Pele slicing open her own throat on the spine of Haleakalā as payment to the shadows for her daughter's protection …

He shook his head. Couldn't remember any more than that. The old myths were just stories the early people told to explain things they didn't understand anyway. They weren't anything close to facts.

Holding an arm up to protect his eyes against the dawn, he got to his feet and scanned the garden one last time. What *was* a fact was that Ambrosia and Pāhoehoe were chemically identical. If the soil they were in grown wasn't the connection, then he must've been missing something else.

He feared the only one who had the answer was Scott Harris, master of the disappearing act. Manō just hoped he and his siblings could keep up their own disappearing acts. This game of cat and mouse could take a wrong turn toward deadly with the smallest misstep.

CHAPTER NINETEEN

Wednesday, October 8

Ret rolled up to the Alanas' safe house around 9:00 a.m. Kai had sounded strange when she called him. After their argument yesterday in the parking lot at Mahina Surf and Dive, she wasn't sure if he was reluctant to see her or if the aloofness in his tone was because of something else.

She knocked on the door, and Manō opened it. Squinting, he lifted a thick, ripped arm to shield his black eyes from the encroaching sun.

Her breath caught at the sight of him, tall, imposing, and more muscular than she remembered. She'd never seen him shirtless in full daylight. The black tattoos spanning most of his left arm looked dull under the morning's fresh glow, but she admired them. He was inked with Native designs she didn't understand. One day she'd ask about them. But not today.

"Aloha," she stammered, glancing furtively behind him for Kai. She didn't see him. "I didn't realize you'd be here."

He stepped out of the way and invited her inside with an open-palmed gesture. He looked like a loosely observant shark trying to decide if it was hungry enough to pursue prey.

Low-level energy rippled off his skin and threaded through the air, electrifying the hairs on her arms. She rubbed them absently. "Kai around?"

She removed her police cap and ran a hand through her short, flattened hair, trying to pump some life into it amid the fog of humidity clinging to everything.

"He's in the shower," Manō said.

"Keahilani?" she asked, noting the stack of old journals on the coffee table. They were their mother's. All were closed.

He shook his head slowly, bobbing back and forth, shark tail driving the whole of him. "At the shop."

She exhaled and wove her arms like a pretzel over her chest. "Where were you guys last night?" she asked softly, trying to sound casual.

"We had some family business." His narrowed eyes took in her uniform with a slow, appreciative swagger. The power of his gaze slithered over her. Shark skin on silk.

She assumed he meant the family's *other* business, the one Ret the cop wasn't supposed to know about if anyone at work asked. "You're at the top of Chief Hale's to-do list. For a number of reasons."

He nodded as if he already knew.

She shot a glance to the closed bathroom door and lowered her voice. "Can I see you tonight?"

"My house is off-limits," he said.

"Come to mine, then." She hated the eagerness buoying her words. It was the same way she used to fawn over Kai, before she grew a spine and fell in with Manō. Desperate. Pathetic. She dialed back the high school drama and shrugged. "If you want."

Manō leaned closer. "What do *you* want?"

Sloughed water hitting the floor of the tub in the bathroom nearly drowned him out. Or maybe it was the rushing pulse in Ret's ears.

In the days since Bane's death, Manō had been darker and broodier than usual, which she supposed was to be expected. But this morning, he almost glowed with a dark fierceness she hadn't seen from him before. It was hot as fuck. Made her forget she'd come to see Kai.

She slid a tentative finger up his arm, imagining the inked

lines were raised like Braille. His skin was cool and damp with sweat. "Half an hour alone with you."

She surprised herself with the proposition, but he seemed unfazed.

"Gonna be hard right now."

Her gaze fell to his shorts zipper. She lifted a suggestive brow. "That's the point."

A hint of amusement eased across his mouth. His tongue swiped his lips, and suddenly Ret was aware of liquid heat roiling between her legs. He so rarely smiled, this was a real treat.

The water shut off, breaking the spell. Ret stepped back, expecting the door to fling open any moment. "Come over tonight," she whispered.

Manō held her gaze as if considering. He nodded once and slipped down the hall into one of the bedrooms.

Satisfied and more than a little excited about the thought of what they might get up to later, Ret sat on the couch. She studied the journals on the table without touching them. The cover on the top one read, "Mahina Alana, 1990."

The police officer in her was curious about what family secrets lay within the pages, but she wouldn't breach her friends' trust. Especially not when her allegiances to the two brothers shifted from day to day depending on how lovesick or horny she was.

Lately, there had been a lot of need that went unsatisfied, but she hoped it would be remedied tonight. The more she tried to stop thinking about Manō, the louder he rattled the diving cage of her subconscious.

He was getting to her. And Kai was drifting away like a raft without an anchor.

The bathroom door opened. Steam billowed around Kai's freshly showered form. He was shirtless like Manō, but their bodies were polar opposites. Where Manō was bulky with mountains of muscle, Kai was tall and wiry. Both had the same tanned skin, but it looked different on their opposing frames. Kai shook out his mop of hair and noticed

Ret.

"Hey," he said, walking over, his eyes guarded.

"Hey." She stood to greet him and poked her thumb toward the door. "I thought you might like to know what's going down at the station. I buzzed Keahilani last night, but she didn't answer. That's why I called you."

Kai lowered his head guiltily and scratched at his nape. "Yeah, we got busy with some stuff."

What were he and Manō hiding? They were both acting weird.

He glanced down the hall to the closed bedroom doors. "I'm sorry for how I acted yesterday. If you're seeing someone else, that's cool. I shouldn't have made a big deal about it. Not like we're dating or anything, right?"

Flashback to ten years ago, and the last line of this conversation was identical to the one they'd had at the lunch table in the cafeteria at Maui High. That was the day after she'd found out she was pregnant with Kai's baby.

A veil of sadness saturated her eyes, and she blinked several times to hold the sudden swell of emotion at bay. Kai really knew how to locate a long-buried, raw nerve and prod it without meaning to.

She pinned a fake smile to her lips and swatted his arm. "Right," she agreed and quickly changed the subject.

"Forensics department says they pulled a single strand of gray hair from the security office at the hospital where the guard was found unconscious. No one who normally works in that room has gray hair. They're doing genetic analysis on it now. If its owner has any felonies logged, we should be able to match it."

Kai's face brightened at the news. "Excellent."

"I'm going over to talk to the nurse and security guard who were on duty the night of the murder."

"I'll go with you. I want to hear what they have to say."

She shook her head. "You can't. It's police business."

He thrust a finger in the direction of the room Manō went into. "Then my brother can trail you. He'll keep his distance.

He's good that way," Kai said with admiration.

Of course Manō would be able to sneak past watchful eyes. He was a damn Hawaiian ninja.

Kai had no idea how badly she wanted to take him up on the offer, but Chief would have her hide if he found out.

"No, Kai. I—"

"Manō," he called.

Manō wandered down the hall, dragging shadows behind him with the long, lean, sharp lines of sharks, all triangles and menace.

Kai said, "Ret's going to question people at the hospital about Bane's death. You up for some recon?"

Typical Kai, steamrolling right over her, as usual. Except this time, she secretly welcomed it.

"It's not a good id—" Ret protested weakly.

Manō stopped in front of her, his back to Kai. The intensity in his gaze tripped her heart out of rhythm. He subtly leaned in and spoke softly. "You'll never know I was there."

And he ambled out of the house without another word. Deep, guttural groans erupted from his motorcycle, and he peeled out of the driveway. Through the window, Ret watched him go, her stomach twitching with an invasion of butterflies.

She inhaled a full breath to steady herself and faced Kai. He was so handsome, so lean and sexy with a surfer's body and a brilliant mind. Yet, she suddenly felt as if her crush on him had sprouted more from dreams of what she wanted him to be rather than the reality of who he was. Why hadn't she seen him clearly all those years ago in high school?

She had. It was the rose-colored glasses that had betrayed her.

Kai had always been out for number one. He was the free spirit, the journeyman searching for things he'd never find because he didn't realize life was more about the road itself than the destination. The people and things you encountered on the path shaped you. Manō seemed to understand that.

But, did Ret?

She'd neglected the road too. Kai had always been her destination. But somewhere along the way, she took a detour. Manō was her new journey, and she was becoming more comfortable traveling his highway with every private romp they shared.

"You ever wonder what goes on in Manō's mind?" She legit wanted to know.

Kai shook his head, the dreadlocks spilling over his shoulders. His eyes were dull, glazed. He'd probably been smoking weed this morning. Some things never changed.

"Nope," he said. "I've seen the darkness on his outside, and it scares the shit outta me. I'm guessing his insides are made of black holes, patchworked together like skin from a vivisection gone horribly wrong."

Ret laughed at his vibrant description, swung her key ring around her index finger once, and caught the keys. "That's one way to put it."

She imagined Manō's inner workings were more like those of an overlooked child who simply learned to fend for himself out of necessity. Given the right amount of attention and love, even wild animals could be tamed. Maybe even sharks.

* * * *

An hour later at the hospital where his brother was smothered to death only a week ago, Manō found his place in the shadows, which were few and far between in noon daylight, and melted into them.

Harsh fluorescents buzzed overhead, throwing everything from the fresh dirt on the floors to the infrequent dents in the walls under glaring, antiseptic scrutiny. From his dark corner, he observed Ret leaning on the counter, talking with the woman who'd been on duty the night of the murder. The thirty-something ICU nurse sat behind the desk, sliding her short hair behind her ear with nervous fingers.

"Mrs. Frankle, I know this is difficult for you, and you've already answered questions from the officers on the evening of the incident," Ret said, her voice soothing and calm. "I was there that night too, but I just want to clarify what you remember. Maybe we can jog something else loose in the process."

"There was a lot going on," the nurse said, a tremble in her throat. "We had the code blue with the other patient, which sent everyone into a tizzy. There were only three of us working the floor."

Ret drew out a small notebook and pen. She flipped to a blank page and set it on the counter. "Let's back up a bit first. Do you remember seeing the man with the lab cart come off the elevator?"

"Yes, he passed by my station." Frankle paused as if gathering her thoughts, retracing steps of a routine that refused to follow routine rules. She gesticulated frequently, her hands sometimes saying more than her mouth. "He was wearing plain green scrubs. That part I remember. I looked at his badge, but I didn't pay attention to his name or his face. I think he was older, but I'm not sure. We keep the lights dim at night for the patients."

"How old? Fifties? Sixties?"

The nurse paused as if searching her memory. "Early fifties," she decided. "He went into the last room on the right."

"What number was that?" Ret asked, looking over her shoulder in the direction the other woman pointed.

"Room 10."

Ret nodded. "Then what?"

"I didn't see him leave, but a few minutes later, the patient in ten flatlined. Everyone who was available ran in."

"So, the other patients on the floor were left unmonitored."

"It was only for a couple minutes," the nurse insisted. A flush of red burst up her neck, coloring her cheeks.

Ret laid a gentle hand on her arm. "I know. No one's

accusing you of anything. I just need to establish a time frame."

The woman nodded and continued. "That was around 4:45. By the time we finished with the patient in ten, the Alana boy was already dead."

"Which nurse was assigned to him?"

"Me." Nurse Frankle's voice pinched. A little gasp escaped her mouth. She covered it with her palm. Tears welled in her eyes. "His brother Kai had been sitting with him, but he'd gone for a quick break. I found Bane with a pillow over his face. He was my responsibility, and I failed him."

Anger swirled like a dark tornado in Manō's chest. He wasn't angry at the nurse. She was a victim like Bane, only her punishment was far less eternal. He was furious that someone had the balls to kill his brother right under their noses like a giant fuck-you to the 'ohana.

The murderer botched the job the first time when he shot Bane in his home, so he had to come to the hospital to finish what he'd started. His need to kill spoke to either the suspect's unhinged mental state or clear, unadulterated vengeance. Maybe both.

"I know this is hard," Ret said with an apologetic tone. "Do you remember anything at all about the man in the scrubs? You said they were green. Any stains, patterns, or different-colored piping? Was he a big guy or smaller?"

Frankle shook her head and withdrew a Kleenex from her pocket. She blew her nose. "I don't know."

"How about jewelry? Did he have on a necklace? Bracelet? Wedding ring?"

"I don't think so. He blended in."

"Any tattoos? Can you picture his shoes?" Ret pressed.

The nurse shook her head again, but then she stopped mid swing. Dabbed at her nose with the tissue. A faraway look came over her eyes. "Wait."

Ret shifted weight between her feet. Her stance tightened. "His shoes? You remember them?"

The skin between Frankle's eyebrows tensed, forming a little ridge. "Yes," she finally said. "He was wearing shoes that didn't fit."

"They were too big?" Ret asked, pen poised over the notebook.

"No, I mean, they didn't go with the scrubs." The nurse lifted her eyes to Ret's and recognition seeped into them. "Most nurses and lab personnel wear tennis shoes. We're on our feet for hours at a time, but that guy had on something different. Brown ..." She seemed to be wading through days of memory, sifting through irrelevant flotsam for something important.

"Dress shoes?" Ret said eagerly.

The woman nodded. "Yeah, maybe. With some kind of writing near the toes," she added.

Ret unlocked her phone and typed something. "Take a look at these." She flashed the screen to the nurse. "Anything familiar?"

The woman flipped through pages of what appeared to be an online shoe catalog. She stopped a moment later, and her eyes lit up. She pointed. "That pair. The man's shoes looked like those. They had writing on them."

Ret studied the image. "Well, I'll be damned. Our suspect has expensive taste. Italian Berlutis ain't cheap. And the Scritto engraving gives us something else to bite into. This is good." She wrote furiously in her notebook.

As he blended into the shadows, Manō's brain snagged on a similar tidbit of information dangling in the dark corners of his memory. The morning after he and Ret first hooked up, he'd seen a well-dressed businessman at Kahului Airport. His bodyguards called him Mr. Lowden. An internet search led Manō to believe he was Grant Lowden, CEO of Waialua Kope, a new coffee company home-based on O'ahu.

He closed his eyes, forcing himself to remember what the man had been wearing. Designer suit. Tie. Briefcase. Sunglasses. Coffee logo on a folder in his bodyguard's satchel.

But what about the shoes, damn it?

The man moved slowly like he had a limp. Manō strained to remember. *Look down,* he told himself as he replayed the memory over and over. *Watch the limp.*

He remembered a black limousine. The chauffeur opening the door for Lowden. The lifted foot as he slid inside the car. The pant cuff rising …

There. There it was. A brown designer shoe with writing on it.

Bingo.

On his way to the elevator, he heard the nurse say, "I told you before, I saw a Waialua Kope key ring dangling from his pocket too," confirming what Manō already knew.

Next stop, some undercover work at the coffee company offices here on Maui.

CHAPTER TWENTY

Keahilani rubbed her forehead as she hung up the phone. All of Sophia's references checked out. The only thing that stuck out about the girl, aside from her affinity for goth hair and her punchy attitude, was the fact that she was only twenty-one. Her age wasn't a problem, but Keahilani found it unusual.

According to her application, Sophia graduated from high school at sixteen, got her undergrad by the time she was nineteen, and earned an MBA from the University of Hawai'i at Hilo at twenty-one this past spring semester. Her master's program advisor raved about her sharp mind and quick wit.

Keahilani couldn't help but smile at the thought of nabbing a prodigy to run the store while the Alanas were busy with the other business. Of course, Sophia would never take Bane's place, but he and the girl shared a lot of similarities, not the least of which was their intelligence and ingenuity. And Sophia being a lesbian that Kai couldn't get his paws on was icing on the cake.

Keahilani wandered over to the door to flip the sign to OPEN and noticed someone in the parking lot, squatting with a nozzle in a gloved hand beside a two-gallon white canister. With a huge smile, she pushed the door open and instantly shielded her eyes from the sun's intensity with a flat hand. Damn, it was bright out here.

"I was about to dock your pay for being late," Keahilani

teased, "but I see that might've been premature."

Sophia turned around and grinned. "What's up, boss?"

She stood up wearing a pair of khaki shorts and a black tank top. A pair of oversized Jackie Onassis sunglasses covered her eyes. Her mass of hair was piled into a haphazard bun on top of her head. Miniature chopsticks with skulls on the ends held the nest in place. A thin sheen of sweat dotted her skin. She must've been out here for a while.

Keahilani walked over, taking in the scene. A big jug of Roundup sat beside a crack barfing up weeds on the pavement. "Damn, Sophia. You read my mind."

Sophia laughed and indicated the deeply veined asphalt. "I figured the best place to start on my new project—*our* new project," she corrected herself, "was the outside. If the outside looks inviting, more people will be drawn to see what's inside."

"Agreed," Keahilani said. "I like this plan. What's next?"

Sophia nodded to a pile of gardening tools sitting at the edge of the pavement and then walked Keahilani to the entrance of the building. "I'm gonna hit the home improvement store and local nursery. You could use some color up front. I downloaded plans for how to make cheap but attractive flower boxes. They'll fit perfectly under the big windows."

"Impressive," Keahilani remarked. "And who's paying for all this stuff?"

"You are, of course," Sophia said, cracking her knuckles. "I'm saving receipts."

Keahilani liked the girl's initiative, but money was tighter than ever right now. And something about buying flowers felt wrong when the front of Mahina's garden was full of them. She'd dig up some proteas next time she went there.

"Go ahead with the boxes but hold off on the flowers. I know where I can get some."

Sophia nodded. "Absolutely, boss."

Keahilani reached for the door handle and said, "Take a break and have a Coke or something. I don't want you passing out. It's not like we have insurance or anything."

Sophia's face paled and expanded in slow-motion shock like a rolling plume of nuclear fallout. "Please tell me you're joking about the insurance."

Keahilani's mischievous snicker turned into a full-blown laugh. It felt good.

Sophia exhaled and laughed too. "Nice one."

"Oh, I got you a key," Keahilani said, digging in her shorts pocket. She handed it over. "You're officially the new manager of Mahina Surf and Dive. Welcome to the 'ohana."

Sophia's smile widened. "Thanks, boss. I'm looking forward to turning this place around."

"Me too."

A permanent female presence around the shop would be welcome. Keahilani had been so used to living and working with her brothers since Mahina's death, she'd almost forgotten that other women existed, let alone how to interact with them. Except maybe for Ret, but she wasn't most women. She was more like one of the boys.

Keahilani went inside, grateful for the air conditioning and a respite from the sun's biting rays zapping her eyeballs.

Her phone buzzed on the counter with a text from Manō: *Working late. Won't be home for dinner.*

Translation: *I'm following a lead on Bane's killer that'll probably keep me out all night. Don't wait up.*

Normally, Manō's comings and goings didn't bother her in the least, but with so many eyes watching the family's every move, she worried for his safety. Of the three of them, he was least likely to get caught doing something he shouldn't. Still, she was already a mother and a brother short and not prepared to lose anyone else.

And a Blake short, her conscience reminded her.

"Shut up," she said softly.

Blake was the last thing she wanted to think about, yet the memory of him falling dead at her feet played over and over on a loop in her mind. There was no blood in this version. No thud or any other sound when he hit the grass.

Just his face. A twisted mask of pain and shocked betrayal.

Manō might've tortured Blake physically, but Keahilani had squeezed the life out of his heart in more ways than one when she pulled the trigger.

He deserved it, the shadows hissed.

Maybe. But what he deserved didn't matter. Blake screwed her over by covering up for Scott.

Fucking Scott.

She tightened her fist. The pencil between her fingers snapped in two. She sighed and tossed the wooden bits into the trash can.

Mahina's journal caught her attention. It had been a week since she'd last inhaled the smell of the old paper within or read her mother's faded words. Butterflies with moons on their wings fluttered in her mind's eye. Chest tightening, Keahilani stroked the supple leather cover. Sometimes she missed Mahina so much, she couldn't breathe.

She picked up the journal. This one was from 1994. Mahina would've been thirty-three then, just seven years older than Keahilani was now.

Though she'd already scoured a few of her mother's other journals from earlier in her life, it still felt like an intrusion, like she was crossing a line by reading Mahina's most intimate thoughts. There were some things that weren't meant for your children's eyes. The story of how Mahina killed their father and made it look like a surfing accident was one. Yet, it was a hard truth Keahilani and her brothers deserved to know.

Justin Jacobs was a lying, evil piece of shit. Was it any wonder his kids had murder in their blood?

That wasn't exactly fair. Keahilani had only killed twice, and both times were justified.

Were they? a voice in her head asked. *Was Blake's murder deserved?*

At the time, when rage coursed through her veins, singing its song of vengeance, yes, it had been deserved. But in the days since she'd killed him, she questioned her own judgment more than once.

Had she turned into her mother, exacting final vengeance on the man she loved?

Or worse, had she become her *father*, a man who killed an innocent hiker in cold blood to prevent him from revealing some measly marijuana plants?

Fuck.

She flicked open the cover to the first page.

January 7, 1994

Two and a half weeks ago, I killed him. Two and a half weeks ago, my children had a father. Now we are on our own, and I'm eight weeks pregnant.

Though being a single mother is hard, I am fine with all of this. It's not like Justin was around much before he died.

Palani stopped by this afternoon. It's been an age since I last saw him—at Mom and Dad's for their thirtieth wedding anniversary celebration, if I remember correctly. I haven't seen them in years either, but my parents tend to stay in closer touch than my brother, which is why Palani's visit was a surprise.

Of course, he wanted to see the kids. He took them to the beach and gave Manō bodyboard tips while Kai and Keahilani surfed. Manō isn't even four yet, but he took to the ocean like a shark. The twins drank in the sun while I watched. Pride swelled in my chest at the sight of them.

Three babies by Justin. Keahilani and Kai seemed to have dodged his evil streak, but I'm beginning to worry about Manō. Sometimes he sleepwalks in the middle of the night. Long after bedtime, I found him wandering in circles around the kitchen table last week with a knife in his hand and a vacant look in his eyes. I've since moved all sharp objects up high, out of reach.

He thrashes fitfully if Keahilani or Kai don't sleep with him. Their presence seems to soothe his demons. Sometimes he cries out and wakes up in a full-body sweat. He comes into my room and crawls into bed with me, his skin slick and clammy. I hold him close, wrapping my arms around him, and whisper prayers to our ancestors, our 'aumākua, *begging them to watch over him.*

Today, he seemed as normal as any other four-year-old, running along the sand, splashing in the waves, laughing. I rubbed my belly as I watched him and his siblings learning techniques from their uncle. The new baby will be different. That's not a bad thing.

After they'd gotten their fill of surfing, Palani brought the children inside. They ran into the living room, chanting songs, while he sat at the table, arms crossed, watching me expectantly.

"Well?" *he said.*

"Well, what?" *I answered. I poured him a glass of lemonade and settled in the seat across from him.*

"You went and got yourself knocked up by him again."

I haven't told anyone, so I'm not sure how Palani would know I was pregnant, but there was no point in lying. "It's not his."

Palani cocked a brow in surprise. "Who's the father? Another* haole*?" *he said with derision.* "You couldn't have done much worse than Justin Jacobs."

I turned on him, irritated by this familiar line of bullshit. My brother has always been a purist when it comes to protecting our family's Hawaiian blood. "Yes, Palani. It's another* haole.*"*

"I don't understand why you can't keep your legs together," *he scoffed.* "Do the white men have magical dicks or something?"

"Who I fuck isn't any of your business." *It was just like high school again with him playing the overprotective brother and me starring as the damsel-in-distress sister. Only difference is, I am no damsel. Not anymore.*

"It became my business when you fell in with Justin and muddied our line with whatever filth pollutes his veins."

"My children do not bear his 'filth.' Something under the mountain made him evil," *I snapped, furious he would imply my kids are somehow tainted simply because they have* haole *blood.* "For someone who claims to love his niece and nephews, *you have a strange way of showing it."*

Palani's eyes narrowed. *"For all your powers of divination,* kahuna kilokilo, *you're awfully naïve. It has nothing to do with his race. It has to do with the purity of his soul."*

My brother has no idea what I am capable of. He has no idea about what I've seen. If he did, he wouldn't be scolding me like a little girl. He'd praise me for my insights and hug me in grief for what's coming.

"Darkness lurks around those children," Palani warned, *lowering his voice so none of them would overhear. I already knew of the darkness, but hearing it from my brother drove their curse home with a sense of foreboding finality. "I can already see it manifesting in* Manō. *It clings to his skin. The only way to keep it from sinking in is through the light."*

Palani's words gave me pause. He is a kahuna kilokilo *too. Maybe he's seen something I haven't. Lately all my divination energy has been centered around the baby in my womb, not the ones outside of it.*

"Manō is tangled up in the same darkness as his father's," Palani continued. *"You've witnessed it too, but you refuse to recognize it for what it is. Dreams of his dead father haunt him. Soon he will awaken from those dreams with violence in his heart, if he hasn't already."*

I swallowed over my denial. It would've been a lie. Manō did have violence in his heart. I've dismissed what I've seen as the result of nightmares children have from time to time. I don't want to believe something darker is infiltrating my little boy's soul. All I can do to stave it off is offer soothing words and hugs and kisses when he wakes up in strange places, wondering where he is or how he got there. I have only love for him.

But Palani is having premonitions of things I don't, and that scares the hell out of me. Did Justin find a way to hide the signs from me? Is his spirit lingering over Manō's bed at night, tempting him into darkness and covering up his hold over my boy?

Spirits can be very powerful. Any kahuna *worth her salt*

knows that.

"What do you suggest I do?" I asked my brother, trying not to sound scared. My children are the most important things in the world. The thought of one of them slipping away from my protection and into danger is unacceptable.

Palani took my hands. His fingers were warm, and his eyes were sincere. "Call on Manō's 'aumākua *for help. Offer the shark libations in exchange for his protection."*

This was a reasonable suggestion. "Okay," I said, nodding. "I'll make the proper offerings tonight."

"You must do it regularly, or the 'aumākua *will be displeased."*

"I will."

"And pay attention to your dreams. Especially ones with fish or sharks. Our ancestor will speak through their mouths. Listen to what they say." Then Palani added quickly, "Has he eaten any shark?"

"No." I shook my head. "No fish of any kind. I know better than to upset the ancestors by breaking kapu.*"*

Palani seemed relieved. "Your offerings will be enough to appease his guardian, but you must remain watchful of Manō."

"I will be watchful of all three," I said.

The children's laughter from the other room reached us, and Palani let go of my hands. I glanced through the doorway to where the children sat on the floor with a book in front of them, Manō propped between Keahilani's stretched legs, staring up at her with adoring black eyes. Arms encircling him, Keahilani sang to him, but she mixed up some words. Kai giggled and jumped around behind them, teasing her and swatting her hair.

I would die if I lost any of them to Justin's darkness.

I looked down at my belly and patted it gently. Bane would at least be spared from the family curse.

Or, would he?

The vision I saw yesterday of a great shadow overtaking a young man who had my eyes flirted with the edges of my consciousness. Like most visions, its symbolism was unclear. It

*could have been Manō or even Kai, but I felt the man was
Bane, the child in my womb, many years from now. I couldn't
interpret whether the darkness consumed the man or lent the
man the dark power to consume others.*

I shook my head, not wanting to think about such things.

*The baby is King's. He's the only one I've been with since
Justin's previous visit.*

*"May the ancestors watch over you, Mahina," Palani
said, standing up.*

*I joined him and gave him a quick hug. "When will I see
you again?"*

*Palani stared into the other room, his eyes focused on
Manō. "I'll be back when you need me."*

*He kissed my forehead sweetly, and I was overwhelmed by
the kindness of the gesture. Palani and I have never been very
close, but in that moment, I yearned for him to stay. He could
be a strong father figure for the children. But he had his own
life to live, his own responsibilities. It wouldn't be fair to ask.*

"I love you," I called after him as he walked to the door.

"I love you too, Mahina." And then he was gone.

The jangle of the bell above the shop door had perfect
timing. Keahilani closed the book, marveling at what she'd
read, just as Sophia came inside. She snatched off her
sunglasses and blinked pointedly at Keahilani. Then she
shifted her gaze sharply to the side.

Keahilani screwed up her face trying to figure out what
was wrong. Then she noticed the two police officers striding
up to the door behind Sophia. Their hands rested casually on
their guns.

"Shit." She shoved the journal under the cash register.

Sophia rounded the counter just as the officers entered.
Her eyes darted as if looking for somewhere to land in the
throes of a blinding blizzard.

All Keahilani could think about were the opening words
of her mother's journal: *Two and a half weeks ago, I killed him.*

She eased past Sophia and mouthed, "Hide this,"

pointing discreetly to the journal. She snatched her phone and greeted the officers with her most innocent expression.

"Can I help you?" she asked, losing track of Sophia in her periphery.

Please, Sophia, just move the journal out of sight.

The female cop removed her hat and stuffed it under her arm. "Officers Gillman and Tighe." She gestured to herself and then her partner. "Are you Keahilani Alana?"

"Yes."

"We'd like to ask you a few questions about a man named Butch Kelly."

And if things couldn't get any worse, at that moment, a text came through. She glanced down. Lui had sent her a blurry Skype screenshot of Bane with the vague image of a shadowy man lifting a gun behind his back.

CHAPTER TWENTY-ONE

The Waialua Kope office in Kahului was a stand-alone three-story building with an attached, covered parking garage. Turquoise fabric awnings over repurposed warehouse windows accented its façade of tasteful brown and red brick. Not too over-the-top, but it was clear from the décor and the expensive cars invading the lot that the place was home to big money. Though, that was true of most businesses on Maui.

Manō parked on the street, turned off his motorcycle, and searched for the company website on his burner phone. After a few minutes of tapping links, he found the names of the board of directors. He dialed the Maui office. A customer service rep answered.

"This is Kevin Statler from the Board," Manō said in his best uptight *haole* voice. "I'm having trouble reaching Mr. Lowden's personal line. I heard he was on Maui and need to speak with him. Can you patch me through?"

"Of course, Mr. Statler," the perky receptionist said. "Just a moment."

The line went quiet for a few seconds, then, "Kevin. Good to hear from you," a deep voice said. Lowden hadn't spoken when Manō saw him at the airport, so he had no way of knowing if this was the same guy. But his gut told him it was.

"You have the documents I requested?" the man asked.

"Yes, sir," Manō said. "I thought I'd deliver them in

person if you're available this afternoon."

There was a pause.

"That's not necessary." The voice grew tighter, harder. Lowden didn't buy his impersonation. "Email everything, and I'll have a look tonight."

"Of course, sir. I'll send them right over."

The line clicked dead. Apparently, Grant Lowden was a man of few words and a low tolerance for bullshit. Manō respected that, but he'd hoped to pull more information out of the guy. There was a good chance the CEO was in the building right now, which meant Manō could either wait outside for him to leave, or he could go into the snake den and see what turned up.

He dropped the burner on the street into incoming traffic. It took all of five seconds for a car to crush the device.

His regular phone rang, and he answered with a grunt.

Ret said, "You ditched me. Not cool."

Manō wasn't sorry. "Lowden is at Waialua Kope in Kahului. I'm going in."

"Manō, don't." Ret's voice took on heightened urgency. "I know you want to find Bane's murderer. I do too. But we gotta do this by the book. You can't obtain any evidence illegally. It'll just be thrown out in court."

"Who says I plan to use it in court?"

Truth was, Manō wasn't looking for evidence. He wanted vengeance. If he found anything to remotely link Lowden to Bane's murder, he'd kill the fucker here and now. No questions asked. Though he had nothing concrete to suggest there was a connection, his gut wouldn't stop nagging him about this Lowden character. Ever since he'd seen the businessman at the airport, accusations had been gnawing at him.

He was grasping at straws, yes, but if Scott Harris had a legit alibi for Bane's murder, Lowden was his only other lead.

"I'm heading over right now," Ret said. "Wait for me."

He didn't answer.

"Please," she said, desperation perforating the word.

"If he leaves, I will follow him."

"Fair enough. I'll be there shortly."

Manō hung up, muted the phone, tugged his cap low over his eyes, and went inside. The lobby was outfitted with oversized chairs and ottomans surrounded by plenty of low tables. All of this served as seating for the adjacent coffee shop sprawling the entire length of the right wall. People sat buried in their phones, sipping iced coffee, shopping bags scattered around their feet, oblivious to the beauty of Haleakalā watching them from the east and the stunning view of the north shore.

Fucking tourists.

Manō stepped up to the counter and ordered a cup of black coffee. He casually inquired from the barista where the restroom was, and the young woman pointed him around the corner to the right. He nodded his thanks and took his coffee to one of the chairs in the corner of the lobby closest to the elevators.

From under his hat, he scoped the floor plan for the ground level and watched the people coming and going. To the left of the bathrooms was a door with a sign that read "Employees only." He waited to see who went in and came out. After several minutes, a custodian exited, pushing a mop in a bucket. He cleaned up a spill just outside the coffee shop and returned the items to the closet, which didn't appear to have a coded lock.

Perfect.

When a boisterous group of six women entered the building, he used their shrill voices and the attention they drew as cover and wandered toward the restrooms. He casually checked the janitor's closet door. Locked. But Manō came prepared. He removed the Swiss Army knife from his pocket, jabbed it into the flimsy lock, and jimmied it open in seconds. He slipped inside just as the loud women shrieked with delight over the barista's latte art.

Score.

Not only was there a cleaning cart within, but he also

found several pairs of coveralls stacked on the shelf. He donned the work attire over his street clothes, flipped up the collar to hide his shark tattoo, and sloshed some water from the utility sink in the corner through his hair to slick it back under his hat.

Next move would be finding Lowden's office.

He pushed the cart out toward the elevator. While he waited for it to open, a man in a suit passed by and gave Manō the once-over. He scowled and said, "Service elevator not working?"

Shrugging, Manō feigned ignorance. "I'm new."

"Where are you heading?" the man asked, checking his watch.

"Mr. Lowden's office to clean up a spill."

The guy directed him around the corner to another elevator. "Third floor." Then he walked off.

Manō hid a smile and followed the man's directions. On the way up, he tugged the shadows around him tightly like a second skin, silently asking them to keep him hidden. He wouldn't be invisible, but when the shadows were close, it was easier for him to blend in and avoid people.

When the door opened, he pushed the cart out and quickly scanned the reception area for a map, a directory, a name plate, a massive glass office with an evil, gray-haired bastard laughing behind a huge desk—anything that might indicate where Lowden was.

What he found was a lone, frazzled-looking admin sitting behind a coffee-cup-emblazoned welcome desk. Two short corridors on either side buttressed the reception area, and that was it. The woman stood up and headed for the copier with a folder full of documents in her hands. With her back to him, he was free and clear to go whichever way he wanted.

Left or right?

Security cameras silently observed from their darkened domes above. There were no fewer than six of them. He couldn't tell which way they pointed, but he assumed he was being watched from every angle.

With no indication of which way to go, he jerked the bill of his hat lower and turned right, pushing the cart down the corridor. He nodded to a passing employee, but the man either didn't notice him or was too far up his own ass to acknowledge the lowly custodian. Fine by Manō.

He found the men's restroom and propped its door open with a rubber wedge from the cart. He grabbed some window cleaner and sprayed the mirrors while casually watching the hallway and listening. Random chatter about reports and sales figures and human resources filings filtered through the hall. He wasted as much time in the men's room as seemed appropriate and then moved on to the ladies' room, repeating the procedure.

The frazzled admin from reception passed hurriedly down the hall, her arms full of more files. Manō casually peered around the corner after her. She knocked on the door at the end of the corridor. A male voice said to come in. Manō was almost positive it was the man he'd spoken to earlier on the phone.

He shot his gaze around the bathroom, looking for vents and settling his sights on the ceiling tiles. He twisted the lock on the door, shut off the lights, and dove into the welcoming arms of darkness like a shark into the depths.

The dark embraced him. He smiled with relief.

He couldn't see anything with his own eyes, but he didn't need them. Using the shadow escorts as his guide, he sensed his surroundings just fine. He climbed on one of the toilet seats and reached up to the ceiling to push a tile aside. He couldn't get up there without support, and the flimsy rafters would probably collapse under his weight anyway.

He supposed that meant he'd have to lighten his load.

He opened his mind and body to the shadows, welcoming them inside.

Whispering like bat wings, the darkness eagerly accepted his offer of flesh. Manō blended into it like a drop of black dye into a cup of filthy water.

Welcome home.

His body elongated, stretching from solid form into shreds of wispy air. He became the shadows, the darkness, the night. His black spirit floated into the vent and swam through the ductwork until it reached the room at the end of the hall. There, he poised over the vent, listening, thrumming with wild energy he wasn't sure he could control.

"Oh, and please sign here too," the assistant said.

From above, Manō studied the figure behind the desk, but with his gray-haired head bent down, it was hard to see him, let alone get a read on him. He inched as close as the metal grate would allow without actually going through.

The man's pen scrawled across the page. He was a lefty. When he finished signing the page, he laid the pen down and stood up slowly, craning his neck around as if a strange noise had tipped off his ears to something that shouldn't have been there.

The shadows gently tugged Manō away from the vent, their amorphous "fingers" sliding over his nonexistent lips. *Hush,* they seemed to say. Manō stilled.

The man lifted his gaze through the grate, targeting him. It was Lowden. And he wasn't alone behind those eyes.

Heavy, sinking dread seeped into Manō like a poison-tipped arrow, spreading threat and foreboding promises of dark pleasures at the expense of life and/or limb.

Curiosity prickling to the point of madness, Manō closed in for one last look. A shiver ran through his shadow as its gaze connected with Lowden. The CEO's narrowed eyes were cast in shadows of their own. They were all Manō saw. Though he couldn't make out their color or even their shape, he'd never forget the depths of their darkness.

He had no conclusive evidence—only his gut to rely on—but Manō was certain Grant Lowden murdered Bane.

Just before the shadows dragged Manō into the recesses of the ventilation duct, he caught a jagged smile that beamed like an epiphany of death.

CHAPTER TWENTY-TWO

Keahilani pretended to think. "I don't know anyone named Butch Kelly," she said to the police officers. She leaned an elbow on the counter.

"How about Blake Murphy?" Officer Tighe asked. The short white man had a voice like a cheese grater tossed into a garbage disposal. Must've smoked several packs a day.

"Now, I *do* know him," Keahilani confessed. She'd been seen with Blake in public and had his signed waiver on file here at the shop from the day she gave him surfing lessons. If, God forbid, they brought a warrant or decided they had probable cause to search the place, they'd find evidence that he'd been there. She couldn't afford to lie when they were literally standing so close to the truth.

"Great," Officer Gillman said. Her smile didn't reach her eyes. "Would you mind coming down to the precinct to talk about him?"

"As you can see, I have a business to run." Keahilani indicated the store with a nod.

"Shouldn't take long." Gillman's fake smile faded. She looked at Sophia. "Besides, you have help. She can mind the store while you're gone."

Keahilani's mind raced. She needed to let Kai and Manō know the cops were here. She also needed to get a better look at the picture that had just come through from Lui, but checking her phone now was out of the question.

"I know my rights," she said, keeping her tone carefully neutral. "I don't have to answer your questions. Unless, of course, you intend to arrest me, in which case, I'll call my lawyer."

Total bluff. She couldn't afford a fucking lawyer, but they didn't know that.

Tighe lifted a hand in a calming gesture. "No need to get worked up."

Keahilani's insides rumbled with anger. Worked up? If Gillman thought *this* was worked up, Keahilani should introduce her to Pele.

"And we're not here to arrest anyone," Gillman soothed. "We just need to ask a few questions."

"Ask away." Keahilani folded her arms over her chest. "I've told you I don't know the first guy you mentioned. I know Blake. What about him?"

Tighe glanced to Sophia. "Can we speak in private?"

Keahilani nodded toward the door, grabbing her keys. "Let's go outside."

The officers trudged out behind her. Keahilani leaned a hip against her car parked in the shade of a tree in the back lot and waited with a defiant huff.

"How do you know Blake Murphy?" Gillman asked.

Keahilani shrugged. "He came in here for surf lessons. I gave them to him."

"When was that?" Gillman said.

"I don't remember. A week ago? Maybe two? I can check my records. He signed a waiver."

"You give him anything other than surfing lessons?" Tighe asked, casually glancing inside the car window.

She straightened and settled her fists on her hips. "What are you suggesting, *officer*?" It was hard to keep the rage from her voice, especially with the shadows dancing behind the pair like playful demon cubs in search of souls to munch.

Go ahead, she thought. *They probably taste like bacon.*

The black, blobby forms seemed to smile at that.

"I'm suggesting you had some kind of relationship with

Blake Murphy that involved more than just a boogie board. Maybe you did some body surfing elsewhere. Like between the sheets at the Westin."

"Is that a crime I'm unaware of?" Her smart-ass sarcasm bit like a wild mule.

"So, you had sex with Murphy," Gillman stated, jotting in her notebook.

"Yes. A couple of times. Is there anything else?"

"When was the last time you saw him?" Gillman asked.

"Like I said. A week ago, maybe two. We did our business, and I left. Haven't seen him since. What's this about?" Keahilani engineered an air of reluctant curiosity. She couldn't come off as *too* interested, but she also needed to appear shocked when they dropped the bomb she knew was coming.

"He's missing," Gillman replied. "Your name came up as a possible witness."

Witness. That was a laugh. Scott had sicced the cops on her after their little family reunion on O'ahu. He'd no doubt told them she'd killed Blake, but without a body, it would be impossible to prove. *Mahalo, Manō.*

Keahilani furrowed her brow and painted on an expression of concern, which, surprisingly, wasn't that hard to do. She wrapped herself in a make-believe body outside of her existing one and imagined what a better version of Keahilani, free of darkness—free of shadows—would feel if the police had just told her Blake was missing.

She would be bereft.

She'd cared for him—maybe even loved him. She just loved her brothers more.

Her breath hitched, and this time it wasn't for show. She snapped her fingers to the necklace around her throat and worried the butterfly charm there. "When?" she asked.

"He was last seen at a bar in Lāhainā with another guy we can't find."

She snapped her eyes to Gillman. "Who?"

The policewoman consulted her notebook. "Pekelo

'Ōpūnui. You know him?"

She shook her head and absently answered, "No."

She hadn't met Pekelo, but she recognized the name. He worked on the farm. She didn't monitor day-to-day hands-on Pāhoehoe operations, but Kai and Manō mentioned him in passing at some point.

So, this Pekelo guy was connected to Blake. Now that Jezzy was no longer on the payroll, it would be hard to find out how. Loose ends like this bugged the shit out of Keahilani. Complications arose from unknowns. At the moment, the Alanas had enough complications to outlast a nuclear winter.

"You know, it would be a hell of a lot easier for us to put the pieces of this puzzle together at the precinct," Tighe said, returning his gaze from the inspection job he was doing on the car to Keahilani.

"What pieces?" she asked. "Sounds to me like you got two separate missing persons cases and a murder. I don't see how any of it relates or how it involves me."

"I'd agree with you," Tighe said. "Only problem is we never said anything about a murder."

Keahilani's blood lurched, searing her veins like fire. Her pulse pounded painfully in her ears. Her face heated.

This was it. In her preoccupation with hiding the truth, she got cocky. They knew she was a fucking liar.

"Would you like to rethink your answer to the Butch Kelly question?" Tighe's self-righteous smirk jabbed the underside of her skin like a thousand needles. The shadows under the tree became agitated, and the green canopy above shook, though there was no wind.

Keahilani willed herself to cool off and cleared her head of all thoughts about Butch, Blake, and the shadows. She scrambled for a lie they'd buy. Then her get-out-of-jail card magically appeared in her hand.

"I was talking about my brother, Bane," she said, thinking fast. She hoped it was enough to cover her guilt. "You know, the guy whose murder you're supposed to be investigating?"

When neither answered, she fired off, "Yeah. That's what I thought."

She walked away, but Tighe's words stopped her halfway to the shop door. "This your car?"

She could lie and say it wasn't hers, but all it would take was a quick search on their squad car computer or a call to a dispatcher to see the Prius was registered to her.

She sighed and glanced over her shoulder. "Yeah."

Tighe straightened and cupped his hands over the window, peering inside. "Got anything in it I should know about?"

"I'm not sure what you're insinuating," she sassed back.

Then it hit her in the gut so hard, she actually bent forward from the impact.

The weed. She always kept weed in her purse and in the glove compartment as a backup in case she met with a dealer who wanted to sample Pāhoehoe. On her way to the shop this morning, she'd hit the brakes a little too hard at a stoplight, and her open purse had tumbled off the seat. It never occurred to her that anything might've spilled out. The contents seemed intact when she parked and got out.

Fear latched on to her throat while thick dread weighed down her limbs like a barnacle-covered anchor.

She squinted at the officers. It was too fucking bright out here. She couldn't see what they were doing.

Shadows. She needed the shadows.

Kill them, she thought. *Kill them!*

In her desperation, she willed the darkness to obey her. But it had no more power in full daylight than she did.

Besides, what the hell was she thinking, telling shadows to kill police officers? First of all, if they *could* do such a thing, she'd be an accessory to yet another unscheduled murder. Second of all, they were goddamn shadows. They only had life in her imagination, right?

The inky specters gave no answer.

Keahilani felt cornered. If she ran, the cops would chase her. If she submitted, they'd have grounds to arrest her. If she attacked, they'd Taser her. Or worse.

Just then, an orange-and-black shape that looked like two vividly painted triangles stuck together flitted past. Keahilani's breath caught. Her 'aumākua. Mahina.

"Can you please open your car door, Miss Alana?" Tighe's condescending tone rankled her.

Keahilani stomped over. "No."

He leaned against the side and nodded to the passenger seat. On the floorboard lay a little plastic baggie with a bud inside.

"You wanna tell me what that is?" he asked.

"I won't say another word until I speak to my lawyer," Keahilani snarled.

Officer Gillman eased closer, reaching for her handcuffs. "Ma'am, we have probable cause to investigate what's in that bag. Please unlock your vehicle and step aside."

"You don't have permission to look in my car," Keahilani protested, agitation rising from her core like a fever. They couldn't do this to her.

"Miss Alana, if you fight me, you'll only make things worse. Open the door," Gillman said firmly, handcuffs dangling from her fingers.

Tighe covered Keahilani's back while she fought off Gillman's advances with the cuffs. Pressure mounted in Keahilani's gut. Darkness descended from the trees above, but it was weak. The shadows mimicked her jerky motions as she slapped and clawed at the officers.

"Let me go!" she screamed.

The front door to Mahina Surf and Dive flew open, and Sophia rushed out, her eyes big and round, her mouth in the shape of an O. "What are you doing to her?"

"Call my brothers," Keahilani shouted to Sophia as Tighe wrestled her to the pavement, shoving her face into the ground.

The latent heat from the blacktop burned. Pebbles, broken bits of glass, and other debris cut into her cheek. She kicked and flailed, reaching for the shadows.

They tried to meet her halfway, but the sun was too strong. The police were too strong. The whole world was against her.

"Leave her alone! You're hurting her!" Sophia begged, her splayed fingers trembling. The pleas fell on deaf ears. She caught Keahilani's eyes as tears flooded her own. She seemed to say, *I'm so sorry.*

Keahilani moaned as the cops roughed her further, kicking her legs aside, straddling her, slapping cuffs on her wrists. The shadows raged above, trying to get to her, but they couldn't cross the sun.

Her brother was dead. Her lover was dead. And if the police found out what else she'd done, she'd be as good as dead.

The officers lifted her to her feet and dragged her to the patrol car. Just before the door shut, she snagged Sophia's gaze one last time. "Call my brothers," she shouted.

Sophia's grim nod was her only answer as Keahilani was ripped away from the safety of Mahina's Surf and Dive and tossed into a bottomless pit of despair.

CHAPTER TWENTY-THREE

The timing couldn't have been a coincidence. Manō had just escaped the Waialua Kope offices and turned on his phone when a call came through. Caller ID flashed the number for the surf shop.

"Your sister," Sophia said breathlessly. The woman sounded like she was having a panic attack. "She … They … The police took her away."

"Slow down," Manō said, trotting toward his bike. "What happened?"

"They came in asking questions about a guy. Something with a B. Two Bs, actually. Butch. And another guy. Brock?" Sophia seemed to argue with herself and finally settled on names. "No, Blake. It was Butch something-or-other and a Blake something."

Manō released his held breath. Unless the cops had been to Kaho'olawe, they didn't have Blake's body. Hard to prove a murder without a corpse. Butch, on the other hand, was a different story.

"They went out to the parking lot, but I was watching through the window," Sophia continued. "She must've had something in her car because they got handsy with her after they looked inside."

Weed. Had to be.

Fuck. How could Keahilani be so careless?

"Which station did they take her to?" Manō asked.

"I don't know."

"Did you hear the officers' names?"

"Gillham and Tighe," Sophia said. "No, wait. Her name was Gillman, I think."

"*Mahalo.*"

He was about to hang up when Sophia said, "Manō, wait. Keahilani asked me to hide something for her. Looks like a journal. I didn't read it," she added quickly. *Yeah, right.* "But she seemed adamant about keeping it away from the police. What do you want me to do with it?"

Double fuck. He had to assume whatever information lay in the pages of Mahina's diary was information Sophia was now privy to. He didn't care how sweet she seemed. The list of people Manō trusted was exactly two names deep, and sometimes even his brother and sister were questionable.

"I'll send Kai over for it." He hung up and peeled out of the Waialua Kope parking deck in a cloud of black smoke.

Once he was a considerable distance from the coffee company and Grant Lowden's creepy-as-fuck eyes, he pulled off at a gas station to text Kai.

K's been arrested. Need you to pick up journal at shop.

Then he opened the Maui County Government page on his web browser and ran a search for the officers' names.

They were from District 1, Wailuku, where Ret worked. He texted her too: *Keahilani arrested. Meet me at station.*

His phone rang. Kai stammered, "What the fuck happened?"

"Best I can tell, they questioned her about Butch and Blake, then found weed in her car. She left Mahina's journal with Sophia. Pick it up and meet me at the Wailuku station."

"We are fucked," Kai moaned, his voice trembling. "We are so fucking fucked!"

Manō ignored Kai's outburst. "We'll figure it out when we get the facts. I'm on my way now."

"Okay." Kai inhaled heavily. "I'll be there shortly."

They hung up. Then Ret texted a terse "OMW." She was pissed at him for ditching her at the hospital, but he didn't have time to deal with a butt-hurt girlfriend's feelings.

He backed up the train on that thought. *Not a girlfriend. A friend. With privileges.*

He arrived at the Wailuku police station and located an admin. When he asked about his sister, the woman said she was being held for questioning and directed him to take a seat.

Thirty minutes later, Ret walked past, barely acknowledging him. He couldn't tell if she was intentionally ignoring him or trying to keep up appearances of neutrality where the Alanas were concerned. The latter would be preferable for any number of reasons, but the former was probably more in line with reality.

A few minutes later, she texted: *They booked her on drug charges, but they're more interested in murder. Got a lawyer?*

No, he texted back.

Get one. I'll do what I can, but it ain't much.

I need to see her, he typed.

Gonna be a while.

If they had evidence that Keahilani was behind Butch's murder, they'd be snooping around her house and the safe house soon, assuming they weren't already. Manō's time would be best spent covering tracks rather than watching the clock here.

He quickly ran through what he knew of both murders. Butch had tried to sexually assault Keahilani at the condo they rented a couple nights a month in Kā'anapali. She'd blown his balls off and then shot him in the head when he wouldn't die quick enough. She'd been dressed as Pele that night.

Shit. Pele.

He stood up and exited the building as fast as he could without drawing attention, texting Kai as he walked. *Change of plans. Going to K's.*

Kai acknowledged, and Manō sped toward Keahilani's. When he got there, it was too late. The place was already marked off with police tape and crawling with cops. Lots of activity around the county forensics van too.

Damn, they got a warrant fast. They must've already had

it written up and ready to execute, which suggested they were on to Keahilani, if not all three siblings, before the incident this morning.

If they hadn't found Keahilani's Pele wig and costume yet, they would soon. Too late to salvage anything here, but he and Kai might be able to beat them to their places. He watched the scene as he dialed Kai.

"I got the journal. I'm at the safe house," Kai said.

"They're searching her apartment," Manō said. On the off chance Keahilani had moved her garb, he asked, "Is her costume with you?"

The sound of heavy footfalls followed by rustling echoed through the speaker as Kai searched. "I don't see it in her room."

Manō clenched his fists. "Get rid of the Enforcer gear and any other trails that might lead them to us."

"What do you want me to do with it?" Kai asked.

"Burn it. Shred it. Bury it. I don't give a fuck. Just get it off the property."

His order signaling the end of an era cut deeper than he expected. Though he and Kai didn't assume their supernatural guises often, and then, only for drug deals, Manō would miss playing the role of Pele's Enforcer. Even though he could kill a man with his bare hands (and had on more than a few occasions), the only times he truly felt powerful were when he and Kai, wearing the giant tiki masks and designer suits, flanked their sister masquerading as the volcano goddess. Separate, the siblings were strong in their own individual ways. But together, the trio was invincible.

Not anymore.

Kai interrupted his racing thoughts. "Ret says they got her on possession, and depending on what the warrant turns up, they might have enough to charge her with Butch's murder."

Irritation burned the spaces between Manō's ribs. So, Kai had already talked to Ret, and she'd seen fit to give him additional information.

And you're pissed because ... what? She likes Kai better than she likes you? Boo-hoo.

This was no time for jealousy. He slammed the door in envy's face and tried to think.

"Does Keahilani have any weapons we need to take care of?"

"I don't think so. She left the one ..." Kai trailed off, but Manō understood what he meant. She left Butch's murder weapon at the scene, wiped of prints, its serial number, and any other identifiers.

"What about her phones?"

"I assume she had them with her."

Not good. Not good at all.

"Check her room for any others and destroy them as well as your burners. Delete any texts, emails, or IMs that might raise suspicion. Assume they're monitoring everything."

"Okay." Kai's voice strengthened. Maybe he was pulling his shit together. Finally.

"I'll do a sweep of Bane's house. You make sure the safe house is clean," Manō said.

"Understood."

Manō hung up and resumed his mission, speeding toward Bane's.

Multiple crimes had been perpetrated, and it was hard to keep track of what happened where. On the night of Bane's death, Keahilani had told the police a man broke into their brother's house and shot him. She claimed she shot the suspect in self-defense, but he got away.

In truth, she'd arrived to find Blake standing over their brother as he bled from a gunshot wound to the chest. Furious, Keahilani had popped a round in Blake's leg. Manō himself had dragged the wounded Blake out of the house, intentionally leaving a blood trail that would serve as a treasure trove of Blake's DNA should the pigs come calling.

If they had him in a database, they'd know Blake had been at the scene. That would provide solid evidence to build a case against him for murdering Bane, even though Keahilani didn't believe Blake had really done it. After what Manō had seen at the coffee company today, he didn't believe Blake was guilty either.

Keahilani's plan seemed a good idea at the time, back when Blake was still alive and could take the fall, but now that he was dead, the picture was blurry. Scott had told the cops Keahilani had something to do with Blake's disappearance. With a missing person report filed on Blake and his blood all over Bane's property, she would look much more like a suspect, especially since she'd lied about shooting a retreating "*haole* guy in a hoodie" rather than calling Blake by name.

Keahilani needed to appear as a credible witness to an unfortunate series of events, but Manō feared she'd already screwed that pooch. There would be no take backs.

One thing was clear: the cops had evidence that could implicate Keahilani at the very least, or the entire *'ohana* at worst.

He saw only one solution. It was a favor he'd hoped he wouldn't need to call in. When he arrived at Bane's and saw all the little markers beside dried blood stains, he knew he'd have to.

He dialed Ret.

"I'm kinda busy here," she said, irritation frosting her quiet voice.

He paused. Closed his eyes. Focused on his breathing. God, he was so damn tired.

"I need you," he said, defeated. The shadows curled around him like a comforting blanket.

"Meet me at the Best Western in Wailuku tonight at midnight," she replied softly and hung up.

He glanced at his jittery hands and once again thought of Blake's body exposed to the elements, his spirit roaming restlessly across the channel. The gods would exact vengeance on Manō for his disrespectful treatment of the dead. If the cops didn't dig up Blake's corpse first.

Guilt sliced through him as he pointed his bike toward the office of John Mendelson, a lawyer who owed him a favor.

Who needed sleep anyway?

CHAPTER TWENTY-FOUR

Ret Rogers rubbed her eyes as she skimmed over Keahilani's open file on her desk for the fifth time. While Manō went gallivanting across the island doing God knew what, she'd spent the morning and part of the afternoon questioning people at the hospital about Bane's death, turning the same details over to look at them under different lenses, but getting the same results.

And then Keahilani went and got arrested.

Fuck, if that woman didn't have a pair of brass balls on her. Trouble was, those shiny clackers got in the way of good sense more often than not lately. She used to have her shit together. Since Bane's death, not so much.

And Blake's death. Ret couldn't forget about him.

She slapped the file closed and pushed it aside. Along with resisting arrest, Tighe and Gillman nabbed Keahilani with drug possession and intent to distribute. That was all they needed to keep her locked up for the night. They'd pick her brain some more about the murders tomorrow. Not that she'd answer. She hadn't given up anything beyond the occasional "fuck you" since they brought her in around noon.

"Rogers, can I see you in my office," Chief called through his open door. It was not a request.

"Yes, sir." Ret rolled back her chair and pushed up to stand. A glance at her watch explained her exhaustion. It was after 9 p.m. Twelve-hour days could bite her.

She ambled into Chief Hale's office and leaned against the door frame. He looked up from the neatly organized papers on his desk and gestured to the chair across from him. "Sit."

She did.

After he finished signing a form, he laid the pen aside and removed his glasses to clean them with his shirt sleeve. "I know you're close to the Alana case. I'm sorry about your friend, but the threads of this web are a tangled mess. Drugs, missing persons, murder. We need to get Miss Alana to talk. I might be willing to drop one of the lesser charges with a little cooperation."

"Chief, I've known Keahilani for ten years now. If she ain't singing now, she won't be singing tomorrow."

"That's unfortunate."

Ret nodded. The deeper her fellow officers dug into the Alanas' background, the harder it would be for Ret to distance herself from either side. With each passing day, the vortex of truth pulled her closer and closer to its funnel. She scrubbed her face.

"A couple detectives got it in their minds that the Alanas are growing illegal marijuana somewhere on the island," Chief said. "They sent the weed they found in Keahilani's car off for testing."

Shit-damn-fuck, this was bad news. Medical marijuana was legal in Hawai'i, but recreational wasn't. If the detectives discovered Keahilani's brothers were involved, they'd go to jail too.

And the fact remained that Keahilani had committed murder. Twice.

"What do you want me to do, Chief?" Ret said with exasperation. She was screwed no matter what.

He narrowed his wise brown eyes on her. What did he see when he looked at her? A good cop? Or a good friend? Trapped between the two, she didn't feel like either.

"Get her to talk," he said. "I can't promise much, but a confession would help her case."

"I'll see what I can do." Ret stood up. "Anything else?"

Chief paused as if thinking through the best way to answer. "This job is hardest when people we know and care about enter the scene. Remember the oath you swore to serve and protect, Officer Rogers."

Was that a threat?

"Be careful," he said.

"Yes, sir." She left his office angry. Guilty.

Ret's mother, God rest her soul, had been a cop all her adult life. When she was killed by a mugger in Central Park a few years ago, Ret vowed to do exactly what Chief said: serve and protect. But what was she supposed do when people she loved like family were the ones making the world less safe for others? The *right* thing would be to put them away. But in this situation, right was a matter of perspective.

The Alanas were drug dealers. They only dealt in weed, yeah, but it was powerful weed.

Worse, they were murderers. At least, Keahilani was. Ret was pretty sure Manō had killed people too, but she didn't have any evidence. She didn't know about Kai.

Question was, did their victims deserve it? Vigilante justice was against the law, but if it served a higher purpose and helped society in the end, was it excusable?

Many women had called the law on Butch Kelly before Keahilani got a hold of him. He was a known rapist, drug dealer, and killer who had the best lawyer money could buy. He was meticulous about not leaving behind evidence at the scenes of his crimes. He wore condoms with the women he sexually assaulted. He was a real piece of shit who deserved to die, and Ret celebrated the day it happened.

If Keahilani's story was true, Butch tried to rape her too. That, in Ret's mind, was all the justification her friend needed to pop one cap between his legs and another between her eyes. Fuckers like Butch Kelly deserved far worse.

As for Blake, Ret didn't know. Keahilani said she caught him at the scene of Bane's shooting, but there was no other evidence of who else might've been there. Did that give her sufficient reason to shoot him? Maybe. It wasn't like Blake was an angel either. He had a felony record for cocaine possession, and he was suspected of a couple murders, neither of which was supported by evidence.

The Alanas' weed business was supposed to help them financially, not hurt anyone. People weren't busted for DWI while on that shit. Once you smoked Pāhoehoe, you weren't going anywhere but to bed so you could fuck your brains out. Theirs provided the most sexual high around, and it kept users fapping and diddling in the comfort of their own homes, not plowing through the streets, smashing up storefronts.

Bottom line: When you smoked Pāhoehoe, you fucked. And you fucked good.

Ret went to the holding tank and found Keahilani sitting alone on the concrete bench in cell 3. Shadows bowed around her like a cape as she stared through the glass window at nothing. Or everything. It was hard to tell.

"Hey." Ret waved, clasping the door handle. She hated these damn cells. Without the door open, you could hardly hear through them. She removed a key from her belt and opened the bean slot so they could talk.

Keahilani stood and walked over, her head lowered. "Hey."

"You hanging in there?"

Her friend nodded. "Yeah. Your boss send you here to try to get me to talk?"

Ret laughed gently. "How'd you know?"

Keahilani glanced casually up to the surveillance camera in the corner and then angled away from it. "Can they hear us?" she whispered.

Ret barely turned her head, following her gaze. The solid red light assured her it was watching their every move. Keahilani turned her back to it.

"No audio," Ret said softly. "No money in the budget for it. But if, God forbid," she crossed herself, "you end up at the correctional facility, keep your voice down. They got audio and video galore. Not to mention it's overcrowded as fuck."

"I need my phone," Keahilani said.

"No can do. They're watching me like a hawk."

"Then bring Manō up here. If you tell him where it is, he can get it."

Ret tensed. "What, is he gonna walk through walls using his super X-ray powers? He can't sneak past the cameras and staff."

Keahilani flashed a wicked smile. "Wanna bet?"

Ret frowned, unsure what she meant by that. "Why do you need your phone?"

"Someone sent a picture right before I got busted. I didn't get a good look at it, but I think it's the killer, taken right before Bane died."

"That makes no sense. Why would a killer selfie his crime?"

"I don't think he did. I'm pretty sure it was a screenshot. Like from a video chat or something. I won't know until I get a good look at the image. You gotta help me, Ret. This is my little brother we're talking about. His murderer is still out there. He might be plotting another death as we speak."

Ret felt her loyalties being stretched like a criminal tied to horses for drawing and quartering. Her heart bled for her friends and the loss they'd endured, but if she got caught helping them, her career was over. Police work was the only thing she'd ever been good at. Not only that, but she'd promised her mom she'd be a great cop—one who'd make her proud.

Mom would never have approved of her helping criminals, friends or otherwise.

"Forget about being promoted to detective. I could lose my job over this," Ret said weakly.

Keahilani nodded. "I understand."

"If you'd just talk to them, they might go easier on you," Ret tried, though she recognized the fatalism in the words. Keahilani was fucked no matter what.

Keahilani snapped her eyes up to meet hers. The green

irises were ringed with unnatural black. Ret gasped and took a step backward. Had Keahilani's eyes always looked that way? Must've been a trick of the low light.

"Look at me, Ret," Keahilani said, grasping the door frame, her arms trembling under the strain. "I'm an uneducated Hawaiian woman facing drug charges with the possibility of two murder charges adding to the pile. When has the system *ever* worked in favor of someone like me? Even if I admitted to all of it, I'd still be looking at years of prison time." She turned away disgustedly. "Maybe if I were a rich white man like my half brother, things would be different."

Ret pressed her lips together to keep from screaming. Her friend was right.

But her friend was also guilty.

"I'll talk to Manō," Ret said quietly.

Keahilani turned toward her, stepped into the light, and lifted her fingers as if to touch her through the glass. She notched her head a few degrees in deference to the camera and dropped her hand. The black disappeared from her eyes. "*Mahalo*," she whispered. "I won't forget this."

Emotions broiling, Ret nodded and left the holding area, heading toward her car. She slipped into the driver's seat and pounded the steering wheel with a fist. Inhaling a deep, calming breath, she turned the car on and drove to the motel. She sat in the parking lot for a few minutes. She heard the growl of Manō's motorcycle before she saw it, and her heart leapt.

With the engine still running, Manō scanned the lot like a predator. Dressed in black, he did things to her body no one had ever done. The scars, the tattoos, the rugged, dark look. He was huge and imposing. If she'd been someone else, she'd never have even considered hooking up with him. But the more time she spent with him, the harder she fell under his spell.

So much darkness trapped under that glorious brown skin. Ret was willing to take it on. All of it.

His eyes passed over to Ret's car. He texted her a few

seconds later.

Room 116. Wait a few minutes after I go in.

The engine revved, and Manō circled to the back lot facing the even-numbered rooms. A trail of shadows followed like a cloud of exhaust in his wake. Manō was made of the kind of darkness she had no business playing with. Kai would've been so much easier, if she just could've separated her feelings for him from her desires for him.

But was her relationship with Manō any different?

It had been at first. Now, she didn't know. Every time she looked at him, something deep inside her ached to dabble in his darkness. Or maybe shine a light on it in hopes of saving him.

Always the hero. Just like Mom.

Or was antihero a better descriptor?

Ret rubbed her tired eyes. "What the hell are you doing, Beretta?" she asked herself aloud.

She didn't answer. Because she knew exactly what she was doing.

She popped open the door and marched fearlessly into the darkness.

CHAPTER TWENTY-FIVE

The door opened before Ret had a chance to knock. With no lights emanating from the motel room, Manō stood in a halo of darkness, the undisputed king of night.

He grabbed her by the wrist and pulled her across the threshold, his roughness triggering a spark of primal need deep within her. His hands fell around her waist. The scent of a nondescript soap wafted off his freshly cleaned skin, tempting her closer. She inhaled deeply, wanting more.

His lips hovered above hers. She couldn't see much, but she felt his restless, black energy climbing all over her, and that was enough. Skimming her fingers up the inside of his body-hugging white tank top, she traced and tested every rigid groove of tight muscle she could find.

She wanted him so badly, but she needed to talk to him about Keahilani before she got carried away by his charms.

"Your sister," she breathed heavily. "She says someone texted her a picture of who she thinks is Bane's killer. The cops came in before she could get a good look. Her phone's locked up with her other belongings at the station."

Manō didn't say anything for a long moment. Then, "I'll get it."

"I can help you access the storage room, but I can't take the fall if you get caught."

"I won't be caught." Always so sure of himself. She wished she shared his certainty.

"And you don't need to get me inside," he added.

"How the hell are you gonna—"

"That day back in high school when I picked you up on the side of the road," he said, cutting her off and angling closer. His feet bumped into hers. He pulled her by the belt loops and left the promise of a kiss dangling like a lure half an inch above her mouth. "Where had you been?"

She couldn't think straight. Surely he didn't mean *that* day. "Wh-what are you talking about?" she stuttered as the memories unleashed a whirlwind of agony she preferred to leave buried in the past.

Hoohana Street. May 13. The day she'd never forget.

Manō came out of the Safeway on the corner of Kamehameha Avenue. Clutching her stomach as it roiled with a bitter combination of physical and emotional pain, she watched him mount his motorcycle and pull out of the parking lot. When he rounded the corner, they locked eyes. A question passed between them. Then an answer.

Are you okay?

No.

"Don't play coy with me, Ret," he said gruffly. "It was after school. The only time I ever picked you up. I saw you walking down Hoohana by yourself. Hair a mess. Eyes lost. You looked like you'd just been told you were dying."

Conflicting emotions cascaded over her anew—worry, regret, fear, sadness. Ret swallowed hard and pushed away, but Manō snatched her hands, covering them with his. His skin was cool and abrasive. *Shark skin.* His shiny black eyes peered through the darkness and found hers.

"You'd just come from the clinic." Manō's voice lost its sharp edge.

She wanted to shut down all the noise raging between her ears, but the inner voices were too loud. Manō opened the lock that had kept them in check for so many years. They would not be silent for a second more.

Sinner.

Murderer.

Baby killer.

"It was Kai's baby," he said.

Tears flooded Ret's eyes and poured past the dams of her lids. She barked a sob and broke down in his arms.

Manō didn't flinch. He guided her to the bed. Sitting on its edge, he took her into his arms and held her as vicious tremors wracked her body.

It felt as if an avalanche had jarred loose a decade's worth of haunting memories and sent them spilling down from her heart. Her worst, most closely guarded secret was out.

But Manō had known all along. It wasn't a secret between them. It was a reality that tied them together even more than their illicit affair.

Manō knew. He'd known for a decade.

She turned her tear-soaked face up to his and sobbed into his neck. The shark tattoo grinned down at her, emotionless. But he wasn't. His arms tightened, holding her against his chest. He rode out the storm alongside her.

Despite everything that had happened today—Keahilani's arrest, Ret and Manō investigating leads on Bane's killer, her talk with Keahilani in the station holding tank—Manō was here. With her. Comforting her, even.

He could've been anywhere else, yet he'd chosen to be here.

A fresh round of tears sprung from her eyes, but she wasn't embarrassed anymore. He cradled her in his strong arms, rubbing her back in small circles, his steady heart beating under her ear, until the bulk of the sadness drifted away.

She'd been to confession more times than she could count, asking God to have mercy on her for aborting the baby. It wasn't until now that she finally felt forgiveness was within her grasp.

"We were just kids," she said, sniffling. "I was sixteen. We were both stupid."

"You never told him. Or anyone else," he said gently.

She curled her arms around him and held on as if life might slip through her fingers if she let go. All this time, she thought she'd been in love with Kai, but she hadn't. She'd been in love with the *ideal* Kai—a gorgeous, green-eyed Hawaiian surfer with a heart of gold and a body that wouldn't quit who loved her for her—but that Kai didn't exist.

Kai was selfish when it came to relationships. He never loved her. He just loved fucking her. And every other girl he dipped his wick into.

"When you picked me up that afternoon, I was so dazed, I hardly remembered it," she confessed, wiping her nose with an arm. She leaned away to try to get a look at his face, but she couldn't see him clearly. In the dark, he was a collection of vague black outlines and blurs. Just as well. She hated appearing like a victim. Or worse, weak.

"Did I even say thank you?" she asked. Her memory was foggy around that time. And she didn't know what she was saying now. Too much heartache and awful feelings to process.

"You had a traumatic experience. You're excused from politeness when bad shit happens," he said.

She laid a balled fist against his hard chest. "I'm Catholic, Manō. Catholics don't murder babies. I'm going to hell."

"You're not going to hell. You're a good person who made a mistake. And I don't mean the abortion," he added.

"Not a day goes by that I don't think of that tiny life being ripped from inside me," she moaned. "Not a single day. He or she would be nearly ten now. I think about what they'd be learning in school, what movies and TV shows we'd watch together, where we'd go for vacation …"

"If you're a Catholic, then you know God forgives. Even the worst crimes. Everyone's a sinner, Ret."

She lifted her gaze to the sketchy darkness of his face and laid a palm on his cheek. Rough whiskers bristled under her fingers.

"I should've told Kai," she whispered. "Things might've turned out differently if I had. But it's too late now. I don't want him to ever know. I couldn't deal with the fallout that would come with the confession."

He nodded. "It's your choice. I respect it."

"*Mahalo*," she said. "And thank you for picking me up and driving me home on one of the worst days of my life. You don't know what a kindness that was. And this. Now. This is also a kindness."

She fell into him again, and he bent his arms around her in a steel-gripped hug. She listened to his strong heartbeat thudding steadily. She reveled in the newfound comfort of his head resting on top of hers, the feel of his skin enfolding her everywhere they touched.

In that long moment of silence, Ret realized her heart had let Kai go long ago. It was her head that held on all this time. In Manō's embrace, she was finally free of Kai and the guilt she'd borne because of her teenage obsession with him.

God forgives.

But would He forgive her for breaking the law? For covering up crimes to save her friends? For ignoring her own pledge to protect and serve her community?

The press of tender lips to her temple stilled her spinning thoughts and unleashed a sudden inferno of explosive need. She pulled back to look at him. Her eyes had adjusted to the darkness, and now she could make out Manō's impressive dark form well enough to know where to target her kiss.

She leaned up, tipping her head back and melted into his mouth with slow, hungry demand. His body stiffened as if caught off guard, but then he loosened up as she pushed him to the bed, crawling on top of him. Straddling his hard cock, she bumped noses with him in her urgency for more of his mouth. She dipped her tongue in, insisting on a reply. The one she got surprised her.

Manō's answer was a softer, slower brush, a deepening of their internal connection rather than the external one. The long drawl of a lick ignited a fire low in Ret's belly, and her mouth got greedy. Driven by a rising swell of lust, she raked her fingers through his short hair and inhaled his clean scent. Then she jerked up, staring down at his godlike body, toying with the ropes of muscle and caressing his washboard abs.

"Why did you pick me up that day?" she asked. The thrill of the moment stole her senses, made her ache for the truth. Her chest heaved with labored breaths.

"I could tell you were hurting," he said.

"Why would you care? You never talked to me back then. Whenever I came to your place, you left right after I set foot in the door." She shoved a wad of droopy blond spikes out of her eyes.

"I recognized some of myself in you that day." His deep voice was softer than an angel's wing. "I'm sorry I didn't see it sooner."

She sighed, trying to cover the panic rising up her throat. More exposure. More wounds on display.

Her mom was gone. She was alone. On her own. She had no one.

No one except the Alanas and a few coworkers who would turn on her the moment they discovered her treachery.

"I know you got a lot going on right now with Bane and Keahilani," Ret said, "but I gotta know where I stand. Where *we* stand."

"You're here with me," he said simply.

"That's it? Are we together? What is … *this*?" She gestured between them, desperate for an answer that would let her down easy if it had to go that way.

"We're whatever you want to be." He sat up inches from her face, staring at her. Somehow darker than their surroundings, his black eyes caught a glint of the light from the parking lot beyond the curtained window. He flinched as if in pain. Then he ducked so her head blocked the light from his eyes.

She cupped his cheek as tears began to well again.

I recognized some of myself in you that day.

The day Kai walked around after school high as a kite with no clue she'd just killed a tiny part of him. The day she'd killed more than a little of herself. The day she'd killed what remained of her innocence.

Maybe Manō was right. They did have something in

common. They were both hurting.

"Right now, all I wanna be is with you," she breathed over his lips just before tagging them.

His arms unfurled like black wings, draping her shoulders and back. She relaxed into them. He was warm now, and he tasted like cinnamon.

They explored each other's mouths amid racing pulses and feverish grasping, tearing, and yanking. Clothes fell to the floor or hung off the sides of the mattress. Manō ripped the covers aside, palmed her hips, and positioned her ass-up near the edge of the bed.

Her nipples ached as she licked a finger and slipped it between her legs. Her body reacted just in time to welcome Manō inside. He eased in slowly, pushing forward an inch, then pulling back a little to spread her natural lube around. After a few strokes, she was more than ready to take all of him.

And all, she did. She gritted her teeth as he plunged the depths of her channel, splitting her wide, exposing her like she'd been exposed with Kai. But here, things were different. There was no one-sided expectation of promises that wouldn't be kept. She and Manō were a detour-free, two-way street.

She hiked up her hips to shift the angle of entry. The small adjustment made all the difference. Her insides opened like a flower, waking her senses with it. Manō's fingers dug into her flesh as he thrusted. He'd leave marks. She prayed they'd stick around, if for no other reason than to admire his handiwork later.

But the sex was different from the few other times they'd been together. None of the animalistic possession showed its face now. The aggression from last time—not that she minded it—was gone. There was only tenderness underscored by a mild kind of worship on his part. He took care of her. He put her needs before his own.

The thought made her want to weep again.

Instead, she focused on how to return the pleasure. She

matched his hips' rhythm. When he upped the pace, she got the impression he was doing his best to hold back.

"It's okay," she panted. "You don't have to be gentle."

A barrage of ideas flickered across the ticker tape running in her mind. Let him destroy her with his desire. Let it wash away her sins. Let his touch make her whole again.

His grip on her hips tightened, and the darkness swelled. The shadows came to life, falling on the bed like little monsters, climbing the windows, blotting out the light from the parking lot.

That made no sense. Shadows couldn't exist without light, and they certainly didn't move without their source moving too.

Manō's thrusts quickened. Darkness slithered over Ret's back like cold-blooded sharks full of dead-eyed menace and promises of death. Dread seeped into her skin.

"Manō?" she whispered, stilling.

He continued pounding her from behind, oblivious.

"Manō," she said, louder this time. The cold sliding and skittering over her flesh truly freaked her out. "Stop. Something's in here. We gotta turn on the lights."

It took him several thrusts to catch up with what she said. He pulled out with a grunt. She turned around. What she saw was the stuff of nightmares.

Manō wasn't there. In his place was a collage of black, pulsating shapes in the vague outline of his body.

Ret cut off the scream poised for ejection at the top of her throat and snatched two handfuls of linen to cover her nakedness.

"Oh my God." She crossed herself as the dark form shimmered.

"It's me," Manō said. But it wasn't exactly his voice. Like a box of rusty nails clinking together, it was more a chorus of metallic feedback.

She kicked, crab-crawling backward to the headboard, her eyes wide in an effort to see more.

"What the hell is going on?" A tremble excised the

toughness out of her voice like a scalpel.

Where was her gun? They'd lost their clothes in such an all-fire hurry, she couldn't remember where she'd laid her purse.

"I'm here."

"You and who else?" she demanded, lowering her hand off the side of the bed to feel around for her bag.

"I can see you." Still with the creepy voice. Every hair on her body stood bristle stiff.

"You're scaring me," she said as her trembling fingers brushed the canvas strap. If he was telling the truth, he knew she was going for her gun. Question was, would he try to stop her?

"I'm sorry, *eleu*," he said.

"Turn on the light." Her voice was low and cold.

"The light hurts."

"Turn on the fucking light," she shouted. She found the butt of her beloved Beretta and dragged it out, clasping it in her unsteady grip.

The bed dipped as he stood and padded to the window. He opened the curtain enough to let a sliver of light from the parking lot in. Ret gasped.

Manō was covered in writhing black shapes. Some looked like malevolent creatures from a sci-fi movie, but most manifested as sharks. All of them shrunk from the light, darting behind him like frightened children behind their mother's skirts.

Her gun dropped to the floor with a thud, and she flung her body over the side to grab it, falling in the process.

He stepped forward to help, but she thrust a defensive hand at him in warning. "Don't touch me."

Under the spell of a barely waning gibbous moon, the sharks surrounding him reflected slices of light off their twisting, shiny skin. The other shadows—the mischievous ones—made a game of chasing the glints as if toying with prey.

She stood, gun snug in the saddle of her palm and pointed

it at him. "Tell me what's going on right this fucking minute, or I'll plug you."

The shadows tittered behind him like angry, taunting chipmunks.

He dropped his hands to his sides and stepped closer, pressing his chest into the gun's muzzle. "You'd be doing me a favor."

He settled his thumb over her index finger on the trigger, inviting her to pull. Heart hammering in her ears, she jerked the Beretta, aiming it at the ceiling, and twisted the switch on the lamp sitting on the bedside table.

Manō lurched away from the onslaught of brightness filling the room. The shadows scurried off him into the four corners. Wide-eyed, Ret tracked their movements. She targeted the gun on one of the dark patches and said, "Am I hallucinating?"

"No." He angled his head down and squinted up at her. Then he gathered his clothes and shoved a foot into a leg of his black jeans.

She spun and grabbed his shoulders. "If I'm not crazy, then what the hell are those things? Why were they clinging to you like that?"

He paused his dressing and turned toward her, but the light still seemed to bother his eyes. He looked like the Manō she knew. Not a monster or a man covered by monsters. Just Manō.

"They've been hanging around me for as long as I can remember. They've gotten more … aggressive lately."

Ret's mouth dropped open. "They're like shadows."

"Not like. They *are* shadows." He tugged up his pants, zipped, and buttoned. Then he grabbed his motorcycle keys.

"Where are you going?" she asked, unable to wrap her head around what he was saying.

"To find Keahilani's phone." He pocketed the keys and pulled on a black shirt from a bag on the floor.

Ret straightened on the outside. Inside she was crumbling, one cell at a time. "No. Not without me."

"I don't need your help." He finally met her eyes even though it seemed to hurt. She saw regret and sadness in them.

Ret touched his wrist with her free hand. "Manō, I can get you inside. Just tell me what the hell is going on."

After a moment's consideration, he shook his head. "You wouldn't understand."

"Then show me," she begged.

"If that's what you want." He tossed her dark uniform shirt over the lampshade and stretched to his full six feet. With each clench of muscle, a new layer of shadow scurried out from a corner and draped over him, suffocating the muted light from the room.

Ret's jaw trembled as she gazed up at a rippling, monstrous black form swimming with sharks from the depths of the ocean. The shark tattoo on his neck gleamed just before the darkness absorbed it.

Manō backed away from her to the door. When his hand twisted the knob and pulled, the night outside devoured him.

Ret was left standing alone and naked with her finger on the trigger, the gun pointing at nothing.

CHAPTER TWENTY-SIX

The hungry shadows ushered Manō away from the motel room. His corporeal form blinked to life each time it landed inside a new splotch of night. He shadow-hopped that way down the street, into a stand of trees where lingering darkness made it easier to move.

The shadows had scared the hell out of Ret at a time when she needed comfort. The murderous hunger in Manō's gut was eating him from the inside out. If he didn't unleash his pent-up aggression soon, he might lose his already tenuous control. He'd come close to hurting Ret, and that was unacceptable.

When the shadows got insatiable like this, they subdued his fight and replaced it with their own. There was one of him and too many of them, and their end games rarely synced with his. Tonight, they'd become too restless to contain with the flaring passions and tempers. Between the sex with Ret and his need to free Keahilani from prison before she lost her own containment to the shadows, he'd lowered his defenses enough for them to attain the upper hand. With his heart-driven mind focused elsewhere, it had been easy.

Manō was losing his grip on reality and on the shades. He was starting to wonder if the shadows were actually his masters instead of the other way around.

Popping under the shroud of a banyan tree with countless ponderous arms, he mourned the loss of the connection he seemed to have finally forged with Ret. She'd opened up about the baby, revealing why she'd been stuck on his brother for so long. She'd allowed herself to be vulnerable in front of him—something he doubted she did with anyone else—and he'd blown it.

"Fuck," he cursed under his breath. Oblivious to his regret, the shadows tightened their shapeless limbs around him, hugging, nipping, possessive. They whisked him away to the next stop on the path to his destination.

Don't leave us for her, they hissed, petting his head. *She's not worthy of you.*

Wrong. *He* wasn't worthy of *her.*

He rode the black waves, floating from one dark blotch to the next, a passenger rather than the driver. He was an afterthought to darkness, just another shark doing its bidding by gobbling up all the light. He'd been a fool to think he had control over anything in his life.

The drugs. His nightmares. The shadows. They all owned more of him than he did.

Several minutes later, the shadows spat him out behind the police station in Wailuku where the lights were less glaring. They fanned out from Manō like a pack of giggling delinquents. They slithered up poles and smothered the lights under a mess of gangly black limbs and razor teeth. Those fangs bit into the bulbs, bursting the halogens in showers of glass and poison gas.

Go on, they chided, pushing against his back. *We'll show you the way in.*

He had no choice. He did as he was told.

When he got to the exit, they nodded to a window up high. Rubbery "hands" descended on his skin. His body lifted, lost its form, and passed through the window like it was made of air.

Manō emerged from his shadow—whole again and considerably heavier—inside a medium-sized room. Despite the pitch blackness, he slunk easily through aisles lined with floor-to-ceiling metal shelving. His night vision had improved enough in the last few days that he could read the labels and scribbles on the stacked folders and boxes. Recovery dates, content lists, incident types, and barcodes told him this was a property room.

Perfect.

Glancing around, he found a box of latex gloves mounted over a sink on the west wall. He snagged a pair and put them on. Then he wandered the aisles until he found the most recently dated boxes. He dragged the top one out. Its contents had been collected last week. Moving down a couple shelves, he tried another. These items were from three days ago. Finally, he found the newest box. He picked through the plastic bags until he came upon one marked "Keahilani Alana."

He snatched the plastic, opened it, and shook out her phone. He pocketed the device and slunk toward the exit. Light seeped in from under the door. The shadows scampered off him as if he were nothing more than a termite mound. Some of them slid across the floor, sneaking peeks at whatever was on the other side of the door.

A small legion slithered into the hall. Seconds later, the sudden, faraway sound of shuffling feet followed by the clang of a heavy, metallic item crashing to the floor destroyed the quiet of the station. Someone shouted, "Shit! We got a runner!"

The lights went out. Surprised shouts echoed over the tile.

Time to leave.

He opened the door quietly, eased out, and stuffed the gloves in his pockets. Staying close to the wall, he blended in enough not to be noticed by third-shifters at the other end of the hall fumbling in the dark for the apparent runaway. Ahead, a patrol of shadows stopped to assess the next junction. They waved Manō onward and pointed left.

A uniformed officer ahead of him shouted, "Everybody calm down. Do not panic."

Everybody panicked.

As personnel clambered for order, the shadows covered Manō's trek to the holding cells. All attention was elsewhere, so it was easy to surf from one shadow to the next until he reached his sister.

As if waiting for him, she stood next to the cell's window. Black circles rimmed her irises like kohl. The shadows clinging to Manō grinned and squirmed under the small space between the door and the floor. They wriggled up the walls and enveloped the camera watching. Manō marveled at their forethought. They were sentient—*intelligent* enough to know when the electricity came back on, the cameras would too.

With a dramatic flourish, the remaining shadows opened a dark conduit between the hall and the other side of the door. Manō slipped through the barrier like it was nothing more than a wispy curtain.

Keahilani's eyes widened. She threw her arms around him and squeezed.

"We don't have much time," Manō whispered as she pulled away. "Here's your phone." He placed it in her hand.

She gazed up at him with questions written all over her face. Instead of saying what was on her mind, she opened the text message with a trembling finger. "It's from Lui: 'I found you a trio of sexy mules. Text for an appointment. And this just landed in my inbox.'"

She turned the screen so they could both study the picture. Palpable fury quaked over Keahilani's skin and rolled into Manō's like chain lightning. The room heated with her rage.

"This is the fuck who killed Bane," she hissed.

Manō tried to piece together the clues in the image staring up at him. Someone had snapped a picture of a laptop screen. It appeared the person was logged into Skype, chatting with Bane. A man with a gun stood behind Bane. The shadows around him were thick, but Manō recognized him.

"Text it to Kai and me," he said hurriedly. "And Lui's number. I have to go, but I'll send updates. Mendelson, your lawyer, should be here first thing in the morning."

Keahilani's glossy eyes shone with tears. "You recognize that prick?"

He clenched his jaw. She had enough to worry about right now. "I got this. Trust me." He nodded to her phone. "Might wanna shut that off to save your battery."

She gaped and stared at the phone. "Like they aren't gonna find it on me with these goddamn cameras everywhere."

Manō waited beside the door for the shadows to power up their supernatural engines. "They'll take care of you."

A shock of disbelief clubbed her in the face. Manō grinned, and his dark escorts pulled him under the steel barrier into the hall. They parkoured their way through the shadows and right the fuck out of the station to a chorus of chaos.

When they reached the back egress they'd come through, Manō stopped short at the sight of Ret in her uniform, leaning against the lamppost the shadows had neutered earlier.

Run, one of the shadows buzzed.

No, hit her. She likes it, a silver-tongued voice taunted.

Break her jaw with your fist, jeered another.

Give her what you both want, the silver-tongued one said. *Fuck her.*

He cut the air with a slice of his hand to silence them. They backed off, but only a little.

Ret stepped into the light of the fat moon, hands out so he could see them. "I just wanna talk."

This was an epically bad idea. The longer she hung around with him, the harder she'd crash when he had to let her fall. It was inevitable.

He let out a long, heavy breath and took her hand. He guided her away from the building, into the dark where it was nominally safer. She looked as tired as he felt. Worn down by her job and the pressure he and his siblings had inadvertently dumped on her in the last week or two, he guessed.

"I don't know what happened in there," Ret said, "but

I'm not giving up on you. Please let me help."

He thought about the picture Lui had sent. If he turned it over to the police, it might aid their investigation into Bane's death. But Ret wasn't high enough up the chain of command to pull any big favors for the Alanas. While before he might have considered it an unfortunate side effect of commiserating with known drug dealers, suddenly Manō didn't like the idea of her taking the fall. For any of them.

Besides, Manō preferred to handle sleights of this particular nature himself. Nothing like making punishment personal with his very own boot stamp of approval.

No, he needed Ret out of the Alanas' circle before she got hurt—in the crossfire or otherwise. They should never have let her inside in the first place.

"There are things I can't explain, even if I wanted to," he said gently. "It would be best if you and I took a break."

She shook her head. "If you don't want to see me anymore, I'll accept it. But there are things *you* don't know, Manō. The forensics team that hit Keahilani's house earlier? They found evidence that links her to Butch's murder. They're gonna charge her tomorrow. I just got the call." She waved her cell phone.

His heart collided with his stomach.

They must've found her costume at the apartment. Or fingerprints at the scene. Or DNA.

Keahilani was going down.

And he'd been standing in the goddamn property room only minutes before, probably within a few feet of the evidence that would convict his sister of murder. Hell, he might've even touched the box it was in.

Snarling, he curled his hand into a ball and cut loose the fury the shadows had been itching for a taste of. He launched his fist out to the side and into a tree branch as thick as his thigh, unleashing a hail of plumeria petals and a loud crack. A gash in the side of his palm dripped blood on the fallen petals. The drooling shadows tripped over each other to get closer to him.

Before Ret could react, the inside lights blinked on, blinding him for a moment. He shuffled backward into the waiting arms of darkness and his damned shadows. The little sharks swam protectively around him in circles, watching Ret out of the corners of their black-hole eyes.

We don't need her, they declared. They seemed so certain.

Clotted, thick pain spread outward from his chest, down his arms and legs. It took every ounce of control not to scream.

The shadows were right. He didn't need her. But he wanted her.

The problem with wanting was eventually, he wouldn't be able to say no to the urges. He'd either fall asleep or fall victim to madness from not sleeping. Either way, if Ret was there, she'd pay for his curse with her blood.

"Go home, Officer Rogers," he said, turning away. "And stay out of this."

CHAPTER TWENTY-SEVEN

Thursday, October 9—Shortly after midnight

"Who has the audacity to call Monsieur Lui at this ungodly hour?" a femme voice huffed over the phone. Sounds of soft *fap, fap, faps* suggested Lui was either fanning himself with a limp-wristed hand on the other end or jerking off. Manō couldn't be sure.

"Manō Alana," he said from the beach outside Lui's room at the Wailea Four Seasons.

A pause. A shifting of fabric against the quiet squeak of fine leather. Lui's head jerked up from the couch inside his oceanfront suite. "Mr. Alana," he cooed flirtatiously. "To what do I owe this *plaisir?*"

More fapping. The hand was now visible through the glass door. Lui was definitely fanning himself. Thank God for small favors.

"Cut the theatrics, Lui. You know Keahilani's in jail. I'm calling about the appointment you mentioned to her."

"Let me just grab my diary, and we'll get you all set up," Lui said. He grunted as he struggled to free himself from the sunken Italian leather sofa. A second later, he grabbed a notebook off the coffee table and settled the phone between his head and shoulder while he picked up a pen. "How are the accommodations over in the Wailuku holding tank, by the way? Up to the Alanas' expectations?"

Manō didn't answer.

"Strong silent type," Lui remarked. "I forgot. And did I mention how sexy I find that? Shiver me timbers, I think I'm blushing."

Manō waited.

"What did you think of that little Polaroid I transmitted?" Lui asked casually.

"Where did you get it?"

"I have my sources."

"So do I," Manō said. "Speaking of, how are *your* accommodations at the Four Seasons in Wailea? I hear the room service is decent but expensive. Like everything at that place. How'd you like your steak tonight? Up to snuff?"

Lui's face lost its color. He fell deathly silent. Manō curled his lips into a satisfied grin. He loved fucking with people who thought they couldn't be fucked with.

When Lui didn't answer, Manō continued. "We're not blind. Like you, the Alanas have eyes everywhere."

Lui inhaled a quiet breath. "I had your sister pegged the moment I met her, but you, Mr. Shark?" he said with a finger wag and the condescending tone a mother might use on a naughty toddler. "I underestimated you. Don't worry. Won't happen again."

"There won't be an again. Our *business arrangement*," Manō sneered over the last two words, "will end once we finalize this last deal."

"Say it ain't so," Lui crooned with mock sadness, clutching the collar of his bright orange, red, and pink aloha shirt. "I was *so* looking forward to conducting more deals with you and your lovely siblings. Well, the whole ones, at least. That half brother of yours can suck my Tetons."

Manō smiled. "And here I thought your relationship with Scott was tighter than a clam's ass at high tide. What happened? Did he threaten to release that picture of you with the late state senator? You remember the one. You. Him. The muzzle of the murder weapon fucking the hole it made in him? Blood makes beautiful ink. Smile, you're on candid camera."

The shadows got a real hard-on with that line. They shot up his legs and hugged him from every angle. He shook them off like annoying gnats.

"Tell me who sent you the picture of Bane," Manō said, his tone low and threatening.

Lui stopped pacing and spun toward the floor-to-ceiling glass separating his room from the lanai. He tugged the curtains across the hurricane-proof doors, cutting off Manō's view. Didn't matter. He'd planted the seed of paranoia. That was good enough.

"I don't know," Lui said, dropping all pretense. "It came from a dummy email account. When I tried to reply, the message was returned."

"What did our friend Jezzy have to say about that?"

"I haven't discussed it with her."

If anyone could uncover the sender's identity, it was Jezzy. She dealt with some heavy hitters across the islands. Though she readily accepted money for her work, she used the secrets she unearthed as her personal currency. She stockpiled information—from the tiniest white lies to classified messages sent from the highest levels of security in the federal government—and saved it for the moment when she'd need it.

"When did you last talk to her?" Manō asked.

"Yesterday," Lui said. "She's busy with another client, working on a big deal."

If Lui was telling the truth, Manō reckoned Scott was the mystery client, which was supremely bad for the Alanas. You couldn't fight a Jezzy. She was a cyber ninja with powers far superior to Manō's—even with the shadows to back him up. If she'd teamed up exclusively with Scott, the Alanas could kiss any chance of escaping incarceration goodbye.

They were fucked six ways to Serotoninville.

Manō shifted gears. "About that appointment …"

"Yes, yes," Lui huffed. "I told your sister I'd help you this one time because our mothers share a past, but this is the end of the line."

Keahilani had found a picture in one of Mahina's journals of the three Alana siblings with a young Lui. Apparently, their mothers had been close when they were young. The picture had been Keahilani's ticket to talk Lui into helping them find distribution for Pāhoehoe in the first place.

"Understood," Manō said.

"I have a quartet lined up for you. After the unfortunate loss of the last distributor I set you up with," he got snippy with the last few words, "I hand-picked these strapping young bucks to meet your … shall we say, *unique* needs."

"Who are they?"

"I'll text you their names and contact information shortly. Trust that these boys are the best of the best. If they can't move your product, no one can."

Awfully sure of himself. But Lui always projected an air of mentally deranged dominance. It usually worked for him too. After this most recent round of whack-an-Alana-distributor, however, Manō had a bad taste in his mouth. He wasn't ready to trust Lui so easily again. He'd proceed with extreme caution.

"Once you have their info, you should set up a meeting. And be extra nice to Dallas. He treats me like the queen I am. A *top*-notch fellow," Lui purred. His throaty emphasis on "top" made Manō squirm.

"What you do in your dungeon isn't my business."

Lui giggled at that. "Touché. Now, I know you're working against a tight timeline. A rush job will require a higher payment."

"You're not getting a penny until every ounce is out in the wild," Manō said.

"Ooh, I love it when you get sassy," Lui breathed. "Do it again. This time, with feeling."

Manō was done with the flirty antics and passive aggression. "You know the *haole* in the photo you sent Keahilani?" he asked.

Lui made an ear-splitting screeching noise. "Whoa, there,

partner. You're shifting tracks and not slowing down enough for me to catch my breath."

"Tell me who he is." Manō already knew, but he wanted to see if Lui would lie.

The big man sighed. "If my peepers do not deceive, that hunk of burning garbage dump is none other than Mr. Grant Lowden, CEO of Waialua Kope, and you'd be wise to stay away from him. I'd hate for him to melt off that gorgeous mug of yours. He has a penchant for using battery acid or scalding water on the fools who cross him, and he always aims for the face."

Lui told the truth and then some. How very interesting.

"How does he know Scott?"

"What?" came Lui's high-pitched answer. Intermittent pounding and scratching noises followed. They were intentional, probably perpetrated by a thumping thumb and his long fingernails scraping the phone's mic. "I think our connection is blinking out. I'll text you. This is Lava Girl signing off. Bye, Shark Boy."

Click. And the line went silent.

Manō stared at his phone. Lui might've assumed the conversation was being monitored. Or someone walked into his room while they were talking. Or he really didn't want to discuss the suggestion of a relationship between Scott and Lowden.

Mental illness notwithstanding, any number of distractions could've set the psycho off, but right now Manō had more important things on his mind. Grant Lowden was the man in the screenshot pointing a .45 at Bane's back.

What he wouldn't give for Jezzy's help. But wishing for things he couldn't have was a pipe dream.

He'd dosed earlier, so he was wide awake. He could use the computer at the safe house to try to get a look at the finer points of the image. It would have a date and time stamp. That would reveal plenty.

Then he'd find Lowden.

The relative peace and quiet on the Scott front gave Manō

pause. No one had seen or heard from Harris since Keahilani threatened him on Oʻahu Monday. He'd had plenty of time to fly back to Maui. If he wanted to get at Keahilani, he must've known she was incarcerated. Manō felt certain Scott had pull with the Maui PD higher-ups. He could've tracked the *ʻohana* down with little effort.

Yet he'd remained in the shadows.

What was he planning? His next move would be a bold one. The silence gave him plenty of cover for the moment, but once that was blown, he wouldn't have the advantage of surprise again. They'd be expecting him.

Lui's text came through with the distributors' info. They called themselves the Gang of Eight. If there were only four of them as Lui had said, that moniker seemed odd. Whatever.

He texted Dallas, the guy Lui mentioned: *Meet Fri nite. ʻIao Valley Park entrance 11:30.*

Lui would have already sent Manō's credentials ahead, so names weren't used on texts.

Come alone. No weapons, Dallas replied.

Well, that was that. Meet and greet with new distributors Friday. Lawyer to visit Keahilani in the morning. Scott was planning a surprise attack. Grant Lowden killed Bane.

And all Manō could think about was the hurt look on Ret's face when he told her to go home hours ago.

He wandered down the beach, absorbing the breezes through his pores, feeling pinpricks of himself going black, essentially blending in to his surroundings wherever the dark defied the light.

Keahilani used to have to talk Manō into taking walks on the north shore when they were kids. He didn't like going to the beach when he was little. It scared him. She always held his hand and promised the sea wouldn't get him as long as she was around.

What she didn't know was that he wasn't afraid of the ocean swallowing him. He was afraid of the darkness beneath its depths and what it might drive him to do if he ever got too close to it.

He found out when he was four in the kitchen with the knife, feeding the hungry shadows, and life hadn't been the same since. He'd lived in fear and awe of what lurked inside of him. His darkness kept him from enjoying much.

His true pleasures were the ones that didn't involve guns, drugs, or death. Like time spent with his *'ohana*. Or finding a quiet place where he could observe nature's stunning beauty in silence. And maybe the warmth that washed over him when Ret was around. Those were reliefs, antimatter to the matters of serious consequence that dominated nearly every breath he took.

He'd been a real dick to Ret when she needed a friend. But he'd have to hang on to his apology until Keahilani was out of jail and they no longer needed to depend on Ret for anything. He'd used her enough.

He gave her an opening to leave, and now he had to let her go no matter how much he wanted her to stay.

The black sharks nuzzled him sympathetically, grazing his arms and legs with soft bumps. They almost felt like hugs. But they lacked Ret's warmth.

Manō was tired of being cold.

He stared over the ocean. Kaho'olawe loomed, craggy and inscrutable, reminding him of yet another failure he'd left simmering on the back burner.

"Soon, Blake," he whispered.

With a sigh, he leaned against the night's arms and let the lifeless shadows absorb him.

CHAPTER TWENTY-EIGHT

"Keahilani, they have evidence that links you to the scene of Butch's murder," Ret said in the tiny meeting room at the station. They were waiting for Keahilani's lawyer, who was running late. "Your height and build match the woman in the surveillance footage. The clothes—"

"Yes, I own a dress like the one in the video," Keahilani snapped. "And a trench coat. But have you seen the snobs who prance around Kāʻanapali at night? *Anyone* could have those things in her closet. The same for the wig. Those images are of a woman who looks like me."

They both knew the woman *was* her, but neither would admit it here.

Ret shook her head. "Add to that the blood they found on Bane's property, and we've got a stew with way too many onions."

"Have they processed the DNA yet?" Keahilani asked.

"Usually takes twenty-four to seventy-two hours, but if there's something you want to tell me about who that sample might've come from before we get the results back, now might be a good time." Ret pressed a meaningful look into Keahilani's eyes.

Her friend glanced up to the eavesdropping camera above. "I have nothing to say."

Damn Keahilani and her stubbornness.

Ret stood up. "Okay. Your choice. I don't need to remind

you how serious this is. If you want to talk after your lawyer leaves, let the guard know. I'll be here in a jiffy."

Keahilani lowered her head in a defeated nod. Ret reluctantly left her for the chief's office. There she tapped on the open door frame. Hale looked up from his neat desk and waved her in.

"Shut it behind you," he said.

A closed door meant he had news, probably not the good kind.

Ret settled into the seat across from him.

"Regarding the Alana kid's murder," Hale said, "the DNA on the hair we found in the security office at the hospital turned up a partial match in CODIS. That person could be a close relative of the hair's owner. We're also picking through Waialua Kope employee rosters, but without a motive or obvious connection to the victim, it's a needle in a haystack.

"Bane's sister, on the other hand …" He plucked a file from the edge of his desk and slid it across the surface to her.

It was the DNA report. Several of the blood samples collected at Bane's house triggered a hit in SDIS, the state DNA database. The blood from the scene matched DNA of a convicted felon named Blake Murphy from O'ahu.

Ret worked hard to contain the disappointment on her face, but the chief caught it.

"Well, that's a real bummer," she said.

"We haven't found a body," Hale said, studying her closely from behind his specs, "but there was a good bit of blood. Keahilani admitted she had a relationship with Blake Murphy. His friend Scott Harris says he's missing. He claims she killed Murphy and bragged about it in his office on O'ahu. Flight records show she flew to Honolulu over the weekend, which supports Harris's story, at least in part."

Chief removed his glasses and cleaned them with his tie. "Whether this Blake guy turns up alive or dead, I bet he'll have plenty to say to help us put Keahilani Alana in prison either way. I'm sorry, Rogers."

Ret drew in a deep breath and let it out slowly. "I still don't think she's guilty. Butch was a known rapist and drug dealer who was too greasy to catch. Even if she did do it, he got what was coming."

"That's not for us to decide," the chief said carefully. "We have a warrant to search the Alanas' property in Kula. It's being executed now."

So, the police had the evidence they'd need to convict Keahilani of not only Butch's death but Blake's too, if his body turned up. It would eventually. Unless Manō had completely destroyed it. Ret shivered at the thought.

Regardless, without new evidence or a witness who could prove her innocence, Keahilani was fucked on the Butch case. Ret didn't think Manō or Kai could handle another loss after the string of failures and bad news that had fallen in their laps.

Would Manō completely lose himself without his sister to balance him? Would he walk into the darkness and never come out the other side? And did Ret even care?

Of course, she did. She didn't love Manō, but maybe someday she might. He gave himself to her with no expectations. He accepted her as she was. She never had to put on airs with him.

And deep down, under the shadows and tattoos and sharks, he was a good person. She'd seen his soul, and despite the darkness covering its outside, the inside was full of light. Just like his mother, God bless her.

Ret hoped she was right about Manō. His crazy shadow thing pushed her willing suspension of disbelief to the very edge of shit she could deal with—and that was only because she cared about the guy. A lot. She mentally crossed herself.

"Let me know if there's anything else I can do to help with the investigation," Ret said as she stood up.

"We'll handle things from here," Chief said casually. The implication under the words was clear: *Back off and stay out of our way. You're off this case.*

She nodded deferentially and headed out of the office to her desk. Normally, she'd be on the beat with her partner

Harry at this time of day, but he was on vacation, and Chief was breaking in a couple new hires who were currently patrolling anyway. Putting another car on the mostly quiet streets would've been a waste of tax payers' dollars. Gas on Maui wasn't cheap.

Harry had left behind a mountain of paperwork that needed to be completed before he returned next week. She sat down and thumbed through the waiting folders. Theft. Burglary. Sexual assault. Battery. Another assault. She sighed. Unmotivated by the prospect of writing reports, she pulled up the digital file on Butch Kelly.

A wave of disgust rolled over her as she scrolled through the mire of his exploits. He'd been linked to dozens of violent crimes, none of which ever made it to court due to lack of evidence.

She thought about Keahilani facing this big thug alone with no one to protect her but herself. Keahilani wasn't a small woman, but she was a hell of a lot smaller than Butch, who had a penchant for punching his victims unconscious and raping them in every orifice. He wore condoms and rubber gloves, which severely limited investigators' chances of retrieving DNA.

Countless accusations by victims were withdrawn shortly after their initial filings. Butch, or someone higher up the food chain he fed on, paid them off for their silence. And the few who tried to sing were swept under the rug and dropped through the cracks.

Butch was a rapist piece of shit. Keahilani was justified in killing his sorry ass.

Ret closed the file and tossed all of her paperwork into the overstuffed tray beside her computer. She knew what she had to do.

* * * *

Manō had lost track of how many days had passed since he last slept. A rising tsunami of exhaustion threatened to drag him under. The shadows' whispers had been intermittent yesterday, but now they were chattering nonstop. Taunting, teasing, goading him to hurt, maim, kill.

He popped a quarter tab of LSD and willed them to shut the fuck up.

Their babbling got louder.

When Manō pulled up to the safe house shortly after noon, Kai was outside talking to two uniformed officers.

What the fuck? He checked his phone for the messages he must've missed. The battery was dead.

After leaving Lui, Manō had been out all night and morning, meeting with contacts and gang members, arranging contingency plans, questioning, gathering information in preparation for his meeting with Lui's guys. In the process, he discovered that several of the Alanas' usual Pāhoehoe customers had bailed on them in favor of Ambrosia, saying it was cheaper and more potent. None of the handful of dealers he'd hired to move their product could be found. If the Alanas didn't have payment rendered in full to their investors in a few days, none of this would matter. Because all three of them would be dead.

Manō was running out of physical and emotional currency, and now more cops were on his doorstep looking for God knew what.

He hopped off his bike and strode toward a frantic-looking Kai who was accentuating his words with big flourishes to emphasize a point.

"Finally. This is my brother, Manō," Kai said. Relief erased some of the lines in his face, but not all of them. "Where have you been?"

Manō turned to the officer in charge. "What's going on?"

"We're just wrapping up," the man said. "Your brother has the warrant. We'll be out of here in a few minutes. Sorry for the intrusion."

Manō faced Kai as the guy wandered off to talk to another officer. "What did they find?"

Kai's cheeks reddened with anger. "I don't know. I got

home an hour ago, and they were all over the backyard with kits and swabs and rubber gloves and covered shoes …"

Manō narrowed his eyes and lowered his voice. "They go inside?"

Kai nodded. "They hit the living room, kitchen, both bedrooms."

"So, everywhere."

"Pretty much." Kai watched after the men and nervously curled his arms over his chest.

"They get Mahina's journals?"

Please say no.

"I don't think so. I have the one from the shop in my car, and Keahilani stored the others in the hall closet."

Manō pushed past Kai toward the house.

"Where are you going?"

"To charge my phone," he grumbled. He paused at the door and turned back. "You deal with them." He gestured to the police with his chin and went inside.

If he had to handle one more goddamn thing, he'd give the shadows the blood they wanted.

He plugged the phone in and waited for it to wake up. Four texts from Kai demanded to know where he was. The only text from Keahilani read: *Please tell me you took care of that package I gave you last week.*

"Package," meaning Blake. Manō scrubbed his face.

He hurled the phone at the wall. Its screen shattered with a sickening crunch. If only that sound had been the police officers' heads going through the front window. Maybe bodies thrown against the gravel lining the garden and crushed under his boot would make a similar, satisfying splat.

Imagine all that crimson, spreading out slowly in a mesmerizing pattern—

Yessss … The writhing shadows licked their lips, surging and ebbing like a black tide having its way with a pristine shoreline. Their palpable agitation bordered on sexual.

The chomping of tires eating small rocks in the driveway diverted Manō's attention from the swelling in his jeans. He glanced out the window. The red tail lights of the forensic officers' vehicles disappeared into the early afternoon sun. Not a moment too soon.

The door flung open, and Kai stomped into the room. "They were all over the spot in back where ... You know," he said, dropping like a bomb into the seat across from Manō. He looked *stick-a-fork-in-me-I'm-done* done.

The spot in question was the one where Keahilani had shot Blake through the chin and splattered his DNA like a rainbow all over the backyard.

Kai and Manō had hosed it down, but it was possible they'd missed some spots. Blake bled a lot. Not to mention, Manō had used his tools on Blake's fingers and left a sodden mess in the guest room that might not have been as cleaned up as it should have been. Luminol would shine all kinds of lights on the shadows there.

The cops would come back for Kai and Manō. It was just a matter of time.

"What are we gonna do about Keahilani?" Kai moaned, leaning forward and scooping a handful of dreadlocks out of his face.

"My phone's broken, but she has hers now," Manō said as the shadows settled around his feet, gazing up with pure adoration. "Text her. Tell her we have everything under control."

"That's a lie, and you know it. We are fucked beyond belief," Kai said.

"Yes. We are. But she doesn't need to hear that right now," Manō said simply.

Shaking his head, Kai thumb-typed the message and set the phone on the table. "Okay, now what?"

"Did you get the picture she sent?"

Kai nodded. "Who is that guy, and how are we going to end him?"

The corners of Manō's lips kinked upward. He was glad Kai was on the same page. "Based on the date and time stamp on the image, it's definitely Bane's killer. Name is Grant

Lowden, the guy I told you about at the coffee company."

"Who took the pic?"

"No idea. Lui says it came from an unknown number."

"If we can find whoever snapped it, maybe they'll be willing to testify and help us put that dick in jail for life."

"Nobody's going to jail, brother," Manō said, his voice low with threat. The shadows billowed around him like an army of darkness, turning daylight into dusk. "He's going to hell. And we're buying his one-way ticket."

Kai looked away and pressed his lips together.

"We need to work out a plan of attack on Lowden. I have a meeting with the Gang of Eight tomorrow night. It'll be good to go into that meeting with the fresh taint of death on my hands. Keeps me on my toes." Manō glanced to the shadows. "Them too."

Kai's Adam's apple shuttled down and up with a swallow. "Why did this Lowden guy kill Bane? To get to us? What are we to him, anyway?"

"He's connected to Scott Harris. My guess is they're partnering to meet the narcotic needs of Hawai'i's elite and trying to create a monopoly on the streets with Ambrosia to put us out of business. From what I hear, Harris is doing a damn good job. We're gonna have to lower our prices to compete."

"We can't afford that," Kai protested. "We barely make enough to cover costs at the current price."

"We don't have a choice," Manō replied. "Once we wrap this meeting with Lui's guys and send the last of the Pāhoehoe out the door, we can focus on tracking down Harris and Lowden. But we gotta get the investors off our backs first."

"What about Keahilani? She's our sister. My goddamn twin. We can't leave her locked up for another night."

"They've got her on drug charges and Butch's murder. They're waiting to see what turns up with Blake. Barring a miracle, I don't see her getting out of this."

Kai lifted anguish-filled eyes to him. "So, we just let her rot in jail for the rest of her life?"

"No," Manō said, stroking a black shark circling his calf. "We bust her out."

"How the hell are we gonna pull that off?"

"We aren't," Manō replied, relishing the darkness bleeding into his eyes. He looked down at the shark smiling up at him with two-rows-too-many teeth. "*They* are."

CHAPTER TWENTY-NINE

Manō and Kai strode into Mahina Surf and Dive shortly after five. Manō came to gather some of Keahilani's belongings and other items he didn't want the cops putting their grubby hands on. He brought Kai along to provide distractions should Sophia become curious about what he was doing.

"Sorry we bailed on you yesterday. *Mahalo* for stepping up under pressure and keeping the doors open," Kai said to Sophia as she flitted to the headwear display to straighten a cockeyed hat after helping a customer find the right size fins.

Five people currently browsed the merchandise. That was five more customers than Manō had seen in here every other time he popped in over the last week.

"It's no problem," Sophia said with a smile. Then she dropped her voice. "How's Keahilani doing? Any news about when she'll be back?"

Kai shook his head and shot a glance at Manō. "Hopefully soon."

Manō kept one ear open while he did his thing behind the counter, pretending to check the till. Keahilani had a safe installed when they first opened years ago. It contained some of Mahina's journals, important papers related to the business, backup cash, and a gun.

Sophia squatted before the sunblock display, checking dates and sorting tubes into "expired" and "unexpired" piles. Given free rein to reorganize and develop a management plan for the store, she seemed to be in her element.

"I've been conducting an informal inventory and made a list of items I think we should stock. Or restock," she said over her shoulder to Kai. "You guys really ought to consider getting reef-safe sunscreen. Did you realize that regular sunscreen contains oxybenzone and octinoxate that damages coral reefs? You gotta go green, especially here where the ocean is one of the most vital contributors to the state economy."

Kai nodded, pretending to be fascinated by her sales pitch. Manō had seen that look before. Kai must've thought he could flip Sophia to the dick side. Always on the prowl for a piece of ass, even in a room full of nope.

Sophia had a good point, though. Manō listened as she offered suggestions to Kai. She had innovative ideas and could be a valuable asset if she stayed on. Hell, if she turned the store around, they might even be able to drop their illegal business. What a dream that would be. As it was …

He opened the safe and shucked everything into one of the plain brown shopping bags they used for customers. If the police decided to serve a warrant here, they wouldn't find anything to help their case against Keahilani.

"If you guys have a minute, I've been working on some marketing ideas I wanted to run by you," Sophia said to Kai.

Kai loosened his stance. "Sure."

Sophia beckoned him to follow. She opened a notebook sitting on the corner of the counter. Tabs stuck out of the side in no-nonsense block print. The slip of paper loaded in the clear plastic cover bore a series of nine Mahina Surf and Dive logos, all different except for the words.

"Damn." Kai whistled appreciatively. "You've been busy."

Sophia shrugged. "I had nothing better to do last night, so I started playing around with images and fonts. You guys need a major marketing overhaul." She pulled the paper out. "See anything that strikes your fancy?"

Manō leaned over for a better look. Sophia tensed just

enough for him to notice. So, he made her uncomfortable. Good. Best to keep everyone at arm's length, especially the help.

He had to admit, the girl had an artistic eye. All of the designs were clean, simple, and direct. The one with the crescent moon snagged his attention.

Kai *ooh*-ed and *ahh*-ed over the images, but in the end, he pointed to the black moon with a woman's silhouetted face shaping the inside of the crescent in negative and the shadow of a star-like plumeria flower where an ear would be.

"Mahina, our mother—her name means moon," Kai said, the corners of his eyes glistened with a hint of wetness. He blinked. "This one fits perfectly. What do you think, Manō?"

He nodded. It was a lovely tribute.

Sophia studied the graphics with a wide smile. "I like that one too. I can have promotional materials printed with the logo. I mean, if Keahilani agrees. I'll wait to see what she says."

Manō and Kai exchanged glances. "Don't worry about her. Use the company credit card," Kai said, fishing out the plastic from his wallet. He passed the card over.

Sophia gave Manō some shy side-eye. "Okay. If you're sure."

Manō added his stamp of approval on the purchase with another curt nod.

"I'll hop on this as soon as I finalize the design," she said. "I think handled shopping bags would be a good start. These plain old craft paper ones aren't much to look at. You need something that'll draw people in and also give you free advertising."

Kai grinned. "I like the way you think."

"I have other ideas too," Sophia said. "All require minor funding, but if executed properly with my business plan, the return on investment will be through the roof by this time next year."

"Give me the highlights," Kai said.

"For starters, the outside needs tidying up," Sophia began. "I knocked out the weeds in the parking lot, but the cracks have to be tarred over. We should revamp the signage with the new logo too.

"Inside, I'd like to redesign the men's and women's sections with attention to market research and what styles and brand names are selling. We'd provide educational materials for every product. Little things like matching hangers, a lemon-water cooler for customers, and music would help. Not the usual Hawaiian music, but grungy stuff to attract the younger crowd."

Sophia had a point about the hangers. The mishmash of shapes, colors, and styles was embarrassing, but Keahilani had bought hangers when and where she could, usually when they were on sale. Consistency in branding was a real problem at Mahina Surf and Dive.

"On the business side, we need to work on your infrastructure. For example, your manual inventory system using spreadsheets is rudimentary and inefficient. It would be great to upgrade to something fast and user friendly. We can also hire a web designer and create email accounts for all employees. Once sales pick up, we should find someone to develop an online marketplace to supplement storefront sales." Sophia paused to gauge Kai's reaction. She shrugged. "I have other ideas too, but maybe we could start with these."

"Wow," Kai said. "All of that sounds ... wonderful."

Manō had to agree. Sophia's excitement was contagious. The few employees they'd hired in the past never lasted more than a couple weeks. It wasn't that the Alanas were bad employers. They just didn't have time to devote to the shop or training its employees. Without direction, workers got bored, and with only minimum wage pay, very few found reasons to stick around.

Two of the customers approached the checkout counter with a couple items apiece. Sophia snapped to attention and darted over. She made friendly small talk with them as she tallied up their purchases.

Movement outside dragged Manō's attention away from the high-priced transaction taking root at the register. A Maui Electric van pulled into the lot and parked in front. A man wearing a tan, short-sleeved company shirt under a neon-yellow safety vest with a pair of khaki shorts and an ME baseball cap hopped out of the vehicle. He slung a tool bag over his shoulder. Clutching a clipboard and a meter reader, he nodded at Manō through the glass as he made his way around the building to the meter.

Sophia finished with her customers, thanked them on their way out, and moseyed over to a trio of women browsing the swimwear. She asked if they needed help finding anything.

While they talked, Kai leaned over to Manō and said, "Shame about her being a lesbian." He appreciatively followed the swing of Sophia's ass as she engaged in an animated discussion with the customers about the pros and cons of various rash guards and which brand offered the best UV protection.

"What happened to Ret?" Manō blurted.

He didn't know why he asked. Maybe guilt had him feeling protective of her after they'd parted on less-than-desirable terms. It was that, or straight-up jealousy.

Kai frowned. "She kicked me to the curb again."

A shark-shaped shadow swam away from the rest of the shiver pooling around Manō's feet, past the counter and dove under the office door. He'd never seen one do that before. It could've been a hallucination. He was getting some nice tracers from the glints off the van's window in the front, and Kai didn't track the shark's trail.

"I'll never understand women," Kai complained. "You think you got 'em figured out, so you ask one out because she's sending all the right signals. You take her on a date. Things escalate—at least, you *think* they do. But then she says she's not ready to go further. Or she wants her space. Or you're too fucking immature."

Manō could picture Ret saying all those things to Kai. It was hard not to smile. Though, he felt a little bad for his brother. If Kai had been anyone else, Manō would've gloated.

"Then you start to notice things. The whiff of men's cologne drifting off her when a breeze hits just right. A vague text from an unknown number that she turns her back to hide from you. A sudden string of unavailable calendar dates when she was wide open before." Kai shook his head regretfully.

"So, go after her," Manō said, casually watching for Kai's reaction. His brother's lips twitched in the throes of defeat. Manō couldn't tell if Kai's fascination with Ret was fueled by genuine infatuation or if he was settling for what he *thought* he wanted.

"Maybe once we get past the shitshow that is our lives, I'll call her," Kai continued. "For now, though, I'm a second-class citizen to the douchebag she's seeing."

Manō didn't have time to flinch at that accusation. The shark shadow returned from the office, shot toward him, gills popping frantically, and bumped his leg with physical force.

Manō jumped, barely containing the "What the fuck?" alarm bell ringing in his head. The shark looked up at him with its black hole eyes, swam to the office, and circled frantically in front of the door, slashing its tail and fins in a sharp, high definition the shadows rarely displayed.

Manō's hackles shimmied to attention. He darted to the door, the shark at his heel like a loyal pet. Looking through the back window from an angle, he caught sight of the meter reader hurriedly shoving tools into his bag.

"What is it?" Kai asked, brow furrowed. He eased over to join Manō. They looked at each other, then to Sophia.

The bell above the door rang, signaling the three customers' departure.

Manō snatched his bag and yelled, "Run!" as he pushed Kai forward.

A chain reaction ensued. Kai bumped into Sophia and grabbed her around the waist, dragging her toward the exit. In slow motion, Manō watched the Maui Electric van peel out of the parking lot into oncoming traffic, tires squealing in protest, eliciting a chorus of honked horns and shaking fists from car windows. He snapped a mental picture of the license plate, which wasn't one for commercial vehicles.

His feet pounded the floor alongside Kai and Sophia. He shoved the door open with all his strength and pushed them out. Both of them tripped, barely keeping their balance as they stumbled across the blacktop. Sophia stared at Manō, confusion and anger plastered over her face. "What the hell—"

Her reprimand was cut off by a deafening explosion behind them that backhanded the trio across the parking lot. They landed several yards away in a shower of broken glass and billowing black smoke. From the gaping maw that had been a monument to Mahina Alana seconds before, an inferno blazed, eating everything in its path.

Mahina's Surf and Dive was no more.

CHAPTER THIRTY

"Hey, Donnie," Ret said as she passed Traskell leaving the restroom, furiously rubbing his left eye. She stopped. "You okay?"

"Yeah," he groaned. "This stupid eye is driving me nuts. I splashed some water on it, but it won't stop itching."

Ret's ears pricked up. Traskell was a civilian hired to man the property room at the station. She'd been trying to figure out how to get in there all day. Thinking fast, she said, "Mind if I take a look?"

He shook his head and stepped closer, leaning down.

She angled her neck up, left, right, carefully examining her coworker. She nearly pissed herself with anticipation.

"I'm no doctor," she said, "but that looks like conjunctivitis to me. Pink eye is extremely contagious. You might want to head over to the doc-in-a-box and have it checked out before you spread it around to everyone. Chief wouldn't take kindly to an outbreak."

"Seriously?" Traskell whined. "It's my anniversary, and I'm supposed to be meeting my wife for dinner at six. I still have to file and barcode a few more pieces of evidence. I don't have time for this shit."

"Wow," Ret said smiling. She clapped the back of his arm. "Congrats. How many years?"

"Fifteen," he replied, knuckling the eye again.

"That's amazing." She gestured to his hand. "Hey, the

more you rub it, the worse it'll be."

She casually scanned the hallway to see if anyone was close. All clear.

"You know what? I don't have to be anywhere tonight. Chief told me to go home early after pulling a late one yesterday, but I don't mind covering the property room and logging your last few pieces of evidence. That was my job when I first got here. I know the protocols. Shouldn't take long. And it would free you up to hit the doctor and get home early enough to bang your wife before dinner," she joked.

His expression shifted from irritation to appreciation. "Are you kidding me? Ret, that would be awesome."

"It's no problem at all. Consider it an anniversary present." She grinned.

"*Mahalo*, my friend. I'll tell Chief I'm leaving early," he said.

She held up a hand. "Don't worry about him. I got you covered. Get outta here and remind your wife why she married your ass in the first place. And have a drink for me, okay, buddy?"

His smile widened as he passed her the keys to the property room. "What time are you in tomorrow morning?"

"Bright and early. Keys will be at my desk first thing." She mock saluted. "Now, go get your eyeball fixed. And enjoy your anniversary."

"The stuff that needs filing is in temporary storage. I owe you, Rogers," he said, pointing as he trotted backwards down the hall.

Wrong. She owed him. Big time.

She pocketed the keys and grinned. "I'll remember that."

And suddenly, all of Ret's problems were solved.

She stopped at her desk to pick up her oversized purse from the drawer and slung the open bag over her shoulder. Then she sauntered to the property room, unlocked the door, and subtly swept the stuffy space to pinpoint all the camera locations. Surveillance covered the room from every corner as well as several places in the ceiling. By her count, there were eight spots to avoid, and even avoidance wouldn't completely hide what she was doing. She had to be very careful.

Keeping her back to the nearest camera, she unlocked the temporary storage locker and picked through, searching for the items the police had confiscated from Keahilani's apartment. At the top of the pile, guns, evidence bags stuffed with questionable contents ranging from soiled clothing to children's toys, and other ephemera lay among the ruins of both victims' and criminals' lives.

It took a minute of digging to produce the wig, dress, and trench coat she was hunting for.

Ret hid her smile when she found them. With some slick sleight of hand, she created a distraction for the camera by dropping the bag on top. She bent over with an exaggerated sweep of her left arm to pick up the plastic while simultaneously stuffing the evidence that kept Keahilani behind bars into her open bag with her right hand. She dragged the other things to the computer, set her purse on the floor, and pretended to catalog them.

Using her body to keep the computer's screen shielded from the camera, she quickly logged in using one of her colleagues' usernames and passwords—she wasn't gunning for detective for nothing. Ret had a small fortune's worth of login credentials she'd collected over the years. Never had a reason to use them until now. She accessed the digital evidence records and pored over them until she found the security feed from the condominium where Butch was murdered. Then she made it disappear.

Several trips to the temporary locker later, she finished cataloging the items Traskell had left and stored them neatly in their proper places on the shelves, barcodes displaying in front. She checked her watch. It was six o'clock already. Though she should've been tired from two long work days in a row, Ret was wired. She was so close. If she could sneak out of there without being caught, she'd have it made.

She stepped out of the property room, locked the door

behind her, and started toward the exit. Paying more attention to the bag on her shoulder than where her feet were going, she ran straight into Chief Hale.

Heat rose in her cheeks, a dead giveaway of her guilt.

"I thought you left hours ago," he said, brow arched. This man made it his mission to bust criminals. He was intimately familiar with the many faces of shady behavior, and Ret was wearing one like it was going out of vogue.

She covered her fumble with a big smile. "Sorry, Chief. Didn't see you. I forgot my purse." She patted the bag and realized her mistake a second too late.

He would assume "forgetting her purse" meant she'd left and come back for it, which the security feeds and Traskell would easily disprove. But it was too late to correct that line of bullshit now.

The instant his eyes narrowed suspiciously on hers, Ret felt the walls of guilt squeezing her like a rat trapped in an unwinnable maze. He knew she was lying.

Never one to jump to conclusions, however, he'd check out his hunch before pursuing her. Hale was methodical in his approaches, which sometimes meant loosening his hold on a lead long enough for the dog to run away. But he had a sensitive nose for crime, and she wouldn't have long before he picked up her trail again.

That meant Ret had to get the hell outta Dodge and find somewhere to destroy Keahilani's stuff fast.

Hale nodded thoughtfully and said, "See you tomorrow."

"You bet." Ret continued down the hall, willing her feet to move slower than they wanted to.

She got in her car as casually as she could, her mind racing the entire time in search of disposal options. Simply throwing the evidence away wouldn't be good enough. She needed to obliterate all traces of it.

"Burn it," she said to herself as she keyed the ignition. "Where to burn?"

She eased out of the lot, running through a list of places on the island that kept fires going. She didn't have a chimney, of course, nor did anyone she knew. A few of the hotels had fire pits, but they were way too public. So were the picnic spots with fire pits along various highways. Too many people.

She headed south down Highway 30 toward Māʻalaea, aimless but still taste-testing ideas. The hospitals probably had incinerators, but getting access to one would be hard.

Then she remembered the resort village she'd stayed at in Kāʻanapali while on vacation last year. She'd taken her recycling to the refuse closet and marveled at the incinerator then, never having seen one before.

"Perfect." She slapped the steering wheel with glee, plotted her course, and hit the gas. Keeping an eye on her rearview mirror, Ret watched for tails but didn't notice anyone suspicious.

As the adrenaline rush dissipated, truth settled uncomfortably into her conscience. She swallowed hard, trying to push the guilt away, but the closer she got to her destination, the heavier the severity of her actions hung like an anvil on her back.

She'd just deleted digital evidence and stolen physical evidence from a criminal investigation to protect a friend. The chief knew it was her, and regardless of whether he could pin it on her or not, she'd tampered with evidence. Though that charge was a misdemeanor in Hawaiʻi, the punishment could be up to two years in prison and/or as much as $10,000 in fines.

Ret had broken her oath of loyalty to not only the citizens of Hawaiʻi but also to the law, her commanding officer, and her late mother.

Bile rose in her throat. The muscles there constricted, threatening to choke her. Tears welled.

This was it. Not only had she killed any chance of ever making detective, but she'd most likely earned herself free rent on a cell in the county jail. She hadn't covered her tracks like she should have. In her rush to get out of the station, she'd left too many loose ends dangling.

She grabbed a hank of blond spikes and gritted her teeth.

"What the hell have I done?"

In that moment of reckoning, she tossed the repercussions around in the cerebral sandbox between her ears and decided it was too late for second chances. She'd done the deed to protect her friend, and no amount of apologizing or denial would make it right.

Justice had been delivered in a roundabout way. Butch got what he deserved. She would have to be okay with that and accept whatever consequences came her way. She just prayed the chief would find it in his heart to have a little bit of mercy on her. Not that she'd earned it.

A fire truck zinged up behind her flashing its red and white lights, siren screaming for everyone within a half-mile radius to get the hell out of its way. Ret eased over to let the vehicle pass. Smoke billowed up ahead from Lāhainā. She debated whether to stop and see if they might need assistance, but the matter of the wig and clothes was too urgent.

Traffic backed up quickly with the fallout from the fire, so Ret snuck down a side street, zigzagging through back roads toward her destination farther north.

When she got to the resort, her phone rang. She checked the caller ID, already knowing it was Chief Hale. She didn't answer. He left her a voice mail. Then the phone rang again. She turned it off.

Ret parked, checked her surroundings for people nearby, and finding no one close, quickly shrugged out of her uniform into the T-shirt and shorts she kept in the back seat. She donned a wide-brimmed sun hat. Then she shifted the evidence from her purse into one of the cloth shopping bags she kept on hand for grocery visits.

Pulling on a pair of sunglasses, she got out of the car with her bag and hustled into the lobby. She caught an elevator to the third floor and headed toward the rubbish closet. Once she was sure no one was around, she opened the door and dropped the wig and clothes into the incinerator, keeping her head down and away from the eye of the camera above.

Then she shot from the resort like a bat out of hell,

tumbled into her car, and headed toward home. Once she got a few miles out of Lāhainā, she turned her phone back on at a stop light. Seven phone messages and four texts awaited.

She wasn't surprised by the urgent requests for her to return Chief Hale's calls. But she quit breathing when she read the text from Kai: *Fire at Mahina's. Please call me.*

CHAPTER THIRTY-ONE

"Where are you?" Ret asked when Kai picked up the phone. She turned around and made for Mahina Surf and Dive. Jesus, the fire truck that had passed her not thirty minutes before must've been on its way to the scene. Her gut twisted for the hundredth time today.

"At the shop." He sounded out of breath. "It's fucking gone, Ret. Vaporized." A choke cut off the last syllable.

Fuck. "Is anyone hurt?"

"Manō and the new girl Sophia and me were the only ones inside."

Another stranglehold latched onto her heart at the mention of Manō.

A long string of red brake lights lit up like a Christmas tree in front of her. Damn traffic in Lāhainā. She laid on the horn, willing the cars in front of her to move. None of them did. These people were on Maui time, oblivious to the tragedy ahead.

"We're banged up, a few cuts and bruises, and none of us can hear very well after the explosion, but we're okay," Kai continued.

"Explosion?" Ret demanded. "As in a gas leak or something else?"

"With everything going on lately, what do you think?" Kai said.

Of course, it was arson. The Alanas had any number of

enemies ganging up against them, not the least of which was Scott Harris. Number one on her suspect list.

"Fire truck got here a while ago. And a few cops," Kai said. "Can you come? Please? I'm begging you. As a friend, Ret." He sounded desperate. Defeated.

But the mention of cops tossed Ret's willingness to help under the bus where it was promptly *bump-bumped* like small-fry roadkill. Chief was looking for her. He'd surely heard about the fire. He'd expect her to show up at the scene for her friends' sake.

She clenched the phone tighter, swiveling her head around, checking the street for blue lights. A side street a few dozen yards ahead could serve as an egress away from this mess.

"Kai," she drew out his name slowly, "I did something bad. The police are looking for me. I can't come now."

"Are you fucking kidding me?" Kai practically shouted.

She got that he was hurt and devastated, but he didn't have to be a complete dick. She'd just sacrificed her career by helping his sister.

"I'm sorry," she lobbed back. "I'll have to explain later. Are you going to the hospital?"

"Manō needs stitches, but he's refusing treatment. Sophia and I are going to get checked out. We could really use your help," Kai pressed, a little less aggressively this time.

She sighed heavily. "I want to help you." *I did help you,* she wanted to say. "Can we meet tonight? After sunset? You, Manō, and me?"

A long pause followed. "Yeah. Whatever." Then he hung up.

"Fuck," Ret screamed at her windshield as she inched toward the right-turn getaway. Traffic rolled to another full stop. Her blood boiled at her inability to make just one simple fucking thing in her life work right.

She texted Manō: *I'm so sorry about the shop. Need to see you asap. It's important.*

Lavender farm entrance. 8:00.

That was upcountry, not far from the Alanas' safe house. The farm would be closed by then, and it would be dark and remote enough to keep away from prying eyes.

She typed, *U ok?* and then deleted the query. Of course he was okay. He was Manō. Even when he wasn't okay, he was.

She sent back a quick thumbs-up emoji and left it at that.

As she waited through several light cycles for traffic to move, the repercussions of her deception weighed heavily on her soul. She couldn't go home. The cops would be watching her apartment in Wailuku. She had no clothes other than her uniform in the back and what she'd slapped on at the resort. She wouldn't have a job tomorrow, which meant no money, and very likely, a stint in prison.

But instead of worrying about what she'd done, she shifted her panicked thoughts to what she needed to do: help her friends. She had to remain focused on that goal.

By the time she escaped the traffic and stopped at a drive-through for a burger, she barely had ten minutes to pull over at an ocean lookout and scarf dinner down before she drove upcountry to meet Manō.

Someone had torched Mahina Surf and Dive. With people inside. Whoever it was intended to kill all of them. Would he go after Keahilani next? Pressure to call the station and ask about her welfare was almost too much to resist, but they could track her phone to within a mile or two using cell towers.

Shit. They could track her phone.

She detoured into the nearest parking lot, deleted all of her text messages, dropped the phone in front of her front left tire, and rolled the fuck over it.

Awareness on hyperalert as she resumed course, she scoured every street she passed. The only good thing about the fire was that most of the Lāhainā police were working the crime scene instead of looking for her. Once she got closer to her district, she'd have to be more careful.

She drove past the turnoff for the lavender farm, keeping

a close watch on her rearview. The only car that had been behind her was now gone. She pulled over on the twisty road and turned around in a driveway. Then she parked near the gate, walked to it, and waited behind a small cluster of trees.

Lights off, Manō's revving motorcycle announced his approach just before eight o'clock. He walked straight toward her, shadows gathered around him like a second skin. It was so dark, she could hardly see him, but he seemed to have no trouble spotting her.

The rotund moon spied on them from above. A breeze carried the chill of higher altitude to her skin, coaxing goose bumps to the surface. When Manō's dark shape reached her, she shivered again.

With a soft swipe of his deeply scabbed cheek, she stumbled into his open arms. He bent around her, enfolding her in warmth. She was safe with him. They held the pose for several seconds during which the only things she heard were his heartbeats and the occasional rustle of wind through trees.

The heaviness of his arms around her and the primal drumbeat in her ear made all the bad things disappear, if only for a few moments. She reluctantly pulled away and stared up into his face. She couldn't see him. She needed to see him. Why did it have to be so dark?

"Did they find any evidence of who did it?" she asked.

He shook his head.

His lips crashed into hers without warning, and she surrendered.

Commanded into submission by his mouth, her body felt as if it lost substance as she merged into him one agonizing molecule at a time. The smells of blood and leather gathered in her nose, prickling her brain with sympathetic needles of tragedy and despair. Everything—the fire, Keahilani's incarceration, her own duplicity—swirled into a maelstrom that threatened to rob her of happiness.

As Manō's soul bled into hers, she reached the conclusion of the first chapter in her adult life and flipped the page to the next one.

She had lost everything.

Except for Manō.

His rough hands were chastened now, roaming her body with assured but slow strokes, first on her hips, sliding around to the small of her back, drawing her into his mouth and his shadow. He might have a dark soul, but it was beautiful to her. Its rippling power danced over her, shielding her from lighter darkness. Inside his circle, she was protected.

Through the deepening of their kiss, his soft exhalations remained steady, tickling her cheeks, mocking her rushing breaths. The more time she spent with him, the giddier she became.

She'd felt like this with Kai when they were kids.

But she and Kai were done. For good. If nothing else proved it, this fucking kiss did.

She snapped her head back, panting. "I stole the evidence they had against Keahilani. I burned the clothes and deleted the video."

"*Mahalo*," he said, his throat a little hoarse. He leaned in to hug her and squeezed hard. "*Mahalo*," he whispered into her neck.

Her hands scaled his chest up to his broad, leather jacket-covered shoulders and encircled them. A tear spilled down her cheek for the impending loss of her job, the destruction of her friends' dream business, and for the end of her and Kai.

No regrets.

She took Manō's hand in hers and stared into the pools of his eyes. Under the fading moonlight, they looked almost completely black. "I probably won't have a job tomorrow, but I want to help your *'ohana*. What can I do?"

He brought the ball of their entangled fists to his lips and kissed her fingers. Then he let go and stroked her cheek with his knuckles. "You've done enough."

She shook her head. "You ain't getting off that easy. You're stuck with me till you get sick of me."

Please don't get sick of me.

Manō was all she had left.

He gently brushed his lips across hers, smuggling the sense right out from under her. Ret went all in with him, clasping his neck and pressing her breasts into his chest with the fever of a thirsty teenager.

He scooped her into his arms, enfolding her in his darkness. Everything went black, and for a microsecond, Ret panicked. But the strength and sureness with which he carried her settled her nerves, and she allowed him to whisk her away. Anywhere he went was okay with her.

The riot between their mouths cut off all the questions she wanted to ask. They could wait. As fired up as she was in the pants, it wouldn't take long.

There was something magical about Manō. The way the shadows seemed to curl around him like armor was eerie, but Ret couldn't resist him, not even after the freaky shit that happened the last time they were together. The power he exuded called to her.

The rough scratch of bark on her back returned her senses to her control as Manō pinned her against a tree. Its leaves sweated a pleasant, earthy smell. Hands fell to her hips and worked up the inside of her shirt, mapping the skin at her sides with calloused fingers. He leaned into her for another deep kiss, kneading her breasts through her bra. When he pinched a nipple, it was like opening the flood gates on the levee down below.

She couldn't wait another second. She unzipped her shorts and let them fall around her ankles, then went for his fly, fumbling in the dark for his erection. He sighed as she stroked him, reading and memorizing every contour and ridge like Braille. With a quick flick of his wrists, he shrugged out of the leather jacket. Steam rose off him, warming the cool air that permeated this higher elevation.

His hips fell into a steady rhythm. He pumped into her curled fingers that barely made it all the way around his girth.

"I need you inside me, Manō," she breathed beside his ear. "Everything else can wait."

She felt him nod. She opened her thighs to the pressure at her entrance and welcomed him inside. Slow, easy thrusts morphed into faster, urgent ones. His body was as tight as a wet suit on a monk seal, and she owned it.

They might've been from different backgrounds, but together, they were perfection. Two strong, determined loners who found the right spark within each other to keep them connected. His darkness became hers, and she reveled in it.

At the motel, his shadows had scared the hell out of her. But under the umbrella of his shadow tonight, she felt safe, protected, treasured. Whatever was between them deserved a chance to grow, and she was determined to see it flourish.

She weathered the brutal lunges hammering her back into the tree as their lips tangled in frenetic rapture peppered with pleasure-filled grunts and occasional curses. She unhooked the front clasp of her bra, exposing her breasts to the darkness and urged him to latch on. Every tongue stroke and pull dragged her closer to the finish line.

He broke away and rested his damp forehead on her shoulder, upping his pace. She swung her hips to meet his rhythm, swallowing every inch of him in a maddening cycle of catch and release until the pressure approached the breaking point.

The night shimmered with agitation. It became a living thing—a shiver of black sharks in a feeding frenzy, fighting for a bite of Ret's soul. Sudden flicks of fins and sharp tail swishes made waves in the air. She could almost feel their sandpaper skin scraping against her.

Manō lifted his hand to her throat like he'd done the other night, and for a single heartbeat, she was afraid. But she remembered how exciting the shock of being choked had been—not knowing when or if he'd let go, the pleasure between her legs building to a crescendo, the wild thrill of being tossed completely out of control, her very life resting at the mercy of his whims.

The fingers clamped around her neck and slowly

tightened like a vise. She gulped as much air as she could, knowing what was coming. Dizziness took up residence in her spinning head. She met his gaze, and her heart took a stumble.

Two black holes where his eyes should've been sucked in every lumen of light within reach. There was nothing but soul-devouring darkness feasting on everything in its path.

Ret launched a hand to his arm, digging her short nails in, urging him to let go. The shadows leaped and hopscotched over him, deviant little imps tittering with delight. She actually heard them. It sounded like another language spoken through high-pitched feedback.

"Manō," she gasped. The word came out with as much weight as air.

The intensity in his jet stare relented. His hand flew away from her throat as if it had touched a hot stove. His expression struggled under the gravity of apology. The impish shadows scattered, leaving behind the circling sharks.

The moon climbed out from its prison behind the clouds. Manō slowed his thrusts and spilled into her. Her nose flared as she inhaled gulps of oxygen coupled with the scent of his arousal and release. Undone by the cocktail of adrenaline and endorphins fistfighting with her emotions, she gave in. Her thighs tightened and trembled, barely keeping her anchored to reality as she drifted on waves of pleasure.

He held her through the climax. She was safe again, his arms around her, cradling her like a precious gift. They stood there, joined at the hips, him supporting her quivering body. He wouldn't let go of her, and she was just fine with that.

"I'm sorry, *eleu*," he mumbled over and over into her neck, the soft exhalations tickling her skin. Tension rose off him like steam.

"There's nothing to be sorry about," she assured him, though she didn't sound convincing.

He pulled back, allowing her a brief peek through the windows of his eyes into the depths of his soul. What she saw there gutted her. Anguish. A prisoner trapped by his circumstances. And so much darkness. How did he bear it?

Desperate to shoulder some of the weight threatening to crush him, she kissed him. He was clearly tortured by whatever secrets he harbored. She needed him to see that she was with him even though she didn't know what he was going through. She cared too much about him to let him go.

He accepted the kiss with gentle thanks, pulled out of her, and turned away.

She grabbed his arm. "Don't leave. Please."

Avoiding her gaze, he licked his lips and shook his head. "We can't do this again."

She was getting really fucking tired of that little escape clause. She pulled her shorts up and refastened her bra.

"Whatever this is," she gestured vaguely to their surroundings, which wasn't near adequate to convey or quantify *this*, "I'll get you through it. But you gotta help me understand."

He wouldn't look at her as he zipped up. "I lost control. I can't stop them when I'm with you."

She inhaled a steadying breath, afraid of the answer to the question she needed to ask. "What are *they*?"

"A curse," he spat and turned away.

"No," she said in a commanding voice behind him. "You don't get to walk away from me without an explanation, Manō Alana. I sacrificed everything for you. I deserve the truth for once."

He swung around and thundered into her personal space, black eyes wide, daring the moon to even think about shining on them. The moon was a total pussy.

"This darkness is my cross to bear, Ret. When I lose control of the reins, bad things happen."

He lifted an arm, and slick, inky blobs wriggled over his skin as if showing off, gazing up with empty yet knowing glances. The evil things *smiled* at her. Their malevolence was palpable.

Out of a sudden, demanding sense of self-preservation, she stepped back, aghast. The blood circulating through her head took a detour south, flooding her feet with unsteadiness. She lost her balance as tunnel vision stalked her. Grabbing the tree he'd just nailed her into, she sucked air through her nose and blew it out through her mouth.

The shadows scattered at the sounds of footsteps coming toward them. A gun snapped into Manō's hand from nowhere, pointing at the approaching figure. That slapped some life back into Ret. She straightened, focusing on her breathing.

In. Out. In. Out.

"Officer Beretta Rogers," a familiar voice said from behind the glint of a gun's muzzle. A sliver of moonlight fell on Chief Hale's face. "You have the right to remain silent."

CHAPTER THIRTY-TWO

"How'd you find me?" Ret's voice was weak, her face pale.

Manō and his bloodthirsty shadows waited for her boss to give them an excuse to end him.

Hale tossed her a small black device. She caught and examined it. Her face fell. "You wired my fucking car? That's low, Chief."

"Put the weapon down," Hale ordered Manō.

In his dreams. One of them wasn't leaving here alive, and Manō fully intended to walk away with Ret by his side when all was said and done.

"You first," he said.

Hale scrutinized him, then volleyed his gaze to Ret.

"Come on, guys, you can put your dicks and yardsticks away," she said with an exasperated sigh. "You both win."

Manō lowered his arm but held on to the .38.

Hale took his time holstering his gun. "I said you have the right to remain silent," he said dryly. "Take my advice."

The tired, watery eyes behind Hale's glasses told the story of a man who'd seen it all, including betrayals of trust from loyal employees. He balanced the world on his thin, aging shoulders. Those shoulders somehow remained straight despite the weight.

Ret walked over to Hale. She held her head high and boldly met his gaze. "You get a warrant for this?" She dropped the GPS tracker into his open palm.

"No. I won't need it," he said.

"You're not taking me in?"

"Not today. Not for this."

Ret's taut stance relaxed as she blew out a long exhale.

"Let's talk," Hale said, walking with a subtle limp toward the gate where she'd parked. He turned and gestured at Manō. "You can leave your friend here."

"His name is Manō Alana," she replied. "And I did it for him. He stays." She glanced to him, her open expression inviting him to join her.

How could he not?

He followed the officers to her car and leaned against it as they talked.

Chief Hale crossed his arms and stared over the top of his glasses at Ret. "I bugged your car when I noticed you spending a lot of time with your friends." He nodded toward Manō. "I wanted to trust you, but some signals you sent told me I shouldn't. Guess I was right."

The disappointment was evident on his face.

Ret hung her head like a beaten dog, but after a moment, she lifted it and met his eyes. Fearless. Decisive.

Hale may have gambled on her loyalty and lost, but Manō and his siblings had hit the jackpot with Ret. By destroying the evidence against Keahilani, she'd proven she was willing to go all in with the Alanas. It was their duty to accept her as one of them now.

Her bravery on the *'ohana's* behalf moved Manō. No one they'd ever trusted had demonstrated this degree of support. Ret was one of a kind. And that was all the reason he needed to keep her in his personal life too—if she wanted to stay.

"I've come to the conclusion that the line between lawful and unlawful is pretty damned blurry," she said. "When I joined the force, I believed there was right, there was wrong, and nothing in between. But that's not the case. Sometimes criminals get away with murder. Sometimes innocents are hurt, despite our best efforts to keep them from harm.

"Butch Kelly was a prime example of the system's

failures. That prick raped countless women and got away with it due to lack of evidence. Whoever killed him—Keahilani or someone else, I don't know—did our community a favor. We, the police whose job is to protect the innocent, failed those victims. That's on us.

"As a police officer, I'm sworn to uphold the law, but the law isn't always right or ethical. I can't in good conscience continue to serve in a job that lets bad guys win."

"I'm glad we're on the same page," Hale said. "Because you can't come back. Tampering with evidence is punishable with jail time and fines."

"I know, sir," Ret said. "And while I'm sorry I let you down, I'm not sorry for what I did."

He nodded. Hale seemed like an honorable man who understood Ret's position, even if he didn't agree with her.

"So, where do we go from here?" she asked.

"You tell me," Hale replied. "Without evidence, we can't prosecute your friend, so it looks like I'll have to cut her loose on the murder count. The drug charges are minor. She has no priors, so the judge will probably slap her on the wrist and send her on her way.

"I'm more concerned about the trouble brewing between your friends and Scott Harris." He narrowed his eyes on Manō. "He's a well-known businessman with ties to major CEOs and more than a few senators, representatives, and other government higher-ups."

"Harris blew up Mahina Surf and Dive," Manō said quietly.

Hale arched an eyebrow. "No offense, but nobody's gonna believe a respected millionaire had a reason to commit arson to destroy a rinky-dink surf shop. You got any evidence to back up that claim?"

Manō shook his head. "Aside from the numbers on the license plate, which was probably stolen, only what's in here." He laid a fist over his heart.

"That won't cut it," Hale said. "If you want me on your side, I need to know everything."

Airing out his *'ohana's* dirty laundry on the police's clothesline would definitely land one or all of the Alanas in jail. "Can't help you there."

"Because you don't know, or you don't want to tell?"

"Both."

Hale nodded. "Well, if you change your mind, give me a call. Ret has my number. Until I hear otherwise, we're treating this as an ongoing arson investigation whose only lead is a guy disguised as a Maui Electric worker driving a van with jacked-up signage that's probably already been stripped of its labels and plates."

"I'd be happy to come in to ID the bastard if you find him," Manō said.

And break his knees on the way out, the shadows giggled.

"As for you," Hale turned to Ret, "I want your badge and gun on my desk first thing tomorrow."

"Yes, sir," she said.

"And your resignation letter," he added.

"Wait." She screwed up her face when the words sunk in. "Resignation? I thought you were firing me?"

"You thought wrong," Hale snapped.

In the span of a heartbeat, something passed between Hale and Ret. A kind of mutual understanding. A reminder of some forgotten pact they'd negotiated. Manō could almost read the fine print in the subtle lift of Ret's shoulders.

Then it hit him. Ret held something over Hale's head. She knew something he didn't want to get out, and he was offering her this escape clause as payment.

Hale continued as if nothing happened. "I'm going to have to bury this lost evidence fiasco—pin it on an administrative glitch or some such. Only reason I'm covering for you is because I believe you thought you were doing the right thing. Hell, maybe you really were doing the right thing. But you broke the rules. You're gonna make it up to me."

Ret straightened. Her glossy eyes brightened and shone in defiance of the darkness. "I'll do my best. What do you need?"

"You're a decent cop, Rogers," he said. "You got a nose for sniffing out bad guys, and," he glanced at Manō, "you have connections with people I can't get close to. While I need good cops on my team, sometimes informants provide us with better information than we can get the old-fashioned way. I can't help you find a new job, but if you happen to see something you think would help our cause, I want you to tell me. You do that, and you won't be wasting space inside the prison."

"I can do that, sir," she smiled. "Absolutely."

Manō sensed satisfaction washing over her. This would be an opportunity for Ret to get a new start. Regardless of whatever secret he wanted to keep out of plain sight, her boss seemed willing to risk his own job to help her, which spoke to his faith in her abilities.

"I'm doing this as a favor because I like you, and I'd hate to see your life ruined over one stupid—and I do mean *stupid*—mistake." The weight of the pause that followed seemed to be directed at himself as much as Ret.

"Don't make me regret my decision, Rogers. I promise, it won't end well for you."

She nodded adamantly. "Yes, sir. Thank you, sir. I appreciate your confidence in me and understand your job's on the line. I will not let you down." Her voice was shaky with sincerity.

"As for you"—Hale faced Manō—"tomorrow morning when we discover the evidence against your sister is gone, I'll have to release her on bond. Make sure she doesn't screw up again. Next time you're on your own."

"*Mahalo*," Manō said quietly, reaching out to shake his hand.

Hale accepted. "Now get the hell out of here. This is private property. Let the Lāhainā district know if you think of any other leads for the arson investigation. If they find evidence of explosives, as I expect they will, they'll bring in the feds. They may call you to identify a suspect if they find one."

Ret stepped forward into the moon's light and held out her hands to the chief. "Thank you, sir. I enjoyed working with you at the station and learned so much under your watch."

Hale reluctantly hugged her, then he returned to his car and drove away.

Ret stared at Manō with wonder splashed across her face. "I can't believe he let me off."

"When you earn someone's respect, they can overlook a lot of bullshit."

Holding on to someone else's secrets for safekeeping doesn't hurt either.

He took her hand. She squeezed a silent reply as he rubbed a thumb over her knuckles. "You have my respect, Ret."

"*Mahalo*," she said.

He nodded.

Things were bad for the Alanas at the moment, but this small favor Ret had done for them might've been all they needed to turn the tide. He shifted his gaze to the darkness surrounding them and marveled at the moon. It always made him think about Mahina.

Mahina.

The shadows cowered from the illumination pouring off the cratered orb, but Manō embraced it despite the burn in his eyes. His mother kept lots of secrets, many of them hidden in her journals. Something she'd written in the one Keahilani had left at the shop jostled loose a forgotten memory. The tiredness plaguing him drifted away like dandelion seeds on the wind. Purpose filled in the empty space.

It always came back to Mahina, didn't it? Because as a *kahuna kilokilo*, Mahina had seen things no one else could have.

'Ohana is everything.

A smile scaled Manō's face, dragging the corners of his lips upward as pieces from various puzzles settled into place.

Stuffing her hands in the back pockets of her shorts, Ret said, "What are you so happy about?"

He dragged her closer until their bodies touched. The shadows gave him room, heeling at his ankles. "I know where to go now."

"For what?"

"Answers."

"What happens next?"

He dropped his lips to hers and kissed her long and hard. "We go to your place."

A huge smile sprouted on her mouth. "And what are we gonna do there?"

"We're gonna finish what we started and do it all over again until you get tired of me."

Ret's smile turned surly, and she ground her breasts into his chest. "I'm riding an adrenaline high that hasn't even spiked yet. It's gonna be a long night."

"I was hoping you'd say that."

CHAPTER THIRTY-THREE

Friday, October 10

"We got some new information related to your case, Miss Alana," Detective Blasingame said as she sat down with Keahilani and her lawyer, John Mendelson.

Keahilani had received a text from Manō saying that Ret had resigned under threat of being fired for destroying evidence. She had breathed the biggest sigh of relief in her life on seeing that news, and she wouldn't ever forget the sacrifice her friend had made to help her out, no matter how this debacle ended.

Ret was a fucking hero.

Blasingame opened a folder and picked through the pages until she found the one she was looking for. She summarized the contents. "The DNA retrieved from your brother Bane's house matches that of a man named Blake Murphy, who's currently considered a missing person. We also matched DNA from your family's home in Kula to the same man." She looked up at Keahilani. "You wanna revise your story about what happened when you arrived at the scene of your brother's shooting?"

Fuck.

Keahilani looked to Mendelson for advice about what to say. He shifted uncomfortably in his seat beside her.

"Tell them what you know," Mendelson said, droplets of

sweat dotting his balding pink head. He'd already given her a heads-up about this meeting and advised honesty. The cops had her number, so there was no point in denying Blake was at Bane's house. It would only get her in more trouble.

Fucking lawyers.

She sighed. "The man I shot was Blake Murphy. When I got there, he was standing over my bleeding brother, out of breath and holding a gun. I assumed he'd killed Bane, so I shot him in self-defense."

"Did he threaten you?"

"Yes," she lied.

"What did he say?"

"He told me to put my gun down or he'd shoot me."

"What did you do then?"

"I told him to back off and plugged him in the thigh when he was distracted."

"Why there?" Blasingame interrupted. "Why not the chest? Or head?"

"Because I wanted to scare him, not kill him."

Blasingame narrowed her eyes, leaned back in her chair, and folded her arms over her chest. "Then what?"

"When he grabbed his bleeding leg, he accidentally dropped his weapon. I grabbed it so he couldn't shoot me. Then he took off."

"He'd just shot your brother, and you let him go?"

"Yes. I let him go."

"Why?"

"Because ..." She scrunched up her face. Surprisingly, she didn't have to command tears to fall. They did so on their own. Despite everything Blake had done to fuck her and her *'ohana* over, she had cared for him. "Because I loved him."

Blasingame laughed humorlessly and tossed the paper back into its folder with disgust. "You *loved* him? Your definition of love must be pretty different from mine."

Mendelson lifted a hand in warning. "That's unnecessary."

Blasingame returned to Keahilani. "Did anyone see what

happened?"

"No."

"How many rounds did you fire?"

"Just the one."

"You're sure?"

"Yes." All of this was true. The killing blow came later, at the safe house.

"Why did we find Murphy's blood at your place in Kula?" Blasingame demanded. "There were traces of it in the backyard."

Keahilani shook her head. "I have no idea," she lied. "If that's true, you'd have to ask Blake what he was doing there. I didn't bring him home. As far as I know, he wasn't even aware I had a house in Kula."

"Kinda hard to do when Blake hasn't been seen in days."

Keahilani was playing a dangerous game with the police, but sometimes you had to take a risk. On the one hand, they had pretty compelling DNA evidence suggesting she was Blake's murderer, but they didn't have a body. That complication was all she needed to maintain the illusion of innocence. But her innocence would be shattered if they found his remains.

She trusted they wouldn't. Manō was very thorough.

"I'm sorry to hear he's missing," Keahilani said softly, her heart squeezing. She really was sorry. For everything. But right now, it was her life on the line, and a dead Blake served the purpose of her ongoing narrative surrounding Bane's murder. "But as far as I can tell, Blake Murphy and Scott Harris are the only suspects in my brother's death. I want those assholes found as much as you do. One of them needs to answer for his crimes."

If she'd been thinking clearly when she confronted Blake at the safe house, things might've played out differently. But Scott had sent him to kill Bane, and Blake probably would have done it if someone else hadn't gotten to him first.

She couldn't keep playing this game of chess with her dead lover. He was a bad guy. She was a bad guy too. With the odds evenly stacked, it could've just as easily gone in his favor if she hadn't snuffed him first.

No regrets.

Easier said than done. Bane's real killer was still out there, getting away with murder.

Mendelson broke the ensuing silence. "Are you going to charge my client or not, Detective? She's been wasting away in a cell for days. It's time to put up or shut up. Where's the evidence for the murders you're accusing her of?"

Blasingame sucked in a deep breath, picked up her folder, and stood. She nudged a clump of brown hair out of her face and stared down her nose at Keahilani. "Circumstances have changed since yesterday. We determined we don't have sufficient evidence to charge you for the murder of Butch Kelly. We have plenty of evidence to build a case against you for the murder of Blake Murphy, but without a body, we'll have to wait." Her voice strained under the weight of her admissions.

"As for the weed," she continued, "since we found less than an ounce in your car, we'll charge you with possession for personal use."

Mr. Mendelson smiled his relief. "That's a petty misdemeanor. Punishment is up to thirty days in jail or a fine. If you plead guilty, the judge might go easy on you since you're a first-time offender."

Keahilani nodded and wiped away a stray tear. "Does that mean I can leave?"

"If you post bail, you'll be free to go," Blasingame said. "Lucky for you, the judge has a light load today. Your arraignment is in thirty minutes." She straightened her file and laid a hand on the doorknob.

"*Mahalo*," Keahilani said, doing her best to suppress the bite in the word.

The door opened from the other side, and another officer ducked his head in. "This just came in. It's relevant to your case." He passed a folder to Blasingame, who nodded her thanks as she opened it. The series of expressions morphing across her face ranged from confusion to consternation to surprise.

Lips parted, she lowered the folder and shoved it under her arm with the other one. She wiped her mouth with the back of her wrist. "It seems this case just got more complicated."

Keahilani fidgeted. *Please, please, please* let someone have come through for her.

"What is it?" she asked cautiously.

"It doesn't concern you."

"If it pertains to her defense, it does concern her," Mendelson objected. "Is there new evidence?"

Blasingame huffed. "We've received a cell phone SIM card from an anonymous source. It appears to belong to Butch Kelly."

Keahilani felt the blood drain from her face. Butch's final text to Blake was on that card, and it implicated her as Pele in Butch's murder, calling her by name. She'd never forget Butch's last two messages. He'd typed "911" at 7:22 p.m., followed immediately with "Pele."

But there was no way the police could've gotten Butch's SIM card. She'd removed it and destroyed his phone after the murder. Then she'd sent it to …

Jezzy.

Manō had given the SIM card to Jezzy so she could determine who Butch's contacts were.

That fucking bitch had sold Keahilani out to the cops to protect Scott's ass!

"What's on the card?" Mendelson asked, still sweating. Keahilani wanted to scream for him to shut up.

She was going down in the worst way. Scott must've told the cops that Pele and her Enforcers were dealers on Maui. All they had to do was ask their informants to confirm they were three Hawaiians—a woman and two big men. While those descriptions could've fit any number of people, with Scott's accusation, it wouldn't be hard for the cops to assume they were the Alanas.

Without the actual costumes, the evidence was circumstantial, but it might give the police more reason to dig deeper into the Alanas' operations.

Now her freedom wasn't on the line. Her brothers' freedom was too.

What had she done?

Blasingame pursed her lips, reopened the folder, and scanned the page. She shook her head with disbelief. "Phone company records confirm the card belonged to Kelly. The forensics team retrieved Kelly's texts, contacts, call history, and deleted data. Looks like he was as bad as his victims said he was."

Mendelson lifted a brow. "And?"

"And your client is free to go," she said.

This couldn't be right. If it really was Butch's SIM card, then they should be throwing her back in a cell, not sending her home.

Was it a fake? If so, someone went to great lengths to weave such an elaborate lie.

Based on the detective's unrestrained display of disgust with the contents of the folder, Keahilani assumed something within its pages exonerated her, which wouldn't have been the case if it were the real card.

Could Jezzy have doctored the evidence on an immutable piece of technology? Or—*holy shit*—altered the data on the phone company's servers to display completely different information?

This was Jezzy she was talking about. Jezzy's superpower was making shit that didn't happen, happen, and vice versa. Her fellow hackers from the most distant corners of cyberspace and the depths of the Dark Web hadn't bestowed the handle "Command/Control" on her for nothing. Jezzy was God.

And God had answered Keahilani's prayers.

Mendelson stood up as a frustrated Blasingame shouldered the door open.

"A word of advice? Stay out of trouble," the detective

said to Keahilani. "You seem to be really good at attracting it. We'll be watching."

When she left, Keahilani and her lawyer expelled two huge lungfuls of air. What she wouldn't give to know what was in that folder.

She silently thanked Jezzy, wherever she was.

Mendelson walked her out to the administrative area to finish her paperwork. He then had her transported to the courthouse just down the street. Once arraignment and bail were wrapped up, Keahilani was free again. Finally.

She hugged Manō and Kai, who'd come to pick her up. Despite the bandages on various appendages and assorted bruises from the explosion at the surf shop, they were all smiles too—even Manō. Maybe they had more good news.

"Where's Ret?" she asked. She fired several semiautomatic rounds of side-eye at the courthouse on the way out. If she never set foot inside that place or the police station again, it would be too soon. She couldn't wait to get home and take the longest bath ever.

"Cleaning out her desk," Kai said. "We'll catch up with her later."

"Good. I owe her a big *mahalo* for what she did."

When they got in Kai's car, she assumed they'd head to Mahina Surf and Dive, but he turned in the opposite direction. Based on what Kai and Manō told her after the explosion, the shop was no longer there. The entire place had been razed.

So many memories just … gone.

That soured her mood.

"Where are we going?" Keahilani shifted her gaze between Kai in the driver's seat and Manō behind him. "What are you two up to?"

"We found Uncle Palani," Kai said.

Whoa.

"No way." Keahilani didn't even know he was still alive. Mahina said she hadn't spoken to him since shortly after their father died.

"Manō tracked him down. He says he may have some information that could help us," Kai said. "And there's more. Ret's detective friends filled her in on your case before she turned in her resignation this morning. Looks like the SIM card from Butch's phone had texts, contacts, call history, and deleted data that proved he was not only running drugs but also bragged about his exploits with the women he raped. There's also damning evidence that implicates Scott in several murders."

"So Jezzy really did come through for us," Keahilani marveled.

"Yeah, she completely erased all traces of you from Butch's phone," Kai said. "The pigs will be looking for Scott now, which lifts some of the pressure off us. Once we get past this deal tonight, we can take a break and regroup until the dust settles."

Keahilani nodded. "That sounds great. But aside from the fire, Scott's been out of the limelight for a few days. I'm sure he'll show up again when we least expect it. We gotta be at the top of our game on the Pāhoehoe front while maintaining an appearance of innocence everywhere else. No more making waves. Not even a ripple. We can't afford another run-in with the police, especially now that Ret can't protect us."

"Caution," Kai agreed. "Until we find Scott. Then I say we cut loose and let the shadows bury him like they did to that car near the garden."

If the shadows had their way, they might not have a choice.

It had come down to a backhanded admission of the truth: The shadows were real, and they had power Keahilani didn't yet grasp. The path to understanding lay in the execution of their desires. Once she figured out how the shadows operated, what set them off, and what they were capable of doing, Keahilani would learn how to control and bend them to her own will.

Then no one would stand in the way of the House of

Mahina.

Or the House of Justin Jacobs, as the case may be.

CHAPTER THIRTY-FOUR

The nursing home was a flat, nondescript one-story building made of tired, weeping red bricks. Surrounded by palm trees that reflected an illusion of happiness, the place had been infiltrated by sounds and smells that belonged in a circus rather than a home for the aged.

Manō's nose twitched at the thin layer of antiseptic trying its best, and epically failing, to cover the stench of urine, vomit, and an assortment of various other bodily secretions almost thick enough to wade through.

It didn't help that he'd dosed before meeting Kai at the courthouse, and his senses were heightened to the point of pain in this chamber of too-bright light and stomach-turning funk.

The shadows had upgraded their bloodthirsty demands from whispered taunts to full-blown threats of violence if he didn't feed them. The sights, sounds, and smells of this place made them even hungrier than usual.

Keahilani inquired at the front desk about their uncle, and a nurse led them to his room. Wiggly nervousness trekked across Manō's skin, searching for a soft spot to sink its teeth into. The shadows didn't like it here. He was on the verge of running when the nurse opened the door and waved the siblings inside the dark room. No lights except for faint glimmers of sun feebly trying to push through the closed blinds.

The first thing Manō noticed was the medical cart beside the frail man lying in the bed. The monitors on it were lit up with blipping red dots, a clear signal that his uncle was not in good shape. A sign on the wall with big letters read *Danger: oxygen in use. No smoking or open flames.* Crackly wheezing like biological static filled the air. Plastic tubes connected to a green oxygen tank threaded around Palani's head and into his nostrils, but he seemed to be struggling to breathe despite the help.

"Your uncle is resting," the nurse said, "but you can sit with him for a while."

Eyes wide with concern and lips slightly parted, Keahilani stepped forward to study the stick-thin figure dwarfed by white linens. "Is he …?"

Dying? echoed through Manō's thoughts.

A tight smile from the nurse was her only answer. She backed out of the room and shut the door behind her.

To say Uncle Palani looked bad was an understatement. Manō didn't remember much about him from his childhood, only that he had a bright smile and always pulled a shiny quarter from each of the kids' ears when he came around, to their delight.

Now there were no smiles or gleaming quarters. Just a fragile twig of a man being eaten alive by an insidious assassin living inside him.

Keahilani dipped her hand over the guard rail on the bed and scooped up Palani's gnarled fingers. She stared down sadly at him as she stroked each knuckle and fold of skin with her thumb.

"Uncle Palani," she ventured softly. "It's Keahilani. Your niece. Mahina's daughter."

For a moment, only the whirring machinery and the sour smell of death answered.

Then a pair of wide, rheumy brown eyes fixed on her with the suddenness of an afternoon rainstorm.

Palani shrank back from Keahilani, squinting. He assessed her, then Kai, and finally Manō the way one might stare at a horrible car accident—with morbid curiosity and deep-seated fear for the people involved.

Are they alive? Manō imagined him thinking. *Will they live? And if so, how long will their pain last?*

A gurgle escaped Palani's throat, and he struggled to push up to sit.

Keahilani studied the controls on the metal arm holding him in the cage of the bed, found the button to raise the mattress, and pushed it. Palani never took his startled eyes off them as his top half rose.

"Keahilani," he said weakly. Then he looked to Kai. "Your twin, Kai." When he shifted to Manō, warnings went off like bombs behind his eyes. He didn't care for whatever he saw. Manō couldn't blame him. A whole lot of bad lived inside him.

"Manō," he said, his voice like kindling being slowly devoured by flames.

Manō dipped his head with respect, hoping to ease some of the old man's fears, but the gesture had the opposite effect. Palani became agitated. His hands shook as they sunk into the mattress in an effort to find a more comfortable position.

"It's been so long since I saw my sister Mahina," Palani said, avoiding Manō. "She used to visit before the cancer got bad." He absently patted his chest.

The old man must've been hallucinating. Mahina had died six years ago, and as far as Manō knew, she'd never visited her brother, with or without cancer.

"She's gone," Keahilani said simply.

A web of lines etched around Palani's eyes with a sudden smile. "No, she's not. She's right there." He pointed behind them. Nothing but a paint-chipped wall with a small whiteboard displaying the names of his nurses and his meal choices for the day.

Kai and Manō exchanged glances but said nothing. They were both fine with letting Keahilani do the lying.

Their sister smiled and nodded as if she'd made a mistake and then continued. "We heard you were sick and wanted to pay our respects."

Uncle Palani lurched up, ramrod straight, and grabbed her arm. His yellowed, talon-like fingernails dug into her flesh. She startled but didn't pull away.

"Your father is a very bad man," Palani declared, his eyes darting to Manō and back at Keahilani. "Mahina was forged from goodness and light. She was impulsive and foolish, but after she fell in with Justin Jacobs," he spat the name, "his darkness tried to steal her light. He robbed her, tried to rape her soul after he claimed her body. But she was too strong for him." He smiled proudly as if reliving a memory he'd just unearthed from the annals of a centuries-old oubliette.

A coughing fit ensued, a horrible rattling that stoked the fire the shadows had lit under Manō's impulse control. Palani watched Manō through the jerking spasm and the rising phlegm. He wiped his mouth with a tissue and pointed at Manō's chest.

"You see that, Mahina?" He glanced to the spot where he'd indicated his sister before. "That's Justin's ink on your boy's soul. You knew it would happen. You never should have laid with him."

He seemed to listen to her reply, though Manō didn't see or hear anything that looked or sounded like Mahina. Then Palani diverted his attention on Manō. Lifting a bony finger to point at his chest, Palani said, "Shadows die in darkness and thrive in light."

A shiver raced up Manō's spine. Not just any shiver. A shiver of sharks. The dark versions of his ʻaumākua. They swam up and down the column of his body, flicking their tails across his nerves, scraping his muscles with their dorsal fins, grazing bones with their teeth.

Palani sat straighter, and his voice gained strength. "Yes," he marveled. "Yes, bring them out. They need the light."

Keahilani and Kai joined their uncle in the staring contest, sweeping their gazes over Manō from head to boots, wide-eyed, enthralled.

"Do you see what I see?" Kai asked Keahilani out of the

corner of his lips. Mouth agape, Keahilani nodded.

Manō looked down at himself. This was not a hallucination. This was not a drug-induced cartoon playing on a loop inside his head. They saw the sharks swimming over, above, under, and through him. The sharks were real.

"Wh-what is that?" Keahilani asked Palani.

Their uncle's grin broadened. "That's my sister, our parents, and grandparents. Our *'ohana*. The light."

"What do you mean?" Kai asked.

Palani held out a trembling hand to the sharks. The drab blue hospital gown fell away to reveal a stick-thin arm mottled with bruises from botched attempts to place IV needles. Murky gray veins shone through paper-thin light brown skin that should've been much darker if old pictures of him were to be believed.

But as Manō fixated on those blood-carrying superhighways winding and crisscrossing, they transformed into sinewy lines that moved with the fluidity of an eel. They slithered off his skin into the air touching it.

"Your *'aumākua*," Keahilani gasped, pointing at Palani's arm, which did indeed resemble a long, slick, darkly spotted moray in the dim light. "*Puhi* the eel is your *'aumākua*."

Palani nodded slowly. He spread his fingers and admired the mottled pattern, pleased that she recognized his personal family protector.

A hint of color returned to his face, putting a hearty dent in the greenish pallor. "Shadows are not evil," he intoned with a voice that didn't belong to him. For all Manō knew, it was the ancestor speaking through the *puhi* clinging to his body. Under its grip, Palani gained strength.

"Shadows are natural. Part of the order of things. They obey the laws of physics." Palani nodded to the sharks still swimming up and down, circling tightly, protecting Manō.

Protecting me from what? he wondered.

"You got the well-behaved shadows from Mahina. Her light kept your shadows alive. Like the full moon."

Mahina means moon.

When they got older, their mother had asked them to call her by name. Not *Makuahine* or even Mom. Mahina.

"Words have power," Palani said, reading his mind.

Had he read Manō's mind? Palani had been a *kahuna* like Mahina. Was he *kahuna kilokilo*, one who could prophesy the future? Or maybe *po'i 'uhane*, a person who could catch spirits (shadows?) and trick them into doing what he wanted?

Either way, Manō straightened and paid close attention to his uncle's words. Sick and dying or not, the man was a font of knowledge, and right now, the *'ohana* desperately needed answers to the many questions that remained in the wake of Mahina's and Bane's deaths.

"But what you got from the other half of you is not natural," Palani continued. "It springs from another kind of darkness altogether. Not of this world.

"Your father's shadows are mutts. Hybrids. His kind came from unattended nightmares left to fester in the psyche and wallow in anger and hatred. His kind doesn't need light. It soaks up the bad and uses it for its fuel."

Trying to keep up with Palani's ever-derailing logic while microdosing LSD proved challenging, but Kai summarized Manō's scattered thoughts more succinctly than he could have.

"Are you saying our …" Kai held up an arm. Manō was caught off guard by the dark shapes of turtles crawling slowly along his brother's flesh. "Our *shadows*," Kai continued, "come from *both* of our parents? How can that be?"

And then it clicked. Manō tracked the shadows wriggling around him. With tighter scrutiny, he was able to pick out differences, much like staring in frustration for several minutes at one of those 3-D posters composed of dots. Nothing makes sense until you catch a corner standing out from the flat plane of space and trace it to the bigger image boldly popping out from the second dimension like a middle finger, giving it depth as well as height and length. Once the holographic pattern emerges to reveal a detailed picture, you never have to try as hard to see it again. You know what to look for.

That was how Manō finally saw the whole picture of himself.

The shadows curling and swimming and circling and protecting were in fact two different breeds—those belonging to his ʻaumākua, the shark spirits of his Hawaiian forebears, and the amorphous ones. The latter variety were darker, more demanding. They constantly flirted with his control, hoping to trigger a meltdown.

Manō's jaw dropped when he recognized his father's genetic legacy permanently staining his soul like the blood from a demon's inkwell.

Sign on the dotted line, motherfucker.

Two kinds of shadows.

Light and dark.

Natural and unnatural.

Good and evil.

The sharks were his ancestors from Mahina's line, assigned to watch over him, while the nondescript ones from Justin goaded him to hurt people.

The bad ones thrived on blood and murder.

This revelation sent his mind tumbling through possibilities and explanations and truths he'd never considered. If what Palani said was true, then his ancestors could manifest inside his shadows. Maybe *they* were the ones who opened the pathways that allowed him to travel between stretches of darkness, not the shadows from Justin's side.

All this time he'd hated his shadows for the crimes they forced him to commit, but in reality, those from his *haole* side were causing him harm. The Hawaiian ones were protecting him.

Shadows die in darkness and thrive in light.

Next time the darkness tried to take control, all he had to do was find enough light to let the ʻaumākua out.

He'd missed the bulk of the ensuing conversation between his siblings and Uncle Palani while he was fixated on unscrambling this new information, but presently, the old man's words drew him back in.

"When they were teens, your mother fell in love with Justin. I tried to dissuade her, but she was too hardheaded. She was in love. Blinded by it. I knew they wouldn't last. I saw how he flirted with other girls when she wasn't looking. I hated him, but I couldn't break my sister's heart by telling her the truth.

"Justin went away when your mother was sixteen or so. When he returned years later, he had changed. Your father became a player. He banged every betty he could stuff his dick into," Palani reminisced with a frown. Keahilani smiled grimly at his word choice. "Something stole what little light he had and replaced it with evil. When that evil shone, it transformed darkness into a spiraling hell that destroyed everything good around him.

"Rumors of his dalliances with women across the islands were legendary. My friends used to joke that when my niece and nephews got old enough, they'd have to ask potential suitors for a detailed family tree to avoid incest. I was embarrassed for my sister and stopped talking to her.

"The day Justin Jacobs died, though, I hunted her down and hugged her, grateful that Justin's curse—his hold over her—was finally broken. But his death was just the beginning. She started having disturbing visions after he drowned."

"You think Justin was the cause of these visions?" Keahilani asked.

Palani shrugged and fell prey to a coughing fit. When his lungs cleared a bit, he answered, "I don't pretend to understand the cycle of life and death. I just know she faced an internal uphill battle once he was gone."

Manō turned over this information. He'd started having nightmares shortly after his father died. Could Justin have somehow possessed him? Mahina too?

"I'm not sure if you knew, but our brother Bane was recently murdered," Keahilani said.

Palani lowered his head but didn't seem shocked by the news. "I'm very sorry to hear that."

"But not surprised," Kai said.

"No," Palani said.

"How did Bane figure into all of this?" Keahilani asked, leaning closer as if her entire existence depended on Palani's answer.

"Justin was not Bane's father," Palani said, confirming Manō's suspicions. "His real father was a priest named King."

"Whoa," Kai exclaimed. "Hold up. Our mother was seeing a priest? And Dad didn't know about it?"

Palani waved off his question like a fly buzzing around his head. "Justin was rarely around, but the timing of Mahina's pregnancy matched the timeline of his final visit to Maui. Everyone figured Bane was his. But she told me the truth. She didn't want anyone to know. There would have been damaging repercussions for both sides. Mahina never spoke of King after Bane was born.

"Your brother was different from the three of you," Palani said. "But you knew that already."

"Where is this King now?" Kai asked.

"I don't know. Maybe he's retired. Or dead. The ancestors come for all of us eventually." Palani blinked, and the light of lucidity faded from his tired eyes, filling them with confusion and accusation.

He threateningly wagged a finger at Manō. "You need to take those shadows down a notch, boy. There's no place for that kind of darkness here."

Manō glanced at his feet. He switched his vision into decipher mode and teased the sharks away from Justin's shadows. So much made sense now. His nightmares, his dark desires, his sadistic need to hurt. All of it came from Justin.

His father had cursed him.

But the curse hadn't fully latched on to Kai or Keahilani yet. And it was his job to ensure it never did.

"We should let you rest, Uncle." Keahilani joined Manō, laying a hand on his arm. She was trying to comfort him as she'd done when he was a boy. He appreciated the gesture. The warmth flowing between them felt good. His sharks and her butterflies—yes, now he could clearly see her shadows were butterflies—circled and danced around each other. Kai's turtles joined in too.

A menagerie of shadows sent as a gift from their mother. It was the best present Manō had ever received.

All of this new, dark movement was subtle, and no one entering the room would have noticed if they weren't looking for it. But Palani saw it. The confusion on his face melted into satisfaction. He closed his eyes.

"*Mahalo*, Uncle," Kai said, gently pressing his palm to Palani's shoulder. "I hope you find peace."

Manō could tell by the pinched look on Keahilani's face that she wanted to say many more things. She wanted to learn more about Justin and Mahina, Bane and his father. She wanted to know how the shadows got here, what they could do, and whether she could control them. She wanted to tell him they'd be back to see him again soon, but time wasn't on Palani's side.

Instead, she kissed his forehead and held his hand as she hummed "Hawaiian Lullaby" to him over the wet gurgles emanating from his chest.

She used to sing the lullaby to Manō, and later Bane, at bedtime. So many songs. So many hugs. Kisses on bruises and cuts. Piggyback rides through the ocean when he was too small to stand in the water. Keahilani—and Kai too—still carried Manō today, in a different way.

Manō was a lucky man to have an *'ohana* such as this.

Starting tomorrow, no more dosing. No more shadows controlling him. From here on, he owned every minute of this life.

CHAPTER THIRTY-FIVE

Keahilani insisted on driving the Mustang home. Kai didn't protest. The ride was quiet. Manō assumed his siblings were chewing on the information Uncle Palani had revealed about the shadows, so he left them to their thoughts.

He seized on the silence to do some mental churning of his own. He was supposed to meet Dallas and the Gang of Eight tonight. With all the chaos surrounding the *'ohana*, Manō didn't have a good feeling about selling illegal drugs to people he didn't know.

Keahilani trusted Lui, but he was a wild card. Not only was he a selfish, psychotic narcissist who only cared about himself, but he also worked for Scott, albeit reluctantly. Lui was in the business of earning money, and if that meant making people disappear in the process, he considered them collateral damage.

Though their mothers had deep ties through mutual history, if it came down to him or the Alanas, Lui would choose himself.

"What time is the meeting again?" Kai asked absently from the seat behind him.

"Eleven thirty," Manō said.

"Then we need to be there at eleven," Keahilani said. "I want the area scoped ahead of time. We aren't taking any chances with these guys."

She read Manō's mind.

"About Uncle Palani," Kai began carefully, as if trying to slip past an active beehive with a pissed-off queen inside. "If what he said about our ... shadows is true, then maybe we can use them to our advantage."

"How?" Keahilani asked.

To some degree, Manō knew how to command the shadows, but he wasn't sure he could explain this technique to his siblings. It wasn't like flipping a switch. He just thought about it and directed the darkness using gut instinct. Though, with the new knowledge that some of the shadows came from Mahina, he might be able to manage them better now. If he could just keep Justin's side on lockdown.

Even as he pondered ways to suppress them, the inky blobs protested from the patches of darkness around the floorboards of the Mustang. Keahilani's eyes left the road for a split second to look at them and then shot Manō a quick glance.

She'd seen them just as he could see similar shapes clinging to her feet too.

The shades they inherited from Justin would be a hell of a challenge to contain, let alone control.

"I don't know, but I don't have a good feeling about this meeting," Kai said, flipping dreadlocks out of his eyes. "We were able to surf the shadows before. Maybe we can use them as an escape if we need to. It'll be plenty dark in ʻĪao Valley tonight, and there shouldn't be any tourists around after closing. I want to have a fail-safe in place in case shit goes south."

"We bring guns," Manō said, though Dallas had told him not to. He'd also insisted Manō come alone, but that wasn't happening either. "Lots of them. Fail-safe secured."

Kai sighed. "You two may be comfortable shooting first and asking questions later, but I'm not." Kai wasn't comfortable shooting anything or anyone, period.

Keahilani's phone rang. She glanced at it, frowned, and answered. "Lui. Please tell me you're calling to confirm our date among the stars."

She listened for a long moment, staring blankly at the road as she drove. "Are you fucking kidding me?"

Another pause. Lui's fast, high-pitched chatter escaped the confines of the receiver. Manō couldn't make out details, but judging by the speed of Lui's speech and Keahilani's reaction, he guessed the news wasn't good.

"Fine," she snapped. "We'll see you in thirty." She ended the call and threw the phone into a cup holder. "The deal's been compromised."

"Great," Kai said coldly. "Now what are we gonna do?"

"We're going to meet Lui and see if we can salvage it," Keahilani barked.

"Do you seriously think that asshole is being straight with us?" Kai asked. "He's a bloodthirsty psycho. The wind could change, and he might decide to bite a guy's ear off. Fuck this shit. I say we ditch Lui and ..."

"And?" Keahilani prompted when Kai didn't finish his thought.

Kai flung his gaze out the window as if the answer lay woven within shifting cloud patterns or lines in the asphalt on the road beneath them. "And find someone else to distribute Pāhoehoe."

"So, you want me to call the thirty dealers who've already turned us down and tell them we'll give 'em a bigger cut on our already discounted merchandise because Ambrosia has eclipsed our sales and we're desperate?" Keahilani snarled. "No, Kai. We don't *have* any other dealers. Scott scared them off or snapped them up to distribute for himself, and he killed the rest. If we don't move this shit tonight, the investors are going to murder *us* in our sleep."

"No one's getting murdered," Manō said, though he wasn't so sure. "Let's see what Lui has to say. He may be psycho, but he's inventive with his crazy."

"I agree," Keahilani said. "We're not canceling anything until we have more details."

After a long minute of silence, Kai said, "Do we want Ret involved?"

Manō hid his flinch. He didn't want her near the meeting or any of the Alanas' dealings, for that matter. She'd taken major shit and suffered plenty by simply being close to them.

"Ask if she can be on standby," Keahilani said, gutting Manō with a swift, merciless stab. "The more guns on our side, the better. Ret's pretty badass with a Beretta."

"Her momma didn't name her that for nothing," Kai mumbled as he dialed her number and lifted his phone to his ear.

The conversation was short and to the point: *Meet us at the safe house tonight, bring a weapon, prepare to guerilla the shit out of this meeting.*

Manō deeply regretted her involvement, but Keahilani was right. They'd need every available gun on their side.

Thirty minutes later, the siblings met Lui at a private residence in Wailuku. The home bore all the opulence and garishness one would expect from Lui, which made Manō think it was his own house. Inviting them to his turf was a magnanimous gesture and signaled his willingness to be open and honest with the *'ohana.*

"Welcome to my humble abode," Lui crooned from the impeccably landscaped front yard as the trio marched up the walkway.

Suspicions confirmed. Lui just earned several brownie points.

The big Hawaiian wore his usual attire: a garish pink, purple, and yellow aloha shirt with designer black slacks and orange slippas that didn't match any of it. He air-kissed both of Keahilani's cheeks and went for Kai's, but Kai held up a hand between them to decline. Lui scraped his gaze down Manō's body, but he didn't bother trying to kiss him.

Smart man.

"Come in, come in," Lui said, flitting inside and kicking off his slippas inside the door. Manō, Keahilani, and Kai removed their shoes as was Hawaiian custom.

Lui guided them to a spacious living area and gestured for them to sit on the sofas. "Aloha, my friends. May I interest you in drinks? Crudités? A snort of blow?"

Keahilani waved him off. "Get to it, Lui. What's going on with the Gang of Eight?"

Lui pouted and settled straight-backed into a huge chair shaped like a hand, its palm upturned, fingers and thumb forming a supportive cage of digits around him. Its fingers loaded with glitzy-jeweled rings, the chair could've served as a throne. Lui fancied himself a king. The chair worked for him.

Lui crossed his legs with a flourish and propped his folded hands atop a knee. "As you know, Dallas and Co. are scheduled to meet Manō tonight. I've used the Gang of Eight for jobs before, but only in a pinch. They can be ... impulsive at times, and that shit don't fly with my operations. I'm the only one around here who's allowed to be impulsive—"

"Can you get to the point?" Keahilani hissed.

"Fine, Miss Bossypants." Lui paused for a dramatic lip pursing and then continued in a cold voice. "I heard from an associate that my personal chum and part-time butt bum Dallas was seen talking to Scott Harris yesterday. *Very* disappointing. He was a fantastic lay. But when it comes to business, Lui don't play."

"Where were they spotted?" Keahilani demanded.

"Waialua Kope offices in Kahului."

Manō tensed. He and Keahilani exchanged worried glances.

"What was he doing there?" she asked.

Lui shrugged. "Don't know, don't care. What I *do* care about is my business. My friend says Scott's hired the Gang to capture Manō and use him as collateral to get to you," he pointed dramatically at Keahilani, "my dear Pele. Now, I don't give a flying fox fuck whether he takes any of you out or not—"

"You're all heart," Keahilani interrupted dryly.

"—but I was supposed to get a 25 percent cut from this deal—"

"Uh, it was 8 percent last time I checked," she said.

Lui's lids lowered with queenly derision as he stared down his nose at Keahilani. "I upped my service and handling fees. Dealing with you people stresses me the fuck out."

"Feeling's mutual," Kai grumbled.

"We'll up it to twelve." Not giving him a chance to counter, Keahilani pressed, "Go on."

His panties were clearly in a wad, but Lui didn't argue. "Scott's got a vendetta against your 'ohana, and he plans to kidnap Shark Boy to find out where your farm is. It's my understanding he's in the process of diversifying—"

"Ambrosia," Kai interrupted with a huff.

Lui nodded. "Weed is passé, and our business won't be as viable once it becomes legal and regulated. Ambrosia is shiny, new, and hella concentrated. It has a bright future if the horny addicts on the street are any indicator."

Lui sighed forcefully and lifted a gold chalice encrusted with gaudy jewels—which looked to be authentic—to his mouth. He pulled a long draught of whatever was inside and licked his lips daintily.

"I thought Scott wanted us dead because of the shit with his wife and Bane?" Kai said.

Lui waved a limp-wristed hand. "Oh, he does. But he also got a hold of your Pāhoehoe and found it to be comparable to Ambrosia, which he's already dipped his dick into. Since Ambrosia is so scarce, he plans to cull it directly from your weed. He's already got a chemist on hand perfecting the process. Hence the need for the location of your farm."

More suspicions confirmed.

Keahilani shook her head, stood up, and paced over Lui's zebra-skin rug. Real zebra, by the look of it.

"He's not getting Manō. He's not getting our weed. And he sure as hell isn't getting our farm," she declared, ticking off each point on her fingers. "That asshole killed our brother and burned down our surf shop."

"Ah yes, the one named after your mother," Lui said. "I was sorry to hear that. Mahina was a good woman." His voice drifted off, carried by some memory he didn't share aloud.

He snapped out of his reverie after a moment and wiped the condescending smirk off his face. Leaning forward, he said, "I'll be straight with you—and this is without a doubt the only time I've ever been anywhere near the same zip code as straight, okay?

"Scott hired Dallas—my two-timing lover—and the Gang of Eight to nab Manō. They'll torture him until he gives them the location of the farm, and if he doesn't, they'll kill you, you, and you." He pointed at Keahilani, Kai, and Manō in turn.

"I don't know the specifics of what's up their sleeves, but you don't have to go to the meeting." His voice softened with a kindness Manō had never heard in it before.

Ah. Now he understood. Lui was making amends for something he felt he owed the Alanas for Mahina's friendship with his mother years ago.

"I'm out of contacts to help you with distribution, but I can loan you the money to pay back your investors—at a high interest rate, of course." Lui turned his attention to Manō. "Or you can agree to do a few jobs for me. Starting with Dallas, the traitor." He sucked his teeth dramatically and added, "If you're up for it."

Manō shook his head. "I'm not a hired gun."

Lui burst out laughing, all traces of seriousness instantly evaporated. "Since when?"

"Since now."

"Party pooper." Lui stuck out his tongue.

Keahilani cut the air with a flat hand. "Enough. Manō is taking the meeting. We don't have a choice. *Mahalo* for filling us in on what Scott's up to, Lui."

Lui narrowed his eyes and dropped his voice to a low, serious pitch. "You owe me, Pele."

"I'll buy you breakfast tomorrow morning after I fuck your boyfriend Dallas with my .38," she tossed back.

This meeting was adjourned. Manō and Kai stood to join her.

While Keahilani went for her shoes, Kai studied the

exotic if macabre paintings adorning the walls. A removed heart pumping blood into a gnarled fist. Tigers devouring a vaguely human-looking body in the jungle. A bloodied, aborted baby dressed in gold silk robes.

"You know, you wouldn't even have to be in this loop if you'd give up your informant," Kai proposed. "Who told you about the Gang of Eight's plans?"

A lithe figure appeared in the doorway from the kitchen's shadows. "I did."

Keahilani, Kai, and Manō lifted their heads in sync and pivoted toward the familiar, breathy sex-goddess voice they'd heard countless times on the phone but never in person.

"What?" Kai exclaimed as Sophia stepped into the dim light. She settled hands tipped off with black fingernail polish on her hips and grinned.

Lui sipped his drink and smiled at Keahilani over the top of his chalice. "I told you I had a Jezzy."

CHAPTER THIRTY-SIX

Keahilani eased her foot out of the shoe she'd just slipped on and pivoted toward her brothers. Jaw hanging open, she pointed at Sophia—*Jezzy*—and padded toward her.

"You," she accused, her tone deep and thick with disbelief.

"Yeah," Jezzy breathed. "Me."

She met Keahilani halfway and stopped inches from her. A staredown ensued.

Keahilani narrowed her eyes. "Why didn't you tell me who you were when I hired you to work at the shop?"

"Come on," Jezzy said, dropping the siren voice in favor of the playful one of her alter ego, Sophia. "I thought you knew me better. When have I *ever* given up primo information for free?"

True. Jezzy was all about the paycheck. Yet, here she was, with Lui of all people, warning the Alanas about incoming danger again.

Keahilani should've decked her. Instead, she opened her arms to her. Jezzy barely cocked her head as if deciding whether to accept. She did, but the hug was brief.

"Look at my pretty girls," Lui swooned, clapping with glee and bouncing on the balls of his feet beside them. "Here I expected the cat fight of the century, but instead, the kittens are smitten. What a happy ending to what might've been a tragedy if dear old Lui hadn't intervened. You can both thank me later."

Kai and Manō wandered over, the former looking dazed by the revelation. Manō seemed nonplussed, as usual. Nothing fazed him.

"What are we supposed to call you?" Kai asked.

Jezzy looked thoughtful for a moment. "Sophia would be preferred outside these walls, but here you can call me Jezzy. I think it suits. And speaking of suits, I have some information about your fave that you might find useful."

She whipped out a phone from her back pocket and entered 1-1-1-1 to unlock it. Then she flicked through apps and typed as she talked. "Thanks to your brilliant idea of lighting up the surf shop with surveillance equipment, I was able to pull video from the feeds showing the bomb being set, license plates, van make and model, and even a picture, albeit blurry, of the guy who did it."

She turned the phone to show the siblings grainy video and stills of the perpetrator doing his business.

Keahilani studied the image carefully. She didn't recognize the man. "You think Scott hired this douchebag?"

"I do," Jezzy said. "I'm not positive, but it would make sense, given Scott's obsession with you."

Keahilani crossed her arms over her chest. "Why are you telling us? Judging by your lack of communication, I figured you were sucking his dick, laughing all the way to the bank about how you two fucked over the Alanas in their time of greatest need."

"No such luck, my friend. Turns out Scott is way more of a bad guy than I originally suspected. I decided to pretend to make nice with him while cutting you guys off. That way he'd think I was loyal. Scott's all about loyalty."

"I see," Keahilani said, not sure whether to believe her. Jezzy had fucked them over a couple times that she knew of. Who was to say she wouldn't do it again? Or maybe she was wired, and Scott was listening to their conversation from his ivory tower on O'ahu or from Waialua Kope in Kahului right now.

"I guess Scott and I have something in common beyond sharing the same daddy," Keahilani said. "I'm pretty big on loyalty myself. Prove to me you're not here to take us down. Prove you're really on our side."

Jezzy lowered her head and licked her lips. She played around on her phone some more and passed the device to Keahilani, who thumbed through pages and pages of detailed notes about Mahina Surf and Dive.

"When the bomb destroyed your business, it destroyed mine too," Jezzy began. "I'd already chosen sides when I walked through your door, but I didn't realize how much I needed you and your *'ohana* until you gave me—a total stranger—a chance. You were the first people who've ever paid me to create something good. Up until I started working at the surf shop, I spent my days hiding in shadows, making deals with bad people, breaking laws. I earned a lot of money from Scott. He kept me living comfortably on an island few people can afford.

"But the shit he made me do weighed heavy on my conscience. I covered up his lies, his deceptions, his illegal business deals ... his murders. The last time I spoke to him was the anniversary of his wife's death. He went off the rails with the crazy. I'd never heard him talk like that. He was plotting revenge on you. I knew your family had done bad things too, but nothing like Scott. I decided then and there, he had to pay for his crimes.

"So, I switched sides without telling a soul and applied at Mahina Surf and Dive to get close to you. I thought I could keep an eye on you, maybe secretly let you know in advance if trouble was coming." Jezzy paused and looked away. "I guess I wanted to do the right thing for once."

Keahilani pored over the documents and spreadsheets Jezzy had created. She'd devised a business plan for Mahina Surf and Dive, and it was ... amazing.

Keahilani held up the phone. "You're serious about this."

Jezzy nodded, taking her cell back. "You know, with the video evidence, you could use your insurance money to rebuild the surf shop. And I could manage the fuck out of it."

Mahina would've wanted them to go legit and give up the weed farm. Too bad they only had the most basic insurance required to run a business. Keahilani had dropped their coverage to the bare minimum to save money for the farm. She looked to her brothers in turn. They didn't know there was nothing to cash out.

"We'll have to think about it," she hedged. "In the meantime, where do we find the cocksucker who blew up the shop? I have a few questions for him regarding his employer."

"I have a guess about where you can find him." Jezzy paused a beat, then consulted her phone. "Looks like Houston's got a problem."

Keahilani cocked her head in question.

Jezzy flashed the screen. It was a map with a moving dot. "Houston. Your bomber."

Keahilani stared at her blankly.

"The Gang of Eight members use cities from Texas for their names," Jezzy said.

"Let me guess," Kai said. "The others are Austin, San Antonio, Laredo, Arlington, Pasadena, and Amarillo."

"Nah, there's only four of them. But you got Austin and Pasadena right." Jezzy winked at Kai and turned to Keahilani. "If you hurry, you can catch him before the meeting. Here. Keep this. It has all the evidence from the bombing. And maybe a few other surprises."

Jezzy tossed the phone into Keahilani's palm. "I can't go with you, but if you need anything, my new number's in the contacts. We'll talk when you get back."

"If we get back," Kai muttered.

Jezzy slapped him with a sharp look. "*When* you get back."

Keahilani nodded. "*Mahalo*, Jezzy." Then she glanced to Lui. "And you too."

"My pleasure, Pele." He tittered in that playful way of his like he was delighted simply to have been born.

Keahilani rolled her eyes and waved her brothers to the

door. "Let's go burn a motherfucking arsonist."

* * * *

Ret met the Alanas in the McDonald's parking lot at 8:00 p.m., discreetly transferred a few important items from her trunk to Kai's, and hopped into the back seat of the Mustang beside Manō. It was hard to breathe with all that Hawaiian muscle and Alana *presence* steaming up the car.

After submitting her resignation that morning, she'd signed a new lease on life and was ready to start living. She did her best to keep from staring at Manō's hot body dressed all in black. It was hard. So damn hard.

"What's the plan?" she asked after greetings were exchanged.

Keahilani pitched a phone back to her. Its GPS app was open and tracking a flashing dot. "We're going there first. And we're gonna cash in on this guy's IOU for destroying our shop."

Ret nodded. "Then what?"

Kai and Keahilani exchanged looks in the front seat as she merged into traffic. Manō kept his gaze pointed out the window, but he widened the space between his legs so that his left one touched her right one. Under the cover of darkness, she slid a hand to his thigh and gently squeezed. He pretended not to notice but slipped his fingers between hers, squeezed back, and then retreated.

"We have some *other* business at ʻĪao Valley Park tonight at 11:30," Keahilani said, glancing to her in the rearview. "If you want to come as backup, we'd welcome an extra gun, but no pressure."

"Sounds like my idea of a good time. I'm all in." Ret stretched and patted the trusty 92A1 Beretta holstered under her black hoodie. Seventeen rounds should be plenty, but she'd stocked up on magazines just in case, planting three extras in various pockets of her cargo pants. And she brought her rifle for later. If all that firepower couldn't get the job done, she deserved to die tonight.

She'd been a cop for a couple years, but this was the first time she'd ever experienced the thrill of a manhunt. There weren't many shootings on Maui. Overall, it was a quiet place. Her talents in the marksmanship arena had been vastly underused on the job. No more.

Roles hadn't just shifted. They'd done complete 180s.

With the rise of the moon against the darkness, she felt bad, and it felt good.

Kai remained uncharacteristically quiet as Keahilani filled her in about the job. This so-called Gang of Eight planned to kidnap Manō. Fuck that.

Manō's eyes lingered on her, heavy like a weighted blanket. She mentally promised him she'd do everything in her power to protect him and his siblings. And she vowed to herself if they made it out of this deal alive, she'd confront Kai about her feelings for Manō.

Her history prior to this point felt like a lie, and it had to be tearing Manō up inside too. She wanted to wash the palette clean and start painting new pictures with Manō in the frame beside her.

She slipped a glance at him. He was staring at her. Everywhere his gaze touched, tingles raced through her. His darkness was palpable. It awakened things in her she could neither deny nor define. They'd have plenty of time to create their own personal dictionary later.

Keahilani made a couple more turns, and she rolled to a stop. "Here we are," she said.

She parked on the street of a quiet neighborhood in Pā'ia and passed out black ski masks to everyone. All four were dressed in nondescript black clothes. They donned their hats as Keahilani gave instructions.

"We need to assess who's home first. We'll each take a side of the house. North, south, east, west." She pointed to Kai, Manō, Ret, and herself in turn. "Once you've made your rounds, meet at the front corner by the palm tree."

She popped the door, and the rest of them followed her

into the night. The houses here were fairly close together. They had to be careful not to draw any attention. The Alanas virtually disappeared the moment they left the car. Ret had excellent vision, but she had a hard time keeping track of where they were. She stayed close to the trees on her way toward the east side of the house, but compared to her friends, she stuck out like a sore thumb.

How did they do that? She'd seen Manō blend into darkness, but not his brother and sister. It was damn eerie.

And cool as shit.

She peeked into the windows on her side. Seeing no indications anyone was there, she met her friends at the designated corner, and the team quickly conversed. Kai reported that Houston was on the south side in the kitchen. It didn't appear anyone else was home.

Keahilani removed her gun and motioned them to the front where she quietly tested the doorknob. She grinned when it turned, and she waved them in behind her. All weapons out, the team slunk inside, turning off lights as they went.

Smells of roasting vegetables filled the air. Loud pop music played from speakers in the living area. The four crowded the edges of the doorway where Houston was happily engaged in slicing a hank of meat while swinging his ass to Meghan Trainor's "All About That Bass." Ret shook her head to keep from laughing. Fucking gangster wannabe.

Keahilani slid a hand around the corner to the wall where a light switch might be. Nothing. Kai repeated the movement on the other side. Bingo.

Darkness fell. They capitalized on the few seconds of confusion that followed Houston's "What the fuck?" by storming the kitchen, guns pointed at his head.

"Drop the knife," Keahilani demanded.

Movement. Rustling clothes. Then a *pfft!* whizzed between her and Manō. Actually, it headed straight for Ret, but Manō's reflexes proved faster when he shoved her aside. The flying knife barely missed her chest. Realizing she was totally out of her league, Ret breathed heavily as a scuffle of feet and thunks of punches and pistol whips resounded.

"Get the fuck outta here!" Houston screamed, a tremor vibrating the words.

Ret started for the light switch so she could see what was going on, but Manō's cold hand stopped her. It felt slimy, unreal. Brow furrowed, she searched the dark for his face, but it wasn't there.

Keahilani hissed from behind Houston, "Who hired you to blow up the surf shop?"

They all assumed it was Scott, but it couldn't hurt to confirm the theory before they went on the warpath to kill a guy.

"Fuck you," Houston said between clenched teeth. More thuds of flesh clobbering flesh. Ret couldn't track what was going on, but it sounded like Houston elbowed Keahilani in the gut. She cried out, and Kai or Manō, she couldn't tell, answered his jab with a crack to the face that had surely broken bone.

Whimpers close to the floor. Keahilani's fast breaths. A few coughs. Shadowy movement toward the whining figure. *Stomp!* Another cry as Houston's leg snapped. One of the boys swooped down low. The glint of metal off his gun shone as it pressed to the man's head.

"We asked you a question," Kai said. But it wasn't his voice. Not completely. Kai was in there, but so was someone—*something*—else. "Who hired you?"

Ret blinked several times to get a grip on the scene before her, but nothing made sense. She could make out Houston's vague, writhing form on the floor, but surrounding him were three human-sized blobs of darkness eating away at what little light spilled in through the windows from the street and climbing moon. Neither their voices nor their shapes were right.

Ret backed up a couple steps.

Kai must've thrust his gun into the hollow of Houston's cheek, because the guy's words came out funny. "He said he'd kill me if I told anyone."

"Yeah?" Kai said. "Well, I'm gonna kill you if you don't. Who hired you?"

Kai's inky shape leaned heavily into the prone figure. Houston lifted his hands in surrender. At least, Ret assumed those two pale raised sticks were arms.

"You got three seconds, motherfucker." The black energy racing over Kai amped up, electrifying the room. It was like swimming through a bed of electric eels, each brush commanding the hairs on Ret's body to stand at attention.

"One."

"He'll kill me," Houston muttered weakly.

"Two."

"Please don't—"

"Thr—"

"He didn't say his name," Houston blurted. "I swear to God, I don't know who he is. Only that the money was transferred to my PayPal account from Waialua Kope Enterprises."

Kai's rippling black form oozed back, but he kept the gun's muzzle pointed at Houston. "Was it Scott Harris?"

"Harris?" Houston sounded confused. "No, he didn't have anything to do with the surf shop. He hired us for something else."

What?

Keahilani stepped into the fray, her voice also altered by something malevolent. "He hired you for the Alanas tonight. What's their plan?"

"I'll tell you everything," Houston begged. "Just don't kill me."

"Survival is dependent on how satisfied we are with your answers," Keahilani said. She sounded like something from beyond the grave.

"Are you them? The Alanas?" Houston sniveled.

Keahilani's ink-stain body leaned closer. "We're your shadows. You wouldn't lie to your shadow, would you?"

The creepy, high-pitched whine punctuating her voice

sent Ret's fear over the edge. She had to get out of there.

Trembling all over, she holstered her gun and ran outside. She bent over, bracing hands on knees, and gulped in breath after breath of cooling night air.

When she finally felt like she could breathe somewhat normally, she straightened. Manō stood beside her. He'd appeared out of nowhere.

Ret screamed, but he covered her mouth to silence her. He leaned forward and said, "We need to talk."

CHAPTER THIRTY-SEVEN

While Keahilani and Kai dealt with Houston, Manō took Ret
by the arm and walked her away from the street to the side of
the house where he could keep an ear open for his siblings
and watch the neighborhood for signs of trouble. He
removed his mask. Ret did the same.

"He wasn't Kai," Ret rasped. Her body shook. He gently
tightened his grip, trying to calm her. "And Keahilani wasn't
herself either. It happened with you last night, but not like
this. Wh-what … *are* you? The truth, Manō. No more
seducing me and sweeping shit under the rug for later."

"We're …" How to explain they were possessed by two
kinds of shadows at war with each other from both sides of
the family?

Finding no other words adequate to convey the truth, he
blurted, "We're possessed by two kinds of shadows at war
with each other from both sides of the family."

She blinked.

He sighed.

"You're a … shadow," she said carefully.

"Not exactly. Kind of."

"So, when we were inside"—she pointed her thumb over
her shoulder—"in the dark, you … melted into it?"

"Maybe. I don't know. It's just who we are."

"How long have you … been like this?" She stepped
back, ran her gaze down his front, and poked his arm like she

wasn't sure if it was real.

"As long as I can remember. Since my dad died."

"Was Mahina a ... *shadow* too?"

He shook his head. "I don't know, Ret. Maybe."

He hated not having concrete answers, but having lived like this most of his life, he no longer questioned what he was. He accepted his lot and evolved with it when situations required him to do so.

"I'm just ... me." He lifted his arms, the black sharks swimming silently beside their lengths, and stared. "Darkness made flesh."

He could see the wheels turning in Ret's mind. She didn't say anything for a long moment. Then her resolve solidified. He actually saw it harden into her features.

"Do you care about me, Manō?"

"Yes." He didn't waste a second answering. "Yes, I care about you."

"Are you gonna hurt me?"

"Never." He spoke the word both gently and resolutely, like a promise. Because that's what it was. He stepped closer, tentatively lifting a hand to her face. When she didn't resist, he cupped her cheek. She leaned into his touch and closed her eyes.

"I care about you too," she said, grasping his hand tightly. "And that's all that matters, isn't it?" When her topaz eyes opened, and she gazed at him with such pure honesty and acceptance, he thought his heart might explode.

He fell for her. Hard.

A kick in the chest from a bee-stung mule would've had less impact.

"That's all that matters," he agreed.

She kissed him, and his tumble into whatever this was picked up speed. His stomach dropped like a skydiver jumping from a plane. But it felt good. Not scary or threatening. Exhilarating.

Their mouths moved in tandem, built for one another. Built to survive a lifetime together, no matter how long or short.

Was this what love felt like? He'd known familial love all his life. He'd been cherished by his siblings and mother, no matter what, and he cared deeply for them too.

But this was different.

This feeling plucked some rogue organ buried deep inside his gut, undiscovered as yet, strumming its odd striations in a swell of beautiful music. Each reverberation bounced within him until his body thrummed like a tuning fork set to a pitch that matched Ret's unique frequency. It wasn't like the explosion of an orgasm, blindingly bright but lasting only a few precious seconds. No, this was much more. It was volume and amplitude. High crests and deep troughs all at once. It was the slow awakening of a sun that promised to light up his solar system for the duration.

Was this love? he asked himself again.

He didn't know the answer. But he was willing to find out.

The front door opened, and Manō jerked away, instantly regretting the parting of their lips. The lurch in his stomach was like the pull of a magnet crying out for its opposite, buried within Ret.

His south needed her north.

Putting their masks on, they feigned disinterest when Kai and Keahilani left the house. They followed his brother and sister to the car and slid into the back seat. The shadows hid his hand on her knee.

"What's the deal?" Ret asked, somewhat breathless.

Keahilani removed her hat and started the car. "Scott didn't blow up the shop."

"We need to find out who at Waialua Kope did," Kai said, tossing his mask onto the dashboard as Keahilani drove away.

"My money's on Grant Lowden," Manō ground out.

"We'll go after Lowden soon enough," Keahilani said. "Jezzy should be able to dig up some dirt on that prick. For now, we need to stay the course. Scott orchestrated tonight's deal. Dallas is actually Prince Seamus, the guy behind the influx of Ambrosia on Maui. He's working for Scott. We're gonna take him and his little Gang of Eight out before they even *think* about laying a finger on Manō."

So, Dallas had used Lui to get to them. Lui already hated Scott, but this double-cross would put Lui firmly in the Alanas' corner for any future confrontations. Manō supposed they could have far worse allies in this drug war.

"How do you want to handle these pickle dicks?" Ret asked. Some of the nervousness left her voice. "Ambush? Snipers? I'm mean as hell with a rifle."

Keahilani glanced at her in the mirror and smiled. "I have something else in mind."

Manō knew what that meant.

Keahilani pulled off into an empty parking lot, and the team made plans.

CHAPTER THIRTY-EIGHT

Prince Seamus—*Dallas* tonight, he reminded himself—and three of his co-conspirators climbed out of the black van and waited near the sign at the entrance of ʻĪao Valley State Park for the rest of his people to show up. It was a quarter past eleven. His crew was late.

Typical.

As Whiskey drove away to park off the main road, Austin texted that he and Pasadena were running a few minutes behind. Duh.

Though Dallas was loaded with a fresh set of extras, the only ones he'd worked with before were Whiskey the driver and Yankee, one of the three sharpshooters twiddling his thumbs beside him. X-Ray and Zulu were new hires, and reluctant ones at that. They'd heard about what happened to Victor after Lui got a hold of him and ripped—literally *ripped*—his balls off on the golf course. The cleanup after that incident had been legend among those in the Gang of Eight's hiring orbit, and not in the good way.

X-Ray and Zulu had demanded extra to sign on. Danger pay, they said. Fucking pussies.

You couldn't hire good help these days without an ass-ton of money. And insurance. Always with the insurance.

This replacement squad just had to do their job. Once the Alana bitch was captured, Dallas didn't give a fuck what happened to the hired grunts. Hell, if they were sloppy, he'd do them afterward and save himself the hassle of hiring a cleaner. In addition to being a kingpin and an expert at playing many sides, Dallas was a feverish planner. His deliveries ran like a well-oiled machine. He didn't tolerate messes or missteps.

Which was why all this lateness put him in a royally bad mood. He'd spent days setting up tonight's operation to go smooth as a baby's ass after butt cream, but so far, this shit was cellulite-spackled with three days' stubble.

He sucked on the cigarette dangling from the corner of his mouth. The cherry on the end lit up the night with an eerie red glow. He rubbed his arms and exhaled a stream of gray smoke that was kidnapped by a sudden breeze. The air down here in the valley was heavier than near the coast, and the fog on nights like this gave it an extra-creepy Scooby-Doo feel.

It's a rain forest, he reminded himself. Of course, there would be gobs of moisture in the air. But the science behind the ghostly pall hanging between every branch and leaf didn't make the weight of the humidity bearing down on him any easier to heft. The massive palms, banyans, and bamboo trees dotting the land bore the eyes and gaping mouths of giant tiki monsters. They seemed to look with disdain upon the measly humans lingering unwanted after dark.

X-Ray, Yankee, and Zulu clustered together on the parking lot blacktop, leaning on their rifles, watching him warily. Yeah, well, he didn't care much for them either.

Zulu spat the toothpick between his lips to the ground and sucked his teeth. He was a short white guy with a bigger right eye than the left. Said it helped his targeting. Dallas thought it was more helpful at getting him date rejections than shooting shit.

"Did you know King Kamehameha I invaded Maui and fought its chiefs right here in this valley at the Battle of Kepaniwai a couple hundred years ago?" Zulu asked no one in particular.

X-Ray cocked a brow at him but didn't answer. Zulu's dark clothes effectively blended him into the night, but his pale face and unusual tan-colored eyes destroyed any chance at complete camouflage.

Yankee grabbed the bill of his cap, yanked it up, and tugged it down low over his eyes. "Yep. So many dudes caught the pinch from Kamehameha's big-ass cannon, their bodies blocked the 'Īao Stream." He chin-pointed toward the sound of rushing water beyond the trees.

"I heard the Maui chiefs got their asses handed to them down here," X-Ray said quietly. "Kamehameha was a bad motherfucker."

Dallas's phone vibrated with a text from Whiskey: *Lights heading our way.*

Seconds later, Pasadena texted. He and Austin were parking near the patch of overgrowth they'd scoped out earlier in the day.

Where the fuck was Houston?

He dialed the asshole's number.

Ring. Ring. Ring. No answer. Voice mail.

So, Dallas texted.

By the time Pasadena and Austin trudged through the underbrush to join the group, Dallas still hadn't gotten a reply from Houston. He checked his watch. Ten minutes till the meeting. He couldn't wait another second.

"Fuck it." He waved the team over. "We're going forward without Houston. Get into positions. We've been over this several times. You know the drill, yes?"

The five men nodded.

"The boss should be here any minute," Dallas continued. "Just do it like we planned, and everything's copacetic. We all get paid real good, and everyone can go home, get high, bang your girl, and go to sleep knowing you did your part to rid the island of the Hawaiian vermin trying to take it over."

His thoughts flickered to Lui, and he stifled a laugh. He'd been so easy to manipulate. Insert dick into ass. Agitate. Release.

Voilà. Instant trust.

Idiot.

"That was an incredibly racist and generally awful thing to say, man," X-Ray argued as he lowered a pair of night vision goggles over his eyes.

Dallas shrugged. "Sue me." *Or sue Scott Harris. He's the one who wants to make it rain Alana blood.* "Now get the fuck outta here."

X-Ray scowled at him over his shoulder as he hefted his rifle and headed for the trees. Yankee and Zulu donned their goggles and split off in opposite directions.

A minute later, the three sharpshooters signaled that they were in place, triangulated around the small clearing where Dallas stood.

Fucking Houston. If that asshole wasn't dead or at least bleeding to death in an alley somewhere, he would be when Dallas found him.

Austin and Pasadena trudged up from their hidden parking space to join Dallas. "Where's Houston?" Pasadena asked, looking around.

Dallas waved the question away. "Don't ask."

"Guess that means no steak dinner like we were promised," Pasadena whined, rubbing his stomach. "Damn. I'm starving."

Dallas ignored the grumble. He was hungry and pissed off too, but bitching about it wouldn't change the fact that Houston was MIA.

"We're down one man from the original plan, but if Alana does as I told him, we'll be fine. We have plenty of firepower backing us up."

"You honestly believe he ain't coming alone? Or armed?" Pasadena asked dubiously. "That would be stupid."

Dallas smiled and glanced around the forest to the spots where X-Ray, Yankee, and Zulu were perched in trees above. "I have eyes everywhere. If anyone else shows, they'll be dead before they hear the gunshot."

Just then a pair of headlights swung around, fending off the darkness. A Mustang parked at the edge of the forest. A wall of man-shaped muscle got out, slammed the door, and casually strode toward them, hands in leather jacket pockets.

"Put 'em up where I can see 'em," Dallas called. Austin and Pasadena stood in stone-cold silence beside him.

The man slowly raised his hands and lifted his shirt. Dallas couldn't see him clearly with all the shadows, but he looked like a big Hawaiian, which was exactly what Harris said their target was.

"A man of honor," Dallas said. He didn't believe for a second that Alana was unarmed, but it didn't matter.

"Are you?" Manō asked.

Dallas smiled and lifted his shirt in the same manner, nodding for Austin and Pasadena to follow suit. He held out his open hands. "See, everybody's playing nice."

Manō settled his gaze on each of the three men in turn. "What happened to the other five members of your so-called 'gang'?"

The clouds parted and light from the moon spilled among them like a silver waterfall, refracting and scattering on the ground and splashing off the huge leaves surrounding them. It should have illuminated Alana's face, but it didn't. He'd masterfully positioned himself within the shadows so Dallas couldn't read his expression. That bugged him more than the thought of Manō having a hidden gun.

"Let me guess," Alana said, taking a step forward, repelling the light like a shield. "The first little piggy went to market and got shot in the head by a hungry butcher."

Another step.

Dallas slipped his hand around to rest on the gun butt stuffed down the back of his jeans. Despite the moon bathing the scene in light, he still couldn't see Manō's face. Dallas gritted his teeth.

The Hawaiian continued. "The second piggy stayed home and got so scared of the dark that the terror of it forced him to turn the gun on himself."

The next step brought Alana up beside the crew. All three turned to watch him, but it took constant adjustments.

Alana was circling them. Like a shark.

Pasadena's hand headed for his gun too.

"The third little piggy choked to death on a hunk of roast beef and vegetables he was cooking for his comrades, and the fourth one got none."

What the—

He couldn't be talking about Houston.

Houston, the foodie who'd said he was preparing a grand meal for the crew at his house for the after-death party tonight.

Holy fuck, Alana had killed him. And no doubt tortured him for information about the meeting tonight.

Now Manō stood opposite of where he'd come in to join the group. The realization that this deal had gone horribly wrong settled like frostbite into Dallas's bones.

Lui. The Hawaiian had double-crossed *him* instead of the other way around.

God damn it.

The breeze kicked up again, accentuating the chill, forcing thousands of leaves around them to giggle quietly. A shiver sunk its teeth into Dallas's nape and shook him all the way down to his tailbone.

"And the last little piggy"—Alana paused dramatically as if to give Dallas's panic a fighting chance to rise up the column of his throat and lodge like a cannonball over his windpipe—"drowned in a sea, sea, sea of darkness, all the way home."

Alana turned his head. Two eyes, blacker than pitch, fell on Dallas. They judged him. Condemned him. They did not pity him.

Dallas swallowed and snapped out the gun. He targeted Alana's head—or where he thought the man's head was. The clouds chose that moment to drift in front of the moon, obscuring the only source of light, and Alana blended into the ensuing darkness.

"Show yourself, you pussy," Dallas said, forcing false bravado into the words.

He reminded himself with a quick, cleansing breath that

he wasn't alone. He had plenty of backup. There might be a few casualties, but he'd make it out of here. He had a job to do, and when he finished, his bank account would be shitting Ben Franklins like an incontinent polymath with a prune juice addiction.

With an adrenaline-spiked infusion of greed-tinged courage, Dallas said, "Where's the Pāhoehoe farm?"

They'd been instructed not to kill Manō—Scott needed him alive to negotiate for his sister—but Dallas valued his life more than a throwaway job. If it came down to Manō Alana or Prince Seamus, Scott could fuck himself.

The clouds parted again. Hands up, Manō eased into the returning light above. His eyes were depths-of-hell black. Even the whites were black.

Oh, hell fucking no. What in the literal fuck was up with those eyes? Dallas's blood turned to ice water. Austin and Pasadena lifted their shaky weapons, targeting Manō's face.

"I don't know anything about a farm. I came here to conduct a deal," Alana said casually. "Is there a problem?"

Dallas tightened his grip on the gun to keep the tremors under wraps. "No problem for me. Big problem for you. See, I think you know exactly where the farm is, and you're gonna take us there. If you don't … well, the consequences of that decision might weigh pretty heavy on your eternal soul."

Beside him, Austin and Pasadena laughed nervously, but their confidence was painfully, obviously fake.

Dallas stuffed two fingers in his mouth and whistled, giving X-Ray, Yankee, and Zulu the signal to pop off warning shots as they'd planned.

Nothing happened.

Dallas, Pasadena, and Austin exchanged worried looks.

Dallas whistled again, shoving the muzzle of his gun into Manō's chest.

This time, there were sounds, just not the right ones. *Thunk, crack-crack-crack, splat!* came from Yankee's direction, followed by a muffled cry from the vicinity of X-Ray's tree. Two *pew-pews!* of exploding bullets dimmed by a silencer rounded out the final chapter in this nightmare of a story, and another heavy *thud* resounded as something man-sized hit the ground near Zulu's station.

Manō's shark grin widened, displaying too many sharp teeth to count. "Was that supposed to be a signal?"

He tossed his head back and laughed. The sight of him standing like that, back arched, arms outstretched with moonlight sliding down him like rain off oiled skin made Dallas's butt cheeks clench.

The silent lack of firepower plinking bullets around them had a far worse effect. No more trembling. His hands hardcore *shook* now.

"Dallas," Austin said carefully, taking a step back. "Where are they?"

"Allow me to demonstrate how signals are *supposed* to work." Manō lifted a hand and snapped his fingers once.

Pop!
Pop!
Pop-pop!

Austin jerked on Dallas's right, grabbed his stomach, and dropped. Several rounds flew from the mouth of his gun on the way down. A microsecond after, Pasadena screamed. His face scrunched in pain as he fell on Dallas's left.

A flood of hot liquid cascaded down Dallas's leg. In his shock, he couldn't tell if it was blood or piss. It took a full three seconds to determine it must've been the latter, otherwise he wouldn't be standing. In those three seconds of self-assessment, Manō had vanished.

Austin cried out weakly, rolling in the dirt, clutching the hole just below his sternum that was pumping dark blood out of his body and onto the ground with alarming efficiency. His breaths came short and fast. His slick, black-stained fingers grabbed Dallas's ankle. "Please ... please ... help me ..."

Dallas kicked Austin's hand free and glanced to Pasadena. He wasn't moving. No sound. Presumed dead.

Fuck. Dallas grabbed both of their guns—he had to fight Austin for his but wrangled it free after a couple jerks—and stuffed them into his pockets. Then he dove for cover under the nearest patch of vegetation, lying flat on his belly to watch from the ground.

Austin's hurried breaths transformed into horrible rattles, but Dallas was grateful for the sounds. They drowned out his own terrified pants.

"I'm gonna huff," Manō called, his deep yet now tinny voice echoing from everywhere, "and puff," the trees came to life with a little help from the wind, "and blow your house down, Prince Seamus."

What in the living fuck had Dallas gotten himself into?

His skin felt like it supported an army of bugs, their legs skittering without direction, on a mission to take him down with fear alone.

Their mission was working.

He glanced to the three spots where his marksmen had been. No movement or sound from Yankee or Zulu's posts, but something slunk along the ground where X-Ray had been stationed. Someone was dragging a body.

Fuck this shit.

Dallas targeted the dark-clad figure and pulled the trigger once, twice, three times. He saw frantic movement but couldn't define what or who it was. Just looked like a black, gelatinous blob that was there one second and gone the next.

The air behind him shifted suddenly. The heat steaming off him met a torrent of icy wind that covered the length of his back. He tried to contain his jerk so as not to give away his location, but it was too late.

"You should have built a stronger house," a male voice intoned right behind his ear. The same terrifying, high-pitched whine as Manō's accented the words.

Dallas flipped to his back and blindly unleashed another three rounds into the figure. No one was there.

Then another voice, this one female, from the opposite side sneered, "Straw, sticks, and poorly equipped hired guns have proven your downfall, my friend." She tsk-tsked as Dallas hit the trigger repeatedly, emptying the magazine into darkness.

A black shimmy blurred the air in front of him. He reached for the gun in his pocket. A combat boot descended with agonizing swiftness on his wrist. This time his attacker was quite solid. His arm, however, no longer was. Bone jutted from the skin of his forearm like a tent pole.

He didn't bother trying to contain the excruciating roar emitted from the depths of his soul. Its echo hopscotched off tree bark and leaves, causing a stir in the dozing bird community.

Dallas tried to snatch the other gun with his free hand, but as soon as he made contact, another boot landed there, pinning him to the ground like a butterfly in an insect collection. The weapon skittered just out of reach. He arched up, screaming, tears rolling down his temples.

A dark-clad woman dropped to the saddle of his pelvis and straddled him. She smoothed his sweaty hair with the gloved hand holding her gun. He tried to head-butt her, to kick his way free, but she leaned out of range, easily dodging his attack.

Her face was a silhouette with no definition. Blank. Black.

The smell of her plumeria perfume brought his nose unexpected sweetness amid a reeking cloud of urine and burnt gunpowder.

"We've let you have your fun," she cooed. "Now it's time for ours. Where's Scott Harris?"

He had nothing left to fight with. Dallas lifted his head, stared into the nothingness of her face, and spat.

But not even a ball of phlegm lobbed at close range could hit her. The woman lost form for a split second. The spit flew through the wispy black space where she should have been and landed on the dirt with a splat. Then she was back, her full weight holding him down. He dropped his head to the ground and moaned.

He was dead. There was no way out of this. If these crazy fucks didn't kill him, a heart attack would. Because this shit was so far outside the realm of possibility, he wondered if he had stepped into an actual horror movie.

People couldn't just melt into darkness. It wasn't real.

The pressure on his broken arm increased, drawing another vicious scream from his lips. "She asked you a question," the man said.

Okay, maybe it was real.

He had to buy time. Distract them long enough to get away and run to the van. Whiskey would be ready to drive him the hell away from this insanity.

"Can you repeat the question?" he said, initiating a fake coughing fit while his fingers stretched along the ground toward the gun that had tumbled out of his pocket.

"Where's Scott Harris?" the woman said through gritted teeth. Hot fury rippled off her.

The air puffed quietly, like the pump of an owl's wings as it launched from a tree branch.

"Right here," Dallas's boss said, walking toward them from the direction of the parking lot. His voice had the same metallic quality as Alana's.

The siblings—his attackers *had* to be Manō's kin—jumped into formation, three abreast, shifting their aim to him.

Dallas's heart fluttered back to life. He was saved. Thank Christ. He stretched, grabbing blindly for the lost gun. He brushed its handle, but his fingers wouldn't work properly. He couldn't pick it up.

Ignoring the Alanas, Scott walked over, pointed his gun between Dallas's eyes, and shook his head. Blackness from the depths of hell washed over him like a pall crafted from pure darkness. "You fucking idiot."

Dallas swallowed once.

Scott pulled the trigger.

Dallas's protest died on his lips. Along with the rest of him.

CHAPTER THIRTY-NINE

Manō's gut clenched at the explosion of gunpowder and bullets penetrating flesh and bone in his periphery. A spray of red erupted from Dallas's head. Chunks of brain matter dotted the ground.

He whipped his gun up, targeting the ridge between Scott's eyes. Kai and Keahilani caught up a second later. Scott didn't look at them. He just stared down at Prince Seamus's lifeless shell with disgust. Three guns pointed at him—four if he counted Ret's rifle from up in one of the trees—and he couldn't have cared less.

Scott slowly lifted his gaze to the trio surrounding him and smiled. "Ah, my sister and brothers. Good evening."

"Not for that guy," Kai quipped, keeping his weapon steady.

Keahilani scowled and spat on the ground between Scott's feet. "We may be kin by blood, but you're not family."

Scott's grin widened. "What's blood got to do, got to do with it?" he crooned to the tune of Tina Turner's song of a similar name.

The crazy in this one was strong, Manō decided.

"Come now, Keahilani. Don't be mad," Scott chided. "But if you prefer to look at our relationship in a different way, it's not shared blood, but the shared shadows in our veins that makes us *'ohana*. Inked directly into our collective genetic code."

He lifted an arm, rolled up his dress shirt sleeve—who wore an expensive shirt to a planned killing? Scott might've surpassed even Lui's level of insanity—and studied the thin, dark lines pulsing beneath his skin.

"Our father was quite the player," he continued. "He managed to keep dozens of other women out of your mother's sight for years before she found out. She must've been awfully gullible."

A muscle ticked in Keahilani's cheek, and she unloaded four rounds into Scott's head.

Except by the time the first bullet left the chamber, Scott was already gone. He blipped out of existence, and Keahilani shot an innocent tree that protested with a creak as one of its branches split and crashed to the ground.

Manō spun, putting his back to his brother and sister, forcing them into triangle formation. He was acutely aware of Ret's position above. Though he couldn't make out her face from this distance, he knew she was still there, watching. Targeting.

Three Alanas moved as one, each set of arms pointing a weapon into the forest, waiting for Scott to reappear and give them a reason to blow his fucking head off for real.

Puff.

He materialized out of the shadow of a nearby branch and thundered toward them. This time, Kai shot at him, but Scott—damn, he was fast—made his body pliable enough to allow the bullets to pass through shadow rather than flesh.

Manō started to question how the hell Scott could pull off such incredible maneuvers, but the answer was obvious. He learned his best shadow tricks from Dad, just as Manō had. Only difference was, Scott was better at dodging bullets than Manō.

"We already know our father was a sex-starved dickhead," Keahilani said, targeting Scott's chest. "We've dealt with it and moved on. You, obviously, still have some daddy issues you need to resolve, but you'll have to work those out with your therapist. Let's stop beating around the bush and get to the point of your visit."

Seeing Manō and Kai had Scott well covered, she stuck her gun into a pocket on her black cargo pants and boldly entered Scott's personal space. She hiked her hands to her hips and stared up at him, defiant in the way only Pele could be.

"This little turf war between Harris and Alana is getting old and frankly, beyond petty. Bane killed your wife, so you retaliated and had him killed. We have a primo weed farm, and you're a dealer who's jealous of the competition, so you decide to put us out of business by selling Ambrosia at a discount to undermine us. You think you're next in line to inherit the farm, but here's the problem, Scott. The farm belonged to our mother, not Justin Jacobs. You can't have it." Keahilani clearly enunciated the words and pressed her body closer, almost touching Scott. Her eyes assumed the blackness that came when the Alanas invited the shadows out to play. It was unnerving how all of them had the same eyes, even Scott.

In that fleeting moment, Manō couldn't deny they *were* family, no matter how much they wished it weren't so. The connection was obvious.

Scott's lips pulled back in a smile that looked more like a snarl—another indicator that he and Keahilani were related. She'd been using the same move since she was a teenager.

"Firstly, as much as I would've loved to watch the light die in Bane's eyes, someone else executed the hit on your brother," Scott said. "You got to Blake before he could fulfill my request."

The mention of Blake zapped Manō in the gut with a guilt gun.

Keahilani charged into the remainder of Scott's space, thrust a finger in his face, and bared her teeth. "Then who was it?"

"I don't know," Scott spat back. "How many times do I have to say it?"

She was trying to trick him into admitting Grant Lowden

had killed Bane, but Manō now wondered if she was forcing a connection that didn't exist. Might Lowden be operating independently of Scott, and if so, why? They had yet to uncover his motivation for the murder. There were no known ties between the CEO and their little brother.

Fury took hold of Keahilani. It bled off her skin in hot waves. She lunged for Scott, fingers curled like talons, going straight for the jugular.

This time, Scott wasn't as fast. She managed to sink her claws into his neck, but with another *puff*, his corporeal form disintegrated into tarry smoke before she did much damage.

That was when Manō realized this disappearing act wasn't only dangerous, but it was also a distraction. Scott wanted to direct their attention away from his real target: the only one still standing who couldn't just pop into shadow form. The one who'd make the perfect hostage.

Ret.

The darkness swirled as human shadows blended into the forest. Manō snapped his gaze up to where Ret was hiding just in time to see a man-sized blackness converge on her from behind.

"Ret!" he shouted.

Kai and Keahilani were slower to react, but Manō had mastered the art of shadow riding. With a nanosecond's worth of concentration, he wrangled the dark tube swelling around him. It twisted and turned, its end pointing up to where he needed to be.

Just like surfing, he jumped inside the barrel of blackness and rode like Mahina had taught him. He angled his "board" from shadow to shadow, up, up, up toward Ret.

She had a rifle, which wasn't conducive to hand-to-hand fighting, but she put its butt to good use when Scott landed behind her, cracking his face with the hard wood.

But Scott had an automatic and the element of surprise going for him. He shoved her. She lost her balance. She plummeted from her perch fifteen feet up in the tree's canopy. He fired three times at her on the way down. Her body impacted on the forest floor with a heavy thud, the breath flying out of her lips. She was utterly silent.

Now it was Manō's turn to channel fury.

His kill switch flicked on, tinting his vision red. If Ret was dead, Scott would spend the rest of his miserable life strapped to a chair, losing one inch off his body from Manō's tools every day until there was nothing left.

If Ret was dead, he had little to live for. Hadn't he been contemplating ending it all a few short days ago? And hadn't his attitude about life greatly improved in that same week after spending it in Ret's light?

Ret had shown him his own value. She had proven her loyalty to his family over and over again. She had taught him how to care for things beyond his 'ohana.

The cold-blooded killing machine formerly known as Manō was fully operational. The live wire running the length of his body and connecting him to every shadow in the forest bypassed his emotion circuits, giving him free rein to do what he did best.

He charged along the dark zip line, baring his shark teeth, allowing his hunger for death to fuel him. He torpedoed into Scott, knocking them both out of the tree. They fell together, arms and legs wrapped in a death grip around each other.

Manō clenched his teeth as he tried to transform into shadow, but the ground was coming up fast.

Then a funny thing happened. Something embedded deep inside Scott connected with its counterpart within Manō. A sort of two-way mirror slid into place between them, and he saw part of himself in his half brother. Whatever shadows or genetic material they shared linked them on a cellular level.

Manō didn't like the idea of being connected to Scott, but he had no problem with yanking the rope tying them together to see what the tug-of-war would yield to his side.

Flexing his muscles and still falling, he grasped their shared darkness and pulled. Scott's eyes widened, and his mouth fell open. All of this took place in the span of a couple seconds, but it was long enough for Manō to drag his shadowy kill from their father's side of Scott into his own.

Scott's shadows sucked into him in an implosion of darkness just in time for him to surf away unscathed, but Scott hit the ground with a cry of pain not far from Ret. His shocked expression said everything. He'd been robbed of his power by what he considered an unworthy opponent. And he wanted it back.

He rolled to his side, cried out, and tried unsuccessfully to stand.

Kai ran over to check on Ret, and Keahilani shadow-hopped to Manō, who stepped out of a shadow near Scott's feet. He pulsed with black energy that made him wild. Hunger bit into his stomach. His darkness recognized Scott's, and it wanted more. All of it.

The good part of him was desperate to know what happened to Ret, but the shadow part controlled his muscles. He stood over Scott, sampling the painfully orgasmic sensations coursing through his veins, spreading its dark endorphins into every crevice. Scott's shadows called to him like starving little owlets screeching for their mother.

Licking his lips, Manō silenced their cries. He wanted to devour Scott like the shark he was. That would put an end to him once and for all.

He bent over and smelled Scott's fear. Water filled his mouth. He swallowed, but the glut of saliva was relentless.

Hungry.

Eat him!

He would do the same to you.

Scott will die for what he did.

Must feed.

He opened his mouth, trailing his tongue over his teeth, and leaned closer. Scott stared up at him through wide black eyes, pervasive fear darting behind them.

"You ain't much without your daddy," Manō noted as his black pet sharks circled his legs. They smelled the blood in the water as strongly as he did. But they didn't urge him to attack. No, that urge came from the filth Manō had just absorbed from Scott. From their father.

Scott closed his eyes and fell onto his back.

Keahilani stood over him, gun aimed at his head. "You know who wins this war? No one. We fight. You hit us back. We try to run a business. You try to destroy it and take it over for yourself. When does it end, *brother*?"

"It ends now," Manō intoned. He didn't recognize his own voice. Dad's shadows had hijacked it.

Keahilani laid a hand on his shoulder. The gesture piqued the Alana side's curiosity, giving the murderous shadows enough pause to stop him from striking a killing blow with his fist to Scott's face.

His punch would've killed Scott. The malevolent wildfire power burning through him could've razed a small town.

"Tell us what you know about Bane's killer, and we'll make it quick," Keahilani urged gently. Her soft tone matched the one she used when she sang Manō lullabies and kissed his boo-boos and held his hand when he was scared, before the world went to shit and their mother left them with all this … darkness.

"Guys," Kai interrupted from behind them, tension heavy in his voice. "We need to get Ret to a hospital."

Manō's focus boomeranged into place, clearing away some of the mounting cobwebs the shadows had spun inside his brain.

Ret. She was hurt.

He glanced over to where his brother attended to her. She wasn't moving.

"Be honest with yourself," Scott rasped, "and acknowledge the scorecard between us is leaning heavily in your favor. I'm just one man—"

Another distraction.

Scott's sudden spate of dialogue tipped Manō off a second too late.

Hand. Gun. Snap.

BANG!

Scott plugged Keahilani just as she exploded into a flurry of wispy black butterflies that scattered from the bullet with ballet-like agility. Then, faster than a blink, she rematerialized in her whole form, eyes pure darkness, standing over him with the muzzle of her gun pushed flush to his forehead.

Manō smiled. His sister was learning how to manipulate the darkness on a molecular level. And she was damn good at it.

They could thank Mahina for that.

He could also thank Mahina for the wisdom of listening to one's gut. He knew without a doubt that Grant Lowden was the one who'd killed Bane. Whether Scott was aware of this fact or not didn't matter because the truth was, Scott didn't do it himself, and the person he'd hired to do it hadn't succeeded either.

In this instance, Scott was innocent.

With the sharks claiming Manō's flesh as their territory, Dad's shadows lost their appetite for blood. For now.

"Kill me," Scott said. "Go ahead. If you don't, I'll just come back. I want what's under that farm, Keahilani. You owe it to me for what your brother did to Lori and our baby. And for what you did to Blake." Tears filled his eyes and spilled past his lids.

Manō sensed the moment when Keahilani's will softened. His did too in the same instant.

She shook her head. "Too much killing. Don't you think there's been enough death?"

Scott stared at her, tears now streaming. "Justin Jacobs lives in all of us. His blood demands sacrifices. We're just giving him what he wants."

Keahilani snorted. "Justin Jacobs is dead. Whatever's in here," she slapped her chest, "belongs to us now. Not him. He can't control us any longer. You shouldn't let him control you either."

"The only person who ever controlled me is gone, thanks to your brother," Scott said. The vein between his brows throbbed. He was trying to call the shadows Manō stole home. A thrum of energy pulsed between them, a battle for domination over their mutual darkness.

"If I have to follow you every single day and every night, I will find your farm, and I'll take what your mother kept from our father. Your blood owes mine." Scott's irises swirled blue like Justin's and succumbed again to the black.

Kai dragged Ret through the foliage toward them. "We need to get out of here right fucking now."

Manō's heart pounded at the sight of Ret's still body. He glanced to signal Keahilani to wrap it up, but with the break in Manō's concentration, Scott had reclaimed enough of his darkness to negotiate a narrow escape via shadows.

"Shit!" Keahilani hissed at the empty ground between her feet, grabbing at the retreating darkness. Taking flight in the shape of an inky owl, Scott barely escaped her grasp and flew away into the night.

With Ret injured, they didn't have time to go after him. Didn't matter. Scott might've gotten away, but he was weak. He wouldn't be able to follow them tonight. He had a lot of wounds to lick—physical and mental.

Manō raced over to Kai and scooped Ret into his arms. Kai frowned at him, but Manō was bigger and stronger. Kai followed him to the car with a furious Keahilani trotting behind.

Manō stared down at Ret's pale face and scanned her body for bullet holes as he walked. Her shirt was ripped in a couple places in sunburst patterns, but there was no blood. He peered through the fabric. A Kevlar bulletproof vest peeked up from underneath. Damn, Ret was good.

When they reached the car, she stirred, wagging her head a little while Keahilani cleared the back seat. Ret cracked open her lids and stared up, dazed.

His pulse raced at a full gallop. She was alive.

"Manō?" she said weakly, reaching for his cheek.

He felt Kai's flinch beside him, but neither said anything. Manō gently pushed her hand down and carefully laid her in the back seat. "You'll be okay."

Kai met his eyes, and unspoken words passed between them.

I'm sitting with her, Kai seemed to say as he slid in beside Ret, resting her head in his lap.

I understand, Manō's nod acknowledged.

The truth would have to come out soon. Manō loved his brother, and the last thing he wanted was to fight with him—especially over a woman. But his feelings for Ret had grown. It wasn't right to keep Kai in the dark.

Funny. The dark was exactly where shadows thrived, but between them, Kai owned the monopoly on light.

Which side did Ret deserve most?

Light or darkness?

There were no shadows without light. If Manō could recapture his soul's most valuable inheritance from Mahina and shine it to tame his evil shadows' baser instincts, maybe it would be enough. Maybe then *he'd* be enough.

CHAPTER FORTY

Saturday, October 11

The next afternoon, after a long night of much-needed sleep in her own bed with Manō and Kai keeping vigil beside her, Ret sat drinking coffee with the Alanas and Jezzy around the kitchen table at their safe house. Ret was still smarting from the massive bruises she'd sustained after Scott shot her. Crashing to the ground from fifteen feet up hadn't been a picnic either.

One of Manō's doctor friends who owed him a favor confirmed she'd broken a couple ribs and had a mild concussion, but overall, she was okay. Manō and Kai had brought her home and insisted on staying. What, if anything, transpired between them while she was knocked out on pain meds was a mystery, but the brothers were cooler than usual toward each other today.

Having them silently fight over her made her feel like part of the *'ohana.*

In her drug-addled haze, Ret relived the night's events on a loop inside her head. She regretted having to kill the drug dealers, but in her mind, their murders were justified. Even more, she regretted scrubbing the evidence that might lead Chief Hale and his cohorts to the truth. She, Keahilani, and Kai had worn gloves and used ghost guns, which had been cleaned of all prints and left at the scene. Phones were checked for digital trails, confiscated, and destroyed. None of the Alanas' team had lost blood, so there would be no DNA for the cops to trace back to them.

Though he got away, they'd survived Scott's attack. Ret was still breathing. Bones would heal. Life was good.

She still didn't understand how her friends had merged in and out of darkness, but it didn't matter. Though she'd seen things that couldn't be explained with logic, she had no choice but to believe what Manō had told her. The Alanas could control shadows, and apparently, Scott had inherited the trait from their father as well.

Until she found a better explanation, it was what it was. End of story.

"Scott might be out of commission for now, but what about Grant Lowden?" Keahilani asked. She sipped her coffee and ducked her head at the afternoon light pouring in through the window. She stood and flipped the blinds shut. "How do we get to him?"

Jezzy sat up straighter. "I'm the one who sent you the image of Lowden on the night of Bane's death."

The air pressure in the room dropped steeply as everyone turned to Jezzy, a thousand questions written across their faces.

"Hold on," Keahilani said. "You were video chatting with Bane the night he died?"

Jezzy nodded guiltily.

"Why the hell didn't you say something sooner?" Keahilani's face burned red, and her fists balled with white-knuckled anger.

"I did," Jezzy said. "I texted you as it was happening. How do you think I knew he was being attacked?"

"And we appreciate the heads-up," Kai said, "but what—*why* were you talking to Bane? Why didn't you send us the screenshot sooner?"

"My business with Bane was private," Jezzy hedged. "As for the man who did it, I wanted to be sure of who it was before I sent you any details. I'm nothing if not thorough, as my track record proves."

Whoa. What the hell was Jezzy's relationship with Bane, and why was it such a secret that she couldn't tell his grieving siblings? The more Ret thought about it, the more she wondered what else Bane had gotten caught up in beyond Lori Harris's murder. Bane was the classic "good kid." Before the Harris shit, he'd never been in trouble. The stuff coming out about him now signaled deep ties to something dark.

Ret glanced to Manō. Worry lined his face.

"I think we have a right to know what our own brother was up to," Kai said. His hands fidgeted under the table. He didn't like this any more than Keahilani or Manō.

Jezzy shook her head slowly. "In due time. I promise."

"Fine," Kai huffed. "Then, what about Grant Lowden? Why did he go after Bane? Did our little brother kill someone else we don't know about?"

Jezzy sighed. "I'm still digging into Lowden's background. I'm putting together a dossier of information about him, but it's too early to speculate on some of the data. I like facts, not suppositions. I swear I'll tell you everything as soon as I have all the details." She glanced at Keahilani. "You have lots of questions, and I will answer them. For the time being, will you trust me on this?"

Keahilani sighed disgustedly. "So, we're supposed to just let this asshole who murdered our baby brother off the hook? Not my style, Jezzy, and you know it."

"I get it. Action before words. But don't forget, you have an entire precinct of cops watching your every move, waiting for you to fuck up again so they can throw you in jail for real," Jezzy countered. How right she was. "Let me handle your intelligence. Once we have that nailed down, you can do whatever the hell you want with it."

Keahilani shook her head. "Much as I'd love to, we can't afford your services right now."

"Ah, yes," Jezzy said, standing up. She grabbed her computer bag off the counter and removed her laptop. "About that."

Jezzy opened the computer, clicked around, and turned it so everyone could see the screen. "In addition to anonymously turning over to the police damning recordings, documents, emails, and texts that prove Scott Harris is a dope dealer and killer—you're welcome—I also took the liberty of transferring a substantial amount of money from Scott's coffers to a newly opened savings account in John Smith's name, which you have access to. It's enough to pay off your investors, but please do it soon. The account will ghost in a few days to avoid IRS scrutiny. You're welcome again."

Keahilani's jaw dropped. Kai's eyes popped wide open. Manō smiled appreciatively.

Jezzy was a godsend for the Alanas. Ret high-fived her.

"You did *what?*" Keahilani said.

"You haven't even looked at that phone I gave you," Jezzy said with a tsk. "Where is it?"

Keahilani mutely handed the device over, her face a picture of pure shock and reverent amazement. With a couple of taps, Jezzy opened an app and passed the phone back.

Keahilani stared at the screen. "I've never seen so many zeroes in my life. Are you shitting me with this?"

Jezzy grinned. "No shit. And don't worry. I extracted my fee from Scott for this magic show, so you wouldn't have to pay it. If he shows his face on this island again, the police will have all the evidence they need to bust his ass and toss him in the slammer for years."

"They won't catch him," Manō said.

He was right. If the shadows were as real as Ret believed, they'd protect Scott.

"Maybe not," Jezzy replied. "But even if they don't, Scott's in a weakened position. With evidence for drugs and murder against him and his bank account cleaned out, he'll be in hiding for a while."

And as long as the Alanas stayed in the light, Scott would be forced to remain in the dark. Ret smiled at Manō, admiring his handsome, brooding face and tight muscles from across the table. She could help him adjust to the light. And she'd love every minute of it.

"Jezzy, we can't accept this," Keahilani said. "By stealing from Scott and turning over this evidence, you're standing directly in his path. He's already after us, and he's proven he's not afraid to kill. We don't want him coming after you or Ret."

"Scott may know Jezzy stole from him and framed him, but he doesn't know Jezzy's real name, her identity, or what she looks like," she replied. "I'm a big girl with a very big brain. I can take care of myself. Besides, I have a new job working at Mahina Surf and Dive. There's lots to do."

"I'd love for you to take over there, but there's no insurance payout," Keahilani said. "I had to switch over to a bare-bones policy to save money."

Jezzy lifted an index finger. "Wrong again, my friend. You have an insurance policy. And the police have not only the video feed showing the man who set the bomb, but also his confession. It seems Houston had a come-to-Jesus moment last night and decided to turn himself in this morning. I wonder what prompted that."

Manō snickered. Ret found it irresistible every time he let his sense of humor out for a run.

Keahilani and Kai must've left quite an impression on Houston for him to go running to the cops with a confession so fast.

"With Houston's admission, the new insurance policy I took out in your name should pay out nicely," Jezzy said. "Maybe you'll even have enough money to give your manager a pay raise after you rebuild."

Keahilani tossed her head back and laughed. The sound of those warm, hiccupping notes made Ret smile. It was the first time since Bane's death that Ret had seen her genuinely happy.

"After everything you've done for us," Keahilani said, "you have a job for life. *Mahalo*, Jezzy."

She got up and hugged Jezzy for a long moment. Then she turned to Ret and threw her arms gently around her shoulders, careful not to disturb Ret's tender chest. "*Mahalo* to you too, Ret. We couldn't have taken those assholes out without you last night. We owe you big time."

"You know, I'm out of a job too," Ret said thoughtfully. "If you happen to have an opening at your surf shop when it reopens, I might be interested."

"Are you serious?" Keahilani said, wide-eyed.

Beside her, Manō lifted an amused brow.

Maybe he liked the idea of her staying close to the family. Even better.

"Hell, yeah," Ret replied. Excitement gained momentum like stampeding horses at the thought of helping them—and herself—out. "What else am I gonna do?"

Keahilani said, "We'd be honored to have both of you on board. Now that we have the funds to pay the investors, we can focus on getting the shop back on its feet."

"What about the farm?" Kai asked.

His question halted all movement in the room as each person considered it.

"With Scott on the run with nothing to do but fixate further on his obsession with finding Mahina's garden, we'll have to lay low for a while and pause Pāhoehoe operations," Keahilani said.

"Would closing up that chapter of our lives really be that big of a deal anyway?" Kai asked, a note of exhaustion hiding under the question. "Much as I love cultivating plants and figuring out hacks for growing shit, I'm so fucking tired of hiding from the cops, begging untrustworthy people to distribute for us, always feeling like I'm on the run, trying to stay a step ahead of whatever's breathing down my neck at any given moment. I hate to throw away everything I've learned about botany these last few years, but maybe we should just … end this."

That was probably the most responsible thing Ret had ever heard Kai say. Maybe he was finally growing up.

Keahilani opened her mouth to speak, turned to Manō, whose face was grim with acceptance, and closed it.

Manō looked to Jezzy and Ret in turn. "Kai has a point. We've been given a do-over card. We should play it."

Ret saw a world of possibilities opening for everyone in the room. The Alanas had been absolved of their sins—at least for the time being—and they now had an opportunity to rebuild their mother's legacy and leave behind the drug trade and the violence that came with it.

She wanted them to be free of their life of crime so badly. And with a fresh start, she and Manō could focus on figuring out *them*.

"What about Bane?" Keahilani said, her voice tight to the breaking point. "I won't let his death go unpunished. *'Ohana* is everything."

"We'll find Grant Lowden," Manō vowed coldly, "and he'll pay for Bane's murder."

A chill tripped up Ret's spine at the thought of him going after the evil man, yet she couldn't think of anyone better to take him on.

One drama at a time, Ret.

"We're in this together," she said, attempting to steer the Alanas' vengeance to the right side of the law.

She thought of Chief Hale and how he'd covered for her to pay her back for her silence years ago at that traffic stop. He understood mistakes. And forgiveness. He'd help the Alanas if it meant justice would be served.

"I have plenty of friends at the department who'd love a high-profile arrest like Lowden's pinned to the front of their personnel files," she said. "I'll help you put him away. Legally."

"Me too," Jezzy added. "I want Scott behind bars for all the shit he's done, and Lowden deserves the same. Let me work my magic, and we'll take them both out soon enough."

Keahilani inhaled a full breath and let it out in a rush. "It's settled, then. We rebuild Mahina Surf and Dive. Jezzy and Ret will work for us. We'll pay back our investors tomorrow, leave behind the drug trade, and focus on finding Grant Lowden when the sun goes down."

Murmurs of approval bandied among the five of them.

Ret was eager to tell Kai about her and Manō, but this wasn't the right time. Maybe once things settled, she and Manō could talk about how to broach the subject. For now, she was content to let whatever happened between them happen as it would. She passed him a secret smile, and he acknowledged it with a subtle nod.

Manō stood up from the table. "I have things to take care of. I'll be back tonight."

On his way out the door, he caught Ret's eye. He didn't say where he was going or what he had to do, but she knew from the muted hope splashed over his face that he was handling whatever lingering shit still hung over him so that he could begin his first day of a crime-free life tomorrow.

And that was fine by her.

EPILOGUE

The shadows still refused to grant Manō passage on their backs to Kaho'olawe, so he dragged out Mahina's canoe and sat beside it on the beach under a palm tree for the rest of the afternoon in quiet contemplation.

Why didn't the shadows want him to go there?

He turned the question over in his mind and attacked it from every angle, but it only left him with more questions about Grant Lowden's mysterious involvement in Bane's death and an uneasy feeling about Scott's plans for revenge.

After last night and this afternoon's revelations at the safe house, there was much to process.

When the sun inhaled the day's last breath and succumbed to dusk, he dragged Mahina's outrigger into the ocean and paddled, his shadow sharks right alongside, protective as ever.

Along his hours-long journey, he puzzled over the connection, or lack thereof, between Scott Harris and Grant Lowden. Lui said Harris had been spotted at Waialua Kope making arrangements with Dallas to blow up the surf shop, which suggested the coffee company was a front for illegal activity.

If Scott really didn't know Grant Lowden, was it simply a coincidence that two men who happened to be after the Alanas were connected to Waialua Kope but not each other? And what about the shadows? They swarmed around

Lowden too.

Manō didn't believe in coincidences. Not like this.

Nothing made sense.

In the coming weeks while his siblings rebuilt the shop, Manō would lean on his contacts to see what else he could dig up.

He needed a peek at the cards Jezzy was holding so close to her chest. She knew something she wasn't giving up, and for that, Manō couldn't completely trust her, much as he wanted to.

He'd let Keahilani and Kai believe they were done with the Pāhoehoe business. They could wash their hands of it, but Manō had a few more transactions to complete before he would let go for good.

As he approached Kaho'olawe, the shark-shadows escorting him paused near his paddles, refusing to go farther. Like the last time he came here, their agitation triggered his. The ominous slopes of the island in the dark yielded little in the way of secrets.

Manō went on without his 'aumākua and sang the chant, requesting permission to land. The island granted him passage.

He dragged the canoe far up the sand, ensuring it would be safe from incoming tides. Then he removed his shovel and headed toward the spot where he'd lain Blake to rest more than a week ago. He tugged a bandana over his mouth and nose to preemptively dim the smell of rotting flesh. He'd seen his share of week-old corpses, and they were never appealing to any of the senses.

It took him a few minutes to locate the marker. When he found it, he gasped and spun around, scanning the eroded ground, the ocean, the beach for a red-eyed intruder. He saw no one.

The rocks he'd left on top of Blake had been disturbed.

He feverishly tossed them aside, hurling them into a pile, digging through the sand like a dog burying a bone.

The space beneath was empty.

Manō fell back on his heels, mouth agape, mind blown, nerves shattered.

Blake Murphy's body was gone.

ACKNOWLEDGMENTS

I'm incredibly grateful to my friend, sprinting partner, and critique partner, Elle J. Rossi. If not for her, this book might not have ever seen the light of day. Her gentle, supportive presence has been a godsend.

Thanks also to: my editor, Jenn Sommersby Young, whose deep understanding of story structure (and pesky grammar rules) challenges me to be the best writer I can be; Emma Rider at Moonstruck Cover Design & Photography for the stunning vision she brought to the 'Ohana series book covers; and my beta readers for their helpful insights. Kelli Case, Nancy Doublin, Jaime Elaine, Kendra Gaither, Diane McElrath, Courtney Nicholas, Melissa Shank, Emily Snow, Christina Spicer, and Amy Turner, thank you all for helping me iron out the wrinkles in this book.

To Resident Geek and the three Demonlings: Day or night, you are the constant light that tames my shadows. I love you all.

ABOUT THE AUTHOR

A whale warrior, indie freedom fighter, and vodka martini aficionado, Kendall Grey is calm like an F-bomb*. She writes about fierce women and the men who love them. Her aliases include Seven Slade (COMING OUT) and Kendall Day (FALLING FOR MR. SLATER).

Kendall lives off a dirt road near Atlanta, Georgia, with three mischievous Demonlings, a dashing geek in cyber armor, a long-haired miniature Dachshund that thinks she's a cat, and an Aussie shepherd mix whose ice-blue eyes will steal your heart and hold it for ransom.

*Detonation manual not included.

kendallgrey.com
Newsletter: bit.ly/HardRockHarlotsNewsletter
facebook.com/KendallGreyAuthor
twitter.com/kendallgrey1
instagram.com/kendallgrey1

ALSO BY KENDALL GREY

Alpha Prez and the First Lady's Secret Weapon

Ghosts

Asgard Awakening Series

Runed

Hard Rock Harlots Series

Strings
Beats
Nocturnes
Rock
Bang

Just Breathe Series

Inhale
Exhale
Just Breathe

FROM HOWLING MAD PRESS

Coming Out by Seven Slade

Falling for Mr. Slater by Kendall Day

Printed in February 2019
by Rotomail Italia S.p.A., Vignate (MI) - Italy